THE BEST OF
SISTERS
IN
CRIME

THE BEST OF
SISTERS
IN
CRIME

edited by

MARILYN
WALLACE

BERKLEY PRIME CRIME, NEW YORK

THE BEST OF SISTERS IN CRIME

For the entire family of writers, in celebration of the risks and pleasures of storytelling.

A Berkley Prime Crime Book
Published by The Berkley Publishing Group, a member of Penguin Putnam Inc.,
200 Madison Avenue, New York, NY 10016

The Putnam Berkley World Wide Web site address is
http://www.berkley.com

First Edition: December 1997

Library of Congress Cataloging-in-Publication Data

The best of sisters in crime / edited by Marilyn Wallace—1st ed.
    p.   cm.
  ISBN 0-425-16060-2
  1. Detective and mystery stories, American.   2. American fiction—
Women authors.   3. Women—Fiction.   I. Wallace, Marilyn.
PS648.D4B47   1997
813'.0872089287—dc21   97-14219
                                                                   CIP

Printed in the United States of America

10   9   8   7   6   5   4   3   2   1

contents

foreword

The first volume of Sisters in Crime made its appearance in 1989, a year George Bush was president, O.J. Simpson was a rental car spokesperson, and Rent was only a monthly housing expense. The 22 stories in that anthology were pronounced "consistently outstanding" (*Publishers Weekly*), a "literary variety show" (the *New York Times*), and "excellent" (*Newsweek*). Readers were so enthusiastic that four more volumes followed, each featuring short stories written by some of the American women who ushered in what many call the Second Golden Age of the mystery.

This collection of stories, culled from the five volumes of SISTERS IN CRIME, is a sampler of the work of a diverse, unruly, and talented group of writers. Difficult to classify, adventurous, energetic, the contributors include writers who are past presidents of the organization Sisters In Crime, writers who aren't members at all, writers from big cities, rural outposts, and suburban enclaves, writers who fly airplanes, practice yoga, study papermaking, take teaching holidays in Poland.

Inevitably, literary lists are subjective. The label "best" lends a competitive cast to an enterprise that isn't meant to be a contest at all. In the interests of simplicity and consistency, we established a criterion: the writer of each story included in this collection has been short-listed for a major prize. Special recognition is due to every contributor of all five volumes, and to all the writers who have so revitalized the mystery and suspense field in the past decade. During the 1996 Oscar Awards ceremony, Frances McDormand offered thanks for the increase in great roles for women; I offer my own gratitude for these wonderful stories about women, by women, for all readers.

Every year, many organizations confer awards in the mystery and suspense field. These national and international prizes include the Edgar Allan Poe awards, commonly called Edgars, given by Mystery Writers of America; Anthonys, named for Anthony Boucher and presented every fall at the national convention named in his honor, Bouchercon; Agathas, awarded at the annual Malice Domestic convention; Macavity awards, announced each summer by Mystery Readers International; and Shamus awards, given annually by Private Eye Writers of America.

When the first volume of the SISTERS IN CRIME anthologies came out in 1989, many of us, readers and writers alike, remembered when a mystery protagonist whose life, dreams, frustrations, and abilities we recognized was rarer than a virtuous blonde in a noir novel. Some of us were also aware that no American woman had won the Edgar award for Best Novel since Margaret Millar in 1956. But Julie Smith finally broke the barrier in 1990 and won the Edgar for NEW ORLEANS MOURNING, in which she introduces Skip Langdon. Margaret Maron took home the prize in 1992, in BOOTLEGGER'S DAUGHTER, another debut of a new character, Judge Deborah Knott. And in 1995, Mary Willis Walker got the gold for THE RED SCREAM.

My, how things have changed! As the dust settles from the marvelous explosion in the number of mystery and suspense novels written by American women, it's clear the one thing that hasn't changed is that mystery and suspense fiction remains a source of delight to readers everywhere because it tells stories.

As a child, I was filled with a deep hunger to read everything, anything, as long as it told a story. I was one of the lucky kids who got to experience the sweet suspense of anticipation while waiting for the Bookmobile. I'd check the kitchen clock impatiently, worry whether Miss Murphy, with her dark, shapeless dresses, sturdy shoes, and short-cut fingernails, had forgotten that I was depending on her for my infusion of stories. All these years later, some words still paint pictures so vivid that I can trace their impact to the stories I devoured as a girl.

Say the word "well" to me and immediately I'm dropped

into a sandcolored landscape lit by a blistering sun. The air is dry, the odor of straw and warm dates wafts on the gentle breeze stirring the leaves of the palm trees. And in the center of this scene, women are gathered around the well, laughing and talking, holding their clay jars on their hips or atop their heads as they exchange news and advice, solve problems, enjoy the fruits of friendship. Their clothing is simple, decorated at the neck or the hem with a burst of colored thread. They learn about health, child rearing, marriage, the world beyond their village through shared tales. Their stories crackle with the drama of human relationships, and their listeners stand transfixed, rapt with wonder and attention.

The *Sisters In Crime* anthologies maintain that tradition of gathering around the well and sharing tales, of entertaining and beguiling with words. I doubt that those women in their sandals would have imagined Kinsey Milhone or V.I. Warshawski or the courageous heroines of Mary Higgins Clark, but they would recognize a common humanity. They'd understand their daring, their humor, their intelligence.

As the five volumes of this anthology series came together, I discovered that stories weren't the only things developing: Friendships were growing, too. I began to think that this must have been the way it was at the well. In the eight years since the series first debuted, I've met wonderful women and men, laughed, joked, traded information, shared struggle and triumph. It may take a village to raise children, as Hillary Clinton has said, but it also takes a thriving community to give readers a true picture of the world we live in. In this volume, we hope our voices reach past the well to the gathering places and the solitary spaces to entertain, amuse, and provoke you, and to offer the pledge that we'll do our best to keep the stories coming!

Marilyn Wallace
May 1997
New York, NY

THE BEST OF
SISTERS
IN
CRIME

Nancy Pickard's Jenny Cain is smart, funny, brave, and equal measures of shrewd and impulsive. Say No to Murder *won an Anthony in 1985. Since then,* Marriage is Murder *won a Macavity;* Bum Steer *won an Agatha; and the remaining Jenny novels have garnered ten other nominations.* The 27-Ingredient Chili Con Carne Murders, *a delightful departure, followed the exploits of Eugenia Potter, created by Virginia Rich. With typical humor, love, and courage, Jenny returns to face a troubling situation in the recent* Twilight.

Honored by Macavity, Anthony, and American Mystery awards, and Edgar and Agatha nominations, "Afraid All the Time" (not a Jenny Cain story) embodies the uniqueness of the American prairie and the emotions it evokes. Open space becomes one of the significant threads woven into the shocking conclusion.

afraid all the time

by Nancy Pickard

"RIBBON A DARKNESS OVER ME . . ."

Mel Brown, known variously as Pell Mell and Animel, sang the line from the song over and over behind his windshield as he flew from Missouri into Kansas on his old black Harley-Davidson motorcycle.

Already he loved Kansas, because the highway that stretched ahead of him was like a long, flat, dark ribbon unfurled just for him.

"Ribbon a darkness over me . . ."

He flew full throttle into the late-afternoon glare, feeling as if he were soaring gloriously drunk and blind on a skyway to the sun. The clouds in the far distance looked as if they'd rain on him that night, but he didn't worry about it. He'd heard there were plenty of empty farm and ranch houses in Kansas where a man could break in to spend the night. He'd heard it was like having your choice of free motels, Kansas was.

"Ribbon a darkness over me . . ."

• • •

Three hundred miles to the southwest, Jane Baum suddenly stopped what she was doing. The fear had hit her again. It was always like that, striking out of nowhere, like a fist against her heart. She dropped her clothes basket from rigid fingers and stood as if paralyzed between the two clotheslines in her yard. There was a wet sheet to her right, another to her left. For once the wind had died down, so the sheets hung as still and silent as walls. She felt enclosed in a narrow, white, sterile room of cloth, and she never wanted to leave it.

Outside of it was danger.

On either side of the sheets lay the endless prairie where she felt like a tiny mouse exposed to every hawk in the sky.

It took all of her willpower not to scream.

She hugged her own shoulders to comfort herself. It didn't help. Within a few moments she was crying, and then shaking with a palsy of terror.

She hadn't known she'd be so afraid.

Eight months ago, before she had moved to this small farm she'd inherited, she'd had romantic notions about it, even about such simple things as hanging clothes on a line. It would feel so good, she had imagined, they would smell so sweet. Instead, everything had seemed strange and threatening to her from the start, and it was getting worse. Now she didn't even feel protected by the house. She was beginning to feel as if it were fear instead of electricity that lighted her lamps, filled her tub, lined her cupboards and covered her bed—fear that she breathed instead of air.

She hated the prairie and everything on it.

The city had never frightened her, not like this. She knew the city, she understood it, she knew how to avoid its dangers and its troubles. In the city there were buildings everywhere, and now she knew why—it was to blot out the true and terrible openness of the earth on which all of the inhabitants were so horribly exposed to danger.

The wind picked up again. It snapped the wet sheets against her body. Janie bolted from her shelter. Like a mouse with a hawk circling overhead, she ran as if she were being chased. She ran out of her yard and then down the highway, racing frantically, breathlessly, for the only other shelter she knew.

When she reached Cissy Johnson's house, she pulled open the side door and flung herself inside without knocking.

"*Cissy?*"

"I'm afraid all the time."

"I know, Janie."

Cissy Johnson stood at her kitchen sink peeling potatoes for supper while she listened to Jane Baum's familiar litany of fear. By now Cissy knew it by heart. Janie was afraid of: being alone in the house she had inherited from her aunt; the dark; the crack of every twig in the night; the storm cellar; the horses that might step on her, the cows that might trample her, the chickens that might peck her, the cats that might bite her and have rabies, the coyotes that might attack her; the truckers who drove by her house, especially the flirtatious ones who blasted their horns when they saw her in the yard; tornadoes, blizzards, electrical storms; having to drive so far just to get simple groceries and supplies.

At first Cissy had been sympathetic, offering daily doses of coffee and friendship. But it was getting harder all the time to remain patient with somebody who just burst in without knocking and who complained all the time about imaginary problems and who—

"You've lived here all your life," Jane said, as if the woman at the sink had not previously been alert to that fact. She sat in a kitchen chair, huddled into herself like a child being punished. Her voice was low, as if she were talking more to herself than to Cissy. "You're used to it, that's why it doesn't scare you."

"Um," Cissy murmured, as if agreeing. But out of her neighbor's sight, she dug viciously at the eye of a potato. She rooted it out—leaving behind a white, moist, open wound in the vegetable—and flicked the dead black skin into the sink where the water running from the faucet washed it down the garbage disposal. She thought how she'd like to pour Janie's fears down the sink and similarly grind them up and flush them away. She held the potato to her nose and sniffed, inhaling the crisp, raw smell.

Then, as if having gained strength from that private moment, she glanced back over her shoulder at her visitor. Cissy was ashamed of the fact that the mere sight of Jane Baum now repelled her. It was a crime, really, how she'd let herself go. She wished Jane would comb her hair, pull her shoulders back, paint a little coloring onto her pale face, and wear something else besides that ugly denim jumper that came nearly to her heels. Cissy's husband, Bob, called Janie "Cissy's pup," and he called that jumper the "pup tent." He was right, Cissy thought, the woman did look like an insecure, spotty adolescent, and not at all like a grown woman of thirty-five-plus years. And darn it, Janie did follow Cissy around like a neurotic nuisance of a puppy.

"Is Bob coming back tonight?" Jane asked.

Now she's even invading my mind, Cissy thought. She whacked resentfully at the potato, peeling off more meat than skin. "Tomorrow." Her shoulders tensed.

"Then can I sleep over here tonight?"

"No." Cissy surprised herself with the shortness of her reply. She could practically feel Janie radiating hurt, and so she tried to make up for it by softening her tone. "I'm sorry, Janie, but I've got too much book work to do, and it's hard to concentrate with people in the house. I've even told the girls they can take their sleeping bags to the barn tonight to give me some peace." The girls were her daughters, Tessie, thirteen, and Mandy, eleven. "They want to spend the night out there 'cause we've got that new little blind calf we're nursing. His mother won't have anything to do with him, poor little thing. Tessie has named him Flopper, because he tries to stand up but he just flops back down. So the girls are bottle-feeding him, and they want to sleep near . . ."

"Oh." It was heavy with reproach.

Cissy stepped away from the sink to turn her oven on to 350°. Her own internal temperature was rising too. God forbid she should talk about her life! God forbid they should ever talk about anything but Janie and all the damned things she was scared of! She could write a book about it: *How Jane Baum Made a Big Mistake by Leaving Kansas City and How Everything About the Country Just Scared Her to Death.*

"Aren't you afraid of anything, Cissy?"

The implied admiration came with a bit of a whine to it—*any*thing—like a curve on a fastball.

"Yes." Cissy drew out the word reluctantly.

"You *are*? What?"

Cissy turned around at the sink and laughed self-consciously.

"It's so silly . . . I'm even afraid to mention it."

"Tell me! I'll feel better if I know you're afraid of things, too."

There! Cissy thought. *Even my fears come down to how they affect you!*

"All right." She sighed. "Well, I'm afraid of something happening to Bobby, a wreck on the highway or something, or to one of the girls, or my folks, things like that. I mean, like leukemia or a heart attack or something I can't control. I'm always afraid there won't be enough money and we might have to sell this place. We're so happy here. I guess I'm afraid that might change." She paused, dismayed by the sudden realization that she had not been as happy since Jane Baum moved in down the road. For a moment, she stared accusingly at her neighbor. "I guess that's what I'm afraid of." Then Cissy added deliberately, "But I don't think about it all the time."

"I think about mine all the time," Jane whispered.

"I know."

"I hate it here!"

"You could move back."

Janie stared reproachfully. "You know I can't afford that!"

Cissy closed her eyes momentarily. The idea of having to listen to *this* for who knew how many years . . .

"I love coming over here," Janie said wistfully, as if reading Cissy's mind again. "It always makes me feel so much better. This is the only place I feel safe anymore. I just hate going home to the big old house all by myself."

I will not invite you to supper, Cissy thought.

Janie sighed.

Cissy gazed out the big square window behind Janie. It was October, her favorite month, when the grass turned as red as the curly hair on a Hereford's back and the sky turned a steel gray like the highway that ran between their houses. It was as if the whole world blended into itself—the grass into the cattle, the roads into the sky, and she into all of it. There was an electricity in the air, as if something more important than winter were about to happen, as if all the world were one and about to burst apart into something brand-new. Cissy loved the prairie, and it hurt her feelings a little that Janie didn't. How could anyone live in the middle of so much beauty, she puzzled, and be frightened of it?

"We'll never get a better chance." Tess ticked off the rationale for the adventure by holding up the fingers of her right hand, one at a time, an inch from her sister's scared face. "Dad's gone. We're in the barn. Mom'll be asleep. It's a new moon." She ran out of fingers on that hand and lifted her left thumb. "And the dogs know us."

"They'll find out!" Mandy wailed.

"*Who'll* find out?"

"Mom and Daddy will!"

"They won't! Who's gonna tell 'em? The gas-station owner? You think we left a trail of toilet paper he's going to follow from his station to here? And he's gonna call the sheriff and say lock up those Johnson girls, boys, they stole my toilet paper!"

"Yes!"

Together they turned to gaze—one of them with pride and cunning, the other with pride and trepidation—at the small hill of hay that was piled, for no apparent reason, in the shadows of a far corner of the barn. Underneath that pile lay their collection of six rolls of toilet paper—a new one filched from their own linen closet, and five partly used ones (stolen one trip at a time and hidden in their school jackets) from the ladies' bathroom at the gas station in town. Tess's plan was for the two of them to "t.p." their neighbor's house that night, after dark. Tess had lovely visions of how it would look—all ghostly and spooky, with streamers of white hanging down from the tree limbs and waving eerily in the breeze.

"They do it all the time in Kansas City, jerk," Tess proclaimed. "And I'll bet they don't make any big crybaby deal out of it.'' She wanted to be the first one in her class to do it, and she wasn't about to let her little sister chicken out on her. This plan would, Tess was sure, make her famous in at least a four-county area. No grown-up would ever figure out who had done it, but all the kids would know, even if she had to tell them.

"Mom'll kill us!"

"Nobody'll know!"

"It's gonna rain!"

"It's not gonna rain."

"We shouldn't leave Flopper!"

Now they looked, together, at the baby bull calf in one of the stalls. It stared blindly in the direction of their voices, tried to rise, but was too frail to do it.

"Don't be a dope. We leave him all the time."

Mandy sighed.

Tess, who recognized the sound of surrender when she heard it, smiled magnanimously at her sister.

"You can throw the first roll," she offered.

In a truck stop in Emporia, Mel Brown slopped up his supper gravy with the last third of a cloverleaf roll. He had a table by a window. As he ate, he stared with pleasure at his bike outside. If he moved his head just so, the rays from the setting sun flashed off the handlebars. He thought about how the leather seat and grips would feel soft and warm and supple, the way a woman in leather felt, when he got back on. At the thought he got a warm feeling in his crotch, too, and he smiled.

God, he loved living like this.

When he was hungry, he ate. When he was tired, he slept. When he was horny, he found a woman. When he was thirsty, he stopped at a bar.

Right now Mel felt like not paying the entire $5.46 for this lousy chicken-fried steak dinner and coffee. He pulled four dollar bills out of his wallet and a couple of quarters out of his right front pocket and set it all out on the table, with the money sticking out from under the check.

Mel got up and walked past the waitress.

"It's on the table," he told her.

"No cherry pie?" she asked him.

It sounded like a proposition, so he grinned as he said, "Nah." *If you weren't so ugly*, he thought, *I just might stay for dessert.*

"Come again," she said.

You wish, he thought.

If they called him back, he'd say he couldn't read her handwriting. Her fault. No wonder she didn't get a tip. Smiling, he lifted a toothpick off the cashier's counter and used it to salute the man behind the cash register.

"Thanks," the man said.

"You bet."

Outside, Mel stood in the parking lot and stretched, shoving his arms high in the air, letting anybody who was watching get a good look at him. Nothin' to hide. Eat your heart out, baby. Then he strolled over to his bike and kicked the stand up with his heel. He poked around his mouth with the toothpick, spat out a sliver of meat, then flipped the toothpick onto the ground. He climbed back on his bike, letting out a breath of satisfaction when his butt hit the warm leather seat.

Mel accelerated slowly, savoring the surge of power building between his legs.

Jane Baum was in bed by 10:30 that night, exhausted once again by her own fear. Lying there in her late aunt's double bed, she obsessed on the mistake she had made in moving to this dreadful, empty place in the middle of nowhere. She had expected to feel nervous for a while, as any other city dweller might who moved to the country. But she hadn't counted on being actually phobic about it—of being possessed by a fear so strong that it seemed to inhabit every cell of her body until at night, every night, she felt she could die from it. She hadn't known—how could she have known?— she would be one of those people who is terrified by the vastness of the prairie. She had visited the farm only a few times as a child, and from those visits she had remembered only warm and fuzzy things like caterpillars and chicks. She had only dimly remembered how antlike a human being feels on the prairie.

Her aunt's house had been broken into twice during the

period between her aunt's death and her own occupancy. That fact cemented her fantasies in a foundation of terrifying reality. When Cissy said, "It's your imagination," Janie retorted, "But it happened twice before! Twice!" She wasn't making it up! There *were* strange, brutal men—that's how she imagined them, they were never caught by the police—who broke in and took whatever they wanted—cans in the cupboard, the radio in the kitchen. It could happen again, Janie thought obsessively as she lay in the bed; it could happen over and over. *To me, to me, to me.*

On the prairie, the darkness seemed absolute to her. There were millions of stars but no streetlights. Coyotes howled, or cattle bawled. Occasionally the big night-riding semis whirred by out front. Their tire and engine sounds seemed to come out of nowhere, build to an intolerable whine and then disappear in an uncanny way. She pictured the drivers as big, rough, intense men hopped up on amphetamines; she worried that one night she would hear truck tires turning into her gravel drive, that an engine would switch off, that a truck door would quietly open and then close, that careful footsteps would slur across her gravel.

Her fear had grown so huge, so bad, that she was even frightened of it. It was like a monstrous balloon that inflated every time she breathed. Every night the fear got worse. The balloon got bigger. It nearly filled the bedroom now.

The upstairs bedroom where she lay was hot because she had the windows pulled down and latched, and the curtains drawn. She could have cooled it with a fan on the dressing table, but she was afraid the fan's noise might cover the sound of whatever might break into the first floor and climb the stairs to attack her. She lay with a sheet and a blanket pulled up over her arms and shoulders, to just under her chin. She was sweating, as if her fear-frozen body were melting, but it felt warm and almost comfortable to her. She always wore pajamas and thin wool socks to bed because she felt safer when she was completely dressed. She especially felt more secure in pajama pants, which no dirty hand could shove up onto her belly as it could a nightgown.

Lying in bed like a quadriplegic, unmoving, eyes open, Janie reviewed her precautions. Every door was locked, every window was permanently shut and locked, so that she didn't have to check them every night; all the curtains were drawn; the porch lights were off; and her car was locked in the barn so no trucker would think she was home.

Lately she had taken to sleeping with her aunt's loaded pistol on the pillow beside her head.

Cissy crawled into bed just before midnight, tired from hours of accounting. She had been out to the barn to check on her giggling girls and the blind calf. She had talked to her husband when he called from Oklahoma City. Now she was thinking about how she would try to start easing Janie Baum out of their lives.

"I'm sorry, Janie, but I'm awfully busy today. I don't think you ought to come over . . ."

Oh, but there would be that meek, martyred little voice, just like a baby mouse needing somebody to mother it. How would she deny that need? She was already feeling guilty about refusing Janie's request to sleep over.

"Well, I will. I just will do it, that's all. If I could say no to the FHA girls when they were selling fruitcakes, I can start saying no more often to Janie Baum. Anyway, she's never going to get over her fears if I indulge them."

Bob had said as much when she'd complained to him long-distance. "Cissy, you're not helping her," he'd said. "You're just letting her get worse." And then he'd said something new that had disturbed her. "Anyway, I don't like the girls being around her so much. She's getting too weird, Cissy."

She thought of her daughters—of fearless Tess and dear little Mandy—and of how *safe* and *nice* it was for children in the country. . . .

"Besides," Bob had said, "she's *got* to do more of her own chores. We need Tess and Mandy to help out around our place more; we can't be having them always running off to mow her grass and plant her flowers and feed her cows and water her horse and get her eggs, just because she's scared to stick her silly hand under a damned hen. . . ."

Counting the chores put Cissy to sleep.

• • •

"Tess!" Mandy hissed desperately. "Wait!"

The older girl slowed, to give Mandy time to catch up to her, and then to touch Tess for reassurance. They paused for a moment to catch their breath and to crouch in the shadow of Jane Baum's porch. Tess carried three rolls of toilet paper in a makeshift pouch she'd formed in the belly of her black sweatshirt. ("We gotta wear black, remember!") and Mandy was similarly equipped. Tess decided that now was the right moment to drop her bomb.

"I've been thinking," she whispered.

Mandy was struck cold to her heart by that familiar and dreaded phrase. She moaned quietly. "What?"

"It might rain."

"I told you!"

"So I think we better do it inside."

"*Inside?*"

"Shh! It'll scare her to death, it'll be great! Nobody else'll ever have the guts to do anything as neat as this! We'll do the kitchen, and if we have time, maybe the dining room."

"Ohhh, noooo."

"*She* thinks she's got all the doors and windows locked, but she doesn't!" Tess giggled. She had it all figured out that when Jane Baum came downstairs in the morning, she'd take one look, scream, faint, and then, when she woke up, call everybody in town. The fact that Jane might also call the sheriff had occurred to her, but since Tess didn't have any faith in the ability of adults to figure out anything important, she wasn't worried about getting caught. "When I took in her eggs, I unlocked the downstairs bathroom window! Come on! This'll be great!"

The ribbon of darkness ahead of Mel Brown was no longer straight. It was now bunched into long, steep hills. He hadn't expected hills. Nobody had told him there was any part of Kansas that wasn't flat. So he wasn't making as good time, and he couldn't run full-bore. But then, he wasn't in a hurry, except for the hell of it. And this was more interesting, more dangerous, and he liked the thrill of that. He started edging closer to the centerline every time he roared up a hill, playing a game of highway roulette in which he was the winner as long as whatever coming from the other direction had its headlights on.

When that got boring, he turned his own headlights off.

Now he roared past cars and trucks like a dark demon.

Mel laughed every time, thinking how surprised they must be, and how frightened. They'd think, *Crazy fool, I could have hit him. . . .*

He supposed he wasn't afraid of anything, except maybe going back to prison, and he didn't think they'd send him down on a speeding ticket. Besides, if Kansas was like most states, it was long on roads and short on highway patrolmen. . . .

Roaring downhill was even more fun, because of the way his stomach dropped out. He felt like a kid, yelling "Fuuuuck," all the way down the other side. What a goddamned roller coaster of a state this was turning out to be.

The rain still looked miles away.

Mel felt as if he could ride all night. Except that his eyes were gritty, the first sign that he'd better start looking for a likely place to spend the night. He wasn't one to sleep under the stars, not if he could find a ceiling.

Tess directed her sister to stack the rolls of toilet paper underneath the bathroom window on the first floor of Jane Baum's house. The six rolls, all white, stacked three in a row, two high, gave Tess the little bit of height and leverage she needed to push up the glass with her palms. She stuck her fingers under the bottom edge and laboriously attempted to raise the window. It was stiff in its coats of paint.

"Damn," she exclaimed, and let her arms slump. Beneath her feet, the toilet paper was getting squashed.

She tried again, and this time she showed her strength from lifting calves and tossing hay. With a crack of paint and a thump of wood on wood, the window slid all the way up.

"Shhh!" Mandy held her fists in front of her face and knocked her knuckles against each other in excitement and agitation. Her ears picked up the sound of a roaring engine on the highway, and she was immediately sure it was the sheriff, coming to arrest her and Tess. She tugged frantically at the calf of her sister's right leg.

Tess jerked her leg out of Mandy's grasp and disappeared through the open window.

The crack of the window and the thunder of the approaching motorcycle confused themselves in Jane's sleeping consciousness, so that when she awoke from dreams full of anxiety—her eyes flying open, the rest of her body frozen—she imagined in a confused, hallucinatory kind of way that somebody was both coming to get her and already there in the house.

Jane then did as she had trained herself to do. She had practiced over and over every night, so that her actions would be instinctive. She turned her face to the pistol on the other pillow and placed her thumb on the trigger.

Her fear—of rape, of torture, of kidnapping, of agony, of death—was a balloon, and she floated horribly in the center of it. There were thumps and other sounds downstairs, and they joined her in the balloon. There was an engine roaring, and then suddenly it was silent, and a slurring of wheels in her gravel drive, and these sounds joined her in her balloon. When she couldn't bear it any longer, she popped the balloon by shooting herself in the forehead.

In the driveway, Mel Brown heard the gun go off.

He slung his leg back onto his motorcycle and roared back out onto the highway. So the place had looked empty. So he'd been wrong. So he'd find someplace else. But holy shit. Get the fuck outta here.

Inside the house, in the bathroom, Tess also heard the shot and, being a ranch child, recognized it instantly for what it was, although she wasn't exactly sure where it had come from. Cussing and sobbing, she clambered over the sink and back out the window, falling onto her head and shoulders on the rolls of toilet paper.

"It's the sheriff!" Mandy was hysterical. "He's shooting at us!"

Tess grabbed her little sister by a wrist and pulled her

away from the house. They were both crying and stumbling. They ran in the drainage ditch all the way home and flung themselves into the barn.

Mandy ran to lie beside the little blind bull calf. She lay her head on Flopper's side. When he didn't respond, she jerked to her feet. She glared at her sister.

''He's dead!''

''Shut up!''

Cissy Johnson had awakened, too, although she hadn't known why. Something, some noise, had stirred her. And now she sat up in bed, breathing hard, frightened for no good reason she could fathom. If Bob had been home, she'd have sent him out to the barn to check on the girls. But why? The girls were all right, they must be, this was just the result of a bad dream. But she didn't remember having any such dream.

Cissy got out of bed and ran to the window.

No, it wasn't a storm, the rain hadn't come.

A motorcycle!

That's what she'd heard, that's what had awakened her!

Quickly, with nervous fingers, Cissy put on a robe and tennis shoes. Darn you, Janie Baum, she thought, your fears are contagious, that's what they are. The thought popped into her head: If you don't have fears, they can't come true.

Cissy raced out to the barn.

With the introduction of Sharon McCone in Edwin of the Iron Shoes in 1977, Marcia Muller opened the floodgates for the modern woman detective. Appearing in 19 novels, Sharon has left her position with All Soul's Legal Cooperative to become an independent investigator, stretching herself to meet the challenges. The results are exciting. Wolf in the Shadows won an Anthony and was nominated for a Shamus and an Edgar, The McCone Files won an Anthony for Best Short Story Collection, and Marcia herself was given a Life Achievement Award from Private Eye Writers of America in 1993. In her most recent outing, Both Ends of the Night, Sharon (like Marcia) learns of the pleasures and the risks of small-plane flight.

In "All the Lonely People," Sharon, with typical humor and sharp wit, puts herself on the roster of a dating service to solve a crime.

all the lonely people

by Marcia Muller

"**N**AME, SHARON MCCONE. OCCUPATION . . . I can't put private investigator. What should I be?" I glanced over my shoulder at Hank Zahn, my boss at All Souls Legal Cooperative. He stood behind me, his eyes bemused behind thick horn-rimmed glasses.

"I've heard you tell people you're a researcher when you don't want to be bothered with stupid questions like 'What's a nice girl like you . . .' "

"*Legal* researcher." I wrote it on the form. "Now— 'About the person you are seeking.' Age—does not matter. Smoker—does not matter. Occupation—does not matter. I sound excessively eager for a date, don't I?"

Hank didn't answer. He was staring at the form. "The things they ask. Sexual preference." He pointed at the item. "Hetero, bi, lesbian, gay. There's no place for 'does not matter.' "

As he spoke, he grinned wickedly. I glared at him. "You're enjoying this!"

"Of course I am. I never thought I'd see the day you'd fill out an application for a dating service."

I sighed and drummed my fingertips on the desk. Hank is my best male friend, as well as my boss. I love him like a brother—sometimes. But he harbors an overactive interest in my love life and delights in teasing me about it. I would be hearing about the dating service for years to come. I asked, "What should I say I want the guy's cultural interests to be? I can't put 'does not matter' for everything."

"I don't think burglars *have* cultural interests."

"Come on, Hank. Help me with this!"

"Oh, put film. Everyone's gone to a movie."

"Film." I checked the box.

The form was quite simple, yet it provided a great deal of information about the applicant. The standard questions about address, income level, whether the individual shared a home or lived alone, and hours free for dating were enough in themselves to allow an astute burglar to weed out prospects—and pick times to break in when they were not likely to be on the premises.

And that apparently was what had happened at the big singles apartment complex down near the San Francisco–Daly City line, owned by Hank's client, Dick Morris. There had been three burglaries over the past three months, beginning not long after the place had been leafleted by All the Best People Introduction Service. Each of the people whose apartments had been hit were women who had filled out the application forms; they had had from two to ten dates with men with whom the service had put them in touch. The burglaries had taken place when one renter was at work, another away for the weekend, and the third out with a date whom she had also met through Best People.

Coincidence, the police had told the renters and Dick Morris. After all, none of the women had reported having dates with the same man. And there were many other common denominators among them besides their use of the service. They lived in the same complex. They all knew one another. Two belonged to the same health club. They shopped at the same supermarket, shared auto mechanics, hairstylists, dry cleaners, and two of them went to the same psychiatrist.

Coincidence, the police insisted. But two other San Francisco area members of Best People had also been burglarized—one of them male—and so they checked the service out carefully.

What they found was absolutely no evidence of collusion in the burglaries. It was no fly-by-night operation. It had been in business ten years—a long time for that type of outfit. Its board of directors included a doctor, a psychologist, a rabbi, a minister, and a well-known author of somewhat weird but popular novels. It was respectable—as such things go.

But Best People was still the strongest link among the burglary victims. And Dick Morris was a good landlord who genuinely cared about his tenants. So he put on a couple of security guards, and when the police couldn't run down the perpetrator(s) and backburnered the case, he came to All Souls for legal advice.

It might seem unusual for the owner of a glitzy singles complex to come to a legal services plan that charges its clients on a sliding-fee scale, but Dick Morris was cash-poor. Everything he'd saved during his long years as a journeyman plumber had gone into the complex, and it was barely turning a profit as yet. Wouldn't be turning any profit at all if the burglaries continued and some of his tenants got scared and moved out.

Hank could have given Dick the typical attorney's spiel about leaving things in the hands of the police and continuing to pay the guards out of his dwindling cash reserves, but Hank is far from typical. Instead he referred Dick to me. I'm All Souls' staff investigator, and assignments like this one—where there's a challenge—are what I live for.

They are, that is, unless I have to apply for membership in a dating service, plus set up my own home as a target for a burglar. Once I started "dating," I would remove anything of value to All Souls, plus Dick would station one of his security guards at my house during the hours I was away from there, but it was still a potentially risky and nervous-making proposition.

Now Hank loomed over me, still grinning. I could tell how much he was going to enjoy watching me suffer through an improbable, humiliating, *asinine* experience. I smiled back—sweetly.

" 'Your sexual preference.' Hetero." I checked the box firmly. "Except for inflating my income figure, so I'll look like I have a lot of good stuff to steal, I'm filling this out truthfully," I said. "Who knows—I might meet someone wonderful."

When I looked back up at Hank, my evil smile matched his earlier one. He, on the other hand, looked as if he'd swallowed something the wrong way.

My first "date" was a chubby little man named Jerry Hale. Jerry was *very* into the singles scene. We met at a bar in San Francisco's affluent Marina district, and while we talked, he kept swiveling around in his chair and leering at every woman who walked by. Most of them ignored him, but a few glared; I wanted to hang a big sign around my neck saying, "I'm not really with him, it's only business." While I tried to find out about his experiences with All the Best People Introduction Service, plus impress him with all the easily fenceable items I had at home, he tried to educate me on the joys of being single.

"I used to be into the bar scene pretty heavily," he told me. "Did all right too. But then I started to worry about herpes and AIDS—I'll let you see the results of my most recent test if you want—and my drinking was getting out of hand. Besides, it was expensive. Then I went the other way—a health club. Did all right there too. But goddamn, it's *tiring*. So then I joined a bunch of church groups—you meet a lot of horny women there. But churches encourage matrimony, and I'm not into that."

"So you applied to All the Best People. How long have you—?"

"Not right away. First I thought about joining AA, even went to a meeting. Lots of good-looking women are recovering alcoholics, you know. But I like to drink too much to make the sacrifice. Dear Abby's always saying you should enroll in courses, so I signed up for a couple at U.C. Extension. Screenwriting and photography."

My mouth was stiff from smiling politely, and I had just

about written Jerry off as a possible suspect—he was too busy to burglarize anyone. I took a sip of wine and looked at my watch.

Jerry didn't notice the gesture. "The screenwriting class was terrible—the instructor actually wanted you to write stuff. And photography—how can you see women in the darkroom, let alone make any moves when you smell like chemicals?"

I had no answer for that. Maybe my own efforts at photography accounted for my not having a lover at the moment. . . .

"Finally I found All the Best People," Jerry went on. "Now I really do all right. And it's opened up a whole new world of dating to me—eighties-style. I've answered ads in the paper, placed my own ad too. You've always got to ask that they send a photo, though, so you can screen out the dogs. There's Weekenders, they plan trips. When I don't want to go out of the house, I use the Intro Line—that's a phone club you can join, where you call in for three bucks and either talk to one person or on a party line. There's a video exchange where you can make tapes and trade them with people so you'll know you're compatible before you set up a meeting. I do all right."

He paused expectantly, as if he thought I was going to ask how I could get in on all these good eighties-style deals.

"Jerry," I said, "have you read any good books lately?"

"Have I . . . *what*?"

"What do you do when you're not dating?"

"I work. I told you, I'm in sales—"

"Do you ever spend time alone?"

"Doing what?"

"Oh, just being alone. Puttering around the house or working at hobbies. Just thinking."

"Are you crazy? What kind of a computer glitch are you, anyway?" He stood, all five-foot-three of him quivering indignantly. "Believe me, I'm going to complain to Best People about setting me up with you. They described you as 'vivacious,' but you've hardly said a word all evening!"

•   •   •

Morton Stone was a nice man, a sad man. He insisted on buying me dinner at his favorite Chinese restaurant. He spent the evening asking me questions about myself and my job as a legal researcher; while he listened, his fingers played nervously with the silverware. Later, over a brandy in a nearby bar, he told me how his wife had died the summer before, of cancer. He told me about his promise to her that he would get on with his life, find someone new, and be happy. This was the first date he'd arranged through All the Best People; he'd never done anything like that in his life. He'd only tried them because he wasn't good at meeting people. He had a good job, but it wasn't enough. He had money to travel, but it was no fun without someone to share the experience with. He would have liked to have children, but he and his wife had put it off until they'd be financially secure, and then they'd found out about the cancer. . . .

I felt guilty as hell about deceiving him, and for taking his time, money, and hope. But by the end of the evening I'd remembered a woman friend who was just getting over a disastrous love affair. A nice, sad woman who wasn't good at meeting people; who had a good job, loved to travel, and longed for children. . . .

Bob Gillespie was a sailing instructor on a voyage of self-discovery. He kept prefacing his remarks with statements such as, ''You know, I had a great insight into myself last week.'' That was nice; I was happy for him. But I would rather have gotten to know his surface persona before probing into his psyche. Like the two previous men, Bob didn't fit any of the recognizable profiles of the professional burglar, nor had he had any great insight into how All the Best People worked.

Ted Horowitz was a recovering alcoholic, which was admirable. Unfortunately he was also the confessional type. He began every anecdote with the admission that it had happened ''back when I was drinking.'' He even felt compelled to describe how he used to throw up on his ex-wife. His only complaint about Best People—this with a stern look at my wineglass—was that they kept referring him to women who drank.

Jim Rogers was an adman who wore safari clothes and was into guns. I refrained from telling him that I own two .38 Specials and am a highly qualified marksman, for fear it would incite him to passion. For a little while I considered him seriously for the role of burglar, but when I probed the subject by mentioning a friend having recently been ripped off, Jim became enraged and said the burglar ought to be hunted down and shot.

"I'm going about this all wrong," I said to Hank.

It was ten in the morning, and we were drinking coffee at the big round table in All Souls' kitchen. The night before I'd spent hours on the phone with an effervescent insurance underwriter who was going on a whale-watching trip with Weekenders, the group that god-awful Jerry Hale had mentioned. He'd concluded our conversation by saying he'd be sure to note in his pocket organizer to call me the day after he returned. Then I'd been unable to sleep and had sat up hours longer, drinking too much and listening for burglars and brooding about loneliness.

I wasn't involved with anyone at the time—nor did I particularly want to be. I'd just emerged from a long-term relationship and was reordering my life and getting used to doing things alone again. I was fortunate in that my job and my little house—which I'm constantly remodeling—filled most of the empty hours. But I could still understand what Morton and Bob and Ted and Jim and even that dreadful Jerry were suffering from.

It was the little things that got to me. Like the times I went to the supermarket and everything I felt like having for dinner was packaged for two or more, and I couldn't think of anyone I wanted to have over to share it with. Or the times I'd be driving around a curve in the road and come upon a spectacular view, but have no one in the passenger seat to point it out to. And then there were the cold sheets on the other side of the wide bed on a foggy San Francisco night.

But I got through it, because I reminded myself that it

wasn't going to be that way forever. And when I couldn't convince myself of that, I thought about how it was better to be totally alone than alone *with* someone. That's how *I* got through the cold, foggy nights. But I was discovering there was a whole segment of the population that availed itself of dating services and telephone conversation clubs and video exchanges. Since I'd started using Best People, I'd been inundated by mail solicitations and found that the array of services available to singles was astonishing.

Now I told Hank, "I simply can't stand another evening making polite chitchat in a bar. If I listen to another ex-wife story, I'll scream. I don't want to know what these guys' parents did to them at age ten that made the whole rest of their lives a mess. And besides, having that security guard on my house is costing Dick Morris a bundle that he can ill afford."

Helpfully Hank said, "So change your approach."

"Thanks for your great suggestion." I got up and went out to the desk that belongs to Ted Smalley, our secretary, and dug out a phone directory. All the Best People wasn't listed. My file on the case was on the kitchen table. I went back there—Hank had retreated to his office—and checked the introductory letter they'd sent me; it showed nothing but a post-office box. The zip code told me it was the main post office at Seventh and Mission streets.

I went back and borrowed Ted's phone book again, then looked up the post office's number. I called it, got the mail-sorting supervisor, and identified myself as Sharon from Federal Express. "We've got a package here for All the Best People Introduction Service," I said, and read off the box number. "That's all I've got—no contact phone, no street address."

"Assholes," she said wearily. "Why do they send them to a P.O. box when they know you can't deliver to one? For that matter, why do you accept them when they're addressed like that?"

"Damned if I know. I only work here."

"I can't give out the street address, but I'll supply the contact phone." She went away, came back, and read it off to me.

"Thanks." I depressed the disconnect button and redialed.

A female voice answered with only the phone number. I went into my Federal Express routine. The woman gave me the address without hesitation, in the 200 block of Gough Street near the Civic Center. After I hung up I made one more call: to a friend on the *Chronicle*. J. D. Smith was in the city room and agreed to leave a few extra business cards with the security guard in the newspaper building's lobby.

All the Best People's offices took up the entire second floor of a renovated Victorian. I couldn't imagine why they needed so much space, but they seemed to be doing a landslide business, because phones in the offices on either side of the long corridor were ringing madly. I assumed it was because the summer vacation season was approaching and San Francisco singles were getting anxious about finding someone to make travel plans with.

The receptionist was more or less what I expected to find in the office of that sort of business: petite, blond, sleekly groomed, and expensively dressed, with an elegant manner. She took J. D.'s card down the hallway to see if their director was available to talk with me about the article I was writing on the singles scene. I paced around the tiny waiting room, which didn't even have chairs. When the young woman came back, she said Dave Lester would be happy to see me and led me to an office at the rear.

The office was plush, considering the attention that had been given to decor in the rest of the suite. It had a leather couch and chairs, a wet bar, and an immense mahogany desk. There wasn't so much as a scrap of paper or a file folder to suggest anything resembling work was done there. I couldn't see Dave Lester, because he had swiveled his high-backed chair around toward the window and was apparently contemplating the wall of the building next door. The receptionist backed out the door and closed it. I cleared my throat, and the chair turned toward me.

The man in the chair was god-awful Jerry Hale.

Our faces must have been mirror images of shock. I said, "What are *you* doing here?"

He said, "You're not J. D. Smith. You're Sharon Mc-

Cone!'' Then he frowned down at the business card he held. ''Or is Sharon McCone really J. D. Smith?''

I collected my scattered wits and said, ''Which are you— Dave Lester or Jerry Hale?''

He merely stared at me, his expression wavering between annoyance and amusement.

I added, ''I'm a reporter doing a feature article on the singles scene.''

''So Marie said. How did you get this address? We don't publish it because we don't want all sorts of crazies wandering in. This is an exclusive service; we screen our applicants carefully.''

They certainly hadn't screened me; otherwise they'd have uncovered numerous deceptions. I said, ''Oh, we newspaper people have our sources.''

''Well, you certainly misrepresented yourself to us.''

''And you misrepresented yourself to *me!*''

He shrugged. ''It's part of the screening process, for our clients' protection. We realize most applicants would shy away from a formal interview situation, so we have the first date take the place of that.''

''You yourself go out with *all* the women who apply?''

''A fair amount, using a different name every time, of course, in case any of them know each other and compare notes.'' At my astonished look he added, ''What can I say? I like women. But naturally I have help. And Marie''—he motioned at the closed door—''and one of the secretaries check out the guys.''

No wonder Jerry had no time to read. ''Then none of the things you told me were true? About being into the bar scene and the church groups and the health club?''

''Sure they were. My previous experiences were what led me to buy Best People from its former owners. They hadn't studied the market, didn't know how to make a go of it in the eighties.''

''Well, you're certainly a good spokesman for your own product. But how come you kept referring me to other clients? We didn't exactly part on amiable terms.''

''Oh, that was just a ruse to get out of there. I had another date. I'd seen enough to know you weren't my type. But I

decided you were still acceptable; we get a lot of men looking for your kind.''

The ''acceptable'' rankled. ''What exactly is my kind?''

''Well, I'd call you . . . introspective. Bookish? No, not exactly. A little offbeat? Maybe intense? No. It's peculiar . . .
you're peculiar—''

''Stop right there!''

Jerry—who would always be god-awful Jerry and never
Dave Lester to me—stood up and came around the desk. I
straightened my posture. From my five-foot-six vantage point
I could see the beginnings of a bald spot under his artfully
styled hair. When he realized where I was looking, his mouth
tightened. I took a perverse delight in his discomfort.

''I'll have to ask you to leave now,'' he said stiffly.

''But don't you want Best People featured in a piece on
singles?''

''I do not. I can't condone the tactics of a reporter who
misrepresents herself.''

''Are you sure that's the reason you don't want to talk
with me?''

''Of course. What else—''

''Is there something about Best People that you'd rather
not see publicized?''

Jerry flushed. When he spoke, it was in a flat, deceptively
calm manner. ''Get out of here,'' he said, ''or I'll call your
editor.''

Since I didn't want to get J. D. in trouble with the *Chron*,
I went.

Back at my office at All Souls, I curled up in my ratty
armchair—my favorite place to think. I considered my visit
to All the Best People; I considered what was wrong with
the setup there. Then I got out my list of burglary victims
and called each of them. All three gave me similar answers
to my questions. Next I checked the phone directory and
called my friend Tracy in the billing office at Pacific Bell.

''I need an address for a company that's only listed by
number in the directory,'' I told her.

''Billing address, or location where the phone's installed?''

"Both, if they're different."

She tapped away on her computer keyboard. "Billing and location are the same: two-eleven Gough. Need anything else?"

"That's it. Thanks—I owe you a drink."

In spite of my earlier determination to depart the singles scene, I spent the next few nights on the phone, this time assuming the name of Patsy Newhouse, my younger sister. I talked to various singles about my new VCR; I described the sapphire pendant my former boyfriend had given me and how I planned to have it reset to erase old memories. I babbled excitedly about the trip to Las Vegas I was taking in a few days with Weekenders, and promised to make notes in my pocket organizer to call people as soon as I got back. I mentioned—in seductive tones—how I loved to walk barefoot over my genuine Persian rugs. I praised the merits of my new microwave oven. I described how I'd gotten into collecting costly jade carvings. By the time the Weekenders trip was due to depart for Vegas, I was constantly sucking on throat lozenges and wondering how long my voice would hold out.

Saturday night found me sitting in my kitchen sharing ham sandwiches and coffee by candlelight with Dick Morris's security guard, Bert Jankowski. The only reason we'd chanced the candles was that we'd taped the shades securely over the windows. There was something about eating in total darkness that put us both off.

Bert was a pleasant-looking man of about my age, with sandy hair and a bristly mustache and a friendly, open face. We'd spent a lot of time together—Friday night, all day today—and I'd pretty much heard his life story. We had a lot in common: He was from Oceanside, not far from where I'd grown up in San Diego; like me, he had a degree in the social sciences and hadn't been able to get a job in his field. Unlike me, he'd been working for the security service so long that he was making a decent wage, and he liked it. It gave him more time, he said, to read and to fish. I'd told him my life story, too: about my somewhat peculiar family, about my blighted romances, even about the man I'd once had to shoot. By Saturday night I sensed both of us were getting bored with examining our pasts, but the present situation was even more stultifying.

I said, "Something has *got* to happen soon."

Bert helped himself to another sandwich. "Not necessarily. Got any more of those pickles?"

"No, we're out."

"Shit. I don't suppose if this goes on that there's any possibility of cooking breakfast tomorrow? Sundays I always fix bacon."

In spite of having just wolfed down some ham, my mouth began to water. "No," I said wistfully. "Cooking smells, you know. This house is supposed to be vacant for the weekend."

"So far no one's come near it, and nobody seems to be casing it. Maybe you're wrong about the burglaries."

"Maybe . . . no, I don't think so. Listen: Andie Wyatt went to Hawaii; she came back to a cleaned-out apartment. Janie Roos was in Carmel with a lover; she lost everything fenceable. Kim New was in Vegas, where I'm supposed to be—"

"But maybe you're wrong about the way the burglar knows—"

There was a noise toward the rear of the house, past the current construction zone on the back porch. I held up my hand for Bert to stop talking and blew out the candles.

I sensed Bert tensing. He reached for his gun at the same time I did.

The noise came louder—the sound of an implement probing the back-porch lock. It was one of those useless toy locks that had been there when I'd bought the cottage; I'd left the dead bolt unlocked since Friday.

Rattling sounds. A snap. The squeak of the door as it moved inward.

I touched Bert's arm. He moved over into the recess by the pantry, next to the light switch. I slipped up next to the door to the porch. The outer door shut, and footsteps came toward the kitchen, then stopped.

A thin beam of light showed under the inner door between

the kitchen and the porch—the burglar's flashlight. I smiled, imagining his surprise at the sawhorses and wood scraps and exposed wiring that make up my own personal urban-renewal project.

The footsteps moved toward the kitchen door again. I took the safety off the .38.

The door swung toward me. A half-circle of light from the flash illuminated the blue linoleum. It swept back and forth, then up and around the room. The figure holding the flash seemed satisfied that the room was empty; it stepped inside and walked toward the hall.

Bert snapped on the overhead light.

I stepped forward, gun extended, and said, "All right, Jerry. Hands above your head and turn around—slowly."

The flash clattered to the floor. The figure—dressed all in black—did as I said.

But it wasn't Jerry.

It was Morton Stone—the nice, sad man I'd had the dinner date with. He looked as astonished as I felt.

I thought of the evening I'd spent with him, and my anger rose. All that sincere talk about how lonely he was and how much he missed his dead wife. And now he turned out to be a common crook!

"You son of a bitch!" I said. "And I was going to fix you up with one of my friends!"

He didn't say anything. His eyes were fixed nervously on my gun.

Another noise on the back porch. Morton opened his mouth, but I silenced him by raising the .38.

Footsteps clattered across the porch, and a second figure in black came through the door. "Morton, what's wrong? Why'd you turn the lights on?" a woman's voice demanded.

It was Marie, the receptionist from All the Best People. Now I knew how she could afford her expensive clothes.

"So I was right about *how* they knew when to burglarize people, but wrong about *who* was doing it," I told Hank. We were sitting at the bar in the Remedy Lounge, his favorite Mission Street watering hole.

"I'm still confused. The Intro Line is part of All the Best People?"

"It's owned by Jerry Hale, and the phone equipment is located in the same offices. But as Jerry—Dave Lester, whichever incarnation you prefer—told me later, he doesn't want the connection publicized because the Intro Line is kind of sleazy, and Best People's supposed to be high-toned. Anyway, I figured it out because I noticed there were an awful lot of phones ringing at their offices, considering their number isn't published. Later I confirmed it with the phone company and started using the line myself to set the burglar up."

"So this Jerry wasn't involved at all?"

"No. He's the genuine article—a born-again single who decided to put his knowledge to turning a profit."

Hank shuddered and took a sip of Scotch.

"The burglary scheme," I went on, "was all Marie Stone's idea. She had access to the addresses of the people who joined the Intro Line club, and she listened in on the phone conversations and scouted out good prospects. Then, when she was sure their homes would be vacant for a period of time, her brother, Morton Stone, pulled the jobs while she kept watch outside."

"How come you had a date with Marie's brother? Was he looking you over as a burglary prospect?"

"No. They didn't use All the Best People for that. It's Jerry's pride and joy; he's too involved in the day-to-day workings and might have realized something was wrong. But the Intro Line is just a profit-making arm of the business to him—he probably uses it to subsidize his dating. He'd virtually turned the operation of it over to Marie. But he did allow Marie to send out mail solicitations for it to Best People clients, as well as mentioning it to the women he 'screened,' and that's how the burglary victims heard of it."

"But it still seems too great a coincidence that you ended up going out with this Morton."

I smiled. "It wasn't a coincidence at all. Morton also works for Best People, helping Jerry screen the female clients. When I had my date with Jerry, he found me . . . well, he said I was peculiar."

Hank grinned and started to say something, but I glared.

"Anyway, he sent Mort out with me to render a second opinion."

"Ye gods, you were almost rejected by a dating service."

"What really pisses me off is Morton's grieving-widower story. I really fell for the whole tasteless thing. Jerry told me Morton gets a lot of women with it—they just can't resist a man in pain."

"But not McCone." Hank drained his glass and gestured at mine. "You want another?"

I looked at my watch. "Actually, I've got to be going."

"How come? It's early yet."

"Well, uh . . . I have a date."

He raised his eyebrows. "I thought you were through with the singles scene. Which one is it tonight—the gun nut?"

I got off the bar stool and drew myself up in a dignified manner. "It's someone I met on my own. They always tell you that you meet the most compatible people when you're just doing what you like to do and not specifically looking."

"So where'd you meet this guy?"

"On a stakeout."

Hank waited. His eyes fairly bulged with curiosity.

I decided not to tantalize him any longer. I said, "It's Bert Jankowski, Dick Morris's security guard."

*Julie Smith, a former reporter in New Orleans and San Fran-
cisco, is wickedly inventive as she gets her thoroughly contemporary characters out of the sticky situations they've managed
to get themselves into. Julie's wit and charm infuse the fictional adventures of clever, attractive attorney Rebecca
Schwartz (most recently,* Other People's Skeletons*) and en-
liven the foibles of Paul MacDonald, who appears in two
books. New Orleans detective Skip Langdon takes readers on
a tour of the darker side of town in the Edgar-winning* New
Orleans Mourning. *Skip goes into action in five other novels,
including the most recent,* Crescent City Kills.

*In "Blood Types," the irreverent Rebecca discovers just
how risky a potion the milk of human kindness can be.*

blood types

by Julie Smith

"**R**EFRESH MY RECOLLECTION, COUNSELOR. ARE
holographic wills legal in California?"

Though we'd hardly spoken in seven years or more, I recognized the voice on the phone as easily if I'd heard it yesterday. I'd lived with its owner once. "Gary Wilder. Aren't
you feeling well?"

"I feel fine. Settle a bet, okay?"

"Unless you slept through more classes than I thought,
you know perfectly well they're legal."

"They used to be. It's been a long time, you know? How
are you, Rebecca?"

"Great. And you're a daddy, I hear. How's Stephanie?"

"Fine."

"And the wee one?"

"Little Laurie-bear. The best thing that ever happened to
me."

"You sound happy."

"Laurie's my life."

I was sorry to hear it. That was a lot of responsibility for a ten-month-old.

"So about the will," Gary continued. "Have the rules changed since we were at Boalt?"

"A bit. Remember how it could be invalidated by anything pre-printed on it? Like in that case where there was a date stamped on the paper the woman used, and the whole thing was thrown out?"

"Yeah. I remember someone asked whether you could use your own letterhead."

"That was you, Gary."

"Probably. And you couldn't, it seems to me."

"But you probably could now. Now only the 'materially relevant' part has to be handwritten. And you don't have to date it."

"No? That seems odd."

"Well, you would if there were a previous dated will. Otherwise just write it out, sign it, and it's legal."

Something about the call, maybe just the melancholy of hearing a voice from the past, put me in a gray and restless mood. It was mid-December and pouring outside—perfect weather for doleful ruminations on a man I hardly knew anymore. I couldn't help worrying that if Laurie was Gary's whole life, that didn't speak well for his marriage. Shouldn't Stephanie at least have gotten a small mention? But she hadn't, and the Gary I knew could easily have fallen out of love with her. He was one of life's stationary drifters—staying in the same place but drifting from one mild interest to another, none of them very consuming and none very durable. I hoped it would be different with Laurie; it wouldn't be easy to watch your dad wimp out on you.

But I sensed it was already happening. I suspected that phone call meant little Laurie, who was his life, was making him feel tied down and he was sending out feelers to former and future lady friends.

The weather made me think of a line from a poem Gary used to quote:

> *Il pleure dans mon coeur*
> *Comme il pleut sur la ville.*

He was the sort to quote Paul Verlaine. He read everything, retained everything, and didn't do much. He had never finished law school, had sold insurance for a while and was now dabbling in real estate, I'd heard, though I didn't know what that meant, exactly. Probably trying to figure out a way to speculate with Stephanie's money, which, out of affection for Gary, I thanked heaven she had. If you can't make up your mind what to do with your life, you should at least marry well and waffle in comfort.

Gary died that night. Reading about it in the morning *Chronicle*, I shivered, thinking the phone call was one of those grisly coincidences. But the will came the next day.

The *Chronicle* story said Gary and Stephanie were both killed instantly when their car went over a cliff on a twisty road in a blinding rainstorm. The rains were hellish that year. It was the third day of a five-day flood.

Madeline Bell, a witness to the accident, said Gary had swerved to avoid hitting her Mercedes as she came around a curve. The car had exploded and burned as Bell watched it roll off a hill near San Anselmo, where Stephanie and Gary lived.

Even in that moment of shock I think I felt more grief for Laurie than I did for Gary, who had half lived his life at best. Only a day before, when I'd talked to Gary, Laurie had had it made—her mama was rich and her daddy good-looking. Now she was an orphan.

I wondered where Gary and Stephanie were going in such an awful storm. To a party, probably, or home from one. It was the height of the holiday season.

I knew Gary's mother, of course. Would she already be at the Wilder house, for Hanukkah, perhaps? If not, she'd be coming soon; I'd call in a day or two.

In the meantime I called Rob Burns, who had long since replaced Gary in my affections, and asked to see him that night. I hadn't thought twice of Gary in the past five years, but something was gone from my life and I needed comfort. It would be good to sleep with Rob by my side and the sound of rain on the roof—life-affirming, as we say in California. I'd read somewhere that Mark Twain, when he built his mansion in Hartford, installed a section of tin roof so as to get the best rain sounds. I could understand the impulse.

It was still pouring by mid-morning the next day, and my throat was feeling slightly scratchy, the way it does when a cold's coming on. I was rummaging for vitamin C when Kruzick brought the mail in—Alan Kruzick, incredibly inept but inextricably installed secretary for the law firm of Nicholson and Schwartz, of which I was a protesting partner. The other partner, Chris Nicholson, liked his smart-ass style, my sister Mickey was his girlfriend, and my mother had simply laid down the law—hire him and keep him.

"Any checks?" I asked.

"Nope. Nothing interesting but a letter from a dead man."

"What?"

He held up an envelope with Gary Wilder's name and address in the upper left corner. "Maybe he wants you to channel him."

The tears that popped into my eyes quelled even Kruzick.

The will was in Gary's own handwriting, signed, written on plain paper, and dated December 17, the day of Gary's death. It said: "This is my last will and testament, superseding all others. I leave everything I own to my daughter, Laurie Wilder. If my wife and I die before her 21st birthday, I appoint my brother, Michael Wilder, as her legal guardian. I also appoint my brother as executor of this will."

My stomach clutched as I realized that Gary had known when we talked that he and Stephanie were in danger. He'd managed to seem his usual happy-go-lucky self, using the trick he had of hiding his feelings that had made him hard to live with.

But if he knew he was going to be killed, why hadn't he given the murderer's identity? Perhaps he had, I realized. I was a lawyer, so I'd gotten the will. Someone else might have gotten a letter about what was happening. I wondered if my old boyfriend had gotten involved with the dope trade. After all, he lived in Marin County, which had the highest population of coke dealers outside the greater Miami area.

I phoned Gary's brother at his home in Seattle but was told he'd gone to San Anselmo. I had a client coming in five minutes, but after that, nothing pressing. And so, by two o'clock I was on the Golden Gate Bridge, enjoying a rare moment of foggy overcast, the rain having relented for a while.

It was odd about Gary's choosing Michael for Laurie's guardian. When I'd known him well he'd had nothing but contempt for his brother. Michael was a stockbroker and a go-getter; Gary was a mooner-about, a romantic, and a rebel. He considered his brother boring, stuffy, a bit crass, and utterly worthless. On the other hand, he adored his sister, Jeri, a free-spirited dental hygienist married to a good-natured sometime carpenter.

Was Michael married? Yes, I thought. At least he had been. Maybe fatherhood had changed Gary's opinions on what was important—Michael's money and stability might have looked good to him when he thought of sending Laurie to college.

I pulled up in front of the Wilder-Cooper house, a modest redwood one that had probably cost nearly half a million. Such were real-estate values in Marin County—and such was Stephanie's bank account.

At home were Michael Wilder—wearing a suit—and Stephanie's parents, Mary and Jack Cooper. Mary was a big woman, comfortable and talkative; Jack was skinny and withdrawn. He stared into space, almost sad, but mostly just faraway, and I got the feeling watching TV was his great passion in life, though perhaps he drank as well. The idea, it appeared, was simply to leave the room without anyone noticing, the means of transportation being entirely insignificant.

It was a bit awkward, my being the ex-girlfriend and showing up unexpectedly. Michael didn't seem to know how to introduce me, and I could take a hint. It was no time to ask to see him privately.

"I'd hoped to see your mother," I said.

"She's at the hospital," said Mary. "We're taking turns now that—" She started to cry.

"The hospital!"

"You don't know about Laurie?"

"She was in the accident?"

"No. She's been very ill for the last two months."

"Near death," said Mary. "What that child has been through shouldn't happen to an animal. Tiny little face just contorts itself like a poor little monkey's. Screams and screams and screams; and *rivers* flow out of her little bottom. *Rivers*, Miss Schwartz!"

Her shoulders hunched and began to shake. Michael looked helpless. Mechanically Jack put an arm around her.

"What's wrong?" I asked Michael.

He shrugged. "They don't know. Can't diagnose it."

"Now, Mary," said Jack. "She's better. The doctor said so last night."

"What hospital is she in?"

"Marin General."

I said to Michael: "I think I'll pop by and see your mother—would you mind pointing me in the right direction? I've got a map in the car."

When we arrived at the curb, I said, "I can find the hospital. I wanted to give you something."

I handed him the will. "This came in today's mail. It'll be up to you as executor to petition the court for probate." As he read, a look of utter incredulity came over his face. "But . . . I'm divorced. I can't take care of a baby."

"Gary didn't ask in advance if you'd be willing?"

"Yes, but . . . I didn't think he was going to die!" His voice got higher as reality caught up with him. "He called the day of the accident. But I thought he was just depressed. You know how people get around the holidays."

"What did he say exactly?"

"He said he had this weird feeling, that's all—like something bad might happen to him. And would I take care of Laurie if anything did."

"He didn't say he was scared? In any kind of trouble?"

"No—just feeling weird."

"Michael, he wasn't dealing, was he?"

"Are you kidding? I'd be the last to know." He looked at the ground a minute. "I guess he could have been."

Ellen Wilder was cooing to Laurie when I got to the hospital. "Ohhhh, she's much better now. She just needed her grandma's touch, that's all it was."

She spoke to the baby in the third person, unaware I was there until I announced myself, whereupon she almost dropped the precious angel-wangel and dislodged her IV. We had a tearful reunion, Gary's mother and I. We both missed Gary, and we both felt for poor Laurie.

Ellen adored the baby more than breath, to listen to her, and not only that, she possessed the healing power of a witch. She had spent the night Gary and Stephanie were killed with Laurie, and all day the next day, never even going home for a shower. And gradually the fever had broken, metaphorically speaking. With Grandma's loving attention, the baby's debilitating diarrhea had begun to ease off, and little Laurie had seemed to come back to life.

"Look, Rebecca." She tiptoed to the sleeping baby. "See those cheeks? Roses in them. She's getting her pretty color back, widdle Waurie is, yes, her is." She seemed not to realize she'd lapsed into baby talk.

She came back and sat down beside me. "Stephanie stayed with her nearly around the clock, you know. She was the best mother anyone ever—" Ellen teared up for a second and glanced around the room, embarrassed.

"Look. She left her clothes here. I'll have to remember to take them home. The *best* mother . . . she and Gary were invited to a party that night. It was a horrible, rainy, rainy night, but poor Stephanie hadn't been anywhere but the hospital in weeks—"

"How long had you been here?"

"Oh, just a few days. I came for Hanukkah—and to help out if I could. I knew Stephanie had to get out, so I offered to stay with Laurie. I was just dying to have some time with the widdle fweet fing, anyhow—" This last was spoken more or less in Laurie's direction. Ellen seemed to have developed a habit of talking to the child while carrying on other conversations.

"What happened was Gary had quite a few drinks before he brought me over. Oh, God, I never should have let him drive! We nearly had a wreck on the way over—you know how stormy it was. I kept telling him he was too drunk to drive, and he said I wanted it that way, just like I always wanted him to have strep throat when he was a kid. He said he felt fine then and he felt fine now.''

I was getting lost. "You *wanted* him to have strep throat?''

She shrugged. "I don't know what he meant. He was just drunk, that's all. Oh, God, my poor baby!'' She sniffed, fumbled in her purse, and blew her nose into a tissue.

"Did he seem okay that day—except for being drunk?''

"Fine. Why?''

"He called me that afternoon—about his will. And he called Michael to say he—well, I guess to say he had a premonition about his death.''

"His will? He called you about a will?''

"Yes.''

"But he and Stephanie had already made their wills. Danny Goldstein drew them up.'' That made sense, as Gary had dated his holograph. Danny had been at Boalt with Gary and me. I wondered briefly if it hurt Ellen to be reminded that all Gary's classmates had gone on to become lawyers just like their parents would have wanted.

A fresh-faced nurse popped in and took a look at Laurie. "How's our girl?''

"Like a different baby.''

The nurse smiled. "She sure is. We were really worried for a while there.'' But the smile faded almost instantly. "It's so sad. I never saw a more devoted mother. Laurie never needed us at all—Stephanie was her nurse. One of the best I ever saw.''

"I didn't know Stephanie was a nurse.'' The last I'd heard she was working part-time for a caterer, trying to make up her mind whether to go to chef's school. Stephanie had a strong personality, but she wasn't much more career-minded than Gary was. Motherhood, everyone seemed to think, had been her true calling.

"She didn't have any training—she was just good with infants. You should have seen the way she'd sit and rock that child for hours, Laurie having diarrhea so bad she hardly had any skin on her little butt, crying her little heart out. She must have been in agony like you and I couldn't imagine.

But finally Stephanie would get her to sleep. Nobody else could."

"Nobody else could breast-feed her," I said, thinking surely I'd hit on the source of Stephanie's amazing talent.

"Stephanie couldn't, either. Didn't have enough milk." The nurse shrugged. "Anyone can give a bottle. It wasn't that."

When she left, I said, "I'd better go. Can I do anything for you?"

Ellen thought a minute. "You know what you could do? Will you be going by Gary's again?"

"I'd be glad to."

"You could take some of Stephanie's clothes and things. They're going to let Laurie out in a day or two and there's so much stuff here." She looked exasperated.

Glad to help, I gathered up clothes and began to fold them. Ellen found a canvas carryall of Stephanie's to pack them in. Zipping it open, I saw a bit of white powder in the bottom, and my stomach flopped over. I couldn't get the notion of drugs out of my mind. Gary had had a "premonition" of death, the kind you might get if you burned someone and they threatened you—and now I was looking at white powder.

I found some plastic bags in a drawer that had probably once been used to transport diapers or formula, and lined the bottom of the carryall with them, to keep the powder from sticking to Stephanie's clothes.

But instead of going to Gary's, I dropped in at my parents' house in San Rafael. It was about four o'clock and I had some phoning to do before five.

"Darling!" said Mom. "Isn't it awful about poor Gary Wilder?"

Mom had always liked Gary. She had a soft spot for ne'er-do-wells, as I knew only too well. She was the main reason Kruzick was currently ruining my life. The person for whom she hadn't a minute was the one I preferred most—the blue-eyed and dashing Mr. Rob Burns, star reporter for the San Francisco *Chronicle*.

Using the phone in my dad's study, Rob was the very person I rang up. His business was asking questions that were none of his business, and I had a few for him to ask.

Quickly explaining the will, the odd phone call to Michael, and the white powder, I had him hooked. He smelled the same rat I smelled, and more important, he smelled a story.

While he made his calls I phoned Danny Goldstein. "Becky baby."

"Don't call me that."

"Terrible about Gary, isn't it? Makes you *think*, man."

"Terrible about Stephanie too."

"I don't know. She pussy-whipped him."

"She was better than Melissa."

Danny laughed unkindly, brayed you could even say. Everyone knew Gary had left me for Melissa, who was twenty-two and a cutesy-wootsy doll-baby who couldn't be trusted to go to the store for a six-pack. Naturally everyone thought *I* had Gary pussy-whipped when the truth was, he wouldn't brush his teeth without asking my advice about it. He was a man desperate for a woman to run his life, and I was relieved to be rid of the job.

But still, Melissa had hurt my pride. I thought Gary's choosing her meant he'd grown up and no longer needed me. It was a short-lived maturity, however—within two years Stephanie had appeared on the scene. I might not see it exactly the way Danny did, but I had to admit that if he'd had any balls, she was the one to bust them.

"I hear motherhood mellowed her," I said.

"Yeah, she was born for it. Always worrying was the kid too hot, too cold, too hungry—one of those poo-poo moms."

"Huh?"

"You know. Does the kid want to go poo-poo? Did the kid already go poo-poo? Does it go poo-poo enough? Does it go poo-poo too much? Is it going poo-poo *right now*? She could discuss color and consistency through a whole dinner party, salmon mousse to kiwi tart."

I laughed. Who didn't know the type? "Say, listen, Danny," I said. "Did you know Laurie's been in the hospital?"

"Yeah. Marina, my wife, went to see Stephanie—tried to get her to go out and get some air while she took care of the baby, but Stephanie wouldn't budge."

"I hear you drew up Gary's and Stephanie's wills."

"Yeah. God, I never thought—poor little Laurie. They asked Gary's sister to be her guardian—he hated his brother and Stephanie was an only child."

"Guess what? Gary made another will just before he died, naming the brother as Laurie's guardian."

"I don't believe it."

"Believe it. I'll send you a copy."

"There's going to be a hell of a court fight."

I wasn't so sure about that. The court, of course, wouldn't be bound by either parent's nomination. Since Stephanie's will nominated Jeri as guardian, she and Michael might choose to fight it out, but given Michael's apparent hesitation to take Laurie, I wasn't sure there'd be any argument at all.

"Danny," I said, "you were seeing a lot of him, right?"

"Yeah. We played racquetball."

"Was he dealing coke? Or something else?"

"Gary? No way. You can't be a dealer and be as broke as he was."

The phone rang almost the minute I hung up. Rob had finished a round of calls to what he called "his law-enforcement sources." He'd learned that Gary's brakes hadn't been tampered with, handily blowing my murder theory.

Or seemingly blowing it. Something was still very wrong, and I wasn't giving up till I knew what the powder was. Mom asked me to dinner, but I headed back to the city— Rob had said he could get someone to run an analysis that night.

It was raining again by the time I'd dropped the stuff off, refused Rob's dinner invitation (that was two) and gone home to solitude and split pea soup that I make up in advance and keep in the freezer for nights like this. It was the second night after Gary's death; the first night I'd needed to reassure myself I was still alive. Now I needed to mourn. I didn't plan anything fancy like sackcloth and ashes, just a quiet night home with a book, free to let my mind wander and my eyes fill up from time to time.

But first I had a message from Michael Wilder. He wanted to talk. He felt awful calling me like this, but there was no one in his family he felt he could talk to. Couldn't we meet for coffee or something?

Sure we could—at my house. Not even for Gary's brother was I going out in the rain again.

After the soup I showered and changed into jeans. Michael arrived in wool slacks and a sport coat—not even in repose, apparently, did he drop the stuffy act. Maybe life with Laurie would loosen him up. I asked if he'd thought any more about being her guardian.

It flustered him. "Not really," he said, and didn't meet my eyes.

"I found out the original wills named Jeri as guardian. If Stephanie didn't make a last-minute one, too, hers will still be in effect. Meaning Jeri could fight you if you decide you want Laurie."

"I can't even imagine being a father," he said. "But Gary must have had a good reason—" he broke off. "Poor little kid. A week ago everyone thought *she* was the one who was going to die."

"What's wrong with her—besides diarrhea?" I realized I hadn't had the nerve to ask either of the grandmothers because I knew exactly what would happen—I'd get details that would give *me* symptoms, and two hours later, maybe three or four, I'd be backing toward the door, nodding, with a glazed look on my face, watching matriarchal jaws continue to work.

But Michael only grimaced. "That's all I know about—just life-threatening diarrhea."

"Life-threatening?"

"Without an IV, a dehydrated baby can die in fifteen minutes. Just ask my mother." He shrugged. "Anyway, the doctors talked about electrolyte abnormalities, whatever they may be, and did every test in the book. But the only thing they found was what they called 'high serum sodium levels.' " He shrugged again, as if to shake something off. "Don't ask—especially don't ask my mom or Stephanie's."

We both laughed. I realized Michael had good reasons for finding sudden parenthood a bit on the daunting side.

I got us some wine and when I came back, he'd turned deadly serious. "Rebecca, something weird happened today.

Look what I found.'' He held out a paper signed by Gary and headed ''Beneficiary Designation.''

''Know what that is?''

I shook my head.

''I used to be in insurance—as did my little brother. It's the form you use to change your life insurance beneficiary.''

The form was dated December 16, the day before Gary's death. Michael had been named beneficiary and Laurie contingent beneficiary. Michael said, ''Pretty weird, huh?''

I nodded.

''I also found both Gary's and Stephanie's policies—each for half a million dollars and each naming the other as beneficiary, with Laurie as contingent. For some reason, Gary went to see his insurance agent the day before he died and changed his. What do you make of it?''

I didn't at all like what I made of it. ''It goes with the will,'' I said. ''He named you as Laurie's guardian, so he must have wanted to make sure you could afford to take care of her.''

''I could afford it. For Christ's sake!''

''He must have wanted to compensate you.'' I stopped for a minute. ''It might be his way of saying thanks.''

''You're avoiding the subject, aren't you?''

I was. ''You mean it would have made more sense to leave the money to Laurie directly.''

''Yes. Unless he'd provided for her some other way.''

''Stephanie had money.''

''I don't think Gary knew how much, though.''

I took a sip of wine and thought about it, or rather thought about ways to talk about it, because it was beginning to look very ugly. ''You're saying you think,'' I said carefully, ''that he knew she was going to inherit the half million from Stephanie's policy. Because she was going to die and he was the beneficiary, and he was going to die and his new will left his own property to Laurie.''

Michael was blunt: ''It looks like murder-suicide, doesn't it?''

I said, ''Yeah,'' unable to say any more.

Michael took me over ground I'd already mentally covered: ''He decided to do it in a hurry, probably because it was raining so hard—an accident in the rain would be much more plausible. He made the arrangements. Then he called me and muttered about a premonition, to give himself some sort of feeble motive for suddenly getting his affairs in order; he may have said the same thing to other people as well. Finally he pretended to be drunk, made a big show of almost having an accident on the way to the hospital, picked up Stephanie, and drove her over a cliff.''

Still putting things together, I mumbled, ''You couldn't really be sure you'd die going over just any cliff. You'd have to pick the right cliff, wouldn't you?'' And then I said, ''I wonder if the insurance company will figure it out.''

''Oh, who cares! He probably expected they would but wanted to make the gesture. And he knew I didn't need the money. That's not the point. The point is why?'' He stood up and ran his fingers through his hair, working off excess energy. ''Why kill himself, Rebecca? And why take Stephanie with him?''

''I don't know,'' I said. But I hadn't a doubt that that was what he'd done. There was another why—why make Michael Laurie's guardian? Why not his sister as originally planned?

The next day was Saturday, and I would have dozed happily into mid-morning if Rob hadn't phoned at eight. ''You know the sinister white powder?''

''Uh-huh.''

''Baking soda.''

''That's all?''

''That's it. No heroin, no cocaine, not even any baby talc. Baking soda. Period.''

I thanked him and turned over, but the next couple of hours were full of vaguely disquieting dreams. I woke upset, feeling oddly tainted, as if I'd collaborated in Gary's crimes. It wasn't till I was in the shower—performing my purification ritual, if you believe in such things—that things came together in my conscious mind. The part of me that dreamed had probably known all along.

I called a doctor friend to find out if what I suspected made medical sense. It did. To a baby Laurie's age, baking soda would be a deadly poison. Simply add it to the formula and the excess sodium would cause her to develop severe, dehydrating diarrhea; it might ultimately lead to death. But she would be sick only as long as someone continued to doctor her formula. The poisoning was not cumulative; as soon as it stopped, she would begin to recover, and in only a few days she would be dramatically better.

In other words, he described Laurie's illness to a *T*. And Stephanie, the world's greatest mother, who was there around the clock, must have fed her—at any rate, would have had all the opportunity in the world to doctor her formula.

It didn't make sense. Well, part of it did. The part I could figure out was this: Gary saw Stephanie put baking soda in the formula, already knew about the high sodium reports, put two and two together, may or not have confronted her . . . no, definitely didn't confront her. Gary never confronted anyone.

He simply came to the conclusion that his wife was poisoning their child and decided to kill her, taking his own aimless life as well. That would account for the hurry—to stop the poisoning without having to confront Stephanie. If he accused her, he might be able to stop her, but things would instantly get far too messy for Gary-the-conflict-avoider. Worse, the thing could easily become a criminal case, and if Stephanie was convicted, Laurie would have to grow up knowing her mother had deliberately poisoned her. If she were acquitted, Laurie might always be in danger. I could follow his benighted reasoning perfectly.

But I couldn't, for all the garlic in Gilroy, imagine why Stephanie would want to kill Laurie. By all accounts, she was the most loving of mothers, would probably even have laid down her own life for her child's. I called a shrink friend, Elaine Alvarez.

"Of course she loved the child," Elaine explained. "Why shouldn't she? Laurie perfectly answered her needs." And then she told me some things that made me forget I'd been planning to consume a large breakfast in a few minutes. On the excuse of finally remembering to take Stephanie's clothes, I drove to Gary's house.

The family was planning a memorial service in a day or

two for the dead couple; Jeri had just arrived at her dead brother's house; friends had dropped by to comfort the bereaved; yet there was almost a festive atmosphere in the house. Laurie had come home that morning.

Michael and I took a walk. "Bullshit!" he said. "Dog crap! No one could have taken better care of that baby than Stephanie. Christ, she martyred herself. She stayed up night after night—"

"Listen to yourself. Everything you're saying confirms what Elaine told me. The thing even has a name. It's called Munchausen Syndrome by Proxy. The original syndrome, plain old Munchausen, is when you hurt or mutilate yourself to get attention.

" 'By proxy' means you do it to your nearest and dearest. People say, 'Oh, that poor woman. God, what she's been through. Look how brave she is! Why, no one in the world could be a better mother.' And Mom gets off on it. There are recorded cases of it, Michael, at least one involving a mother and baby."

He was pale. "I think I'm going to throw up."

"Let's sit down a minute."

In fact, stuffy, uptight Michael ended up lying down in the dirt on the side of the road, nice flannel slacks and all, taking breaths till his color returned. And then, slowly, we walked back to the house.

Jeri was holding Laurie, her mother standing over her, Mary Cooper sitting close on the couch. "Oh, look what a baby-waby. What a darling girly-wirl. Do you feel the least bit hot? Laurie-baurie, you're not running a fever, are you?"

The kid had just gotten the thumbs-up from a hospital, and she was wrapped in half a dozen blankets. I doubted she was running a fever.

Ellen leaned over to feel the baby's face. "Ohhh, I think she might be. Give her to Grandma. Grandma knows how to fix babies, doesn't she, Laurie girl? Come to Grandma and Grandma will sponge you with alcohol, Grandma will."

She looked like a hawk coming in for a landing, ready to snare its prey and fly up again, but Mary was quicker still. Almost before you saw it happening, she had the baby away from Ellen and in her own lap. "What you need is some nice juice, don't you, Laurie-bear? And then Meemaw's going to rock you and rock you . . . oh, my goodness, you're burning up.'' Her voice was on the edge of panic. "Listen, Jeri, this baby's wheezing! We've got to get her breathing damp air. . . .''

She wasn't wheezing, she was gulping, probably in amazement. I felt my own jaw drop and, looking away, unwittingly caught the eye of Mary's husband, who hadn't wanted me to see the anguish there. Quickly he dropped a curtain of blandness. Beside me, I heard Michael whisper, "My God!''

I knew we were seeing something extreme. They were all excited to have Laurie home, and they were competing with each other, letting out what looked like their scariest sides if you knew what we did. But a Stephanie didn't come along every day. Laurie was in no further danger, I was sure of it. Still, I understood why Gary had had the sudden change of heart about her guardianship.

I turned to Michael. "Are you going to try to get her?''

He plucked at his sweater sleeve, staring at his wrist as if it had a treasure map on it. "I haven't decided.''

An image from my fitful morning dreams came back to me: a giant in a forest, taller than all the trees and built like a mountain; a female giant with belly and breasts like boulders, dressed in white robes and carrying, draped across her outstretched arms, a dead man, head dangling on its flaccid neck.

In a few days Michael called. When he got home to Seattle, a letter had been waiting for him—a note, rather, from Gary, postmarked the day of his death. It didn't apologize, it didn't explain—it didn't even say, "Dear Michael.'' It was simply a quote from *Hamlet* typed on a piece of paper, not handwritten, Michael thought, because it could be construed as a confession and there was the insurance to think about. This was the quote:

> Diseases desperate grown
> By desperate appliance are relieved,
> Or not at all.

I didn't ask Michael again whether he intended to take Laurie. At the moment, I was too furious with one passive male to trust myself to speak civilly with another. Instead, I simmered inwardly, thinking how like Gary it was to confess to murder with a quote from Shakespeare. Thinking that, as he typed it, he probably imagined grandly that nothing in his life would become him like the leaving of it. The schmuck.

hog heaven

by Gillian Roberts

HARRY TOWERS WALKED OUT OF HIS OFFICE BUILD-ing and blinked in the late-afternoon light. The sea of homebound bodies divided around him as he deliberated how, and with whom, to fill the hours ahead.

The redheaded receptionist had other plans. Lucy, his usual standby, had run off to Vegas with a greeting-card salesman. Charlene was back with her husband, at least for tonight. Might as well check out Duffy's.

He stood a little straighter, smoothed his hair over his bald spot, and sucked in his stomach. Duffy's was a giant corral into which the whole herd of thirty-plus panic-stricken single women stampeded at nightfall. Duffy's Desperates, he called them. Not prime stock, but all the same, the roundup saved time.

He walked briskly. Everything would be fine. He didn't need that stupid redheaded receptionist.

"Harry? Harry Towers?"

The sidewalks were still crowded, but Harry spotted the

owner of the melodic voice so easily, it was as if nobody but the two of them were on the streets.

He had seen her a few times before, recently, right around this time of day. She was the blonde, voluptuous kind you had to notice. A glossy sort of woman, somebody you see in magazines or on TV. Not all that young, not a baby, but not a bimbo. And definitely not a Duffy's Desperate.

She repeated his name and continued moving resolutely toward him. He tried not to gape.

"You *are* Harry Towers, aren't you?" A small, worried frown marred her perfect face.

He smiled and nodded, straightening up to his full height. He was a tall man, but her turquoise eyes were on a level with his.

"I thought so!" Her face relaxed into a wide smile. "Remember me?" Her voice was so creamy, he wanted to lick it.

"I . . . well—" In his forty-five years, he had never before laid eyes on this woman, except for the sidewalk glimpses this week. Harry did not pay a whole lot of the remembering kind of attention to most women, but this was not most women. This one you'd remember even if you had Alzheimer's.

She was using the old don't-I-know-you-from-somewhere? line, and it amused him. She'd even gone to the trouble to find out his name. Flattering, to say the least.

"Does the name Leigh Endicott sound familiar?" she prompted.

"Oh!" he said emphatically, nodding, playing the game. "Leigh . . . Endicott. Sure . . . now I—well, it must be—"

"Years," she said with one of those woeful smiles women give when they talk about time. "Even though it seems like yesterday." She shook her head, as if to clear away the time in between. "I've thought about you so often, wondered what became of you." She put her hand on his sleeve, tenderly.

If only the redhead hadn't left the building before him— if only she could see him now!

"I always hoped I'd find you again someday," she purred.

She was overdoing it. Should he tell her to skip the old-

friend business? They didn't need a make-believe history. He
decided to keep quiet, not rock the boat, follow her lead.
"Why don't we find someplace comfortable?" he said. "To,
uh, reminisce?"

She glanced at her watch, then shrugged and smiled at
him, nodding.

"There's a place around the corner," he said. "Duffy's."
The Desperates would shrivel up and turn to dust when they
saw this one. Then they'd know, all those self-important
spritzer drinkers, that Harry Towers still had it. All of it.

They started walking, her arm linked through his. Suddenly she stopped short. "I just had a wonderful idea. I have
a dear little farmhouse in the country. Very peaceful and
private. Would you mind skipping the bar? I'm sure it's too
noisy and crowded for a really good . . . talk. My car's over
there. I can drive you back later—if you feel like leaving."

What a woman! Right to the point! He hated the prelim-
inaries, the song-and-dance routine, anyway. He followed her
to the parking lot, grinning.

I am in hog heaven, he thought. *Hog heaven.*

The ride was a timeless blur. Harry was awash, drowning
in the mixed perfumes of the car's leather, the spring evening, the woman beside him, and the anticipation of the
hours ahead. When Leigh spoke, her voice, rich and sensu-
ous, floated around him. He had to force himself to listen to
the words instead of letting them tickle his pores and ruffle
his hair.

"Almost there, Harry," she was saying. "Don't you love
this area? Open country. Free. Natural. I love the farmhouses,
the space . . ."

Almost there. Free. Natural. Wonderful words.

Leigh, eyes still on the road, voice talking about the wonders of the countryside, placed a manicured hand on his
thigh.

God? he said silently, needing the Deity for the first time
in years. God, let this really be happening.

After dinner she sent Harry into the living room. "Make
yourself comfortable," she insisted, "while I clean up. I'll

bring in coffee.'' No number about sharing the work. He couldn't believe his luck.

The tape stopped, and he picked out a mellow one. Make-out music, they called it a century or two ago when he was young. Why did that seem so funny? He stifled a giggle. He turned the volume to a soft, inviting level, then settled into the rich velvet sofa. He felt a little weird. Almost like a teenager again, that racing high, that thrumming excitement.

What a woman! He couldn't believe his luck. He stretched and enjoyed the memory of the meal. Her own recipe, her own invention. Spicy, delicious, exotic. Like Leigh herself, like the charged talk that had hovered around the table, like the possibilities of a long night in the remote countryside.

''Here you are,'' she announced, carrying a tray with a coffeepot, creamer, sugar bowl, and cups. She bent close and his giddy lightheadedness, the speeding double-time rush of blood through his veins, intensified.

She poured the coffee, then stepped back and spread her arms as if to embrace the room. ''Do you like my place?'' she asked. ''The people at work think I'm crazy to be this isolated, this far from everything. But I love my privacy. Or maybe I like animals better than people.'' She laughed. ''Present company excluded, of course.''

Bubbles of excitement popped in Harry's veins. ''Have a seat,'' he suggested, patting the sofa next to him. He wiggled his lips. They felt thick, a little foreign and tingly. Stupid to have eaten so much. And all that wine, too. Now he was bloated, sluggish.

Leigh, on the other hand, seemed wired. ''This is a working farm,'' she said. ''Cows, pigs, horses. There's a caretaker, of course.'' She stopped her pacing. ''But don't worry—he won't bother us. He's all the way on the other side of the property, and anyway, he's away for the night.''

''Leigh—'' he began. He sounded whiny and stopped himself. But all the same, why couldn't they start enjoying this nice private place before her stupid roosters crowed? He was reminded of his teens, of dates with nervous girls chattering furiously to keep his attention—and hands—off their bodies. It had annoyed him even then. He decided to see if actions would speak louder than words, and smacked at the sofa's velvet.

It worked. She finally sat down. But just out of easy reach.

He considered strategy. He felt planted in the soft cushions. He took a moment to evaluate the pros and cons of uprooting himself.

"Do you know which is the most intelligent barnyard animal?" she asked.

Who cared? Frankly, even a brainless chicken was beginning to seem brighter than this woman. Didn't she remember why they were here?

She refilled his coffee cup. He sipped at it while he tried to figure a way to change the subject.

"Pigs," she said. "It's almost a curse on them, being that smart. They know when they're going to slaughter. They scream and fight and try to prevent their own destruction."

Harry finished the coffee. There was no subtle way to stop her, so he'd be direct. "I don't care about pigs," he said emphatically. "I care about you. Come closer."

"I'm fond of pigs." She stayed in place. "Don't you care about what I care about? About who I am?"

"Of course! I didn't mean to . . ." Damn. She was one of those. He hadn't expected it, from the way she'd come on to him, but she was one more of them who needed to discuss their innermost feelings first, get to know the man, make things serious and important.

"Let's take things slowly," she said. "I've waited years and years to be with you again."

"Ah, c'mon," he said. "We're adults. Don't pretend anymore. I like you, you like me. Tha's enough. Don't need games."

She refilled his cup, then held it out to him.

He stared at her hands, confused.

"Games can be fun, Harry," she murmured. "And so can the prizes at the end." She put his cup in his hands.

It required a great deal of effort to bring it to his lips.

"You still haven't answered the first question, you know," she said with a small smile.

He shook his head. He had no idea what she was talking

about. "I really don't like games," he said. The whole idea made him tired.

"Yes you do." Her voice was a croon, a lullaby. "Sure you do. I know that about you. You just like the game to be yours, the old familiar one. But this one is new. This is mine, and it's called 'Do You Remember Me?' "

She was all smiles and burbles, but he felt suddenly chilled.

"Oh, you look puzzled," she said. "I'll give you a clue." She stood up. "*Campus.*" She clicked musically, sounding like a game-show timer.

"College?" he asked, frowning. "State?"

"Good!" She waited. "Any more? Who am I, Harry Towers? You have fifteen seconds." She began her manic clicking noise again.

"You were there?" His voice sounded remote and dislocated, as if it weren't coming out of his own throat.

She nodded pertly. "A freshman when you were a junior. Think." He was afraid she would begin her timer again, but instead she asked him if he wanted brandy.

He shook his head. "Feel a little . . ." He clutched the arm of the sofa for support.

She nodded. "So, how are we doing with those clues?"

"I . . ." He said her name silently, hoping it would connect with something, but all it did was bang from side to side in his brain. Leeleeleelee . . . a sharp bell tolling painfully.

"Ahhh," she said, "so you really don't remember me. How about that."

He couldn't think of what he should say. She was all snap-and-crackle confusion, and he was fuzzy lint. "Sorry," he whispered. Actually, he decided, she wasn't worth it. Too much time and effort. As soon as he felt a little better, he wanted out.

"Harry," she whispered. "Your mouth is open. You're drooling."

He tried to close it.

"I guess it would be hard to remember one girl out of that crowd of them you had." She smiled down at him, and he felt the tension ease.

There had been so many girls sticking to him as if he were made of Velcro. Such a good time. While it lasted. He wondered where his old letter sweater was, whether it still fit him, then remembered he was supposed to be trying to remember Leigh. But the girls were one big blur of sweet-smelling hair, firm breasts, lips, assorted parts.

She sat down so close to him that her perfume increased his dizziness. "Poor baby," she crooned. "You're woozy. Rest your head in my lap."

She stroked his thinning hair as if she loved every strand. Beneath her hand, his head swirled and popped, as the dinner wine and spices fermented. Maybe she wasn't such a bitch. He couldn't get a fix on her. Maybe it was good she liked the sound of her own voice too much. He needed time. She'd been at State with him. He rummaged again through his memories of all those girls, those legs and arms and shiny hair. Which one had been Leigh? He couldn't remember any of them. Female faces had a way of blurring away by the next morning, let alone after decades.

"Innasorority?" he said in a soft hiss.

She shook her head. "I was so shy. A loner. Until Harry Towers invited me to his fraternity party and everything was magically changed."

Which party? No way to separate out all those drunken, sweaty, wonderful nights. God, but those guys were fun. So many laughs. Best years of his life.

"Except that I never saw you again," Leigh said.

"Musta been outa my mind," he gasped chivalrously. Maybe it would appease her.

She chuckled very softly. "Wish you hadn't been. You can't imagine what a difference it would have made to me if you'd asked me out again."

So he hadn't been the most steady guy. That's how he was, who he was. But he'd never been a fool, so why hadn't he seen as much of this one as possible? Had something happened? Damn, but the memory slate was clean. Not even a chalk smear on it. He tried to sit up, to face her, to say something, but he only made it halfway.

Abruptly, she stood. He flopped down onto the cushions,

then grabbed the back of the sofa and tried to pull into a sitting position.

She was going into the bedroom. Maybe talking time was over, just like that. Maybe they weren't going to have to deal with ancient history and guessing games, after all. He staggered to his feet.

"No. Stay," she called out. "I need something."

Safe sex, he realized. Sure. Okay. His legs wobbled and he couldn't stop swaying. He sank back into the sofa.

She returned and handed him a ragged-edged snapshot.

"Whadoss . . ." He gave up the effort of asking what this had to do with anything.

"It's part of the game," she said. "The last clue."

He focused his eyes with difficulty. When he had managed the feat, he regretted the effort. The girl in the photograph had a moon-shaped face with dark hair pulled back severely so that her ears stuck out like flaps. Sunlight bounced off her glasses, emphasizing the shadows cast by her enormous nose, her chubby cheeks, and her collection of chins. For no reason Harry could think of, she was smiling, revealing teeth that gaped like pickets on a wobbly fence. A real loser. A dog. A pig. Harry let the picture drop onto the coffee table.

"Too bad," she said. "We're out of time. Ladies and gentlemen, our contestant has forfeited the game. But don't turn off that set—we've got a few surprises left! It's not over till it's over!" She loomed above him, a giantess. Then she pushed the picture back in front of him. "Harry Towers, meet Leigh Endicott," she said.

"Wha?" He had an overwhelming sense of wrongness. His mouth was painfully dry. He reached toward the coffee, but his fingers weren't working properly. He sat, arms hanging loose, staring at the old black-and-white snapshot on the table.

"How could you not recognize me?" Her voice was sweet and coquettish. "The only changes have been from time— oh, and a few superficial adjustments, like a diet, a nose bob, contact lenses, ear pinning, chin enlarging, straightening and capping the teeth and bleaching the hair. Nothing compared to what's possible nowadays. But that was a long time ago."

A whoosh came out of the hollowness inside Harry. He'd

taken her—that photo girl—to a party. He felt chilly, then hot. Something wanted to be remembered. Something hovered just above his head, ready to fall.

"I left school to earn the money for the changes," she said. "Took me four years, same as my degree would have." She walked toward the window. "Only thing is, at the end I was still the same girl inside, but who cares about that, right?"

He put up his hand like a traffic cop, to stop her words from falling onto his skull. He was cold again, afraid, needed to explain and defend himself, as if he were on trial, but when he opened his mouth, he gagged. When was it? Why? Did he really remember certain times . . . ? Why did Duffy's Desperates suddenly stampede into his mind in a great cloud of dust?

"Your party," she said. "My first date on campus. My first date, actually. I had such a good time. Every little girl knows the story of Cinderella—why shouldn't it happen to all of us? And Prince Charming had nothing on you, Harry. But when I left the room to powder my oversized nose, I overheard two of your darling fraternity brothers. Very drunk and very happy fraternity brothers. They were laughing so much, I could barely make out the joke, except that they kept repeating one particular word. This is the last question in the game, Harry. Do you know the word?"

His heart was going to explode. Party—ugly girl. Laughing. It all connected, turned fiery and molten. Pig. Pig party. Had forgotten all about them. Probably didn't have them anymore. Defunct, part of the world of the dinosaurs, but back then . . .

"Weren't supposed to know . . ." he said. "Just a . . . prank. Fun. No harm meant."

She loomed over him, stony and enormous. A warrior woman.

"F'give," he begged. "Boys will be . . ." What? What will boys be? What did he mean? Now or then—what? His mind was falling apart, great chunks slopping like mud into heaps. His hands were damp and cold. He tried to smile, although his mouth had become enormous, like a clown's, and rubbery.

"Stop groveling," she said. "There's no point. Or do you still think we're here because I *yearn* for you?" She laughed harshly but with real amusement.

He was freezing. His hands trembled uncontrollably, even while they lay in place.

She waved her arms at her imaginary audience, somewhere outside the windows. "The game is over, folks. Over," she said. Then she turned back to Harry. "You thought you caught a dream tonight, didn't you?" she said. "Maybe I'd make up for everybody else's indifference, would see past the sad slick of failure you wear like skin, past your dead-end job, your saggy gut, your stupid life, your smell of loneliness. You wanted me to find the real you—the special person inside, didn't you?"

Her voice was low and cool, only distantly interested in him, as if he were a specimen. He wished she would scream, maybe blot out the deafening sound of his own pulse.

"I understand it all, Harry," she said, "because that's what I wanted, what I believed, too, the night you asked me to your party. And get this: Neither of us—not me years ago, not you tonight—understood one damn thing that was going on."

His head ached as if she'd physically beaten him.

"I found out accidentally," she said. "You're going to find out very deliberately. That's the only difference." She walked away. "Pig party," she said. "Where all you perfect, self-important fraternity jackasses could observe and be amused by a freak show of imperfect but oblivious females. How sidesplitting of us to think we were actual dates, actual lovable, desirable humans! What fun it must have been to wink and poke each other in the ribs, award the man who'd found the absolute worst, laugh through the night about us. It's quite an experience, Harry, finding out you're a laughing matter. Changes a person forever."

He had to get the hell out of here, but his limbs were boneless, he couldn't stand.

"Of course, it was also a learning experience," she said. "A chance to grow. For years now I've wanted you to share it, have the same chance, but I don't belong to a fraternity, and besides, I'd like to think there aren't any more pig par-

ties. So I had to find a way to return the favor personally."
She came very close, kneeled in front of him.

A wave of nausea engulfed him. He swallowed hard and
struggled to get to his feet.

"You're not going anywhere!" she snapped, pushing him
back in place with one hand. "Do you really think it's the
wine, or a few peppers making you feel so rotten? Aren't
you worried?"

His burning eyes opened wide. "Poison?" he gasped.

She smiled. "It's a possibility, isn't it? I've had years to
prepare for tonight. But why be concerned? This is a party,
Harry. Your very own pig party. In fact, my dear, you *are*
the party—the pig's party."

He nearly wept from the sawtooth edge of screams slicing
the edges of his mind.

"The pigs behind the house, remember? Poor babies, they
can't enjoy the miracles of cosmetic surgery. They're stuck
as pigs forever, so surely they're entitled to a little piggy
treat now and then. You'll give them such pleasure!"

"Hhhhh?"

"How?" Her voice traveled from a great distance and echoed through him, down to his fingertips.

"They eat almost anything, of course. But you—you'll be
the best dish they ever had. Of course, we won't let them
have all of you, will we? Nobody's ever had that. We'll do
it bit by bit. Start with gourmet tidbits. The, uh, choice cuts,
shall we say? The sought-after, prized, yummy parts."

Tears dribbled from his eyes.

"You know what they call pig food? Slops, Harry. How
appropriate."

He heard dreadful, guttural sounds.

"Be still," she said. "And your nose is running. How
disgusting."

He was small and lost and terrified, poisoned and para-
lyzed on a velvet sofa, about to be butchered, to have pigs
eat his—pigs swallow his—

He summoned all of his strength, determined to get free.
But his knees buckled and he dropped to the floor. "Please,"
he said between sobs, "was so long ago . . ."

"Not long enough," she said. "I realized that two weeks

ago, when I saw you downtown. My jolt of pain wasn't old or faded. Some things are forever. You killed a part of me that night. However plain or fat or shy I was, I had an innocent pride and dignity, and you took it away. You turned me into a pig.''

He howled at the top of his lungs.

''Hush. Nobody can hear,'' she reminded him. ''Nobody knows you're here. For that matter, nobody knows *I'm* here. This isn't my house—it's a friend's, and he's away. So is the caretaker.'' She walked around him. ''And for the record, my married name isn't Leigh Endicott. Anyway, we're both going to simply disappear from here. But you'll do it bit by bit.'' She paused in an exaggerated pose of thought. ''Or should we say bite by bite?'' she asked with a grin.

He crawled, crying. An inch. No more.

''Why struggle so?'' she said. ''You are, quite literally, dead meat. On the other hand, you're about to be reborn, to give of yourself at last, to become whole—swine, inside and out.''

The door was impossibly far away. He sprawled, numb and exhausted, gasping as the dark closed in. He could feel himself begin to die at the edges. His fingers were already gone, and his feet.

Through static and splutters and whirs in his brain, he heard her move around, run water, open cabinets.

''All clean now,'' she said. ''Not a trace.'' She leaned down and pulled up one of his eyelids. ''Tsk, tsk,'' she said. ''Look what's become of the big bad wolf.''

He dissolved into a shapeless, quivering stain on the floor. All his mind could see was a pig, heavy and bloated, pushing its hideous, hairy snout into its trough, into the slops, grunting with pleasure as it ate . . . him.

Glass broke, a door slammed, but all Harry heard was a fat sow's squeal of pleasure as it chewed and smacked and swallowed . . . him.

He felt a hand on his shoulder. He gasped, ran his own hands over his body once, then twice. Everything was there. He was intact and whole! He burst into tears.

''Damn drunk. Probably a junkie,'' a voice said. ''Breaks

in to use the place as a toilet. Jesus.'' Harry was pulled to his feet by men with badges. Police.

"Listen, I—'' he began. His head hurt.

"You have the right to remain silent,'' the taller man began. He droned through his memorized piece. Harry couldn't believe it. They searched him and looked disappointed when they found nothing. "Passed out before you could take anything,'' the tall man said.

"But I wasn't—'' They weren't interested. He told them about Leigh. They ignored him. He found out that an anonymous caller—female—had alerted the police to a prowler on the farm. He told them they had it all wrong, that it was her, Leigh. Somebody who'd picked him up, taken him here, drugged him, smashed the window so it'd look like he'd broken in, and called them, setting him up. He explained it to them, to the lawyer they appointed, to the psychiatrist, to the technician who analyzed the drugs in his bloodstream—street drugs they were, nothing fancy or traceable, damn the woman. He explained it to the judge. Nobody listened or believed or cared.

He stopped explaining. He endured the small jail until they released him. He paid for the broken window and the soiled rug. Paid the fine for trespassing, for breaking and entering. Paid through the nose for a taxi back to the city and his apartment.

In his mailbox, the only personal mail was a heart-shaped card with a picture of two enormous pigs nuzzling each other. He burned it.

From that day on, Harry Towers's stoop became more pronounced. He no longer combed his hair over his bald spot or sucked in his stomach. He stayed home nights, watching television alone.

And he never ate bacon or pork chops or ham steaks, for they, along with many other former delights, tasted like ashes in his mouth.

When Pious Deception *introduced Kiernan O'Shaugnessy, a former forensic pathologist, Susan Dunlap became the first woman to write three series featuring each of the major types of detective—a private investigator (Kiernan), a police officer (Jill Smith), and an amateur detective (Veejay Haskell, utility meter reader). Kiernan, who will make her fourth appearance in* No Immunity, *enjoys her material comforts—her San Diego beach house is maintained by a former football player. Berkeley detective Jill Smith, featured in eleven novels including* Cop-Out, *is noted for keen wit, compassion, integrity, and a love of chocolate.*

In "The Celestial Buffet," winner of an Anthony award, offerings of unearthly delight continue to entice the narrator, who doesn't intend to be limited to just desserts.

the celestial buffet

by Susan Dunlap

I HADN'T STEPPED ONTO THE CELESTIAL ESCALATOR WITH the escort of two white-suited angels like I had seen in the 1940s movies, but I did have the sense that I had risen up. I was very aware of the whole process, which is rather surprising considering what a shock my death was. I hadn't been sick, or taken foolish chances. I certainly didn't plan on dying—not ever, really—but in any case not so soon.

I looked down from somewhere near the ceiling and saw my body lying on the floor. I should have been horrified, overwhelmed by grief, more grief than I'd felt at the sight of any other body, but I really felt only a mild curiosity. My forty-year-old body was still clad in a turquoise running suit. It was, as it had been for most of its adult life, just a bit pear-shaped around the derriere. It could have stood to lose five pounds (well, too late now). It was lying on the living room floor, its head about six inches from the coffee table, the stool overturned by its feet. How many times had Raymond told me not to stand on that stool to change the light

bulb? If he had seen me holding the last, luscious bite of a
Hershey bar in my left hand he would have said, "One of
these days, you'll fall and kill yourself." And, of course, he
would have been right. Now, I recalled wavering on that
rickety stool, knowing I should reach up and grab onto the
light fixture, hesitating, unwilling to drop the chocolate. It
was still there, in my hand, clutched in a cadaverous spasm.
How humiliating! I could almost hear Raymond's knowing
cackle. At least that infuriating cackle was not the last sound
I'd heard in life. If I had felt anything at all for that body
on the floor I would have hoped Raymond wouldn't tell anyone how it died.

But the body and the possibility of its being ridiculed
didn't hold my attention for long. I left it there on the floor
and rose up. Exactly how I rose is unclear. I didn't take a
white escalator, or a shimmering elevator, or any more sophisticated conveyance; I just had the sense of ascending till
I reached a sort of landing.

I can no more describe the landing than I can the means
of reaching it. There were no clear walls or floor, no drapes,
no sliding gossamer doors, no pearly gates or streets paved
with gold. Nothing so obvious. Just a sense, a knowing that
this was the antechamber, the place of judgment. I stood,
holding my breath (so to speak). Somewhere in the Bible it
speaks of the moment of judgment when the words each of
us has whispered in private will be broadcast aloud. A distinctly uncomfortable thought. I had rather hoped that if that
had to happen it would be at a mass event with a lot of
babble and confusion, and everyone else as embarrassed at
his own unmasking as I was. But here I was, alone, surrounded by silence. I waited (what choice had I?) but no
public-address system came on. So the celestial loudspeaker,
at least, was a myth.

But even with that out of the way, I still knew (knew,
rather than was told, for it was apparent to me now that
communication in this place was not verbal or written—
things simply were known) that there was a heaven and, God
forbid, a hell, and this was the last neutral ground between
the two. In a short time I would know which I was to reside
in. Forever.

But I had led a decent life. There was no reason to worry. I had worked hard . . . well, hard enough. I'd voted, even in off-year elections. I'd spent Christmas every other year with my parents when they were alive. (Weren't my parents supposed to be here to meet me? Surely their absence wasn't because they were not in heaven? No. More likely, the greetings by all those who had gone on before was another myth.) I realized that my conception of this place was as ephemeral as the room itself. I hadn't given it more than the most cursory of thoughts, being sure that, at worst, I had years to form an idea of it. So what expectations I did have came mostly from Sunday school, and of course, forties movies.

The waiting was making me uneasy. Couldn't I move on to eternal bliss now? Why the delay? I had been a good person. I had followed the Ten Commandments, as much as was reasonable for someone living in San Francisco. I had honored my mother and father on those Christmases and long distance after five and on Saturdays. I had kept the Sabbath when I was a child, before they televised the football games, which is all that could be legitimately expected. I had even gone to a series of Krishnamurti lectures on Sundays a year or two ago.

But my parents and the Sabbath were only two commandments. What of the other eight? What *were* the other eight? That was a question I had considered only in connection with the Seven Dwarfs or the eight reindeer. Commandments? Ah, taking the name of the Lord in vain. Oh, God! Whoops! Admittedly, I'd been less than pure here, but who hadn't? If that commandment had been pivotal there would be no need for this room at all. The escalator would only go down.

Regardless, I felt distinctly uncomfortable. I looked around, searching for walls, for a bench, for something solid, but nothing was more substantial than a suggestion, a fuzzy conception way in the back of my mind.

Then, suddenly, there were double doors before me. With considerable relief, I pushed them open and walked into a large room, a banquet hall. To my right were the other guests. I couldn't make out individuals, but I knew they were seated at festively decorated tables, with full plates before them and glasses of Dom Perignon waiting to be lifted. No words were distinct, but the sounds of gaiety and laughter were unmistakable. Maybe the welcoming of those who had gone on before was *not* a myth. A welcoming dinner!

To my left was a buffet table.

It had been a long time since that fatal chocolate bar. The whole process of dying had taken a while, and the Hershey's had been a preprandial chocolate. Now that I was no longer distracted by apprehension, I realized I was famished. And I couldn't have been in a better place. I was delighted that this was not to be a formal dinner with choice limited to underdone chicken breast or tasteless white fish and a slab of Neapolitan ice cream for dessert. For me a buffet was the perfect welcome.

The buffet table was very long and wonderfully full. Before me were bowls of fruit. Not just oranges or canned fruit cocktail, but slices of fresh guavas and peaches, of mangoes and kiwi fruit, hunks of ripe pineapple without one brown spot, and maraschino cherries that I could gorge on without fear of carcinogens. As I stood pleasantly salivating, I knew that here at the celestial buffet I could eat pineapple and ice cream without getting indigestion, mountains of coleslaw or hills of beans without gas. And as much of them as I wanted. Never again the Scarsdale Diet. No more eight glasses of water and dry meat. Never another day of nine hundred or fewer calories. I could consume a bunch of bananas, thirty Santa Rosa plums, enough seedless grapes to undermine the wine industry, and remain thin enough for my neighbor's husband to covet me.

But that was a topic I did not want to consider in depth. Surely, in business, in the twentieth century, in California, a bit of extramarital coveting was taken for granted. I hadn't, after all, coveted my neighbor's husband (he was sixty, and *he* only coveted a weed-free lawn). I hadn't really coveted Amory as much as I did his ability to make me district manager. After the promotion I hadn't coveted him at all. And his wife never knew, and Raymond only half suspected, so that could hardly be considered Mortal Coveting. Besides, there wouldn't be guavas in hell.

A plate, really more of a platter than a mere one-serving plate, hovered beside me as if held up on the essence of a cart. Balancing the plate and the cup and holding the silver and napkins was always such a nuisance at buffets (and balancing, as I had so recently been reminded, was not my best skill). So this floating platter was a heavenly innovation. I was pleased that things were so well organized here. I scooped up some guava, just a few pieces, not wanting to appear piggish at my welcoming dinner. I added a few more, and then a whole guava, realizing with sudden sureness that at this banquet greed was not an issue. I heaped on cherries, berries, and peeled orange sections soaked in Grand Marnier. Had this been an office brunch, I would have been ashamed. But all the fruit fit surprisingly well on the platter and, in truth, hardly took up much of the space at all. It must have been an excellent platter design. Each fruit remained separate, none of the juices ran together, and I knew instinctively that the juices would never run into any of the entrées to come.

I moved along and found myself facing lox, a veritable school of fresh pink lox, accompanied by a tray of tiny, bite-size bagels, crisp yet soft, and a mound of cream cheese that was creamy enough to spread easily but thick enough to sink my teeth into. And there was salmon mousse made with fresh dill weed, and giant prawns in black bean sauce, and a heaping platter of lobster tails, and Maryland soft-shell crab, and New Jersey bluefish that you can't get on the West Coast, and those wonderful huge Oregon clams. I could have made a meal of any of them. But meal-sized portions of each fitted easily onto the platter. More than I ever coveted.

Coveting again. I may have coveted my neighbor's goods, but I had certainly not broken into his house and taken them. Oh, there had been the notepads and pens from the office, a few forays into fiction on my tax returns, but no one fears eternal condemnation for that. And there was the money from Consolidated Orbital to alter the environmental survey, but that was a gift, not stolen, regardless of what the environmentalists might have said. No, I could rest assured on the issue of coveting my neighbor's goods.

I adore quiche, and for the last three years it has given me indigestion. But there is no need for plop-plop fizz-fizz amongst the heavenly host. And the choice of quiche here was outstanding. Nearest me was Italian Fontina with chanterelle mushrooms, New Zealand spinach, and—ah!—Walla Walla onions that were in and out of season so fast that a week's negligence meant another year's wait. Beside it, bacon. Bacon throughout the quiche and crisp curls decorating the top! The smell made me salivate. I could almost taste it. Bacon loaded with fat and sodium and preservatives and red dyes of every number. I had forced myself to forgo it for years. And crab quiche, and one with beluga caviar sprinkled—no, ladled—over the top. I couldn't decide. I didn't have to. It was truly amazing how much fit onto the platter. I was certainly glad I didn't have to hold it up. Had I even contemplated eating this much on earth, I would have gained five pounds. Ah, heaven! On earth, I would have killed for this.

I smiled (subtly speaking, for my spiritual face didn't move but my essence shifted into the outward show of happiness). *Thou shalt not kill.* Well, I wasn't a murderer either. And that was a biggie. The closest I had come to a dead body was my own. I moved on to the meats—rare roast beef with the outside cuts ready for my taking, and crispy duck with no grease at all. Admittedly, Milton Prendergast, my predecessor as district manager, had killed himself, but that was hardly my fault. I didn't murder him. He was merely overly attached to his job. I added some spareribs to my platter. I could sympathize with Prendergast's attachment to the job. I had aimed for it myself, and there was a lot of money to be had through it. But still, suicide was hardly murder, even if he did tell me he would kill himself if I exposed him. And I had to do that, or even with Amory's help I couldn't have gotten the job. Well, knowing the shenanigans Prendergast had been involved in, at least I knew I wouldn't be running into him up here.

The roast turkey smelled wonderful, a lifetime of Thanksgivings in one inhalation. With that sausage stuffing my Mom used to make. And fresh cranberries. My whole body quivered with hunger at the smell. I took a serving, then another.

There was still room for the muffins and breads—steaming popovers, orange nut loaf, Mexican corn bread with cheese and chiles—and for the grand assortment of desserts beyond.

But I was too hungry to wait. The juices in my empty stomach swirled; and I found myself chomping on my tongue in juicy anticipation. I needed to eat *now*. And this was, after all, a buffet. I could come back—eternally.

I reached for my platter.

It slipped beyond my grasp.

I grabbed.

Missed!

I heard laughter. Those diners at the tables—they were laughing at me.

My stomach whirled, now in fear. Surely this couldn't mean that I was in ... I lunged. But the platter that had been right beside me was suddenly, inexplicably, three feet away. Too far to reach, but near enough for the sweet smell of pineapple to reach me. Despite my fear, my taste buds seemed to be jumping up and down at the back of my tongue. The laughter from the tables was louder.

I didn't dare turn toward the diners. Judgment Day separated the sheep from the goats. And even I, a city person, knew that sheep don't laugh. And there was a definite billy-goat quality to that cackle.

I stood still, smelling the salty aroma of the caviar, the full flavor of that freshest of salmon, the smell of the bacon, of the turkey dressing. The platter stayed still, too, still out of reach. The smell of the cranberries mixed with the tangy aroma of the oranges. I inhaled it, willing it to take substance in my throbbing stomach. It didn't.

If I couldn't capture that platter ... but I didn't want to think about the hellish judgment that would signify. But there was no point making another grab. The laughter was louder; it sounded strangely familiar.

Slowly I turned away from the platter, careful not to glance out at the diners, afraid of what I might see. Head down, shoulders hunched over, I took a shuffling step away from the food. I could sense the platter following me. I took another step. From behind me, the oranges smelled stronger, sweeter. I could almost taste them. Almost. I lifted my foot as if to take another step, then I whirled around and with both hands lunged for the food. The hell with the platter.

The laughter pounded at my ears.

Let them laugh. I'd come up with one hand full of cranberries and the other grasping a piece of caviar quiche. I had my food. Triumphantly, and with heavenly relief, I jammed half the quiche in my mouth. No eternal damnation for me. The laughter grew even louder. I knew that laugh; it came from a multitude of mouths, but it was all the same cackling sound. I swallowed quickly and poured the whole handful of cranberries into my mouth.

That cackle—Raymond's laugh!

I swallowed and pushed the rest of the quiche into my mouth. Then the oranges from the now near platter, and the salmon, and the pineapple, the prawns in black bean sauce, the turkey, and the Oregon clams, and the Walla Walla sweet onions.

But there was no silencing Raymond's knowing cackle. And there was no denying where I was—eternally. I'd got my food all right, but it all tasted exactly the same. It tasted of nothing but ashes—like it had been burned in the fires of hell.

Joan Hess, nominated for an Anthony for Strangled Prose, *offers delighted readers three series. Claire Malloy is featured
in eleven books, including American Mystery award winner* A
Diet to Die For *and the latest,* Holly Jolly Murder. *Theo
Bloomer appears in two books, including* The Deadly Ackee
*(written as Joan Hadley). The ten books in the Arly Hanks
series (including* Mischief in Maggody *and* O Little Town of
Maggody, *Agatha and Anthony nominees, and* Miracles in
Maggody) *recount the hijinks in a small southern town. Fans
would argue that the sprightly and slightly wicked Hess wit is
really the highlight of her books.*

*In "Too Much to Bare," which won a Macavity award,
motivations are stripped to essentials, giving new meaning to
the notion of girls' night out.*

too much to bare

by Joan Hess

"MY HUSBAND IS GOING TO KILL ME,"
Marjorie announced. It was not the first time she'd suggested
the possibility. Anne had lost count. "Oh, honey," Sylvia
said soothingly, "it's not as if we're taking the merchandise
home, or even having a chance to do more than study it from
a respectable distance. Not that I wouldn't object, should the
opportunity arise—if you know what I mean!"

The three other women at the table obligingly giggled at
Sylvia's comment. Marjorie, already damp with perspiration
in her rumpled polyester pantsuit, flapped a pudgy hand as
if to dispel any lingering aura of naughtiness. "You are such
a joker," she said. "I don't know how you think of these
things."

"I would imagine it comes from hanging around outside
the locker room," Bitsy said. Her eyes, heavily accented with
mascara and undulating ribbons of blue and gray shadow,
closed for a moment as a curtain of black hair fell across her
face. She took a sip of beer, wrinkled her nose, and pushed

aside her cup. A Christian in the Colosseum could not have looked less delighted.

"Better than hanging around inside," Sylvia said, "unless we're discussing some little jock's strap."

Anne busied herself replenishing their plastic cups with beer from the pitcher, keeping her face lowered in order to hide her expression. Sylvia's jokes were always crude. Most of the teachers at the school avoided the lounge whenever Sylvia sailed in for coffee and conversation; Anne had discovered she preferred to stay in the library rather than listen to the barrage of gossip and off-color humor. A thermos of coffee sufficed. But tonight she found herself taking a certain pleasure in Sylvia's company. A certain pleasure, yes.

The Happy Hour Saloon was swelling with a large and raucous crowd. The music blared from omnipresent speakers, too loud and senseless for Anne's taste, forcing voices to compete in shrieks. The throbbing, repetitive beat seemed to stir the two hundred or so women, however, with promises of erotica, of good times to come. Lights flashed in a dizzying pattern that lacked discernible organization, changing faces from red to green to blue as if they were hapless chameleons. The tables were littered with cups, pitchers, ashtrays heaped with cigarette butts, and spreading wet circles that glittered like kisses as the lights swept across them.

"Isn't this a hoot?" Sylvia demanded of the table. "I went to one of these last year, and it was beyond my wildest imagination." She flung her blond hair over her shoulder and studied the barnlike room with a complacent smile. "This crowd looks a lot worse. We are in for quite a time this evening, ladies. Quite a time."

Marjorie drained her cup and pushed herself to her feet. "If Hank's going to kill me, I might as well die happily. I'm going for another pitcher, after a trip to the can to powder my nose. Anyone else interested?"

Bitsy picked up her purse and tucked it under her arm. "I'm tempted to stay in the ladies' room until the show is over," she said acidly. "I cannot believe I'm actually here. I don't know why we let Sylvia coerce us into this low-class display of vulgarity, although I can understand why it might appeal to her."

Waggling a finger at her, Sylvia said, ''It's time you saw something more exciting than a kindergarten classroom, my dear. You're beginning to look like one of your five-year-olds.''

Bitsy pursed her lips into a pout. ''This whole thing is nauseating. I should have stayed at my apartment and washed my hair. Let's go, Marjorie. The ladies' room is probably filthy, but I'm not accustomed to beer. Scotch is less fattening, and so much more civilized than this swill.''

Once Marjorie and Bitsy found a path through the crowd of women and vanished around the far corner of the bar, Anne gazed across the table. ''I can't believe I'm here either. It's a good thing Paul's out at the cabin this weekend. Maybe by Sunday night I'll have worked up enough courage to tell him about it.'' Or perhaps she might whisper it in his ear, while he lay in a coffin at the funeral home. Even tell him she'd changed her mind about the divorce—he could file it in hell or wherever he ended up. She bit her lip to hide a quick smile. The irony was delicious.

''What's he doing at the lake?'' Sylvia asked. She lit a cigarette and inhaled deeply.

''He said he had a lot of work to do and wanted to put fifty miles between himself and a telephone. He's been under such stress lately; I hope he has a chance to relax.''

''You still don't have a telephone out there? God, Anne, it's halfway to the end of the world.''

''That's why Paul bought it. I don't really enjoy staying there, but he seems to find ways to amuse himself. I haven't been there in months.'' She crossed her fingers in her lap. She'd been there two days ago, when she'd called in sick and then taken a little field trip, although hardly in a fat yellow school bus. ''He asked if I would drive up this weekend. I told him I absolutely had to finish the semester inventory at the library, but that's only partly true. In all honesty, he's been in a rotten mood for several months, and I have no desire to be cooped up with him in the middle of the woods.''

''Maybe he's in mid-life crisis. My ex went crazy when he hit forty. His shrink said he'd get over it, but I divorced the bastard on general principle. When men get to that age, they don't seem to know what they want—unless it's a combination of cuddle and sizzle.''

"He's not having an affair," Anne replied firmly. "Paul is much too straitlaced to do anything to threaten his stuffy law practice. I do wish he didn't have to work so hard; we haven't had a proper dinner in three months.'' He had, though. She'd opened the bill from the credit card company. Lots of restaurants, but she hadn't been invited for any cozy little dinners with elegant wine. She'd been at home, putting gourmet meals down the garbage disposal.

"The old working-late-at-the-office bit?'' Sylvia raised two penciled eyebrows. "Well, if you're not going to worry about it, then neither am I, but I think you'd better keep an eye on him. Paul's an attractive man, and he knows it. Did you hear what happened this morning in the teachers' lounge when the toilet backed up?''

Anne forced a smile as Sylvia began to relate a bit of gossip that would, without a doubt, end on a crude bark of laughter. The music drowned out a major part of the story, but she didn't care. Sylvia didn't require more than a superficially attentive audience. The bitch. So she was surprised there was no telephone at the cabin. As if she didn't know. Of course what she and Paul did at the cabin didn't require a telephone—only a mattress. Or any flat surface, for that matter. Her smile wavered, but she tightened her jaw and willed it into obedience.

"Hank is going to kill me," Marjorie said as she set the pitcher on the table and sat down beside Anne. "So when do we see the boys?''

Sylvia consulted her watch. "In about ten minutes, I would guess. The management wants to give all of us time to drink ourselves into a cheerful mood.''

Bitsy slipped in next to Sylvia and glared at the rowdier elements of the crowd. "*Cheerful* is hardly the adjective, Sylvia. Nasty and foulmouthed might be closer to the truth. Where do all these women come from? I've never seen so many women about to burst out of their jeans or pop buttons off their blouses.'' She shifted her eyes to Sylvia's ample chest, which was distorting a field of silk flowers.

"This isn't a Sunday prayer meeting," Sylvia said, grinning. "Now you and Marjorie could sneak in the back door of the church if you wanted to, but Anne and I came to have fun. Isn't that right, Anne?"

"Oh, yes," Anne murmured. Oh, no, she added to herself as she once again held in a smile. She had come to put the plan in motion. Sylvia needed to know where Paul was, and how lonely he might be for his cooperative slut. She decided to reiterate the information once again, just in case Sylvia had missed it. "You should have convinced Hank to go fishing with Paul, Marjorie. The poor baby's out at the cabin all by himself for the entire weekend, with no one to entertain him. And he's been acting very odd these last three or four months; I'm worried he might be on the edge of a nervous breakdown."

"So worried that you felt obliged to come to this horrid show instead of bothering to be with him?" Bitsy said coolly.

Anne winced as she struggled to hide a flicker of irritation. It was, she lectured herself, an opening to produce her alibi, even if it had been provided in a self-righteous tone of voice. "He told me he preferred to be alone, Bitsy, and I can't go to the cabin this weekend, in any case. I'm going to spend the next two days locked in the library with Bev to do the semester inventory. We agreed we'd work until midnight Saturday and Sunday if we had to, and send out for sandwiches. Paul will enjoy a chance for relaxation and total solitude."

"Total solitude?" Sylvia echoed, laughing. "Maybe he's having an affair with some nubile specimen of wildlife."

"That's not a very nice thing to say," Bitsy said. "Just because your husband chased every skirt in town doesn't mean that—"

"Paul's banging a raccoon? My ex would have; he banged everything that breathed." Sylvia laughed again, then finished her beer and lit another cigarette from the smoldering butt in her hand. Next to her, Bitsy coughed in complaint and pointedly fanned the air with her hand. Anne covertly studied Sylvia's face, searching for some sign that the blonde's thoughts were centered on the poor lonely husband in the conveniently remote cabin.

Marjorie had managed to mention her impending demise three more times before the music abruptly stopped. A middle-aged man in a pale blue tuxedo bounded onto the stage, a microphone in one hand. The crowd quieted in expectation, as did the four women at the table next to the stage.

"Are you ready?" the man demanded.

"Yes!" the women squealed.

"Are you ready?" he again demanded, leering into what must have resembled a murky aquarium of multicolored faces.

The crowd responded with increased enthusiasm. The ritual continued for several minutes as the emcee warmed up the audience. Anne could not bring herself to join the frenzied promises that she was indeed ready, even though, at a more essential level, the decision had been reached and the plan already set in motion. This man seemed too manipulative to merit response, too crassly chauvinistic—too much like Paul. Sylvia had no such reservations, of course. Marjorie was mouthing the sentiments of the crowd and clapping; Bitsy stared at the tabletop as if she were judging kindergarten finger paintings for potential van Goghs.

"Do you want to meet the men?" the emcee howled. The crowd howled that they most definitely did. The emcee mopped his forehead, assured them that they would in one teeny minute, but first they were going to have the opportunity to order one more round of drinks. Waving good-bye, he bounded off the stage and the music rose to fill the void.

Sylvia began to dig through her purse. "Damn it, I just had that prescription refilled last week," she said as she piled the contents on the table. "Tranquilizers aren't cheap."

But the gaunt blond divorcée was, Anne thought. Too bad she couldn't find her pills, but they had been removed earlier in the week, when Sylvia had negligently left her purse in the lounge. They were a part of the plan, a major part of the plan that would end with a wonderfully melodramatic climax. The other climaxes would occur earlier—in the bed, under the kitchen table, wherever the two opted to indulge their carnal drives.

She really didn't care anymore. Her marriage was a farce, as silly and shallow as the night's entertainment. It would be over by Sunday, and she would be free from Paul's over-bearing hypocrisy and Sylvia's treacherous avowals of friendship. A colleague had told her about seeing the two of them at a restaurant. Although the news had initially para-lyzed her, she had begun within a matter of days to devise the plan. It had taken several weeks to perfect it; the invitation from Sylvia to the male revue had seemed such a lovely, ironic time for the countdown to begin.

"You really shouldn't mix barbiturates with alcohol. The combination can be lethal," she said, hoping she sounded properly concerned. The advice was based on many hours of research, after all, done while sipping coffee from her thermos. An elementary school library held so many fascinating books and magazines. From both sides of the table, Bitsy and Marjorie nodded their agreement.

Sylvia shrugged and began to cram things back in her purse. "It'd take a handful of the things to do any damage. I must have left them in the bathroom at home, or in another purse. Damnation, I feel a really ghastly tension headache coming on; I'll have to drown it in beer."

Just wait, Anne added under her breath. By Sunday night, Sylvia and Paul were going to be far past the point of feeling anything. The bottle was in the liquor cabinet at the cabin, a brand she knew Paul always kept well stocked. The drifting sediment at the bottom would not prevent the contents from being savored, and the effects would take several hours to be felt. By then, it would be much too late.

Sunday night, or perhaps Monday morning, she would telephone the sheriff's department and in a worried, wifely voice ask them to check the cabin. The suicide note she had typed on Paul's typewriter would be found in her bedside drawer, his illegible signature scrawled across the bottom. It was really quite nicely written, with pained admissions that he could no longer bear a life without Sylvia, that he had taken her pills earlier in the week so they could gently pass away in each other's arms. A bittersweet postscript to his wife, begging her forgiveness. She suspected she would shed a few tears when the police showed it to her. Her friends would all assure her that he had had a nervous breakdown, that he hadn't known what he was writing. They would be right, but she wouldn't tell them that.

"Oh, my lord," whispered Marjorie. "Hank really is going to kill me if I have to call him for bail."

Anne yanked her thoughts to the present moment and turned to the stage. A young man had appeared, dressed in a police uniform. His face was stern as he slapped a billy club across his palm. She felt as if it were slamming against her abdomen. Had Paul found the note and realized what she had arranged for the lovebirds?

"I should arrest all of you," he said, scowling as his eyes flitted around the room. "Run you in, book you, and take you to a cold, dark cell. Fling you across the cot and interrogate you until you beg for mercy. Is that what you want me to do?"

"No," screamed a voice from the crowd. "Take it off!"

His mouth softened; dimples appeared in his cheeks. "Is that what you want me to do?" he demanded of the crowd.

"Take it off!"

Like a prairie dog, the emcee popped up on the platform at the back of the stage. "Do you want Policeman Dick to take it off? You'll have to tell him what you want!"

"Take—it—off!" the crowd howled in unified frenzy.

The music began to pulsate as the young man toyed with the top button of his shirt, his hips synchronized with the beat. The crowd roared their approval. Sylvia leaned forward and said, "You turned absolutely white, Anne. Did you think he was a real cop?"

Anne kept her eyes on the man in the middle of the stage. "Don't be absurd, Sylvia. I don't have a guilty conscience," she said distractedly. The first button was undone, and the graceful fingers had moved down one tantalizing inch. A few curly chest hairs were visible now; she felt a sudden urge to dash onto the stage and brush her hand across them. "Is he going to take it all off?"

"I can't believe you said that," Bitsy sniffed. "I think this is disgusting."

Anne had expected to feel the same way, but now, with the darling young blond man who looked so wholesome, so boyish and innocent and pleased with the response from the crowd—it wasn't disgusting. It was very, very interesting.

Marjorie put her cup down, her eyes wide and her mouth slightly agape. "I don't think it's disgusting," she said in a hollow voice.

Bitsy leaned back in the chair and crossed her arms. "The three of you are slobbering like dogs."

Anne barely heard the condemnation from across the table. Policeman Dick was easing out of his shirt, letting each sleeve slide down his arm so slowly she could feel the ripple of his biceps, the hard turn of his elbows, the soft skin of his forearm, the mounded base of his hand, the long, delicate fingers. She heard herself exhale as the khaki shirt fell to the floor.

His hips still moving with the music, the man flexed his arms and turned slowly so the women could appreciate his flat stomach and broad shoulders. He swaggered across the stage to Anne's table and curled his hands behind Sylvia's neck.

"Unbuckle my belt or I'll run you in," he said, smiling to take the menace from his facetious threat. He noticed Anne's stunned expression and winked at her, sharing the joke in an oddly private message.

"You can run me in anytime you want!" Sylvia smirked as she fumbled with the buckle of his belt. Beside her, Bitsy was almost invisible below the table. Her face was stony, and her mouth a pinched ring of scandalized disapproval.

When the buckle was freed, the man backed away to tease the crowd with his jutting pelvis and bare chest. His trousers began to slide down his hips. Again Anne could feel his skin, now so taut with smooth, muscular slopes. It's been such a long time, she thought, panicked by the intensity of her reaction. If only Paul hadn't lost interest when he began the affair with Sylvia. . . . It was his fault she was responding like a silly, breathless, hormone-driven adolescent.

The uniform was off now; only a small triangle of khaki fabric acknowledged the limits of legality. The young man— Policeman Dick, she amended with a faint smile—began to dance with increased insistence, turning often so that all the women could have an equal opportunity to admire that which deserved admiration. The colored lights flashed across his body in silken hues, shadows to be stroked to find their depth.

As he moved toward the table, Sylvia creased a dollar bill and waved it over Anne's head. "Over here!" she called.

Perplexed, Anne frowned across the table. When Sylvia grinned and pointed, she turned back to see the young man dancing directly in front of her. Blue eyes crinkled in amusement. The dimples back again. And the wondrously unclad body, close enough that she could see the faint sheen of sweat. Feathery blond hair. Muscles that swooped like snow-covered hills. Hard thighs. The mysterious khaki bulge.

Despite the sudden grip of numbness, a wave of Novocain that flooded her chest and froze her lungs, she felt the dollar bill in her hand. The man slowly pulled her to her feet. All around them, women were bellowing in approval, their hands banging the tabletops and their feet pounding the floor. The music seemed to grow louder, a primitive command from a wild and unknown place. The young man curled a finger for Anne to move closer to him. Then, before she could consider her actions, she found herself sliding the bill under the narrow strap that supported his only item of clothing. Her fingers brushed his skin. A baby's skin.

He leaned down and caught her head in his hands. His deliberate kiss caught her by surprise, stunned her into acquiescence, and then, as his lips lingered, into unintentional cooperation. When she felt as if she were losing herself in a tunnel of heat, he eased away and met her eyes. After another disturbing wink, he danced away to collect the dollar bills that now waved like pennants all over the room.

"Sit down!" Bitsy snapped. "Everyone's staring at you. I want you to know that I am simply disgusted with you, Anne. And both of you too," she added to Sylvia and Marjorie. "I've had more of this than I can bear. I'm going home."

Anne wiggled her hand in farewell, but she could not unlock her eyes from the young blond dancer. Coals had been lit deep within her; they flamed and glowed, painfully. Her body ached for him. And he seemed to remain aware of her even as he accepted dollars and gave kisses to the screaming women crowding the edge of the stage.

Then, with a dimpled smile and a wink she felt was hers, he left the stage. The emcee introduced a dark-haired young man in a sequined cape, who began to produce gyrations with his hips as he paraded around the stage.

Anne looked at the dressing-room door in one corner of the room. "Will he be back?" she asked Sylvia.

"Probably. I could see you liked what you saw, Anne. You'd better not tell Paul too much about this when he gets home Sunday. He may not approve of his wife kissing a male stripper."

Marjorie sighed. "What was it like, Anne?"

"Just a kiss." But such a kiss. Soft lips and a faint hint of after-shave. A kiss more innocent than a high-school sweetheart's, but promising more than any boy could offer. A cherub without a robe. Every mother's son, every woman's lover. The ache increased until she felt as if she might slip into a fantasy of such erotic delight that she would never willingly return.

"Looks like our Annie is in love," Sylvia said. She pulled out another dollar bill and waved it over Marjorie's head. "Let's see if we can share the good fortune."

While Marjorie laughingly protested and tried to hide, Anne forced herself to watch the man on stage, who was nearing the same state of undress his predecessor had achieved. It did nothing to distract her from the memory of the kiss. She was startled when a waiter tapped her on the shoulder and handed her a folded note. He nodded in the direction of the dressing-room door and left.

Would she wait for "D" after the show?

There was a bit more, but she could hardly see the written letters. Would she? Did she dare? Anne Carter, wife of a lawyer, respected librarian at the neighborhood elementary school, gracious hostess for countless cocktail parties and elegant buffets designed to charm Paul's clients, was hardly the sort to hang around stage doors for male . . . dancers, dimples or not. She had never . . . done such a thing. It was . . . unthinkable. She simply . . . couldn't.

Men continued to dance on the stage. Dollars were waved; women were kissed and convinced not to pull too strenuously on the elastic straps that kept the show marginally legal.

Anne watched it all, sipping beer that had no taste, clapping to music that had no beat, hearing catcalls that had no meaning. Could she be in the blond man's arms while her husband and his mistress unwittingly poisoned themselves with the bottle she had left at the cabin?

Dick appeared during the second half of the show, this time dressed in tight pants and a shirt with flowing sleeves. As he danced at the table next to hers, Anne caught his questioning smile. She nodded. There really was no choice.

She survived the rest of the show, counting the minutes until the room would clear and he would emerge from the dressing room. At last, after a finale of flesh, the emcee thanked the crowd and told them when his show would return to the Happy Hour Saloon. Once the stage was empty, most of the women started for the exits, babbling excitedly about the relative merits of each performer.

"Hank's going to kill me," Marjorie said happily, then pulled herself out of her chair and left.

Anne glanced at Sylvia. "Don't you have a date?" she asked. At a cabin, with a bottle of Scotch and a husband who had strayed too far to ever merit forgiveness. She wanted it to be done.

"I do, and here he comes," Sylvia said, putting her cigarette case in her purse. "But what about you? This is hardly the place for librarians to sit alone and drink beer."

"He's here?" He couldn't be here—he was at the cabin.

Sylvia waved to a man waiting near the door. "My accountant, actually. I've been after him since April, because he saved me an absolute fortune on my taxes this year. If he can get me a refund next year, I may break down and marry him."

"Your accountant?"

"Somebody has to do my taxes. What's wrong with you?"

"I thought—I thought you and Paul—" Anne gasped through a suddenly constricted throat.

"Not me, Annie. Your husband's attractive, but he's more interested in the younger set. Or those who teach them." Sylvia looked at the chair beside her, where Bitsy had sat until she had made the indignant exit. "You'd better ask Paul about his late nights at the office. I didn't want to say anything, but Bitsy's been awfully concerned the last few months about your schedule.''

"Bitsy?" All she could manage was a croak. It couldn't be; the suicide note named Sylvia—not Bitsy. Her literary masterpiece would fool no one, not with the wrong name. The police would realize Paul hadn't written it. They would show it to her, ask her if she had been to the cabin lately, demand to know if she had taken barbiturates from Sylvia's purse and left the empty vial under the note in the night-table drawer. She hadn't worried about fingerprints, or mud on her tires, or any such trivial details. The investigation wouldn't have gone that far. The plan was too good.

She searched wildly for a way to prove Sylvia wrong, to catch her in some horridly devious lie. "But you had dinner with him!"

"He wanted to ask me how I thought you'd react to a divorce," Sylvia said gently. "He made me swear not to mention it to you. It's been Bitsy all along."

"No, it can't be. It can't be Bitsy." She rubbed her face, unable to believe it. "You're lying."

"Sorry to be the one to tell you," Sylvia said as she stood up. "I have to run; my gentleman friend's waiting to hear about the strippers. Don't stay here too long."

As Sylvia left, Anne felt her stomach grow cold with fear. Bitsy had left more than an hour ago, no doubt on her way to the rendezvous Anne herself had suggested. There was no way to telephone Paul, to tell him that the Scotch was filled with barbiturates, that she would no longer contest a divorce if he would quietly pour the bottle down the drain and tear up the damning suicide note.

Perhaps she could drive up there in time to stop them from consuming too much of the Scotch. The two wouldn't start on the bottle immediately. Surely they'd spend a few minutes greeting each other, and Bitsy would relish telling Paul all the details of the vulgarity to which she'd been exposed. Tell him how his wife had actually kissed a stripper. Offer righteous comments about the cheapness of the bar and the ill-bred behavior of the spectators.

Yes, she had time to rush to the cabin and prevent the

Scotch from carrying out its lethal assignment. If she left at once. She grabbed her purse and shoved back her chair. She had enough gas in her car; the route to the cabin was still fresh in her mind. She'd have to confront the two and admit what she'd done, but maybe—

"I'm glad you waited for me," a voice murmured in her ear. A hand touched her elbow and pulled her back down to her chair. "You're the sexiest woman I've ever seen, with your lovely dark hair and little-girl eyes."

"I—I have to leave. Now."

His hand tightened around her elbow, sending a flow of electricity up her arm. As disappointment crossed his face, she said, "An errand has come up, something I really and truly have to do. I'm sorry. I'd like to stay for a drink, but I have to go. Right now. There isn't much time. I'm sorry."

"We leave in the morning and won't be through here for at least six months," he said with a sigh, his blue eyes lowered. "I was very excited about getting to know you, if only for one night. I couldn't believe you'd actually waited for me, but I suppose you've changed your mind." He looked up with a wistful smile. "I wanted to make you happy this one night."

Anne took a deep breath as she studied the sweep of his eyelashes, the faint frown that managed to provoke his dimples, the haze of moisture on his neck from a hurried shower. She knew what his shirt and jeans covered, and she could envision what the khaki triangle had hidden. This—or a frantic drive down a dark, rutted road to the cabin to save two treacherous people from a fate they well deserved?

As the lights swept across the room, her face changed from red to blue to green. "The errand's not all that important," she said in a soft, slow voice.

Sue Grafton's private eye, Kinsey Millhone, plies her trade
from the coastal town of Santa Teresa, which clever Califor-
nians might think is much like Santa Barbara. Kinsey's combination of wit and grit have endeared her to readers as her
exploits take her through the alphabet, via the bestseller lists,
from ''A'' is for Alibi *through the upcoming and yet-to-be-
titled* ''N''. *Along the way, her novels have won four Anthonys,
three Shamus awards, two American Mystery awards, and five
Doubleday Mystery Guild awards; her short stories have collected three Macavitys, an Anthony, and an American Mystery
award.*

''In a Poison That Leaves No Trace,'' *winner of an American Mystery award, Kinsey advises a client that there is no
such thing—until she discovers the toxic nature of certain bitter pills.*

a poison that leaves no trace

by Sue Grafton

THE WOMAN WAS WAITING OUTSIDE MY OFFICE WHEN
I arrived that morning. She was short and quite plump, wearing jeans in a size I've never seen on the rack. Her blouse
was tunic-length, ostensibly to disguise her considerable rear
end. Someone must have told her never to wear horizontal
stripes, so the bold red-and-blue bands ran diagonally across
her torso with a dizzying effect. Big red canvas tote, matching canvas wedgies. Her face was round, seamless, and
smooth, her hair a uniformly dark shade that suggested a
rinse. She might have been any age between forty and sixty.
''You're not Kinsey Millhone,'' she said as I approached.

''Actually, I am. Would you like to come in?'' I unlocked
the door and stepped back so she could pass in front of me.
She was giving me the once-over, as if my appearance was
as remarkable to her as hers was to me.

She took a seat, keeping her tote squarely on her lap. I
went around to my side of the desk, pausing to open the

French doors before I sat down. "What can I help you with?"

She stared at me openly. "Well, I don't know. I thought you'd be a man. What kind of name is Kinsey? I never heard such a thing."

"My mother's maiden name. I take it you're in the market for a private investigator."

"I guess you could say that. I'm Shirese Dunaway, but everybody calls me Sis. Exactly how long have you been doing this?" Her tone was a perfect mating of skepticism and distrust.

"Six years in May. I was with the police department for two years before that. If my being a woman bothers you, I can recommend another agency. It won't offend me in the least."

"Well, I might as well talk to you as long as I'm here. I drove all the way up from Orange County. You don't charge for a consultation, I hope."

"Not at all. My regular fee is thirty dollars an hour plus expenses, but only if I believe I can be of help. What sort of problem are you dealing with?"

"Thirty dollars an hour! My stars. I had no idea it would cost so *much*."

"Lawyers charge a hundred and twenty," I said with a shrug.

"I know, but that's in case of a lawsuit. Contingency, or whatever they call that. Thirty dollars an *hour* . . ."

I closed my mouth and let her work it out for herself. I didn't want to get into an argument with the woman in the first five minutes of our relationship. I tuned her out, watching her lips move while she decided what to do.

"The problem is my sister," she said at long last. "Here, look at this." She handed me a little clipping from the Santa Teresa newspaper. The death notice read: "Crispin, Margery, beloved mother of Justine, passed away on December 10. Private arrangements. Wynington-Blake Mortuary."

"Nearly two months ago," I remarked.

"Nobody even told me she was sick! That's the point," Sis Dunaway snapped. "I wouldn't know to this day if a former neighbor hadn't spotted this and cut it out." She tended to speak in an indignant tone regardless of the subject.

"You just received this?"

"Well, no. It came back in January, but of course I couldn't drop everything and rush right up. This is the first chance I've had. You can probably appreciate that, upset as I was."

"Absolutely," I said. "When did you last talk to Margery?"

"I don't remember the exact date. It had to be eight or ten years back. You can imagine my shock! To get something like this out of a clear blue sky."

I shook my head. "Terrible," I murmured. "Have you talked to your niece?"

She gestured dismissively. "That Justine's a mess. Marge had her hands full with that one," she said. "I stopped over to her place and you should have seen the look I got. I said, 'Justine, whatever in the world did Margery die of?' And you know what she said? Said, 'Aunt Sis, her heart give out.' Well, I knew that was bull the minute she said it. We have never had heart trouble in our family. . . ."

She went on for a while about what everybody'd died of; Mom, Dad, Uncle Buster, Rita Sue. We're talking cancer, lung disorders, an aneurysm or two. Sure enough, no heart trouble. I was making sympathetic noises, just to keep the tale afloat until she got to the point. I jotted down a few notes, though I never did quite understand how Rita Sue was related. Finally, I said, "Is it your feeling there was something unusual in your sister's death?"

She pursed her lips and lowered her gaze. "Let's put it this way. I can smell a rat. I'd be willing to *bet* Justine had a hand in it."

"Why would she do that?"

"Well, Marge had that big insurance policy. The one Harley took out in 1966. If that's not a motive for murder, I don't know what is." She sat back in her chair, content that she'd made her case.

"Harley?"

"Her husband . . . until he passed on, of course. They took out policies on each other and after he went, she kept up the premiums on hers. Justine was made the beneficiary. Marge never remarried and with Justine on the policy, I guess she'll get all the money and do I don't know what. It just doesn't seem right. She's been a sneak all her natural life. A regular con artist. She's been in jail four times! My sister talked till she was blue in the face, but she never could get Justine to straighten up her act.''

''How much money are we talking about?''

''A hundred thousand dollars,'' she said. ''Furthermore, them two never did get along. Fought like cats and dogs since the day Justine was born. Competitive? My God. Always trying to get the better of each other. Justine as good as told me they had a falling-out not two months before her mother died! The two had not exchanged a word since the day Marge got mad and stomped off.''

''They lived together?''

''Well, yes, until this big fight. Next thing you know, Marge is dead. You tell me there's not something funny going on.''

''Have you talked to the police?''

''How can I do that? I don't have any *proof.*''

''What about the insurance company? Surely, if there were something irregular about Marge's death, the claims investigator would have picked up on it.''

''Oh, honey, you'd think so, but you know how it is. Once a claim's been paid, the insurance company doesn't want to hear. Admit they made a mistake? Uh-uh, no thanks. Too much trouble going back through all the paperwork. Besides, Justine would probably turn around and sue 'em within an inch of their life. They'd rather turn a deaf ear and write the money off.''

''When was the claim paid?''

''A week ago, they said.''

I stared at her for a moment, considering. ''I don't know what to tell you, Ms. Dunaway. . . .''

''Call me Sis. I don't go for that Ms. bull.''

''All right, Sis. If you're really convinced Justine's implicated in her mother's death, of course I'll try to help. I just don't want to waste your time.''

''I can appreciate that,'' she said.

I stirred in my seat. ''Look, I'll tell you what let's do.

Why don't you pay me for two hours of my time. If I don't come up with anything concrete in that period, we can have another conversation and you can decide then if you want me to proceed.''

''Sixty dollars,'' she said.

''That's right. Two hours.''

''Well, all right. I guess I can do that.'' She opened her tote and peeled six tens off a roll of bills she'd secured with a rubber band. I wrote out an abbreviated version of a standard contract. She said she'd be staying in town overnight and gave me the telephone number at the motel where she'd checked in. She handed me the death notice. I made sure I had her sister's full name and the exact date of her death and told her I'd be in touch.

My first stop was the Hall of Records at the Santa Teresa County Courthouse two and a half blocks away. I filled out a copy order, supplying the necessary information, and paid seven bucks in cash. An hour later, I returned to pick up the certified copy of Margery Crispin's death certificate. Cause of death was listed as a ''myocardial infarction.'' The certificate was signed by Dr. Yee, one of the contract pathologists out at the county morgue. If Marge Crispin had been the victim of foul play, it was hard to believe Dr. Yee wouldn't have spotted it.

I swung back by the office and picked up my car, driving over to Wynington-Blake, the mortuary listed in the newspaper clipping. I asked for Mr. Sharonson, whom I'd met when I was working on another case. He was wearing a somber charcoal-gray suit, his tone of voice carefully modulated to reflect the solemnity of his work. When I mentioned Marge Crispin, a shadow crossed his face.

''You remember the woman?''

''Oh, yes,'' he said. He closed his mouth then, but the look he gave me was eloquent.

I wondered if funeral home employees took a loyalty oath, vowing never to divulge a single fact about the dead. I thought I'd prime the pump a bit. Men are worse gossips than women once you get 'em going. ''Mrs. Crispin's sister was in my office a little while ago and she seems to think there was something . . . uh, irregular about the woman's death.''

I could see Mr. Sharonson formulate his response. ''I wouldn't say there was anything *irregular* about the woman's death, but there was certainly something sordid about the circumstances.''

''Oh?'' said I.

He lowered his voice, glancing around to make certain we couldn't be overheard. ''The two were estranged. Hadn't spoken for months as I understand it. The woman died alone in a seedy hotel on lower State Street. She drank.''

''Nooo,'' I said, conveying disapproval and disbelief.

''Oh, yes,'' he said. ''The police picked up the body, but she wasn't identified for weeks. If it hadn't been for the article in the paper, her daughter might not have ever known.''

''What article?''

''Oh, you know the one. There's that columnist for the local paper who does all those articles about the homeless. He did a write-up about the poor woman. 'Alone in Death' I think it was called. He talked about how pathetic this woman was. Apparently, when Ms. Crispin read the article, she began to suspect it might be her mother. That's when she went out there to take a look.''

''Must have been a shock,'' I said. ''The woman did die of natural causes?''

''Oh, yes.''

''No evidence of trauma, foul play, anything like that?''

''No, no, no. I tended her myself and I know they ran toxicology tests. I guess at first they thought it might be acute alcohol poisoning, but it turned out to be her heart.''

I quizzed him on a number of possibilities, but I couldn't come up with anything out of the ordinary. I thanked him for his time, got back in my car, and drove over to the trailer park where Justine Crispin lived.

The trailer itself had seen better days. It was moored in a dirt patch with a wooden crate for an outside step. I knocked on the door, which opened about an inch to show a short strip of round face peering out at me. ''Yes?''

''Are you Justine Crispin?''

"Yes."

"I hope I'm not bothering you. My name is Kinsey Millhone. I'm an old friend of your mother's and I just heard she passed away."

The silence was cautious. "Who'd you hear that from?"

I showed her the clipping. "Someone sent me this. I couldn't believe my eyes. I didn't even know she was sick."

Justine's eyes darkened with suspicion. "When did you see her last?"

I did my best to imitate Sis Dunaway's folksy tone. "Oh, gee. Must have been last summer. I moved away in June and it was probably some time around then because I remember giving her my address. It was awfully sudden, wasn't it?"

"Her heart give out."

"Well, the poor thing, and she was such a love." I wondered if I'd laid it on too thick. Justine was staring at me like I'd come to the wrong place. "Would you happen to know if she got my last note?" I asked.

"I wouldn't know anything about that."

"Because I wasn't sure what to do about the money."

"She owed you money?"

"No, no. I owed *her* . . . which is why I wrote."

Justine hesitated. "How much?"

"Well, it wasn't much," I said, with embarrassment. "Six hundred dollars, but she was such a doll to lend it to me and then I felt so bad when I couldn't pay her back right away. I asked her if I could wait and pay her this month, but then I never heard. Now I don't know what to do."

I could sense the shift in her attitude. Greed seems to do that in record time. "You could pay it to me and I could see it went into her estate," she said helpfully.

"Oh, I don't want to put you to any trouble."

"I don't mind," she said. "You want to come in?"

"I shouldn't. You're probably busy and you've already been so nice. . . ."

"I can take a few minutes."

"Well. If you're sure," I said.

Justine held the door open and I stepped into the trailer, where I got my first clear look at her. This girl was probably thirty pounds overweight with listless brown hair pulled into an oily ponytail. Like Sis, she was decked out in a pair of jeans, with an oversize T-shirt hanging almost to her knees. It was clear big butts ran in the family. She shoved some junk aside so I could sit down on the banquette, a fancy word for the ripped plastic seat that extended along one wall in the kitchenette.

"Did she suffer much?" I asked.

"Doctor said not. He said it was quick, as far as he could tell. Her heart probably seized up and she fell down dead before she could draw a breath."

"It must have been just terrible for you."

Her cheeks flushed with guilt. "You know, her and me had a falling out."

"Really? Well, I'm sorry to hear that. Of course, she always said you two had your differences. I hope it wasn't anything serious."

"She drank. I begged her and begged her to give it up, but she wouldn't pay me no mind," Justine said.

"Did she 'go' here at home?"

She shook her head. "In a welfare hotel. Down on her luck. Drink had done her in. If only I'd known . . . if only she'd reached out."

I thought she was going to weep, but she couldn't quite manage it. I clutched her hand. "She was too proud," I said.

"I guess that's what it was. I've been thinking to make some kind of contribution to AA, or something like that. You know, in her name."

"A Marge Crispin Memorial Fund," I suggested.

"Like that, yes. I was thinking this money you're talking about might be a start."

"That's a beautiful thought. I'm going right out to the car for my checkbook so I can write you a check."

It was a relief to get out into the fresh air again. I'd never heard so much horsepuckey in all my life. Still, it hardly constituted proof she was a murderess.

I hopped in my car and headed for a pay phone, spotting one in a gas station half a block away. I pulled change out of the bottom of my handbag and dialed Sis Dunaway's motel room. She was not very happy to hear my report.

"You didn't find anything?" she said. "Are you positive?"

"Well, of course I'm not positive. All I'm saying is that so far, there's no evidence that anything's amiss. If Justine contributed to her mother's death, she was damned clever about it. I gather the autopsy didn't show a thing."

"Maybe it was some kind of poison that leaves no trace."

"Uh, Sis? I hate to tell you this, but there really isn't such a poison that I ever heard of. I know it's a common fantasy, but there's just no such thing."

Her tone turned stubborn. "But it's possible. You have to admit that. There could be such a thing. It might be from South America . . . darkest Africa, someplace like that."

Oh, boy. We were really tripping out on this one. I squinted at the receiver. "How would Justine acquire the stuff?"

"How do I know? I'm not going to set here and solve the whole case for you! You're the one gets paid thirty dollars an hour, not me."

"Do you want me to pursue it?"

"Not if you mean to charge me an arm and a leg!" she said. "Listen here, I'll pay sixty dollars more, but you better come up with something or I want my money back."

She hung up before I could protest. How could she get her money back when she hadn't paid this portion? I stood in the phone booth and thought about things. In spite of myself, I'll admit I was hooked. Sis Dunaway might harbor a lot of foolish ideas, but her conviction was unshakable. Add to that the fact that Justine was lying about *something* and you have the kind of situation I can't walk away from.

I drove back to the trailer park and eased my car into a shady spot just across the street. Within moments, Justine appeared in a banged-up white Pinto, trailing smoke out of the tail pipe. Following her wasn't hard. I just hung my nose out the window and kept an eye on the haze. She drove over to Milagro Street to the branch office of a savings and loan. I pulled into a parking spot a few doors down and followed her in, keeping well out of sight. She was dealing with the branch manager, who eventually walked her over to a teller and authorized the cashing of a quite large check, judging from the number of bills the teller counted out.

Justine departed moments later, clutching her handbag protectively. I would have been willing to bet she'd been cashing that insurance check. She drove back to the trailer where she made a brief stop, probably to drop the money off.

She got back in her car and drove out of the trailer park. I followed discreetly as she headed into town. She pulled into a public parking lot and I eased in after her, finding an empty slot far enough away to disguise my purposes. So far, she didn't seem to have any idea she was being tailed. I kept my distance as she cut through to State Street and walked up a block to Santa Teresa Travel. I pretended to peruse the posters in the window while I watched her chat with the travel agent sitting at a desk just inside the front door. The two transacted business, the agent handing over what apparently were prearranged tickets. Justine wrote out a check. I busied myself at a newspaper rack, extracting a paper as she came out again. She walked down State Street half a block to a hobby shop where she purchased one of life's ugliest plastic floral wreaths. Busy little lady, this one, I thought.

She emerged from the hobby shop and headed down a side street, moving into the front entrance of a beauty salon. A surreptitious glance through the window showed her, moments later, in a green plastic cape, having a long conversation with the stylist about a cut. I checked my watch. It was almost twelve-thirty. I scooted back to the travel agency and waited until I saw Justine's travel agent leave the premises for lunch. As soon as she was out of sight, I went in, glancing at the nameplate on the edge of her desk.

The blond agent across the aisle caught my eye and smiled.

''What happened to Kathleen?'' I asked.

''She went out to lunch. You just missed her. Is there something I can help you with?''

''Gee, I hope so. I picked up some tickets a little while ago and now I can't find the itinerary she tucked in the envelope. Is there any way you could run me a copy real quick? I'm in a hurry and I really can't afford to wait until she gets back.''

"Sure, no problem. What's the name?"

"Justine Crispin," I said.

I found the nearest public phone and dialed Sis's motel room again. "Catch this," I said. "At four o'clock, Justine takes off for Los Angeles. From there, she flies to Mexico City."

"Well, that little shit."

"It gets worse. It's one-way."

"I knew it! I just knew she was up to no good. Where is she now?"

"Getting her hair done. She went to the bank first and cashed a big check—"

"I bet it was the insurance."

"That'd be my guess."

"She's got all that money *on* her?"

"Well, no. She stopped by the trailer first and then went and picked up her plane ticket. I think she intends to stop by the cemetery and put a wreath on Marge's grave. . . ."

"I can't stand this. I just can't stand it. She's going to take all that money and make a mockery of Marge's death."

"Hey, Sis, come on. If Justine's listed as the beneficiary, there's nothing you can do."

"That's what you think. I'll make her pay for this, I swear to God I will!" Sis slammed the phone down.

I could feel my heart sink. Uh-oh. I tried to think whether I'd mentioned the name of the beauty salon. I had visions of Sis descending on Justine with a tommy gun. I loitered uneasily outside the shop, watching traffic in both directions. There was no sign of Sis. Maybe she was going to wait until Justine went out to the gravesite before she mowed her down.

At two-fifteen, Justine came out of the beauty shop and passed me on the street. She was nearly unrecognizable. Her hair had been cut and permed and it fell in soft curls around her freshly made-up face. The beautician had found ways to bring out her eyes, subtly heightening her coloring with a touch of blusher on her cheeks. She looked like a million bucks—or a hundred thousand, at any rate. She was in a jaunty mood, paying more attention to her own reflection in the passing store windows than she was to me, hovering half a block behind.

She returned to the parking lot and retrieved her Pinto, easing into the flow of traffic as it moved up State. I tucked in a few cars back, all the while scanning for some sign of Sis. I couldn't imagine what she'd try to do, but as mad as she was, I had to guess she had some scheme in the works.

Fifteen minutes later, we were turning into the trailer park, Justine leading while I lollygagged along behind. I had already used up the money Sis had authorized, but by this time I had my own stake in the outcome. For all I knew, I was going to end up protecting Justine from an assassination attempt. She stopped by the trailer just long enough to load her bags in the car and then she drove out to the Santa Teresa Memorial Park, which was out by the airport.

The cemetery was deserted, a sunny field of gravestones among flowering shrubs. When the road forked, I watched Justine wind up the lane to the right while I headed left, keeping an eye on her car, which I could see across a wide patch of grass. She parked and got out, carrying the wreath to an oblong depression in the ground where a temporary marker had been set, awaiting the permanent monument. She rested the wreath against the marker and stood there looking down. She seemed awfully exposed and I couldn't help but wish she'd duck down some to grieve. Sis was probably crouched somewhere with a knife between her teeth, ready to leap out and stab Justine in the neck.

Respects paid, Justine got back into her car and drove to the airport where she checked in for her flight. By now, I was feeling baffled. She had less than an hour before her plane was scheduled to depart and there was still no sign of Sis. If there was going to be a showdown, it was bound to happen soon. I ambled into the gift shop and inserted myself between the wall and a book rack, watching Justine through windows nearly obscured by a display of Santa Teresa T-shirts. She sat on a bench and calmly read a paperback.

What was going on here?

Sis Dunaway had seemed hell-bent on avenging Marge's death, but where was she? Had she gone to the cops? I kept one eye on the clock and one eye on Justine. Whatever Sis was up to, she had better do it quick. Finally, mere minutes before the flight was due to be called, I left the newsstand, crossed the gate area, and took a seat beside Justine. "Hi," I said. "Nice permanent. Looks good."

She glanced at me and then did a classic double take. "What are you doing here?"

"Keeping an eye on you."

"What for?"

"I thought someone should see you off. I suspect your Aunt Sis is en route, so I decided to keep you company until she gets here."

"Aunt *Sis*?" she said, incredulously.

"I gotta warn you, she's not convinced your mother had a heart attack."

"What are you talking about? Aunt Sis is dead."

I could feel myself smirk. "Yeah, sure. Since when?"

"Five years ago."

"Bullshit."

"It's not bullshit. An aneurysm burst and she dropped in her tracks."

"Come on," I scoffed.

"It's the truth," she said emphatically. By that time, she'd recovered her composure and she went on the offensive. "Where's my money? You said you'd write a check for six hundred bucks."

"Completely dead?" I asked.

The loudspeaker came on. "May I have your attention, please. United Flight 3440 for Los Angeles is now ready for boarding at Gate Five. Please have your boarding pass available and prepare for security check."

Justine began to gather up her belongings. I'd been wondering how she was going to get all that cash through the security checkpoint, but one look at her lumpy waistline and it was obvious she'd strapped on a money belt. She picked up her carry-on, her shoulder bag, her jacket, and her paperback and clopped, in spike heels, over to the line of waiting passengers.

I followed, befuddled, reviewing the entire sequence of events. It had all happened today. Within hours. It wasn't like I was suffering brain damage or memory loss. And I hadn't seen a ghost. Sis had come to my office and laid out the whole tale about Marge and Justine. She'd told me all about their relationship, Justine's history as a con, the way the two women tried to outdo each other, the insurance, Marge's death. How could a murder have gotten past Dr. Yee? Unless the woman wasn't murdered, I thought suddenly.

Oh.

Once I saw it in *that* light, it was obvious.

Justine got in line between a young man with a duffel bag and a woman toting a cranky baby. There was some delay up ahead while the ticket agent got set. The line started to move and Justine advanced a step with me right beside her.

"I understand you and your mother had quite a competitive relationship."

"What's it to you," she said. She kept her eyes averted, facing dead ahead, willing the line to move so she could get away from me.

"I understand you were always trying to get the better of each other."

"What's your point?" she said, annoyed.

I shrugged. "I figure you read the article about the unidentified dead woman in the welfare hotel. You went out to the morgue and claimed the body as your mom's. The two of you agreed to split the insurance money, but your mother got worried about a double cross, which is exactly what this is."

"You don't know what you're talking about."

The line moved up again and I stayed right next to her. "She hired me to keep an eye on you, so when I realized you were leaving town, I called her and told her what was going on. She really hit the roof and I thought she'd charge right out, but so far there's been no sign of her. . . ."

Justine showed her ticket to the agent and he motioned her on. She moved through the metal detector without setting it off.

I gave the agent a smile. "Saying good-bye to a friend," I said, and passed through the wooden arch right after she did. She was picking up the pace, anxious to reach the plane.

I was still talking, nearly jogging to keep up with her. "I couldn't figure out why she wasn't trying to stop you and then I realized what she must have done—"

"Get away from me. I don't want to talk to you."

"She took the money, Justine. There's probably nothing in the belt but old papers. She had plenty of time to make the switch while you were getting your hair done."

"Ha, ha," she said sarcastically. "Tell me another one."

I stopped in my tracks. "All right. That's all I'm gonna say. I just didn't want you to reach Mexico City and find yourself flat broke."

"Blow it out your buns," she hissed. She showed her boarding pass to the woman at the gate and passed on through. I could hear her spike heels tip-tapping out of ear range.

I reversed myself, walked back through the gate area and out to the walled exterior courtyard, where I could see the planes through a windbreak of protective glass. Justine crossed the tarmac to the waiting plane, her shoulders set. I didn't think she'd heard me, but then I saw her hand stray to her waist. She walked a few more steps and then halted, dumping her belongings in a pile at her feet. She pulled her shirt up and checked the money belt. At that distance, I saw her mouth open, but it took a second for the shrieks of outrage to reach me.

Ah, well, I thought. Sometimes a mother's love is like a poison that leaves no trace. You bop along through life, thinking you've got it made, and next thing you know, you're dead.

Elizabeth George's A Great Deliverance, *winner of an Anthony and an Agatha, and nominated for an Edgar and a Macavity, introduced Detective-Inspector Thomas Lynley and Detective Sergeant Barbara Havers. The sleuths return in eight more bestselling novels, including* Deception on His Mind, *to solve cases in which love, betrayal, and the often unrecognized burdens of the past are key elements. Internationally acclaimed (she won the German Mimi and the Grand Prize for Literature in France), the Lynley and Havers novels abound with British sites and sounds, providing palpable settings for Elizabeth's astute observations of human nature.*

In "The Evidence Exposed," hidden motivations are brought to light after a member of class in British architecture dies on an excursion.

the evidence exposed

by Elizabeth George

ADELE MANNERS GAVE HER ROOM ONE LAST LOOK. The bed was made. The clothes were picked up. Nothing betrayed her.

She shut the door and descended the stairs to join her fellow students for breakfast. The dining hall rang with the clatter of their dishes and silverware, with the clamor of their talk. As always, one voice managed to soar above the rest, shrill and determined to fix attention upon the speaker. Hearing it, Adele winced.

"Hypoglycemia. Hy-po-gly-*ce*-mia. You know what that is, don't you?"

Adele wondered that anyone could avoid knowing since, in their two weeks at St. Stephen's College, Noreen Tucker hadn't missed an opportunity to expatiate upon hypoglycemia or anything else. Seeing that she was doing so once again, Adele decided to take her plate of scrambled eggs and sausage to another location, but as she turned, Howard Breen came to her side, smiled, said, "Coming?" and carried his own plate to where Noreen Tucker reigned, outfitted by Laura Ashley in an ensemble more suited to a teenager than a romance writer at the distant end of her fifth decade.

Adele felt trapped. She liked Howard Breen. From the first moment they had bumped into each other and discovered they were neighbors on the second floor of L staircase, he had been very kind to her, preternaturally capable of reading past her facade of calm yet at the same time willing to allow her to keep personal miseries to herself. That was a rare quality in a friend. Adele valued it. She valued Howard Breen. So she followed him.

"I'm just a martyr to hypoglycemia," Noreen was asserting vigorously. "It renders me useless. If I'm not careful . . ."

Adele blocked out the woman's babbling by scanning the room and engaging in a mental recitation of the details she had learned in her two weeks as a student in the Great Houses of Britain class. *Gilded capitals on the pilasters*, she thought, *a segmented pediment above them*. She smiled wryly at the fact that she'd become a virtual encyclopedia of architectural trivia while at Cambridge. Cram the mind full of facts that one would never use and perhaps they might crowd out the big fact that one could never face.

No, she thought. *No, I won't. Not now.* But the thought of him came to her anyway. Even though it was finished between them, even though it had been her choice, not Bob's, she couldn't be rid of him. Nor could she bury him as he deserved to be buried. She had made the decision to end their affair, putting a period to five years of anguish by coming to this summer session at St. Stephen's College in the hope that an exposure to fine minds would somehow allow her to forget the humiliation of having lived her life for half a decade in the fruitless expectation that a married man would leave his wife for her. Yet nothing was working to eradicate Bob from memory, and Noreen Tucker was certainly not the incarnation of razor intellect that Adele had hoped to find at Cambridge.

She gritted her teeth as Noreen went on. "I don't know what would have happened to me if Ralph here hadn't insisted that I go to the doctor. Always weak at the knees.

Always feeling faint. Blacking out on the freeway that time. On the freeway! If Ralph here hadn't grabbed the wheel . . .'' When Noreen shuddered, the ribbon on her straw hat quivered in sympathy. "So I keep my nuts and chews with me all the time. Well, Ralph here keeps them for me. Ten, three, and eight P.M. If I don't eat them right on the dot, I go positively limp. Don't I, Ralph?"

It was no surprise to Adele when Ralph Tucker said nothing. She couldn't remember a time when he had managed to make a satisfactory response to some remark of his wife's. At the moment his head was lowered; his eyes were fixed on his bowl of cornflakes.

"You *do* have my trail mix, don't you, Ralph?" Noreen Tucker asked. "We've got the trip to Abinger Manor this morning, and from what I could tell from looking at that brochure, it's going to be lots of walking. I'll need my nuts and chews. You haven't forgotten?"

Ralph shook his head.

"Because you did forget last week, sweetie, and the bus driver wasn't very pleased with us, was he, when we had to stop to get me a bit of something at three o'clock?"

Ralph shook his head.

"So you *will* remember this time?"

"It's up in the room, hon. But I won't forget it."

"That's good. Because . . ."

It was hard to believe that Noreen actually intended to go on, harder to believe that she could not see how tiresome she was. But she nattered happily for several more minutes until the arrival of Dolly Ragusa created a diversion.

Silently, Adele blessed the girl for having mercy upon them. She wouldn't have blamed Dolly for taking a place at another table. More than anyone, Dolly had a right to avoid the Tuckers, for she lived across the hall from them on the first floor of M staircase, so there could be no doubt that Dolly was well versed in the vicissitudes of Noreen Tucker's health. The words *my poor blood* were still ringing in the air when Dolly joined them, a black fedora pulled over her long blond hair. She wrinkled her nose, rolled her eyes, then grinned.

Adele smiled. It was impossible not to find Dolly a pleasure. She was the youngest student in the Great Houses class—a twenty-three-year-old art history graduate from the University of Chicago—but she moved among the older students as an equal, with an easy confidence that Adele admired, a spirit she envied. Dolly's youth was fresh, unblemished by regret. This was not a girl who would be so stupid as to give her love to a man who would never return it. This was not a weak girl. Adele had seen that from the first.

Dolly reached for the pitcher of orange juice. "The Cleareys had a real knockdown drag-out this morning," she said.

"About six-thirty. I thought Frances was going to put Sam through the window. Did you guys hear them?"

The question was directed to both the Tuckers, but it was Noreen who answered, looking up from straightening the sailor collar on her dress. "A fight?"

The question was spoken casually enough, but Adele saw how the information had piqued Noreen's interest. She had made no secret of her fascination with Sam Clearey, a U.C. Berkeley botanist.

"It was a doozy," Dolly said. "Apparently, Sam was just getting in. Just getting in at six-thirty in the morning! Can you believe it? He spent the night in someone else's room!" She grinned. "I love these Cambridge intrigues, don't you? It's sorta like high school all over again. Where d'you think he was?"

"Not with me, I'm afraid," Adele replied. "You're a better bet than I am to catch his fancy."

Dolly laughed. "*Me?* Adele, he's at least sixty years old! Come on!" She twirled a lock of hair around her finger and looked reflective. "But he is pretty great for an older guy, isn't he? All that gray hair. The way he dresses. I wonder who snagged him?"

"I saw him in the bar last night with that blonde from the Austen class," Howard Breen offered. "They seemed friendly enough."

Noreen Tucker's lips pursed. "I hardly think that Sam Clearey would be taken in by a forty-nine-year-old divorcée with three teenagers and dyed hair. He's a college professor, Howard. He has taste. And intelligence. And breeding."

"Thanks. You *were* talking about me, I assume?'' Cleve Houghton slid into place next to Dolly Ragusa, carrying a plate heavily laden with eggs and sausages, grilled tomatoes and mushrooms.

Adele felt a quick release of tension at Cleve's arrival. Through mentioning the fact that Sam Clearey had shown interest in another woman, Howard Breen had innocently raised Noreen's ire. And Noreen was not the type of woman to let such a slight go by unanswered. Cleve's presence prevented her from doing so for the moment.

"Ran eight miles this morning,'' he was saying. "Along the backs to Granchester. The rest of you should try it. Hell, it's the best exercise known to man.'' He tossed back his hair and contemplated Adele with a lazy smile. "The *second* best exercise.''

Heat took Adele's face. She crumpled her napkin in her fist.

"Goodness. In mixed company, Cleve.'' Noreen Tucker's gaze was hungrily taking in the most salient aspect of Cleve Houghton's figure: jeans sculpted to muscular thighs. He was fifty but looked at least a decade younger.

"Damn right in mixed company,'' Cleve Houghton replied, digging into his eggs. "Wouldn't consider it in any other kind.''

"I certainly hope not,'' Noreen declared. "There's nothing worse than a man wasting himself on another man, is there? In one of my novels, I deal with just that topic. A woman falls in love with a homo and saves him. And when he realizes what it's like to have a woman and be normal, he melts. Just melts. I called it *Wild Seed of Passion. Seed* seemed appropriate. There's something in the Bible about spilling seed, isn't there? And that's exactly what those homos are up to. If you ask me, all they need is a real womanly woman and that would take care of that. Don't you agree, Howard?''

Adele offered a quick prayer that Howard Breen would see the barb for what it was and would hold his tongue. But Noreen's provocation was too much for him.

"I'd no idea you'd done research in this area,'' he said.

"I . . . research?'' Innocently, Noreen pressed a hand to

her chest. "Don't be silly. It's only reasonable to assume that when a man and a woman . . . Heavens, surely I don't have to point out the obvious to *you*? Besides, a creative artist sometimes has to take license with—"

"Reality? The truth? What?" Howard spoke pleasantly enough, but Adele saw the tightening muscles of his hand and she knew very well that Noreen saw the same.

Noreen reached across the table and patted his arm. "Now confess to us, Howard. Are you one of those San Francisco liberals with half a dozen homosexual friends? Have I offended you? I'm just an old-fashioned girl who loves romance. And romance is all about true love, which as we all know can only exist between a man and a woman. You know that, don't you?" She smiled at him coolly. "If you don't, you can ask Dolly. Or Cleve. Or even Adele."

Howard Breen stood. "I'll forgo that pleasure for now," he said, and left them.

"Gosh. What's the matter with him?" Dolly Ragusa asked, her fork poised in midair.

Cleve Houghton lifted a hand, dropped it to dangle limply from his wrist. "Figure it out for yourself. It shouldn't be tough. Howard's a hell of a lot more likely to chase after me than you."

"Oh, Cleve!" Noreen Tucker chuckled, but Adele did not miss the glint of malicious triumph in her eyes. She excused herself and went in search of Howard.

She didn't find him until eight forty-five, when she went to join the rest of the Great Houses class at their appointed meeting place: the Queen's Gate of St. Stephen's College. He was leaning against the arch of the gateway, stuffing a lunch bag into his tattered rucksack.

"You all right?" Adele tried to sound casual as she took her own lunch from the box in which the kitchen staff had deposited it.

"I took a walk along the river to cool off."

Howard didn't look that composed, no matter his words. A tautness in his features hadn't been there earlier. Even though she knew it was a lie, Adele said, "I don't think she really knew what she was saying, Howard. Obviously, she *doesn't* know about you or she wouldn't have brought the subject up at all.''

He gave a sharp, unamused laugh. ''Don't kid yourself. She's a viper. She knows what she's doing.''

''Hey, you two. Smile. Come on!'' Some ten yards away, Dolly Ragusa held a camera poised. She was making adjustments to an overlarge telephoto lens.

''What are you shooting with that thing, our nostrils?'' Howard asked, and Adele heard in his voice the quick change of mood that Dolly seemed capable of inspiring in people.

Dolly laughed. ''It's a macro-zoom, you dummy. Wide angles. Close-ups. It does everything.''

Nearby, Cleve Houghton was pulling on a sweater. ''Why are you carting that thing around anyway? It looks like a pain.''

Dolly snapped his picture before she answered. ''Art historians always have cameras smashed up to their faces. Like extra appendages. That's how you recognize us.''

''I thought that's how you recognize Japanese tourists.'' Sam Clearey spoke as he rounded the yew hedge that separated the main court from the interior of the college. As had been his habit for all their excursions, he was nattily dressed in tweeds, and his gray hair gleamed in the morning sunlight. His wife, a few steps behind him, looked terrible. Her eyes were bloodshot and her nose was puffy.

Seeing Frances Clearey, Adele felt a perfect crescent of pain in her chest. It came from recognizing a fellow sufferer. *Men are such shit*, she thought, and was about to join Frances and offer her the distraction of conversation when Victoria Wilder-Scott steamed down from Q staircase and rushed to join them, clipboard in hand. Her spectacles were perched on the top of her head, and she squinted at her students as if perplexed by the fact that they were out of focus.

''Oh! The specs! Right,'' she said, lowered them to her nose, and continued breezily. ''You've read your brochures, I trust? And the section in *Great Houses of the Isles*? So you know we've dozens of things to see at Abinger Manor. That marvelous collection of rococo silver you saw in your textbook. The paintings by Gainsborough, Le Brun, Lorrain, Reynolds. That lovely piece by Whistler. The Holbein. Some remarkable furniture. The gardens are exquisite, and the park . . . well, we won't have time to see everything but we'll do our best. You have your notebooks? Your cameras?''

''Dolly seems to be taking pictures for all of us,'' Howard Breen said as Dolly snapped one of their instructor, whirled and took another of Howard and Adele.

Victoria Wilder-Scott blinked at the girl, then beamed. She made no secret of the fact that Dolly was her favorite student. How could she be otherwise? They shared a similar education in art history and a mutual passion for *objets d'art.*

''Right. Then, shall we be off?'' Victoria said. ''We're all here? No. Where are the Tuckers?''

The Tuckers arrived as she asked the question, Ralph shoving a plastic bag of trail mix into the front of his safari jacket while Noreen stooped to pick up their lunches, opened hers, and grimaced at its contents. She followed this with a wink at Sam Clearey, as if they shared a mutual joke.

Her students assembled, Victoria Wilder-Scott lifted an umbrella to point the way and led them out of the college, over the bridge, and down Garret Hostel Lane toward the minibus.

Adele thought that Noreen Tucker intended to use their walk to the minibus as an opportunity to mend her fences with Howard, for the romance writer joined them with an alacrity that suggested some positive underlying intent. In a moment, however, her purpose became clear as she gave her attention to Sam Clearey, who apparently had decided that a walk with Howard and Adele was preferable to his wife's accusing silence. Noreen slipped her hand into the crook of his arm. She smiled knowingly at Howard and Adele, an invitation to become her fellow conspirators in whatever was to follow.

Adele shrank from the idea, feeling torn between walking more quickly in an attempt to leave Noreen behind and remaining where she was in the hope that somehow she might protect Sam, as she had been unable to protect Howard earlier. The nobler motive was ascendant. She remained with the little group, hating herself for being such a sop but unable to abandon Sam to Noreen, no matter how much he might deserve five minutes of her barbed conversation. She was,

Adele noted, even now winding up the watch of her wit.

"I understand you were a naughty little boy last night," Noreen said. "The walls have ears, you know."

Sam seemed to be in no mood to be teased. "They don't need to have ears. Frances makes sure of that."

"Are we to know the lady who was favored with your charms? No, don't tell us. Let me guess." Noreen played her fingers along the length of her hair. It was cut in a shoulder-length pageboy with a fringe of bangs, its color several shades too dark for her skin.

"Have you read the brochure on Abinger Manor?" Adele asked.

The attempt to thwart Noreen was a poor one, and she countered without a glance in Adele's direction. "I doubt our Sam's had much time to read, Adele. Affairs of the heart always take precedence, don't they?" She gave a soft, studied laugh. "Just ask our Dolly."

Ahead of them, Dolly's laughter caught the air. She was walking with Cleve Houghton, her gait like a bounce. She gestured to the spires of Trinity College to their right and bobbed her head emphatically to underscore a comment she was making.

With Sam within her grasp, Noreen's suddenly dropping the subject of his assignation on the previous night and moving on to target Dolly seemed out of character. It was not quite in keeping with Noreen's penchant for public humiliation, especially since there was no chance that Dolly could hear her words.

"Just look at them," Noreen said. "Dolly's digging for gold and she's found the mother lode."

"Cleve Houghton?" Howard said. "He's probably older than her father."

"What does age matter? He's a doctor. Divorced. Piles of money. I've heard Dolly sighing and drooling over those slides Victoria shows us. You know the ones. Antiques, jewelry, paintings. Cleve's just the one to give her that sort of thing. And he'd be happy to do so, make no mistake of that."

Sam Clearey was examining the shine on his well-buffed shoes. He cleared his throat. "She doesn't seem the type—"

Noreen squeezed his arm. "What a gentleman you are, Sam. But you didn't see them in the bar last night. With Cleve holding forth about seducing women by getting to know their souls and appealing to their minds, and all the time his eyes were just boring into Dolly. Ask Adele. She was sitting right next to him, weren't you, dear? Lapping up every word."

Noreen's teeth glittered in a feral smile, and for the first time Adele felt the bite of the woman's words directed against herself. A chill swept over her at the realization that nothing escaped Noreen's observation. For she *had* listened to Cleve. She had heard it all.

"Little Dolly may like to play virgin in the bush," Noreen concluded placidly, "but if Cleve Houghton's doing eight miles in the morning, I'd bet they're right between Dolly's legs."

Sam Clearey's skin darkened. Whether it was rage or embarrassment, it was difficult to tell, for he was careful to let neither color his remark. "How can you possibly know that?"

Noreen favored him with a tender look. "She's right across the hall from me. And I told you, Sammy. The walls have ears."

Sam disengaged her hand from his arm. "Yes. Well. If you'll excuse me, I'd better see to Frances."

Once he had gone, Noreen Tucker seemed to feel little need to remain with Howard and Adele. She left them to themselves and went to join her husband.

"Still think she doesn't mean any harm?" Howard asked. When Adele didn't reply, he looked her way.

She tried to smile, tried to shrug, failed at both, and hated herself for losing her composure in front of him. As she knew he would, Howard saw past the surface.

"She got to you," he said.

Adele looked from Dolly Ragusa to Cleve Houghton to Sam Clearey. She had received Noreen's message without any difficulty. Nasty though it was, it was loud. It was clear. As had been her message to Howard at breakfast. As, no doubt, had been her message to Sam Clearey. Whatever it was.

"She's a viper," Adele agreed.

• • •

The worst part of those brief moments with Noreen was the fact that her cruelty brought everything back in a rush. No matter that there was no direct correlation between Noreen's comment and the past; her veiled declaration of knowledge did more than merely make perilous inroads into Adele's need for privacy. It forced her to remember.

The minibus trundled along the narrow road. Signposts flashed by intermittently: Little Abington, Linton, Horseheath, Haverhill. Around Adele, the noise of conversation broke into Victoria Wilder-Scott's amplified monologue, which was droning endlessly from the front of the bus. Adele stared out the window.

She had been thirty-one and three years divorced when she'd met Bob. He'd been thirty-eight and eleven years married. He had three children and a wife who sewed and swept and ironed and packed lunches. She was loyal, devoted, and supportive. But she didn't have passion, Bob declared. She didn't speak to his soul. Only Adele spoke to his soul.

Adele believed it. She had to. Belief gave dignity to what otherwise would have been just a squalid affair. Elevated to a spiritual plane, their relationship was justified. More, it was sanctified. Having found her soul mate, she grew adept at rationalizing why she couldn't live without him. And how quickly five years had passed in this manner. How easily they decimated her meager self-esteem.

It was two months now since Bob had been gone from her life. She felt like an open wound. "You'll be back," he'd said. "You'll never have with another man what you have with me." It was true. Circumstances had proven him correct.

"You can't get anything inside the bus. There's not enough light."

Adele roused herself to see that Cleve Houghton was laughing at Dolly Ragusa. She was kneeling backward on the seat in front of him, focusing her camera on his swarthy face.

"Sure I can." *Click.* And to make her point. *Click.*

"Okay. Then let me take one of you."

"No way."

"Come on." He reached out.

She dodged him by scampering into the aisle. She moved among the seats, snapping away at one student after another: Ralph Tucker dozing with his head against the window, Howard Breen reading the brochure on Abinger Manor, Sam Clearey turning from the scenery outside as she called his name.

From the front of the minibus, Victoria Wilder-Scott continued her monologue about the manor. "... family remained staunchly Royalist to the end. In the north tower, you'll see a priest's hole where Charles I was hidden prior to escaping to the Continent. And in the long gallery, you'll be challenged to find a Gibb door that's completely concealed. It was through this door that King Charles—"

"Doesn't she think we can read the brochure? We know all about the paintings and the furniture and the silver gee-gaws, for God's sake." Noreen Tucker examined her teeth in the mirror of a compact. She rubbed at a spot of lipstick and got to her feet—intent, it seemed, upon Sam Clearey, who sat apart from his wife.

Restlessly, Adele turned in her seat. Her eyes met Cleve Houghton's. His gaze was frank and direct, the sort of appraisal that peeled off clothing and judged the flesh beneath.

He smiled, eyelids drooping. "Things on your mind?"

Dolly's shout of laughter provided Adele with an excuse not to answer. She was perched on the arm of Ralph Tucker's seat, talking to Frances Clearey. Her face was animated. Her hands made shapes in the air as she spoke.

"I think it's great that you and Sam do things like this together," Dolly said. "This Cambridge course. I tried to get my boyfriend to come with me, but he wouldn't even consider it."

Frances Clearey made an effort to smile, but it was evident that her concentration was on Noreen Tucker, who had dropped into the vacant seat next to Frances's husband.

"D'you two do this sort of thing every summer?" Dolly asked.

"This is our first time." Frances's eyes flicked to the side as Noreen Tucker laughed and inclined her head in Sam Clearey's direction.

Dolly spoke cheerfully. Adele saw her move so that her body blocked Frances's view of Sam and Noreen. "I'm going to tell David—that's my boyfriend—all about you two. If a marriage is going to work, it seems to me that the husband and wife need to share mutual interests. And still give each other space at the same time. Like you and Sam. David and I . . . he can really be possessive."

"I'm surprised he didn't come with you, then."

"Oh, this is educational. David doesn't worry if I'm involved in art history. It's like him and his monkeys. He's a physical anthropologist. Howlers."

"Howlers?"

Dolly lifted her camera and snapped Frances's picture. "Howler monkeys. That's what he studies." She grinned. "Their poop, if you can believe it. I ask him what he's going to learn from putting monkey poop under a microscope. He says looking at it's not so bad. Collecting it is hell."

Frances Clearey laughed. Dolly did likewise. She took another picture and danced up the aisle.

Adele marveled at how easily the girl had managed to bring Frances out of herself, even for a moment. How wise she was to point out subtly to Frances the strengths of her marriage instead of allowing her to sit in solitude, brooding upon its most evident weakness. Noreen Tucker was nothing, Dolly was saying. Other women are nothing. Sam belongs to you.

Dolly's was a decidedly insouciant attitude toward life. But why should she offer any other perspective? Her future stretched before her, uncomplicated and carefree. She bore no scars. She had no past to haunt her. She was, at the heart of it, so wonderfully young.

"Why so solemn this morning?" Cleve Houghton asked Adele from across the aisle. "Don't take yourself so seriously. Start enjoying yourself. Life's to be lived."

Adele's throat tightened. She'd had quite enough of living. *Click.*

"Adele!" Dolly was back with her camera.

When they arrived at their destination, the sight of Abinger Manor roused Adele from her blackness of mood. Across a moat that was studded with lily pads, two crenellated towers stood at the sides of the building's front entry. They rose five stories, and on either side of them, crow-stepped gables were surmounted by impossibly tall, impossibly decorated chimneys. Bay windows, a later addition to the house, extended over the moat and gave visual access to an extensive garden. This was edged on one side with a tall yew hedge and on the other with a brick wall against which grew an herbaceous border of lavender, aster, and dianthus. The Great Houses of Britain class wandered toward this garden with a quarter hour to explore it prior to the manor's first tour.

Adele saw that they were not to be the only visitors to the manor that morning. A large group of Germans debouched from a tour coach and joined Dolly Ragusa in extensively photographing the garden and the exterior of the house. Two family groups entered the maze and began shouting at one another as they immediately lost their way. A handsome couple pulled into the car park in a silver Bentley and stood in conversation next to the moat. For a moment, Adele thought that these last visitors were actually the owners of the manor—they were extremely well dressed and the Bentley suggested a wealth unassociated with taking tours of great houses. But they joined the others in the garden, and as they strolled past Adele, she overheard a snatch of conversation pass between them.

"Really, Tommy, darling, I can't recall agreeing to come here at all. When did I do so? Is this one of your tricks?"

"Salmon sandwiches" was the man's unaccountable reply.

"Salmon sandwiches?"

"I bribed you, Helen. Early last week. A picnic. Salmon sandwiches. Stilton cheese. Strawberry tarts. White wine."

"Ah. *Those* salmon sandwiches."

They laughed together quietly. The man dropped his arm around the woman's shoulders. He was tall, very blond, clear-featured, and handsome. She was slender, dark-haired, with an oval face. They walked in perfect rhythm with each other. Lovers, Adele thought bleakly, and forced herself to turn away.

When a bell rang to call them for the tour, Adele went

gratefully, hoping for distraction, never realizing how thorough that distraction would be.

Their guide was a determined-looking girl in her midtwenties with spots on her chin and too much eye makeup. She spoke in staccato. They were in the original screens passage, she told them. The wall to their left was the original screen. They would be able to admire its carving when they got to the other side of it. If they would please stay together and not stray behind the corded-off areas . . . Photographs were permissible without a flash.

As the group moved forward, Adele found herself wedged between two German matrons who needed to bathe. She breathed shallowly and was thankful when the size of the Great Hall allowed the crowd to spread out.

It was a magnificent room, everything that Victoria Wilder-Scott, their textbook, and the Abinger Manor brochure had promised it would be. While the guide cataloged its features for them, Adele dutifully took note of the towering coved ceiling, of the minstrel gallery and its intricate fretwork, of the tapestries, the portraits, the fireplace, the marble floor. Near her, cameras focused and shutters clicked. And then at her ear: ''Just what I was looking for. *Just*.''

Adele's heart sank. She had successfully avoided Noreen Tucker in the garden, after having almost stumbled upon her and Ralph in the middle of a Noreenian rhapsody over a stone bench upon which she had determined the lovers in her new romance novel would have their climactic assignation.

''The ball. Right in here!'' Noreen went on. ''Oh, I *knew* we were clever to take this class, Ralph!''

Adele looked Noreen's way. She was dipping her hand into the plastic bag that protruded from her husband's safari jacket. Ten o'clock, Adele thought, trail-mix time. Noreen munched away, murmuring, ''Charles and Delfinia clasped each other as the music from the gallery floated to caress them. 'This is madness, darling. We must not. We cannot.' He refused to listen. 'We *must*. Tonight.' So they—''

Adele walked away, grateful for the moment when the guide began ushering them out of the Great Hall. They went up a flight of stairs and into a narrow, lengthy gallery.

"This long gallery is one of the most famous in England," their guide informed them as they assembled behind a cord that ran the length of the room. "It contains not only one of the finest collections of rococo silver, which you see arranged to the left of the fireplace on a demi lune table—that's a Sheraton piece, by the way—but also a Le Brun, two Gainsboroughs, a Reynolds, a Holbein, a charming Whistler, and several lesser-known artists. In the case at the end of the room you'll find a hat, gloves, and stockings that belonged to Queen Elizabeth I. And here's one of the most remarkable features of the room."

She walked to the left of the Sheraton table and pushed lightly on a section of the paneling. A door swung open, previously hidden by the structure of the wall.

"It's a Gibb door. Clever, isn't it? Servants could come and go through it and never be seen in the public rooms of the house."

Cameras clicked. Necks craned. Voices murmured.

"And if you'll especially take note of—"

"Ralph!" Noreen Tucker gasped. *"Ralph!"*

Adele was among those who turned at the agitated interruption. Noreen was standing just outside the cord, next to a satinwood table on which sat a china bowl of potpourri. She was quite pale, her eyes wide, her extended hand trembling. Hypoglycemia seemed to be getting the better of her at last.

"Nor? *Hon*? Oh, damn, her blood—" Ralph Tucker had no chance to finish. With an inarticulate cry, Noreen fell across the table, splintering the bowl and scattering potpourri across the Persian carpet. Down the length of the room, the satin cord ripped from the posts that held it in place as Noreen Tucker crashed through it on her way to the floor.

Adele found herself immobilized, although around her, everyone else seemed to move at once. She felt caught up in a swell of madness as some people pressed forward toward the fallen woman and others backed away. Someone screamed. Someone else called upon the Lord. Three Germans dropped in shock onto the couches that were made available to them now that the cord of demarcation was gone. There was a cry for water, a shout for air.

Ralph Tucker shrieked, "Noreen!" and dropped to his knees amid the potpourri and china. He pulled at his wife's shoulder. She had fallen on her face, her straw hat rolling across the carpet. She did not move again.

Adele called wildly, "Cleve. *Cleve*," and then he was pushing through the crowd. He turned Noreen over, took one look at her face, said, "Jesus Christ," and began administering CPR. "Get an ambulance!" he ordered.

Adele swung around to do so. Their tour guide was rooted to her spot next to the fireplace, her attention fixed upon the woman on the floor as if she herself had had a part in putting her there.

"An ambulance!" Adele cried.

Voices came from everywhere.

"Is she . . ."

"God, she *can't* be . . ."

"Noreen! Nor! Hon!"

"Sie ist gerade ohnmachtig geworden, nicht wahr . . ."

"Get an ambulance, goddamn it!" Cleve Houghton raised his head. His face had begun to perspire. "Move!" he yelled at the guide.

She flew through the Gibb door and pounded up the stairs.

Cleve paused, took Noreen's pulse. He forced her mouth open and attempted to resuscitate her.

"Noreen!" Ralph wailed.

"Kann er nicht etwas unternehmen?"

"Doesn't anyone . . ."

"Schauen Sie sich die Gesichtsfarbe an."

"She's gone."

"It's no use."

"Diese dummen Amerikaner!"

Over the swarm, Adele saw the blond man from the Bentley remove his jacket and hand it to his companion. He eased through the crowd, straddled Noreen, and took over CPR as Cleve Houghton continued his efforts to get her to breathe.

"Noreen! Hon!"

"Get him out of the way!"

Adele took Ralph's arm, attempting to ease him to his feet. "Ralph, if you'll let them—"

"She needed to eat!"

Victoria Wilder-Scott joined them. "Please, Mr. Tucker. If you'll give them a chance . . ."

The tour guide crashed back into the room.

"I've phoned . . ." She faltered, then stopped altogether.

Adele looked from the guide to Cleve. He had raised his head. His expression said it all.

Events converged. People reacted. Curiosity, sympathy, panic, aversion. Leadership was called for, and the blond man assumed it, wresting it from the guide with the simple words, "I'm Thomas Lynley. Scotland Yard CID." He showed her a piece of identification she seemed only too happy to acknowledge.

Thomas Lynley organized them quickly, in a manner that encouraged neither protest nor question. They would continue with the tour, he informed them, in order to clear the room for the arrival of the ambulance.

He remained behind with his companion, Ralph Tucker, Cleve Houghton, and the dead woman. Adele saw him bend, saw him open Noreen's clenched hand, saw him examine the trail mix that fell to the floor. Cleve said, "Heart failure. I've seen them go like this before," but although Lynley nodded, he looked not at Cleve but at the group, his brown eyes speculating upon each one of them as they left the room. Ralph Tucker sank onto a delicate chair. Thomas Lynley's companion went to him, murmured a few words, put her hand on his shoulder.

Then the door closed behind them and the group was in the drawing room, being asked to examine the pendant plasterwork of its remarkable ceiling. It was called the King Edward Drawing Room, their much-subdued guide told them, its name taken from the statue of Edward IV that stood over the mantelpiece. It was a three-quarter-size statue, she explained, not life-size, for unlike most men of his time, Edward IV was well over six feet tall. In fact, when he rode into London on February 26, 1460 . . .

Adele did not see how the young woman could go on.

There was something indecent about being asked to admire chandeliers, flocked wallpaper, eighteenth-century furniture, Chinese vases, and a French chimneypiece in the face of Noreen Tucker's death. Adele had certainly disliked Noreen, but death was death and it seemed that, out of respect to her passing, they might well have abandoned the rest of the tour and returned to Cambridge. She couldn't understand why Thomas Lynley had not instructed them to do so. Surely it would have been far more humane than to expect them to traipse round the rest of the house as if nothing had happened.

But even Ralph had wanted them to continue. "You go on," he had said to Victoria when she had attempted to remain with him in the long gallery. "People are depending on you." He made it sound as if a tour of Abinger Manor were akin to a battle upon whose outcome the fate of a nation depended. It was just the sort of comment that would appeal to Victoria. So the tour continued.

Not that it would have been allowed to disband. Something in Thomas Lynley's face indicated that.

Everyone was restless. The air was close. Composure seemed brittle. Adele had no doubt that she was not the only person longing to escape from Abinger Manor.

The guide was asking for any questions about the room. Dolly cooperatively inquired if King Edward's statue was bronze. It was. She photographed it. The tour moved on.

There was a murmur when Cleve Houghton rejoined them in the winter dining room.

"They've taken her," he said in a low voice to Adele.

"And that man? The policeman?"

"Still in the gallery when I left. He's put out a call for the local police."

"Why?" Adele asked. "I saw him looking at . . . Cleve, you don't . . . she seemed healthy, didn't she?"

Cleve's eyes narrowed. "I know a heart attack when I see one. Jesus, what are you thinking?"

Adele didn't know what she was thinking. She only knew that she had recognized something on Lynley's face when he had looked up from examining Noreen Tucker's trail mix. Consternation, suspicion, anger, outrage. Something had been there. If that were the case, then it could only mean one thing. Adele felt her stomach churn. She began to evaluate her fellow students in an entirely new way: as potential killers.

Frances Clearey seemed to have been shaken from her morning's fury at her husband. She was close at Sam's side, pressed to his arm. Perhaps Noreen's death had allowed her to see how fleeting life was, how insignificant its quarrels and concerns were once one came to terms with its finitude. Or perhaps she simply had nothing further to worry about now that Noreen was eliminated.

She hadn't been at breakfast, Adele recalled, so she could have slipped into Noreen's room and put something into her trail mix. Especially if she knew that Sam had spent the night with Noreen. Removing a rival to a man's love seemed an adequate motive for murder.

But Sam himself had also not been at breakfast. So he, too, had access to Noreen's supply of food. If Noreen had known with whom he had spent the night—and surely that's what she had been hinting at this morning—perhaps Sam had seen the need to be rid of her. Especially if she had been the woman herself.

It was hard to believe. Yet at the same time, looking at Sam, Adele could see how Noreen's death had affected him. Beneath his tan, his face was worn, his mouth set. His eyes seemed cloudy. In each room, they alighted first upon Dolly, as if her beauty were an anodyne for him, but then they slid away.

Dolly herself had come into breakfast late, so she also had access to Noreen's supply of nuts. But Noreen had not given Dolly an overt reason to harm her, and surely Noreen's gossip about the girl—even if Dolly had heard it, which was doubtful—would only have amused her.

As it would have amused Cleve Houghton. And pleased him. And swelled his ego substantially. Indeed, Cleve had every reason to keep Noreen alive. She had been doing wonders to build repute of his sexual prowess. On the other hand, Cleve had come into breakfast late, so he, too, had access to the Tuckers' room.

Howard Breen seemed to be the only one who hadn't had

time to get to Noreen's trail mix. Except, Adele remembered, he had left breakfast early and she hadn't been able to find him.

Everyone, then, had the opportunity to mix something in with the nuts, raisins, and dried fruit. But what had that something been? And how on earth had someone managed to get hold of it? Surely one didn't walk into a Cambridge chemist's shop and ask for a quick-acting poison. So whoever tampered with the mix had to have experience with poisons, had to know what to expect.

They were in the library when Thomas Lynley and his lady rejoined them. He ran his eyes over everyone in the room. His companion did the same. He said something to her quietly, and the two of them separated, taking positions in different parts of the crowd. Neither of them paid the slightest attention to anything other than to the people. But they gave their full attention to them.

From the library they went into the chapel, accompanied only by the sounds of their own footsteps, the echoing voice of the guide, the snapping of cameras. Lynley moved through the group, saying nothing to anyone save to his companion, with whom he spoke a few words at the door. Again they separated.

From the chapel they went into the armory. From there into the billiard room. From there to the music room. From there down two flights of stairs and into the kitchen. The buttery beyond it had been turned into a gift shop. The Germans made for this. The Americans began to do likewise.

Adele could not believe that Lynley intended to allow them to escape so easily. She was not surprised when he spoke.

"If I might see everyone, please," he said as they began to scatter. "If you'll just stay here in the kitchen for a moment."

Protests rose from the German group. The Americans said nothing.

"We've a problem to consider," Lynley told them, "regarding Noreen Tucker's death."

"Problem?" Behind Adele, Cleve Houghton spoke. Others chimed in.

"What do you want with us anyway?"

"What's going on?"

"It was heart failure," Cleve asserted. "I've seen enough of that to tell you—"

"As have I," a heavily accented voice said. The speaker was a member of the German party, and he looked none too pleased that their tour was once again being disrupted. "I am a doctor. I, too, have seen heart failure. I know what I see."

Lynley extended his hand. In his palm lay a half dozen seeds. "It looked like heart failure. That's what an alkaloid does. It paralyzes the heart in a manner of minutes. These are yew, by the way."

"Yew?"

"What was yew—"

"But she wouldn't—"

Adele kept her eyes on Lynley's palm. Seeds. Plants. The connection was horrible. She avoided looking at the one person in the kitchen who would know beyond a doubt the potential for harm contained in a bit of yew.

"Surely those came from the potpourri," Victoria Wilder-Scott said. "It spilled all over the carpet when Mrs. Tucker fell."

Lynley shook his head. "They were mixed in with the nuts in her hand. And the bag her husband carried was filled with them. She was murdered."

The Germans protested heartily at this. The doctor led them. "You have no business with us. This woman was a stranger. I insist that we be allowed to leave."

"Of course," Lynley answered. "As soon as we solve the problem of the silver."

"What on earth are you talking about?"

"It appears that one of you took the opportunity of the chaos in the long gallery to remove two pieces of rococo silver from the table by the fireplace. They're salt cellars. Very small. And definitely missing. This isn't my jurisdiction, of course, but until the local police arrive to start their inquiries into Mrs. Tucker's death, I'd like to take care of this small detail of the silver myself."

"What are you going to do?" Frances Clearey asked.

"Do you plan to keep us here until one of us admits to something?" the German doctor scoffed. "You cannot search us without some authority."

"That's correct," Lynley said. "I can't search you. Unless you agree to be searched."

Feet shuffled. A throat cleared. Urgent conversation was conducted in German. Someone rustled papers in a notebook.

Cleve Houghton was the first to speak. He looked over the group. "Hell, I have no objection."

"But the women . . ." Victoria pointed out.

Lynley nodded to his companion, who was standing by a display of copper kettles at the edge of the group. "This is Lady Helen Clyde," he told them. "She'll search the women."

As one body, they turned to Lynley's companion. Resting upon them, her dark eyes were friendly. Her expression was gentle. What an absurdity it would be to resist cooperating with such a lovely creature.

The search was carried out in two rooms: the women in the scullery and the men in a warming room across the hall. In the scullery, Lady Helen made a thorough job of it. She watched each woman undress, redress. She emptied pockets, handbags, canvas totes. She checked the lining of raincoats. She opened umbrellas. All the time she chatted in a manner designed to put them at ease. She asked the Americans about their class, about Cambridge, about great houses they had seen and where they were from. She confided in the Germans about spending two weeks in the Black Forest one summer and confessed to an embarrassed dislike of the out-of-doors. She never mentioned the word *murder*. Aside from the operation in which they were engaged, they might have been new acquaintances talking over tea. Yet Adele saw for herself that Lady Helen was quite efficient at her job, for all her friendliness and good breeding. If she didn't work for the police herself—and her relationship with Lynley certainly did not suggest that she was employed by Scotland Yard— she certainly had knowledge of their procedures.

Nonetheless, she found nothing. Nor, apparently, did Lynley. When the two groups were gathered once again in the kitchen, Adele saw him shake his head at Lady Helen. If the silver had been taken, it was not being carried by anyone. Even Victoria Wilder-Scott and the tour guide had been searched.

Lynley told them to wait in the tearoom. He turned back to the stairway at the far end of the kitchen.

"Where's he going now?" Frances Clearey asked.

"He'll have to look for the silver in the rest of the house," Adele said.

"But that could take forever!" Dolly wailed.

"It doesn't matter, does it? We're going to have to wait to talk to the local police anyway."

"It was heart failure," Cleve said. "There's no silver missing. It's probably being cleaned somewhere."

Adele fell to the back of the crowd as they walked across the pebbled courtyard. A sense of unease plucked at her mind. It had been with her much of the morning, hidden like a secondary message between the lines of Noreen Tucker's words, trying to fight its way to the surface of her consciousness in the minibus, lying just beyond the range of her vision ever since they had arrived at the manor. Like the children's game of What's Wrong With This Picture, there was a distortion somewhere. She could feel it distinctly. She simply couldn't see it.

Her thoughts tumbled upon one another without connection or reason, like images produced by a kaleidoscope. There were yew hedges in the courtyard of St. Stephen's College. Sam and Frances Clearey had had a fight. The walls have ears. The silver was available. It was pictured in their text. It was in the brochures. They'd seen both in advance. Dolly wanted Cleve. She loved antiques. Sam Clearey liked women, liked the blonde from the Dickens class, liked . . .

Once again Adele saw Lady Helen go through their belongings. She saw her empty, probe, touch, leave nothing unexamined. She saw her shake her head at Lynley. She saw Lynley frown.

The two groups entered the tearoom and segregated themselves from each other. The Americans took positions at a refectory table at the far end. The Germans lined up for coffee and cakes.

"Victoria, can we go back to Cambridge?" Frances asked.

"I mean, when this is over? We've another house to see today, but we can drop it, can't we?"

Victoria was hesitant. "Ralph did specifically want us to—"

"Screw Ralph Tucker!" Sam said. "Come on, Victoria, we've had it."

"There's the minibus to consider, the driver's salary . . ."

"Couldn't we just chip in some money and tip him or something?" Dolly set her camera on the table in front of her. She folded her hands around it, her shoulders slumped. "I mean . . . oh, I guess that's dumb. Forget it."

And there it was in an instant. Right before her. Adele saw it at last. She knew what Noreen Tucker had been saying during their walk to the bus. She knew the source of her own disquiet on the journey to Abinger Manor. She acknowledged what she had seen without seeing from the moment they had arrived at the manor. Thirty-six was the key, but it had been exceeded long ago. The knowledge brought to Adele an attendant rush of wrenching illness. Thomas Lynley had made an assumption from the facts at hand.

But Lynley was wrong.

She pushed herself to her feet and left the group. Someone called after her, but she continued on her way. She found Lynley in the drawing room, directing three workmen who were crawling across the floor.

How can I do this? she asked herself. And then, *Why? With the future a blank slate upon which nothing but hope and success were written. Why?*

Lynley looked up. Lady Helen Clyde did likewise. Adele did not even have to speak to them. They joined her at once and followed her to the tearoom.

"What's going on?" Cleve asked.

Adele didn't look at him. "Dolly, give the inspector your camera."

Dolly's blue eyes widened. "I don't understand."

"Give him the camera, Dolly. Let him look at the lens."

"But you—"

Lynley lifted the camera from the girl's shoulder. Lined along its strap were containers for film. All of them were empty. Adele had seen that earlier, had seen it and had thought no more about it than she had thought about the fact that there had been no film in Dolly's shoulder bag. Nor had there been any in her pockets. She'd been shooting pictures all morning with no film in her camera at all, in order to conceal her real reason for carrying the camera with her to the manor in the first place.

Lynley twisted off the macro-zoom lens. It was useless, hollowed. Two pieces of rococo silver tumbled out.

Howard dropped into the seat next to Adele. "You okay?"

"Okay." She didn't want to talk about it. She felt like a Judas. She wanted to go home. She tried to keep from thinking about Dolly being led off by the police.

"How did you figure Dolly?"

"She took too many pictures. She would have had to change film, but she never did that. Because there was no film."

"But Noreen. Why did Dolly . . ."

Adele's limbs felt numb. "She didn't care one way or the other about Noreen. Probably intended the seeds to make Noreen good and sick, not kill her. She just needed a diversion to get to the silver."

"I don't get it. How could she possibly have known what yew seeds do?"

"Sam. He probably didn't know what he was telling her or why she was asking. He probably didn't think of anything except what it felt like to be his age and to be in bed with someone like Dolly." Even that was hard to bear. Knowing that Dolly's solicitous conversation with Frances Clearey about her marriage had been nothing more than part of the game. Just another diversion, just another lie.

"*Sam* and Dolly?" Howard looked across the aisle to where Cleve Houghton lounged in his seat, eyes half closed. "I thought Cleve . . . when Noreen was telling us that Cleve was talking last night about seducing women . . ."

"She was talking to me. About me. Cleve wasn't with Dolly last night, Howard." Adele looked out the window, said nothing more. After a moment, she felt Howard leave the seat and move away.

I will bury you, Bob, she had thought with Cleve Houghton. *I will end it between us this way.* So she had drunk in the college bar with him, she had walked on the backs and listened to him talk, she had pretended to find him intriguing and delightful, a man of passion, a soul mate, a replacement for Bob. And when he wanted her, she had obliged. Hurried grappling, urgent coupling, a body in her bed. To feel alive, to feel wanted, to feel a creature of worth. But not to bury Bob. It hadn't worked that way.

"Hey." Adele pretended not to hear him, but Cleve crossed the aisle and dropped into the seat. He carried a flask in his hand. "You look like you need a drink. Hell, I need one." He drank, spoke again in a lower voice. "Tonight?"

Adele raised her eyes to his face, trying and failing to force his features into the shape of another man's.

"Well?" he said.

Of course, she thought. Why not? What difference did it make when life was so fleeting and youth without meaning?

"Sure," she said. "Tonight."

Carolyn G. Hart is the recipient of two Agathas, two Anthonys, and a Macavity for her novels, as well as a Macavity for the short story. Annie Laurance Darling, owner of a mystery bookstore, Max Darling, Max's mother Laurel, and the Death on Demand bookstore are featured in nine novels, including Mint Julep Murder. With the introduction of Henrietta O'Dwyer Collins, known as Henrie O., like Carolyn, a former journalist, the American mystery scene is enriched by the example of a seasoned sleuth who knows her way around the world and maintains her vigorous, no-nonsense pursuit of the truth in five novels, most recently Death in Paradise.

In "Upstaging Murder," Annie's motehr-in-law, Laurel, discovers that all the world's become a stage—and one of the players isn't sticking to the rules.

upstaging murder

by Carolyn G. Hart

LAUREL DARLING ROETHKE WAS A LATECOMER TO MYS-teries, but, as with all her enthusiasms, she gave her new interest her all. She subscribed to both *Ellery Queen Mystery Magazine* and *Alfred Hitchcock Mystery Magazine*, belonged to the Mystery Guild, and was on the mailing list of a half dozen mystery bookstores, from Grounds for Murder in San Diego, California, to The Hideaway in Bar Harbor, Maine. Her heart, of course, belonged to Death on Demand, the mystery bookstore so ably directed by her dear daughter-in-law, Annie Laurance Darling. She adored Annie, though it was a bit of a puzzle that Max had chosen such a serious young woman to be his wife. Oh, well, one could never quite understand the squish of another's moccasins.

Still, it was Max's love for Annie that had led Laurel to the mystery. A true thrill was discovering the delights and pleasures of mystery weekends, from the Catskills to the Sierras, from the Louisiana bayous to the Alaskan tundra.

Annie encouraged her, of course. Dear Annie. So thoughtful to send a brochure on that Tibetan weekend, Murder at the Monastery. But she was already committed to Death Stalks the Smokies at this gorgeous inn in southeastern North Carolina, and it would only make sense to visit Annie and Max on her way home. She was so near.

So far, this weekend had been such a wonderful experience, a welcoming dinner devoted to one of Laurel's favorite authors, Leslie Ford, with choice tidbits about three of Ford's most famous characters, Grace Latham and Colonel Primrose and *dear* Sergeant Buck.

Laurel hummed vigorously as she inspected her image in the mirror. What was it that lovely police chief, the guest of honor, had murmured as they danced last night? That she had a Grecian profile and hair that shimmered like moonlight on water? How sweet! Men were so often obtuse, but they added such spice to life. She brushed a soupçon of pale pink gloss to her lips, nodded in satisfaction, and turned toward the door. Not that she expected to encounter anyone else abroad at this hour, but a woman owed it to herself always to look her best.

She slipped quietly down the hall. After all, you couldn't be too careful at mystery weekends. Everyone was so determined to win. Very American, of course, the spirit of competition. Some people (her mind skittered to Henny Brawley, one of the most avid mystery readers to frequent Annie's store) would do almost anything to win. So Laurel felt it was quite fair to scout out the territory in advance.

The Big Ben-like tone of the grandfather clock on the landing tolled the hour. Boom. Boom. So *quiet* at two A.M. Then she paused, one hand lightly resting on the heavy mahogany newel post at the foot of the stairs. Switching off her pencil flash, she cocked her head to listen.

A footstep.

No doubt about it.

How odd.

Perhaps another mystery competitor. She felt a quiver of disappointment. She'd so often triumphed because most people, face it, were slugabeds. She, of course, scarcely needed any sleep to function quite successfully. Darting into the cavernous library, which also served as the inn's lobby and as an auditorium, she found shelter behind heavy red velvet drapes as another stealthy footstep sounded.

Her heart raced in anticipation. Perhaps this weekend would be decidedly special. There were many reports of ghosts in these backwoods. Could it be that she would soon witness a spectral apparition? Laurel considered herself something of an authority on unearthly visitants. She was quite familiar with the works of the Society for Psychical Research, having read the ambitious, two-volume, 1,400-page work, *Phantasms of the Living*, published in 1886, and certainly she was cognizant of the apparitional research of that modern giant in the field, Dr. Karlis Osis.

Eagerly, she peered from behind the drapes. When a gray-robed figure glided into view, she was at once disappointed, yet intrigued. This was no ghost. After all, apparitions have no need of flashlights. But this was decidedly curious! Something was afoot here, no doubt about it. The dimly seen gray figure in the long, sweeping, hooded robe aimed a pencil flash, a twin to the one Laurel carried, down the center of the huge room. Laurel followed the bobbing progress of the light to the small stage where the mystery play would be presented tomorrow night. Such a clever idea, as touted in the brochure. As is customary at mystery weekends, a murder would be discovered shortly after breakfast, teams formed, and an investigation begun. The young actors hired to play suspects' roles would provide grist for the weekend detectives' mills. But, in addition, this weekend would feature a suspense play to be presented after dinner and before the announcement of the winning detective team at, of course, the stroke of midnight.

The hooded figure ran lightly up the steps and the pencil flash illuminated a narrow portion of the stage. The set included a yellow pine nightstand beside a rickety wooden bed with a pieced quilt cover. The figure placed the flash on the bed, the sliver of light aimed at the nightstand.

A gloved hand pulled open the drawer and lifted out a pistol.

Laurel strained to see the robed figure, dimly visible in the backwash of the flash, the sharply illuminated gloved hand, the gun. A crisp click, the gun opened. Another click, it shut. The gun was replaced in the drawer, the drawer closed, and the pencil flash lifted.

The hooded figure passed very near, but there was no visible face, just folds of cloth. There was an instant when Laurel could have reached out, yanked at the robe, and glimpsed the face of the intruder. She almost moved. To unmask the villain now—and the click of the pistol signaled unmistakable intent to Laurel—would perhaps protect the victim in this instance. But what of the future? Laurel remained still and listened to the fading footsteps, and then the figure was gone.

The police chief, such a handsome man and, understandably, a bit confused as to the purpose of her visit, welcomed her eagerly to his room. She soon put things clear, however. Then it took a bit of persuasion, but finally the chief agreed to her plan.

"Damned clever," he pronounced. "And, now, my dear, perhaps, after all your exertions, you might enjoy a glass of wine?"

Laurel hesitated for a moment but, after all, nothing more could be accomplished in her quest for justice until the morrow. She nodded in acquiescence, bestowing a serene smile upon her coconspirator. She couldn't help but appreciate the enthusiastic gleam in the chief's dark eyes.

Over a breakfast of piping hot camomile tea and oat bran sprinkled with alfalfa sprouts, Laurel studied the program of *Trial*, described as "a drama of life and death, of murder and judgment, of passion and power. An abused wife, Maria, is on trial for her life in the shooting death of her husband. A vindictive prosecutor demands a death for a death. Her fate will lie in the hands of the judge." Laurel thoughtfully chewed another sprig of alfalfa and committed to memory the five young faces of the cast.

Kelly Winston, the abused wife, had sharply planed, dramatic features and soulful eyes. She was a drama graduate of a Midwestern college. Beside her studio picture was a single quote: "I want it all."

"Hmm," Laurel murmured as she admired the really very

handsome features of Bill Morgan, the abusive husband slain by Maria. Such an attractive young man, though, of course, handsome is as handsome does. His quote: "George M. Cohan has nothing on me!"

Handsome was not the word for Carl Jenkins, who portrayed the prosecutor. His dark face glowered up from the program, thin-lipped and beak-nosed. "I'll see you on Broadway."

Walter Sheridan beamed from his studio picture, apparently the epitome of charm, good humor, and lightheartedness. He played the judge. "Life's a bowl of cherries."

Jonathan Ravin's face was young and vulnerable. His chin didn't look as if it had quite taken shape. He played the hired man who excites the husband's jealousy. "All I need is a chance."

Laurel did suffer a few pangs of envy as the weekend detectives began their investigation into the murder of a rich playboy at a Riviera château. (The roles played during the day investigation differed, of course, from the roles in that evening's play.) Laurel found the thrill of the chase hard to ignore. But a greater duty called. She consoled herself with thoughts of that great company of fictional sleuths who, like the company of all faithful people, surely were at her shoulder at this very moment (figuratively speaking): Mary Roberts Rinehart's Miss Pinkerton, Patricia Wentworth's Miss Silver (though why one should be dowdy with age mystified Laurel), Heron Carvic's Miss Seeton, Gwen Moffat's Miss Pink, Josephine Tey's Miss Pym, and, of course, Leslie Ford's Grace Latham. (Good for Grace. She, at least, made time in her life for men.)

But Laurel's plan of necessity required that she not be at the forefront of the mystery weekend investigations. In fact, she lagged, and only approached one of the young people playing the mystery roles when the investigators bayed through the inn in search of further elucidation.

She approached by herself, bearing goodies. Did anyone ever outgrow cookies and milk, even if, at later ages, these translated to gin and tonic?

Kelly Winston, who played a countess in the investigations, occupied one alcove in the library. As Laurel approached, the actress made a conscious effort to erase a tight frown and look aggrieved, in keeping with her role of the countess whose diamond tiara had been stolen.

Laurel proffered an inviting Bloody Mary with a sprig of mint. "Hard work, isn't it?" she said cheerfully. "I do so admire you young people. And the life of an actress! So much to be envied, but often such difficult demands, especially when emotions run high. It's so hard with men, isn't it, Kelly?"

Kelly looked at Laurel in surprise, but the drink was welcome. "Aren't you doing the mystery weekend?"

A light trill of laughter. "In a way, my dear. But I'm a writer too. Fiction, let me hasten to add. And I dearly enjoy getting to know my fellow human beings on a personal level. And I can tell that you are *so* unhappy."

The dam burst. Laurel made gentle, cooing noises, such an effective response, and presented an ingenuous face and limpid blue eyes. Kelly admitted that it was too, too awful, the way Walter was glooming around. After all, they'd only dated for a couple of months. Of course, he had helped her get the mystery troupe job, but that didn't mean he owned her, did it? More empathetic coos. And Bill was just the cutest guy she'd ever met!

Laurel found her next quarry, Bill Morgan, with an elbow on the bar. He accepted his drink with alacrity. He was a strapping young man, six foot four at least, with curly brown hair, light blue eyes, and a manly chin. Laurel's glance lingered. She did so admire manly chins. "I do think Kelly is such a dear girl! I hope Walter isn't making things too difficult for you both."

Bill, who was clearly accustomed to female attention from ages six to sixty, expressed no surprise at Laurel's personal interest. He drank half his Bloody Mary in a gulp. "Oh, Kelly's just being dramatic. Actually, it's Carl who gets on my nerves. I didn't even know she'd been involved with him until he got drunk the other night and told me I was a dumb sh—" He glanced at Laurel, cleared his throat. ". . . jerk to get involved with her. He said she went through men like a gambler through chips." He downed the rest of the drink, then looked past Laurel at the main hall and began to wave. "Hi, Jenny. Hey, how about later?"

A tiny, dark-haired girl with an elfin grace paused long enough to blow him a kiss. "Terrific. See you at the pool."

Laurel waited until Bill realized she was still there, not a usual situation for her. Of course, he was crassly young. When he smiled at her dreamily, obviously still thinking of Jenny, she said bluntly, "Do you think Walter is jealous?"

Bill looked at her blankly. "Jealous?"

"Of you and Kelly," she said patiently.

"So who cares?" he asked lightly.

"And Carl?" Laurel prodded.

"Oh, he's just a drunk." Then he frowned. "But kind of a nasty one."

Carl looked like he could be a nasty drunk, with his dark, thin face, prominent cheekbones, and small, tight mouth. As Laurel approached, he smoothed back patent-slick hair (he played a French police inspector in the mystery skit). He stared at the Bloody Mary suspiciously.

"So what's in it?" he snapped. "Ipecac? Valium?"

It was Laurel's turn to be surprised. "Why should I?"

"This isn't my first mystery weekend. People are crazy. They'll do anything."

Laurel lifted the glass to her lips, took a sip. "One hundred percent pure tomato juice, vodka, and whatever," she promised, and smiled winningly.

Carl gave a grudging smile in return. "You aren't one of the nuts?"

"Do I look like a nut?" she asked softly.

He took the Bloody Mary.

"Actually," Laurel confided, "I'm a writer and I'm doing an article on how women mistreat men. Don't you think that's a novel idea? So often, it's the other way around, don't you think?"

Although he looked a little confused, he nodded vehemently. "Damn right. Women mistreat men all the time. Wish they'd get some of their own back."

"Your last girlfriend?" she prompted.

His face hardened. "Should have known better. She two-timed me and made a play for Walter. My best friend. But he's finding out. She isn't any damned good. She'll dump Bill, too, one of these days.''

"Isn't it hard, having to act with her?"

Carl looked at her sharply. "Hey, what the hell? How'd you know it was Kelly? Hey, lady, what's going on here?"

"That's what I'm finding out," she caroled. Laurel gave him a sprightly wave and wafted toward the hall. She ignored his calls. A determined sleuth is never deflected.

The abandoned Walter, a French chef in the daytime skit, was short, plump, and genial. His spaniel eyes drooped at the mention of Kelly. "Gee, I wish I'd never gotten involved with her. She just seems to irritate everybody. It hasn't been the same since she came aboard."

"Were you deeply in love with her?" Laurel asked gently.

A whoop of laughter. "Lady, love is a merry-go-round. You hop on and you hop off. No hard feelings."

She found the fifth member of the troupe, Jonathan Ravin, beneath an umbrella at poolside. He played Oscar, a Polish expatriate. Long blond hair curled on his neck. He had unhappy brown eyes and bony shoulders.

He shook away the Bloody Mary. "I never adulterate my tomato juice."

"Oh, I certainly understand that," Laurel said sympathetically. "So dreadful what is done to food today. I cook only organically grown vegetables."

After a lengthy discussion of the merits of oat over wheat bran, Laurel segued nearer her objective. "Do your friends eat as you do?"

"My friends?"

"The other actors, Kelly and Bill and Carl and Walter."

"They aren't my friends," he burst out bitterly. "I thought Bill was. But when Kelly came along, he didn't even have time to play checkers anymore. Why did Walter have to bring her in? We had a wonderful time before she came."

Mystery teams sat together at dinner, passing notes, engaging in intense conversations with occasional loud outbursts of disagreement. But when the solutions were turned in at eight P.M., there was a general air of relaxation.

Laurel had not even sat with her team. Admittedly a der-

eliction of duty on her part, but more serious matters domi-
nated. Instead, she settled early at the table closest to the
stage, her police chief friend beside her. Their chairs were
only a few feet from the downstage-left stairs. As the house-
lights dimmed, she sat forward, chin in hand, to observe.

As the play unfolded, she was impressed with the skill of
the young acting troupe. Kelly was superb as the abused wife
on trial for the murder of her husband, the handsome, strapping Bill. Slender, blond Jonathan was an effective hired
man, who served as the object of the husband's jealousy.
The play began in the courtroom where the widow was on
trial for her life for the murder of her husband. She claimed
self-defense. Plump Walter, as the judge, looked unaccus-
tomedly stern in his black robe. The prosecutor, played by
the dark-visaged Carl, was determined to see her executed
for the crime. As Carl badgered her upon the witness stand,
she broke down in tears, screaming, "You can't know what
it was like that night!" The stage went dark. An instant
passed and the spots focused downstage on the partial set
containing the old bed and the nightstand. Kelly raised up in
the bed. She was dressed in the cotton gown she had worn
the night of the shooting.

Laurel slipped to her feet and moved toward the downstage-left steps. The police chief, with footsteps as light as a
cat's, followed close behind.

Onstage, the door to the bedroom burst open. The husband, played so well by that handsome young man, Bill Morgan, lunged toward the bed. His face aflame with jealousy
and anger, he accused her of infidelity. Denying it, Kelly
rolled off the bed, trying to escape, but her husband bounded
forward. Grabbing Kelly, Bill flung her toward the bed and
began to pull his belt from its loops. With a desperate cry,
she turned toward the nightstand and yanked at the drawer.
Pulling out the gun, she whirled toward Bill—and Laurel
was there.

Firmly, Laurel wrested the gun from Kelly's hand. She
stepped back.

"Lights." (It had only taken a moment that afternoon to
convince Buddy, a charming young hotel man, that a new
wrinkle had been added to the evening's entertainment. So

many people, it was sad to say, were so credulous. Really, it was no wonder criminals found such easy pickings.)

The stage was bathed in sharp white light.

"What the hell's going on?" Bill demanded.

Laurel held the gun with an extremely competent air. (After all, she had been second highest overall for women at the National Skeet Shooting Association World Championships in San Antonio in 1978.)

"So boring," Laurel trilled, "when everything always goes on schedule. Let's be innovative, listen to the inner promptings of our psyches. What would happen at this moment if this gun were turned upon another? Let us see." She smiled kindly at Bill Morgan, the handsome young man so accustomed to female adoration. "Not you, my dear. You've had your close call for now. But what about Carl? Does he hate you for taking Kelly away?" She swung the pistol toward the dark-visaged actor.

He squinted at her beneath the bright lights. "Lady, you *are* a nut." He folded his arms across his chest and shook his head in disgust.

The barrel poked toward him for a moment.

"No," Laurel said crisply, "not Carl."

The barrel swiveled up to aim at the black-clad judge. "Walter."

"Jesus, lady, get the hell offstage!"

But he made no move to duck or move away. Laurel smiled benignly. "It is important to be open to life. You passed a romantic moment with Kelly, did you not? But you see all liaisons as impermanent. So I think I shan't shoot at you."

She sighed and turned the gun toward the slender young man. Jonathan brushed back a wisp of blond hair. "This isn't funny, even if you think it is," he said pettishly. "What if we don't get paid for tonight?"

"Ah, the Inn will not be unhappy. Mystery lovers prefer excitement in the raw. They wish to experience life upon the edge. And we are now so close to true drama."

She swung around and leveled the pistol, aiming directly at Kelly's heart.

"I believe you will be the victim tonight, my dear. One, two . . ."

Kelly lifted her hands, stumbled backward, turned and began to run. "Stop her, somebody. Stop her before she kills me!"

As Kelly fled down the steps into the hall, Laurel called after her. "My dear, how interesting that you should be afraid. Because all the players know this gun is loaded with blanks."

The police chief, nodding approval at Laurel, hurried after the escaping actress.

Bill's eyes widened like a man who sees an unimaginable horror. "The gun. Blanks. You mean . . ."

Laurel nodded. "I'm afraid so, my dear. She put in real bullets. She would have killed you, of course—and claimed it was an accident, that some malicious person must have made the substitution. It would have been so difficult to prove otherwise. But, fortunately, I was abroad in the still of the night. And the dear police chief and I, such a cooperative man, removed the bullets, just in case, you know, that I didn't move swiftly enough tonight. Though everyone who knows me knows that I am always swift. We have the bullets she put in place of the blanks. They are Exhibits A, B, and C, I believe. The police are *so* efficient."

"Real bullets?" Bill repeated thinly. "My God, why?"

"Oh, my dear young man. You are so young. It would be well to understand that a woman who goes from man to man must do so at her own volition. A woman such as Kelly could never bear to be cast aside." She beamed at the handsome young man. "There is much to be said for constancy, you know." (She forbore to mention her own marital record of five husbands and—but that would be another story entirely.) "In any event, you should be quite safe now. Such a *public* demonstration of evil intent."

Ever since the publication of Where Are the Children? *Mary Higgins Clark has been a premier purveyor of psychological suspense. Three of her novels have been made into feature films and six into films for television. Past president of Mystery Writers of America, winner of the French Grand Prize for Literature, Mary's bestselling noels, including* Loves Music, Loves to Dance; Let Me Call You Sweetheart; Moonlight Becomes Her; Pretend You Don't See Her; *and the forthcoming* You Belong to Me, *are avidly devoured by readers all over the world—and for good reason. Hers is the supreme story-teller's gift, for which her legions of fans are grateful.*

In "Voices in the Coalbin," a young husband tries to still the ominous chorus that haunts his wife.

voices in the coalbin

by Mary Higgins Clark

IT WAS DARK WHEN THEY ARRIVED. MIKE STEERED THE car off the dirt road down the long driveway and stopped in front of the cottage. The real estate agent had promised to have the heat turned up and the lights on. She obviously didn't believe in wasting electricity.

An insect-repellent bulb over the door emitted a bleak yellowish beam that trembled in the steady drizzle. The small-paned windows were barely outlined by a faint flicker of light that seeped through a partially open blind.

Mike stretched. Fourteen hours a day of driving for the past three days had cramped his long, muscular body. He brushed back his dark brown hair from his forehead wishing he'd taken time to get a haircut before they left New York. Laurie teased him when his hair started to grow. "You look like a thirty-year-old Roman Emperor, Curlytop," she would comment. "All you need is a toga and a laurel wreath to complete the effect."

She had fallen asleep about an hour ago. Her head was

resting on his lap. He glanced down at her, hating to wake her up. Even though he could barely make out her profile, he knew that in sleep the tense lines vanished from around her mouth and the panic-stricken expression disappeared from her face.

Four months ago the recurring nightmare had begun, the nightmare that made her shriek, *"No, I won't go with you. I won't sing with you."*

He'd shake her awake. "It's all right, sweetheart. It's all right."

Her screams would fade into terrified sobs. "I don't know who they are but they want me, Mike. I can't see their faces but they're all huddled together beckoning to me."

He had taken her to a psychiatrist, who put her on medication and began intensive therapy. But the nightmares continued, unabated. They had turned a gifted twenty-four-year-old singer who had just completed a run as a soloist in her first Broadway musical to a trembling wraith who could not be alone after dark.

The psychiatrist had suggested a vacation. Mike told him about the summers he'd spent at his grandmother's house on Oshbee Lake forty miles from Milwaukee. "My grandmother died last September," he'd explained. "The house is up for sale. Laurie's never been there and she loves the water."

The doctor had approved. "But be careful of her," he warned. "She's severely depressed. I'm sure these nightmares are a reaction to her childhood experiences, but they're overwhelming her."

Laurie had eagerly endorsed the chance to go away. Mike was a junior partner in his father's law firm. "Anything that will help Laurie," his father told him. "Take whatever time you need."

I remember brightness here, Mike thought as he studied the shadow-filled cottage with increasing dismay. I remember the feel of the water when I dove in, the warmth of the sun on my face, the way the breeze filled the sails and the boat skimmed across the lake.

•   •   •

It was the end of June but it might have been early March. According to the radio, the cold spell had been gripping Wisconsin for three days. There'd better be enough coal to get the furnace going, Mike thought, or else that real estate agent will lose the listing.

He had to wake up Laurie. It would be worse to leave her alone in the car, even for a minute. "We're here, love," he said, his voice falsely cheerful.

Laurie stirred. He felt her stiffen, then relax as he tightened his arms around her. "It's so dark," she whispered.

"We'll get inside and turn some lights on."

He remembered how the lock had always been tricky. You had to pull the door to you before the key could fit into the cylinder. There was a night-light plugged into an outlet in the small foyer. The house was not warm but neither was it the bone-chilling cold he had feared.

Quickly Mike switched on the hall light. The wallpaper with its climbing ivy pattern seemed faded and soiled. The house had been rented for the five summers his grandmother was in the nursing home. Mike remembered how clean and warm and welcoming it had been when she was living here.

Laurie's silence was ominous. His arm around her, he brought her into the living room. The overstuffed velour furniture that used to welcome his body when he settled in with a book was still in place but, like the wallpaper, seemed soiled and shabby.

Mike's forehead furrowed into a troubled frown. "Honey, I'm sorry. Coming here was a lousy idea. Do you want to go to a motel? We passed a couple that looked pretty decent."

Laurie smiled up at him. "Mike, I want to stay here. I want you to share with me all those wonderful summers you spent in this place. I want to pretend your grandmother was mine. Then maybe I'll get over whatever is happening to me."

Laurie's grandmother had raised her. A fear-ridden neurotic, she had tried to instill in Laurie fear of the dark, fear of strangers, fear of planes and cars, fear of animals. When Laurie and Mike met two years ago, she'd shocked and amused him by reciting some of the litany of hair-raising stories that her grandmother had fed her on a daily basis. "How did you turn out so normal, so much fun?" Mike used to ask her.

"I was damned if I'd let her turn me into a certified nut." But the last four months had proved that Laurie had not escaped after all, that there was psychological damage that needed repairing.

Now Mike smiled down at her, loving the vivid sea-green eyes, the thick dark lashes that threw shadows on her porcelain skin, the way tendrils of chestnut hair framed her oval face. "You're so darn pretty," he said, "and sure I'll tell you all about Grandma. You only knew her when she was an invalid. I'll tell you about fishing with her in a storm, about jogging around the lake and her yelling for me to keep up the pace, about finally managing to outswim her when she was sixty."

Laurie took his face in her hands. "Help me to be like her."

Together they brought in their suitcases and the groceries they had purchased along the way. Mike went down to the basement. He grimaced when he glanced into the coalbin. It was fairly large, a four-feet-wide by six-feet-long plankboard enclosure situated next to the furnace and directly under the window that served as an opening for the chute from the delivery truck. Mike remembered how when he was eight he'd helped his grandmother replace some of the boards on the bin. Now they all looked rotted.

"Nights get cold even in the summer but we'll always be plenty warm, Mike," his grandmother would say cheerily as she let him help shovel coal into the old blackened furnace.

Mike remembered the bin as always heaped with shiny black nuggets. Now it was nearly empty. There was barely enough coal for two or three days. He reached for the shovel.

The furnace was still serviceable. Its rumbling sound quickly echoed throughout the house. The ducts thumped and rattled as hot air wheezed through them.

In the kitchen Laurie had unpacked the groceries and begun to make a salad. Mike grilled a steak. They opened a bottle of Bordeaux and ate side by side at the old enamel table, their shoulders companionably touching.

They were on their way up the staircase to bed when Mike spotted the note from the real estate agent on the foyer table: "Hope you find everything in order. Sorry about the weather. Coal delivery on Friday."

They decided to use his grandmother's room. "She loved that metal-frame bed," Mike said. "Always claimed that there wasn't a night she didn't sleep like a baby in it."

"Let's hope it works that way for me." Laurie sighed. There were clean sheets in the linen closet but they felt damp and clammy. The boxspring and mattress smelled musty. "Warm me up," Laurie whispered, shivering as they pulled the covers over them.

"My pleasure."

They fell asleep in each other's arms. At three o'clock Laurie began to shriek, a piercing, wailing scream that filled the house. "Go away. Go away. I won't. I won't."

It was dawn before she stopped sobbing. "They're getting closer," she told Mike. "They're getting closer."

The rain persisted throughout the day. The outside thermometer registered thirty-eight degrees. They read all morning curled up on the velour couches. Mike watched as Laurie began to unwind. When she fell into a deep sleep after lunch, he went into the kitchen and called the psychiatrist.

"Her sense that they're getting closer may be a good sign," the doctor told him. "Possibly she's on the verge of a breakthrough. I'm convinced the root of these nightmares is in all the old wives' tales her grandmother told Laurie. If we can isolate exactly which one has caused this fear, we'll be able to exorcise it and all the others. Watch her carefully, but remember: She's a strong girl and she wants to get well. That's half the battle."

When Laurie woke up, they decided to inventory the house. "Dad said we can have anything we want," Mike reminded her. "A couple of the tables are antiques and that clock on the mantel is a gem." There was a storage closet in the foyer. They began dragging its contents into the living room. Laurie, looking about eighteen in jeans and a sweater, her hair tied loosely in a chignon, became animated as she went through them. "The local artists were pretty lousy," she laughed, "but the frames are great. Can't you just see them on our walls?"

Last year as a wedding present, Mike's family had bought them a loft in Greenwich Village. Until four months ago, they'd spent their spare time going to garage sales and auctions looking for bargains. Since the nightmares began, Laurie had lost interest in furnishing the apartment. Mike crossed his fingers. Maybe she *was* starting to get better.

On the top shelf buried behind patchwork quilts he discovered a Victrola. "Oh, my God, I'd forgotten about that," he said. "What a find. Look. Here are a bunch of old records."

He did not notice Laurie's sudden silence as he brushed the layers of dust from the Victrola and lifted the lid. The Edison trademark, a dog listening to a tube and the caption *His Master's Voice*, was on the inside of the lid. "It even has a needle in it," Mike said. Quickly he placed a record on the turntable, cranked the handle, slid the starter to ON, and watched as the disk began to revolve. Carefully he placed the arm with its thin, delicate needle in the first groove.

The record was scratched. The singers' voices were male but high-pitched, almost to the point of falsetto. The effect was out of synch, music being played too rapidly. "I can't make out the words," Mike said. "Do you recognize it?"

"It's 'Chinatown,' " Laurie said. "Listen." She began to sing with the record, her lovely soprano voice leading the chorus. *Hearts that know no other world, drifting to and fro.* Her voice broke. Gasping, she screamed, *"Turn it off, Mike. Turn it off now!"* She covered her ears with her hands and sank onto her knees, her face deathly white.

Mike yanked the needle away from the record. "Honey, what is it?"

"I don't know. I just don't know."

That night the nightmare took a different form. This time the approaching figures were singing "Chinatown" and in falsetto voices demanding Laurie come sing with them.

• • •

At dawn they sat in the kitchen sipping coffee. "Mike, it's coming back to me," Laurie told him. "When I was little. My grandmother had one of those Victrolas. She had that same record. I asked her where the people were who were singing. I thought they had to be hiding in the house somewhere. She took me down to the basement and pointed to the coalbin. She said the voices were coming from there. She swore to me that the people who were singing were in the coalbin."

Mike put down his coffee cup. "Good God!"

"I never went down to the basement after that. I was afraid. Then we moved to an apartment and she gave the Victrola away. I guess that's why I forgot." Laurie's eyes began to blaze with hope. "Mike, maybe that old fear caught up with me for some reason. I was so exhausted by the time the show closed. Right after that the nightmares started. Mike, that record was made years and years ago. The singers are all probably dead by now. And I certainly have learned how sound is reproduced. Maybe it's going to be all right."

"You bet it's going to be all right." Mike stood up and reached for her hand. "You game for something? There's a coalbin downstairs. I want you to come down with me and look at it."

Laurie's eyes filled with panic, then she bit her lip. "Let's go," she said.

Mike studied Laurie's face as her eyes darted around the basement. Through her eyes he realized how dingy it was. The single light bulb dangling from the ceiling. The cinder-block walls glistening with dampness. The cement dust from the floor that clung to their bedroom slippers. The concrete steps that led to the set of metal doors that opened to the backyard. The rusty bolt that secured them looked as though it had not been opened in years.

The coalbin was adjacent to the furnace at the front end of the house. Mike felt Laurie's nails dig into his palm as they walked over to it.

"We're practically out of coal," he told her. "It's a good thing they're supposed to deliver today. Tell me, honey, what do you see here?"

"A bin. About ten shovelfuls of coal at best. A window.

I remember when the delivery truck came how they put the chute through the window and the coal roared down. I used to wonder if it hurt the singers when it fell on them.'' Laurie tried to laugh. ''No visible sign of anyone in residence here. Nightmares at rest, please God.''

Hand in hand they went back upstairs. Laurie yawned. ''I'm so tired, Mike. And you, poor guy, haven't had a decent night's rest in months because of me. Why don't we just go back to bed and sleep the day away. I bet anything that I won't wake up with a dream.''

They drifted off to sleep, her head on his chest, his arms encircling her. ''Sweet dreams, love,'' he whispered.

''I promise they will be. I love you, Mike. Thank you for everything.''

The sound of coal rushing down the chute awakened Mike. He blinked. Behind the shades, light was streaming in. Automatically he glanced at his watch. Nearly three o'clock. God, he really must have been bushed. Laurie was already up. He pulled khaki slacks on, stuffed his feet into sneakers, listened for sounds from the bathroom. There were none. Laurie's robe and slippers were on the chair. She must be already dressed. With sudden unreasoning dread, Mike yanked a sweatshirt over his head.

The living room. The dining room. The kitchen. Their coffee cups were still on the table, the chairs pushed back as they left them. Mike's throat closed. The hurtling sound of the coal was lessening. *The coal.* Maybe. He took the cellar stairs two at a time. Coal dust was billowing through the basement. Shiny black nuggets of coal were heaped high in the bin. He heard the snap of the window being closed. He stared down at the footsteps on the floor. The imprints of his sneakers. The side-by-side impressions left when he and Laurie had come down this morning in their slippers.

And then he saw the step-by-step imprint of Laurie's bare feet, the lovely high arched impressions of her slender, fine-boned feet. The impressions stopped at the coalbin. There was no sign of them returning to the stairs.

The bell rang, the shrill, high-pitched, insistent gonglike sound that had always annoyed him and amused his grandmother. Mike raced up the stairs. Laurie. Let it be Laurie.

The truck driver had a bill in his hand. "Sign for the delivery, sir."

The delivery. Mike grabbed the man's arm. "When you started the coal down the chute, did you look into the bin?"

Puzzled faded blue eyes in a pleasant weather-beaten face looked squarely at him. "Yeah, sure, I glanced in to make sure how much you needed. You were just about out. You didn't have enough for the day. The rain's over but it's gonna stay real cold."

Mike tried to sound calm. "Would you have seen if someone was in the coalbin? I mean, it's dark in the basement. Would you have noticed if a slim young woman had maybe fainted in there?" He could read the deliveryman's mind. He thinks I'm drunk or on drugs. "God damn it," Mike shouted. "My wife is missing. My wife is missing."

For days they searched for Laurie. Feverishly, Mike searched with them. He walked every inch of the heavily wooded areas around the cottage. He sat, hunched and shivering on the deck as they dragged the lake. He stood unbelieving as the newly delivered coal was shoveled from the bin and heaped onto the basement floor.

Surrounded by policemen, all of whose names and faces made no impression on him, he spoke with Laurie's doctor. In a flat, disbelieving tone he told the doctor about Laurie's fear of the voices in the coalbin. When he was finished, the police chief spoke to the doctor. When he hung up, he gripped Mike's shoulder. "We'll keep looking."

Four days later a diver found Laurie's body tangled in weeds in the lake. Death by drowning. She was wearing her nightgown. Bits of coal dust were still clinging to her skin and hair. The police chief tried and could not soften the stark tragedy of her death. "That was why her footsteps stopped at the bin. She must have gotten into it and climbed out the window. It's pretty wide, you know, and she was a slender girl. I've talked again to her doctor. She probably would have committed suicide before this if you hadn't been there for her. Terrible the way people screw up their children. Her doctor said that grandmother petrified her with crazy superstitions before the poor kid was old enough to toddle.''

"She talked to me. She was getting there." Mike heard his protests, heard himself making arrangements for Laurie's body to be cremated.

The next morning as he was packing, the real estate agent came over, a sensibly dressed, white-haired, thin-faced woman whose brisk air did not conceal the sympathy in her eyes. "We have a buyer for the house," she said. "I'll arrange to have anything you want to keep shipped."

The clock. The antique tables. The pictures that Laurie had laughed over in their beautiful frames. Mike tried to picture going into their Greenwich Village loft alone and could not.

"How about the Victrola?" the real estate agent asked. "It's a real treasure."

Mike had placed it back in the storage closet. Now he took it out, seeing again Laurie's terror, hearing her begin to sing "Chinatown," her voice blending with the falsetto voices on the old record. "I don't know if I want it," he said.

The real estate agent looked disapproving. "It's a collector's item. I have to be off. Just let me know about it."

Mike watched as her car disappeared around the winding driveway. *Laurie, I want you.* He lifted the lid of the Victrola as he had five days ago, an eon ago. He cranked the handle, found the "Chinatown" record, placed it on the turntable, turned the switch to the ON position. He watched as the record picked up speed, then released the arm and placed the needle in the starting groove.

"Chinatown, my chinatown . . ."

Mike felt his body go cold. *No! No!* Unable to move, unable to breathe, he stared at the spinning record.

". . . hearts that know no other world drifting to and fro . . ."

Over the scratchy, falsetto voices of the long-ago singers, Laurie's exquisite soprano was filling the room with its heart-stopping, plaintive beauty.

Dorothy Cannell, who writes about people she likes, behaving the way she'd like to behave if "...something thrillingly chilling..." happened to her, says that she became a writer to avoid learning algebra, and her fans are delighted that she made the choice. Her first novel, The Thin Woman, *introduced Ellie and Ben Haskell;* Down the Garden Path *featured Hyacinth and Primrose Tramwell; and* The Widow's Club, *nominated for an Agatha and an Anthony, brought the four sleuths together. Most recently,* God Save the Queen *continues to provide chills and laughs.*

In "The High Cost of Living," a brother and sister are taxed by the consequences of their plan to keep pace with inflation.

the high cost of living
by Dorothy Cannell

"THEY'RE NOT COMING!" CECIL SAID FOR THE fourth time, peering out into the rain-soaked night. The gale had whipped itself into a frenzy, buffeting trees and shaking the stone house like a dog with a rag doll. On that Saturday evening the Willoughbys—Cecil and his sister, Amanda— were in the front room, waiting for guests who were an hour late. The fire had died down and the canapés on their silver tray were beginning to look bored.

"They're not coming!" mimicked Amanda from the sofa, thrusting back her silver-blond hair with an irritable hand. "Repeating oneself is an early sign of insanity ... remember?"

Her eyes, and those of her brother, shifted ceilingward.

"Cecil, I regret not strangling you at birth. Stop hovering like a leper at the gate. Every time you lift the curtain an icy blast shoots up my skirt."

A shrug. "I've been looking forward to company. The Thompsons and Bumbells lack polish, but it doesn't take much to break the monotony in this morgue.''

''Really, Pickle Face!'' Amanda eyed a chip in her pearl-pink manicure with disfavor. ''Is that kind?''

''Speaking of kind''—Cecil let the curtain drop and adjusted his gold-rimmed spectacles—''I didn't much care for that crack about insanity. I take exception to jibes at Mother.''

''Amazing!'' Amanda wielded an emery board, her eyes on the prying tongues of flame loosening the wood fibers and sending showers of sparks up the chimney. ''Where did I get the idea that but for the money, you would have shoved the old girl in a cage months ago? Don't hang your head. All she does is eat and—''

''You always were vulgar.''

''And you always were forty-five, Cecily dear. How you love to angst, but spare me the bit about this being Mother's house and our being a pair of hyenas feasting off decaying flesh. That woman is not our mother. Father remarried because we motherless brats drove off every housekeeper within a week.''

''Mary was good to us.'' Drawing on a cigarette with a shaking hand, Cecil sank into a chair.

''Brother, you have such a way with words. Mary had every reason to count her blessings. She acquired a roof over her head and a man to keep her warm in bed. Not bad for someone who was always less bright than a twenty-watt bulb.''

''I still think some respect . . .'' The cigarette got flung into the fire.

''Sweet Cecily''—Amanda buffed away at her nails—''you have deception refined to an art. I admit to living in Stepmother's house because it's free. Come on! These walls don't have ears. The only reason Mad Mary isn't shut up in a cracker box is because we're not wasting her money on one.''

''I won't listen to this.''

''Your sensitivity be damned. You'd trade her in for a used set of golf clubs any day of the week. Who led the way, brother, to see what could be done about opening up Father's trust? Who swore with his hand on the certificates of stock that Mary was *non compos mentis*? Spare me your avowals of being here to keep Mary company in her second childhood." Amanda tossed the emery board aside. "You wanted a share in Daddy's pot of gold while still young enough to fritter it away."

Cecil grabbed for the table lighter and ducked a cigarette toward the flame. "I believe he would have wished—"

"And I wish him in hell." Amanda tapped back a yawn. "Leaving his money tied up in that woman for life . . ."

"Mary was halfway normal when Father died. Her sister was the fly in the ointment in those days. Always meddling in money matters."

"Hush, brother dear." Amanda prowled toward the window and gave the curtain a twitch. "Is the storm unnerving you? I'm amazed we haven't had the old lady down to look for her paper dolls. For the record, I've done my turn of nursemaid drill this week. Mrs. Bridger didn't come in the last couple of days, and if I have to carry another tray upstairs I will need locking up."

Her brother stared into the fire.

"No pouting." Peppermint-pink smile. "Beginning to think, dear Cecily, that the world might be a better place if we treated old people the way we do our dogs? When they become a bother, shouldn't we put them out of everyone's misery? Nothing painful! I hate cruelty. A whiff of a damp rag and then deep, deep sleep. . . . Oh, never mind! Isn't that the doorbell?"

Cecil stopped cringing to listen. "Can it be the Thompsons or the Bumbells?"

"Either them or the Moonlight Strangler." Amanda's voice chased him from the room. Hitching her skirt above the knee, she perched on the sofa arm. From the hall came voices.

"Terrible night! Sorry we're late. Visibility nil." A thud as the wind took the front door. Moments later an arctic chill preceded Cecil and the Thompsons into the room. Mrs. Thompson was shivering like a blancmange about to slide off the plate. Her husband, as thin as she was stout, was blue around the gills.

"Welcome." Amanda, crisp and sprightly, stepped forward. "I see you've let Cecil rob you of your coats. What sports to turn out on such a wicked night."

Mr. Thompson thawed. This was one hell of a pretty woman. He accepted a brandy snifter and a seat by the fire. His wife took sherry and stretched her thick legs close to the flames. That popping sound was probably her varicose veins.

"The Bumbells didn't make it." Norman Thompson spoke the obvious. "I told Gerty you wouldn't expect us, but she would have it that you'd be waiting and wondering."

"Our phone was dead," Gerty Thompson defended herself. "Heavens above!" Cheeks creasing into a smile. "Only listen to that wind and rain rattling the windows. Almost like someone trying to get in. I won't sleep tonight if it keeps up."

"She could sleep on a clothesline," came her husband's response.

"Refills?" Cecil hovered with the decanters.

Gerty held out her glass without looking at him. Staring at the closed door, she gave a squeaky gasp. "There's someone out in the hall. I saw the doorknob turn." Sherry slopped from the glass.

Norman snorted. "You've been reading too many spook-house thrillers."

"I tell you I saw—"

The door opened a wedge.

"Damn! Not now." Almost dropping the decanter, Cecil grimaced at Amanda. "Did you forget her sleeping pills?"

An old lady progressed unsteadily into the room. Both Thompsons thought she looked like a gray flannel rabbit. She had pumice-stone skin and her nightdress was without color. Wisps of wintry hair escaped from a net and she was clutching something tightly to her chest. A child terrified of having her treasures snatched away.

"How do you do?" Gerty felt a fool. She had heard that old Mrs. Willoughby's mind had failed. On prior occasions when she and Norman had been guests here, the poor soul had not been mentioned, let alone seen. Meeting her husband's eye, she looked away. Amanda wore a faint smirk, as though she had caught someone drinking his finger bowl. Most uncomfortable. Gerty wished Norman would say something. He was the one who had thought the Willoughbys worth getting to know. The old lady remained marooned in the center of the room. A rag doll. One nudge and she would fold over. Why didn't someone say something?

Cecil almost tripped on the hearth rug. "Gerty and Norman, I present my stepmother, Mary Willoughby. She hasn't been herself lately. Not up to parties, I'm afraid. You never did like them did you, Mother?" Awkwardly he patted Mrs. Willoughby's shoulder, then propelled her toward the Thompsons.

Gerty began shivering worse than when she was on the doorstep. "What's that you're holding, dear?" She had to say something—anything. The old lady's eyes looked dead.

An unreal laugh from Cecil. "A photo of her twin sister, Martha. They were very close; in fact, it was after Martha passed on last year that Mother began slipping. She always was the more dependent of the two. They lived together here after my father was taken."

"Sad, extremely sad." Mr. Thompson would have liked to sit back down, but while the old lady stood there . . .

Nudging Cecil aside, Amanda slid an arm around Mrs. Willoughby. "Nighty-night, Mary, dear!" she crooned. "Up the bye-bye stairs we go."

"No." The old lady's face remained closed, tight as a safe. But her voice rose shrill as a child's. A child demanding the impossible. "I want Martha. I won't go to sleep without Martha."

"Poor lost soul!" Ready tears welled in Gerty Thompson's eyes. "What can we do? There must be something."

"Mind our own business," supplied her husband. He was regretting not keeping his relationship with the Willoughbys strictly business. They had been a catch as investors, money having flowed from their pockets this last year.

The old lady did not say another word. But everyone sensed it would take a tow truck to remove her from the room.

"I give up," Amanda said. "Let's skate the sweet lamb over to that chair in the bookcase corner. She won't want to be too near the fire and get overheated. I expect she feels crowded and needs breathing space. Look, she's coming quite happily now, aren't you, Mary?''

''Ah!'' Gerty dabbed at her eyes with a cocktail napkin as Amanda tossed a rug over Mrs. Willoughby's knees. ''She didn't want to be sent upstairs and left out of things. Being with the ones she loves is all she has left, I suppose.''

''Yes, we are devoted to Mother,'' responded Amanda.

Mrs. Willoughby rocked mindlessly, her pale lips slack, the photo of her dead sister locked in her bony hands.

The others regrouped about the fire. Cecil poured fresh drinks and Amanda produced the tray of thaw-and-serve hors d'oeuvres. Rain continued to beat against the windows and the mantel clock ticked on self-consciously.

''We could play bridge, or do I hear any suggestions from the floor?'' Amanda popped an olive into her mouth, eyes on Norman Thompson.

''How about . . .'' Gerty's face grew plumper and she fussed with the pleats of her skirt. Everyone waited with bated breath, for her to suggest Monopoly. ''. . . How about a séance? Don't look at me like that, Norman. You don't have to be a crazy person to believe in the Other Side. And the weather couldn't be more perfect!''

Amanda set her glass down on the coffee table. ''What fun! My last gentleman friend suspected me of having psychic powers when I knew exactly what he liked in the way of . . . white wine.''

Cecil broke in. ''I don't like dabbling in the Unseen. We wouldn't throw our doors open to a bunch of strangers were they alive—''

''Coward!'' His sister wagged a finger at him. ''How can you disappoint Gerty and Norman?''

Mr. Thompson forced a smile.

Gerty was thrilled. ''Everything's right for communication. This house—with the wind wrapped all about it! What could be more ghostly? And those marvelous ceiling beams and that portrait of the old gentleman with side whiskers . . .'' While she enthused the others decided the game table in the window alcove would serve the purpose. Amanda fetched a brass candlestick.

''Perfect!'' Fearless leader Gerty took her seat. ''All other lights must be extinguished and the curtains tightly drawn.''

"I trust this experiment will not unsettle Mrs. Willoughby.'' Norman Thompson glanced over at the old lady seated in the corner.

"Let's get this over.'' Cecil was tugging at his collar.

"Lead on, Gerty.'' Amanda smiled.

"Very well. Into the driver's seat. All aboard and hold on tight! Everyone at his own risk. Are we holding hands? Does our blood flow as one? Feel it tingling through the veins— or do I mean the arteries? I can never remember.''

"My dear, lay an egg or get off the perch,'' ordered her husband.

Gerty ignored him. She was drawing upon the persona of her favorite fictional medium, the one in that lovely book *Ammie Come Home*. "Keep those eyes closed. No peeking! Let your minds float . . . drift, sway a little.''

"I can't feel a damn thing,'' said Norman. "My leg's gone to sleep.''

"The change in temperature! We're moving into a different atmosphere. We are becoming lighter. Buoyant! Are we together, still united in our quest? The spirits don't like ridicule, Norman.''

"They'll have to lump it.''

Amanda wiggled a foot against his. *Let's see if the old coyote is numb from the waist down.*

"Is anybody out there?'' Madame Gerty cooed. "We are all friends here. With outstretched arms we await your coming.''

Sounds of heavy breathing . . . the spluttering of the fire and a muffled snoring from the bookcase corner.

"Is there a message?'' Gerty called. Only the wind and rain answered. The room was still, except for Norman, who was trying to shake his leg free of the cramp—or Amanda's teasing foot. The clock struck eleven. From outside, close to the front wall of the house, came the blistering crack of lightning. The whole house took a step backward. The table lurched toward the window. For a moment they all imagined themselves smashing through the glass to be swept away by the wind. Gerty went over with her chair, dragging Cecil down with her. The candle, still standing, went out.

It was agreed to call a halt to the proceedings.

"We must try another time." Gerty hoisted herself onto one knee and reached for her husband's hand. "I am sure someone was trying to reach me."

Amanda shivered. "My God, this place is an igloo."

"The fire's out." Cecil righted the chairs.

"Well, get it going again! I'm freezing solid. Someone stick a cigarette between my lips so I can inhale some heat."

"The trouble with your generation is, you have been much indulged. A little cold never hurt anyone. Leave those logs alone. They must last all winter. I am not throwing money on a woodpile."

The voice cracked through the room like another bolt of lightning, turning the Willoughbys—brother and sister—into a pair of dummies in a shop window. Norman Thompson sat down without meaning to, while Gerty resembled a fish trying to unswallow the hook. Otherwise the only movement came from the old lady in the corner. Even seated, she appeared to have grown. Her eyes burned in the parchment face. Glancing at the photo in her hands, she laid it down on the bookcase, tossed off her blanket, and stood up. "There has been a great deal of waste in this house lately." The voice dropped to a whisper but carried deep into the shadows.

"This extravagance will stop. When one is old, people tend to take advantage. It appears I must come out of retirement, get back in harness and pull this team."

Her face as ashen as her hair, Amanda stood hunched like an old woman. She and Cecil looked like brother and sister for once. They wore matching looks of horror—the way they had worn matching coats as children. As for the Thompsons, they resembled a pair of missionaries who, having wandered into a brothel, are unable to find the exit.

"Norman, dear, I think we should be running along; it is getting late. . . ."

"We can get our own coats. . . . Good night!" Husband and wife backed out the door. Never again would Gerty Thompson lift the mystic veil.

"Good night," echoed the voice of Mary Willoughby. "A pedestrian pair . . ." A pause, filled by the banging of the front door. "In future the decision as to who comes into this house is mine. I certainly do not enjoy entertaining in my nightdress, and more to the point . . ." The pale lips flared back. "You, Amanda and Cecil, are uninvited guests here. Don't forget. Whether you go or stay will depend on how we all get on together. A pity, but I don't think either of you can afford to live anywhere else at present. Gambling is your vice, Cecil. The corruption of the weak and indolent. I remember how you never wanted a birthday cake because you'd have to share it. As for you, Amanda, all you're good for is painting your nails and throwing up your skirts." A smile that turned the parchment face colder. "Neither of you are talking and I won't say much more tonight. I don't want to strain my voice. Tomorrow I will telephone lawyer Henry Morbeck and invite him out here—for the record. Your year of playing Monopoly is over. Your father left me control of his money and I want it back in my hands. The capital will come to you both one day, but bear in mind you may have quite a wait." Smoothing a hand over her forehead, Mrs. Willoughby removed the hair net and dropped it in the grate. "Good night, children. Don't stay up late; I won't have electricity wasted."

She was gone. They stood listening to her footsteps mounting the stairs. Finally a door on the second floor closed.

"It's not her!" Amanda pummeled a fist into her palm. "That creature—that monster—is not Mary."

Cecil grabbed for a cigarette, then could not hold his hand steady to light it. "That fool Thompson woman and her fun-and-games séances. She unearthed this horror. We're talking possession. Someone else looked out of Mother's eyes. Something has appropriated her voice."

"We have to think." Amanda hugged herself for warmth. "We gave it entrée, now we must find a way to be rid of it before it sucks the life out of us all. It will bleed the bank accounts dry. We'll be paupers at the mercy of an avenging spirit. We're to be made to pay for every unkind word and deed Mary has experienced at our hands."

"What do you suggest?" Cecil still had not lit the cigarette. "Do we tell the bank manager that should Mary Willoughby ask to see him, she is really a ghost in disguise?''

''We'll talk to Dr. Denver.'' Amanda was pulling at her nails. ''He saw the condition Mother was in last week. He'll know something is crazy. He'll come up with a diagnosis of split personality or . . . some newfangled disorder. Who cares, so long as he declares her incompetent.''

''He won't.'' With a wild laugh Cecil broke his cigarette into little pieces and tossed them onto the dead fire. ''He'll opt for a miracle, and why shouldn't he? Is anything less believable than the truth?''

''Do you never stop kidding yourself?'' The words were screamed. ''We all know who she is, and we know why she has come back. So if you can't answer the question how to be rid of her, kindly shut up. I'll die of cold if I remain in this ice chest. Let's go to bed.''

''I'll sleep in a chair in your room,'' offered Cecil.

''Some protection you'd be. At the first whisper of her nightdress down the hall you'd turn into a giant goose bump.'' Amanda opened the door. ''Remember, she's seeing Morbeck tomorrow.''

They huddled up the stairs like sheep, making more than usual of saying good night before separating into their rooms. After a while the murmur of footsteps died away and the lights went out, leaving the house to itself and the rasping breath of the storm. The stair treads creaked and settled, while the grandfather clock in the hall tocked away the minutes . . . the hours. The house listened and waited. Only the shadows moved until, at a little after three, came the sound of an upstairs door opening . . . then another. . . .

Early the next morning Dr. Denver received a phone call at his home.

''Doctor, this is Amanda Willoughby!'' Hysteria threatened to break through her control. ''There's been the most dreadful accident. It's Mother! She's fallen down the stairs. God knows when it happened . . . sometime during the night! We think she may have been sleepwalking! She was very worked up earlier in the evening. . . . Please, please hurry!''

The doctor found the door of Stone House open and entered the hall, pajama legs showing under his raincoat. Dripping water and spilling instruments from his bag, he brushed aside the brother and sister to kneel by the gray-haired woman sprawled at the foot of the stairs.

"Oh, Lord!" Cecil pressed his knuckles to his eyes. "I can't bear to look. I've never seen anyone dead before. This bloody storm. If she screamed, we would have thought it the wind! I did hear a . . . thump around three A.M. but thought it must be a tree going down in the lane. . . ."

"These Victorian staircases are murder." The doctor raised one of Mrs. Willoughby's eyelids and dangled a limp wrist between his fingers. "One wrong step and down you go."

Amanda's eyes were bright with tears. "Our one hope, Dr. Denver, is that she died instantly."

"My dear girl." He straightened up. "Mrs. Willoughby is not dead."

"What?" Cecil staggered onto a chair that wasn't there and had to grip the banister to save himself from going down. His sister looked ready to burst into mad laughter.

"Your stepmother is in a coma; there is the possibility of internal injuries and the risk of shock." The doctor folded away his stethoscope. "Shall we say I am cautiously optimistic? Her heart has always been strong. Mr. Willoughby, fetch your sister a brandy. And how about taking this photo. Careful, old chap, the glass is smashed."

"She was holding on to it for dear life when she fell . . . I suppose," Cecil said in an expressionless voice.

Dr. Denver stood up. "Get a new frame and put it by her bed. Amazing what the will to live can accomplish. Ah, here comes the ambulance. . . ."

Two weeks later the setting was a hospital corridor. "Often the way with these will-o'-the-wisp old ladies!" Henry Morbeck, lawyer, ignored the no-smoking sign and puffed on his pipe. "They harbor constitutions of steel. Had a word with Dr. Denver this morning and he gave me to understand that barring any major setbacks, Mrs. Willoughby will live."

Amanda tapped unvarnished nails against her folded arms. "Did he tell you she has joined the ranks of the living dead?"

Mr. Morbeck puffed harder on his pipe. "I understand your frustration. She remains unconscious, even though the neurologists have been unable to pinpoint a cause. Small comfort to say that such cases . . . happen. The patient lapses into a coma from which not even the most advanced medical treatment can rouse him."

"They say Mary could linger for years." Cecil's voice barely rose above a whisper. "She looked older, but she is only in her early sixties. What do you think, Henry?" Desperate for some crumb of doubt.

"My friend, I am not a doctor. And remember, doctors are not God. With careful nursing and prayers for a miracle . . . well, let's wait and see." Mr. Morbeck cleared his throat and got down to business. "Since this hospital does not provide chronic patient care, the time comes to find the very best nursing home. Such places are extraordinarily expensive, but not to worry. Mrs. Willoughby is secure. Your far-seeing father provided for such a contingency as this."

Silence.

"The bank, as co-trustee, is empowered to arrange for her comfort and care no matter what the cost. The house and other properties will be sold."

"Oh, quite, quite." Cecil knew he was babbling. "We had hoped to take Mother back to Stone House and care for her ourselves."

"I love nursing." Amanda knew she was begging.

"Out of the question." The lawyer tapped out his pipe in a plant stand and left it stuck there. "Your devotion to Mrs. Willoughby is inspiring, but you must now leave her and the finances in the hands of the professionals. Take comfort that the money is there. She keeps her dignity and you are not burdened. You have my assurance I will keep in close touch with the bank." He pushed against a door to his left. "I'll go in with you and . . . take a look at her."

The three of them entered a white, sunlit room. The woman in the railed bed could have been a china doll hooked up to a giant feeding bottle.

"She would seem at peace," Mr. Morbeck said.

There must be something we can do, Amanda thought. It

always sounds so easy. Someone yanks out the plug and that's that.

Nothing to pull, Cecil thought wearily. She's existing on her own. No artificial support system, other than the IV and no damned doctor is going to starve a helpless old woman.

She has no business being alive, Amanda thought as she gripped the rail. She should be ten feet under, feeding the grubs instead of feeding off us. "Cecil, let's get out of here." She didn't care what the lawyer thought. "And if I ever suggest coming back, have me committed."

Alone with the patient, Mr. Morbeck quelled a shiver and clasped the leaden hand. "Mary Willoughby, are you in there?" His voice hung in the air like a bell pull, ready to start jangling again if anyone breathed on it. And Mary Willoughby was breathing—with relish. Had Mr. Morbeck been a man of imagination he would have thought the pale lips smiled—mischievously. Eager to be gone, he turned and saw that the woman in the photo by the bed seemed to be laughing back. Mary's twin sister, Martha. Or was it . . . ? Mr. Morbeck had always had trouble telling the two of them apart.

say you're sorry

by Sarah Shankman

DOWN IN BATON ROUGE DARKNESS HAD FALLEN, AND
the official State of Louisiana fireworks display could finally
begin. An expectant, sunburned crowd filled the Capitol
lawn. Children sat on their fathers' shoulders dribbling half-
eaten ice-cream cones down their backs. Teenaged couples
held hands, willing their palms not to sweat. Then, for the
fifth time that day, the Capital City High School Marching
Band struck up the opening notes of "The Star-Spangled
Banner" and everyone rose, some more proud than others to
be Americans in this summer whose television stars included
Senator Sam Ervin and the whole panoply of Watergate
crooks.

As the crowd sang the words *bombs bursting in air*, red,
white, and blue rockets shrieked across the clear evening sky,
exploding into mushrooms of light that reflected in the clear
eyes of children and then floated, trailing off into vapor. The
fireworks would continue for half an hour, each barrage of
sound and light more spectacular than the one before, punc-

tuations of *oohs* and *ahs* joining the growing roar until the grand finale that smothered all reverberations except its thunderous self, reminding more than one Vietnam veteran, who leaned against a crutch or sat in a wheelchair, of sounds he'd just as soon forget, but couldn't.

Across town from the Capitol lawn on a narrow street that intersected Front, Loubella Simms sat alone on her porch steps and watched the lights above the treetops. She lighted one long cigarette off another and sipped iced tea from a sweating glass.

Inside the darkened living room, her battered hi-fi repeated the same record over and over, Sweet Emma and her band from the New Orleans Preservation Hall playing Dixieland. Slideman, a trombone player and one of Loubella's friends and admirers, had brought her the record, which was now worn scratchy, but she didn't mind. It didn't have all that much further to go.

With that thought, she ran a hand inside her faded pink seersucker housecoat and trailed her fingers across her pendulous left breast.

The sweet man named Isaac was the one who had found the spot first.

Now who was Isaac? He was the one who bought the River City Hotel (read "whorehouse") from the sheriff who had bought it from Blanche, the former mistress of River City and the woman who, out of misplaced jealousy, had had Loubella locked up.

"Honey," Isaac'd said to her one night when they were lying in bed together, nothing serious, just sipping bourbon and messing around. "Honey, I . . ." And then he'd hesitated as he'd realized he was about to drop a stone into waters whose circles might never stop.

"What?"

"I think I feel something here."

" 'Course you do, sugar. You feel what you always feel when you get the mood on you."

"No I don't." His voice had become serious so that Loubella had sat up in bed and switched on the light.

She'd put her hand atop his, and together their hands moved in a slow circle.

Then she'd slipped her fingers beneath, and she, too, felt what he was talking about. The lump was about the size of her smallest fingernail, but round like an egg yolk.

She took a deep breath, and when she let it out the lie came with it: "Oh, that's been there for a long time. I get them all the time, little old lumps like chicken fat."

"That's not true, Loubella. You know it's not."

She'd waved off his words and pulled him to her, smothering his worrying with her mouth.

But after he'd gone, after he'd looked her straight in the eye and ordered her to see a doctor the very next day, and after she'd nodded that she would, she'd lain awake for a long time tracing her fingertips over and over the spot.

It wasn't gone the next morning or the one after that. In fact, it grew larger all the time, as if it were a child inside her doubling and redoubling until it could draw its own breath.

"The doctor said nothing, it's nothing, just as I told you," she answered her lover when he asked her about it.

Actually the doctor had said nothing because she had never gone to see him. A couple of times she had picked up the phone to call for an appointment, but then had dropped it back into its black cradle as if it were a snake.

There was no way that she was going to let anyone cut off her breast.

Why, she said to herself this Fourth of July night as she watched the fireworks explode into the air, she'd be so lopsided she'd fall off the sidewalk into the street. And she managed a crooked smile at the thought of that.

When she'd been a young girl and these ridiculous things had sprouted themselves like ever larger fruit—oranges, cantaloupes, then finally watermelons—on her chest, she'd been ashamed. The boys had opened their legs as she'd passed, touched themselves, and sniffed after her as if she were a dog permanently in heat. But then when she'd seen that her breasts were to be her meal ticket, as no other opportunity had presented itself, she'd said "So be it." She'd never loved her bosoms even though she'd named them Lou and Bella and had pretended that she appreciated the men who looked at her chest. But in time she'd grown used to her bounty, and parting with half of it was something that she simply couldn't bring herself to do.

She knew the consequences. She didn't need a doctor to tell her that. And before long she could feel the sickness growing, reaching out beneath her armpits, putting feelers into her groin. Now there was no call to remove her breast; it was already too late.

Loubella leaned her back against the step and lit another cigarette, watching the smoke curl into the night air. In a moment she'd get up and flip the record to the other side and put on a pot of water. It was too hot a night for coffee, but she wanted it anyway—sweet and black, the perfect end to a perfect day.

And she couldn't imagine one more perfect. Isaac had come over about noon and they'd had a long, gentle time in bed. Then they'd taken a cool shower together and she'd spread out their holiday dinner: fried chicken, potato salad with sour cream (her secret ingredient), baked beans, and pineapple upside-down cake.

"Honey," Isaac had said, "you should have been a cook."

"I should have been lots of things. But I'm stuck with what I've been. It's a little too late."

"It's never too late, Loubella."

But she'd seen the look in his eyes, and she knew he could see what looked back at her from her mirror these days. She could smell it too. They both knew she was already holding hands with a bad-breathed lover, Mr. Death.

Then they'd sat for a while on the porch playing gin rummy, right out in the open, not caring who came by. Not that Isaac had ever been big on sneaking and hiding, but in some ways he was circumspect. Not this day. Not this Fourth of July, which was also Loubella's birthday. She was forty-six.

"Lordy, lordy, who'd of thought I'd be getting so old?"

"And so beautiful." He'd kissed her and placed among the cards before them a little jeweler's box.

Inside was a diamond solitaire, a big sparkling beauty of an engagement ring.

They smiled at each other, Loubella's gold tooth shining

like a ray of sunlight. They smiled, for they both understood the symbolism and yet knew that in that sense the ring didn't mean a goddamned thing.

For her lover was married, a Baton Rouge businessman who carried considerable weight, and he wasn't about to toss over everything to marry a retired whore. Not that they would have had time to do that anyway, even though divorces could be had now in only six months. Both of them knew that Loubella didn't have that much time left.

She held her hand out before her now that he was gone, watching the diamond catch the fireworks' light, admiring the token of his love like a sixteen-year-old girl. She savored both it and the favor she'd asked of him, which he'd granted—making the phone call without missing a beat.

Loubella, she said to herself now, *all in all you've had a good life.*

The whoring hadn't gotten her, nor the drugs, nor the time in jail. She'd risen above them all like cream coming to the top. And these last few years with Isaac, tending her little house and the bar in his now respectable River City, they'd been all she'd ever hoped for, more than she'd ever dreamed.

And in just a little while it would be over. For Loubella was not waiting for Mr. Death to name the time. She would do that herself. Not for her the long hoping and the slow snipping, a breast here, a womb there, all her hair falling out, what was left of her fading beauty gone, till there was nothing left but the tubes and high hospital bed and the drugs dripping into her veins, the drugs that didn't quite smother the smells or the pain.

She heard the big car coming even before she saw its headlights. She sat up straight and a tingle ran right down the back of her neck.

Oh, it had been such a while since she'd seen her enemy's face. This time was going to be so sweet.

Now the heavy door of the Cadillac slammed, just once, which meant Blanche hadn't brought her husband Aces with her. Well, it would have been nice to have them both, but Aces didn't really matter. Blanche had been the hand behind the hand that turned the key that locked the door that kept her imprisoned eleven and a half years, almost one quarter of her life.

"Evening, Blanche," Loubella called from the steps. She had been sitting there for a while growing cats' eyes and could see into the night.

"Loubella?" Blanche stopped dead still as she recognized the voice.

"Sure 'nuff. Come on in."

Blanche came closer now. Good Lord have mercy, how she'd aged! The golden girl was gone. And here in her place stood a middle-aged pouty pigeon in a blue dress that was too tight, stretched across the bulging stomach and the spreading butt. Ah, beautiful Blanche, Loubella thought, has all that barbecue caught up with you at last?

"Isaac called and gave me this address. Said he wanted to talk some business." Blanche's voice was wary.

"He does."

"Well, where is he?" Blanche stood uneasily, shifting her considerable weight.

"Inside." Loubella gestured up toward the porch, pointing at a wicker chair. "But why don't you sit out here with me for a minute first 'fore you go in? Give yourself a rest."

Loubella watched Blanche's mouth open and close. No, not a pouty pigeon. Now she reminded Loubella of a chicken, an old rusty hen, ready for the pot.

"Would you like some coffee?" Loubella kept her voice ever so light.

"Why, yes," said Blanche, smoothing her dress across her stomach with nervous little hands. She hadn't seen Loubella since before she'd been sent away. "I guess I would. Yes, that would be awfully nice."

Loubella smiled her still-pretty smile, full lips pulled back from teeth that were perfect and white except for that one spot of gold, which was nothing but vanity. Then she disappeared into the house.

Blanche fidgeted in the wicker chair. She smoothed and re-smoothed her lap, adjusted her rings, tried to find a place to plant her twisting feet. Though age had slowed her down, now she felt fourteen again, flighty as a bird just this moment locked in a cage. She hadn't expected Loubella gliding toward her now, carrying a tray with two pretty china cups, so delicate that, between the pattern of violets, they were translucent.

"Oh," Loubella said then, just as her rear end touched her chair. "I forgot the cake. Would you like some?"

"No, I just couldn't. Thank you." Blanche listened to herself playacting that she wasn't unnerved. *Woman*, she thought, *butter wouldn't melt in your mouth.*

"Sure you could." Loubella smiled. "Have some cake."

Blanche wondered if the other woman were mocking her little jelly rolls of fat. She really must go on a diet, but then it always had been hard for her to deny herself anything she wanted to put in her mouth.

"You've got to have some of my birthday cake."

"Your *birthday*. Why, of course it is. The Fourth. I'd forgotten."

And she had, but she remembered now.

When they were girls, even though Loubella was almost ten years younger than she, she'd never missed Loubella's birthday party. It was *the* event of the summer. Loubella's grandmother, who was her entire family, had taken her in when everyone else, for one reason or another, had disappeared, would churn peach ice cream for the whole neighborhood, spread tables with ham and chicken, once even saved to pay a three-piece band who'd played for dancing in the street beneath Japanese lanterns until the last pair of happy feet stopped. After that night Blanche had said to her mother that Loubella was going to grow up thinking the entire country celebrated *her* birthday, not knowing it belonged to the whole United States.

"That little girl has no family but her Mamaw, Blanche, who gives her this one day. Begrudging her that, child, you ought to be ashamed." And Blanche had been. She'd tried to make up for her jealousy by pretending to be the big sister Loubella had never had.

She remembered holding Loubella, a dark-haired little girl, a doll baby, balancing her on her knees while she divided her hair into sections and braided her pigtails. She taught her to swim at the edge of the river, along with a couple of other little kids. She'd baptized them first, pouring water over their heads with a handleless cup, making up the words as she went along.

"And the Baby Jesus watch over you and carry your little soul straight to heaven without no detours if you drown," she'd said. Loubella's brown eyes had grown wide like saucers plopped into her face.

Yes, there'd been a long time when she'd truly loved the girl Loubella, had mothered her and smiled proudly at the mention of her name.

Now, from atop her coffee cup, she slid a look toward the woman and felt a flash of regret, then shame. How fragile friendship could be. How was it you spent years with someone—your minds so intertwined you didn't even need to pick up the phone but could just transmit thoughts—laughed together, loved each other, and then things changed? There was a misunderstanding, an angry word that grew into a great wrong as you carried it around in your hand, blowing on it to give it life until, like a flame, it had a will of its own. But it had been more than a cross word, hadn't it, that thing that had turned her love for Loubella to hate?

It had begun one July when Parnell, then Blanche's husband and owner of River City, decided to pick up where Loubella's mamaw had left off and in a fit of flamboyance treated his girls to a trip on a paddleboat all the way down the river to New Orleans. He'd said that his girls didn't have to work on the Fourth, but Blanche had known that that was just his excuse to throw a party for Loubella.

Before that, when Blanche had come back to Baton Rouge to marry Parnell and had found Loubella in his stable of whores, it had made her sad for a bit, but then a woman had to do what she had to do. For a while she and Loubella had carried on together like they had when they were girls. They'd run into each other on the back stairs, Loubella in a yellow silk wrapper that glowed like fireflies, and then they'd sit right down on the steps, their legs tucked back against them within their encircling arms, gossiping and giggling with no mind for the passing hours, reaching their hands out and patting one another on a knee or a shoulder, little butterflies of affection, easy, easy, old love.

But Parnell had noticed, and he hadn't liked it, not one bit.

"You don't need that whore teaching you tricks, Blanche," he said. "Unless you planning on turning pro."

"Parnell! You know Lou and I've been friends since we were girls!"

"I know what you been. You think I didn't grow up in this very same neighborhood? But Loubella *works* for me, woman. She's my whore. Just 'cause she don't punch no time clock don't mean she ain't on salary. And the lady of the house don't fraternize with the help."

Well. Blanche hadn't believed a word of that. She knew there was something more tiptoeing around in Parnell's big head. She also knew that he sampled the goods from time to time, like a moonshiner sipping his own whiskey, and she guessed that included Loubella too. But then, she enjoyed a taste of other sweetmeat her own self now and again, so she wasn't about to be calling the kettle black.

And every once in a while, like naughty children ignoring all warnings, she and Loubella still slipped off to have a good visit, and whatever quick and dirty passed between her husband and her friend was no part of that.

But then there'd been Loubella's Fourth of July birthday and the paddleboat and—worse than catching them in bed together, because what would that mean, after all, a little roll in the hay between two people who trafficked in flesh—she'd seen their eyes meet.

Again and again throughout that afternoon, she'd watched that connection between them, as simple and direct as plugging in a lamp. Their glances crossed and caught and held, and Blanche had to turn her gaze away, for if Parnell had leaned over and slowly licked Loubella's naked eyeball, the act could not have been more intimate. Everything else in the entire world, including her, oh yes, including her, fell away. And Blanche, who had never had that kind of communion with another human being in her whole life but recognized it when she saw it, hated Loubella from that very afternoon to this.

So she'd punished her, hadn't she, she'd punished her good. Planted a load of dope in her room, then called the cops to raid her own joint. It was hers by then, Aces having already pulled the trigger that morning so long ago, pulled the trigger that had blasted Parnell's head and sent it rolling and tumbling like a child's ball down Front. She'd married Aces right after that, before they sent him up for a little stay in Angola.

Now she looked up at Loubella from the edge of her violet-sprigged coffee cup and all the years fell away. There before her was the face of the little girl with birthday candles shining in her eyes, the little girl she'd loved as her own. Parnell had been dead for so many years, and he hadn't been worth shaking a stick at, anyway. What had all that been about? Blanche wondered what would happen if she reached out and patted Loubella's cheek and said, "I'm sorry I was so mean." Would Loubella understand that if she could do it all over again she'd do it differently?

Loubella caught her look and that old communion of spirits that ran between them straighter than the string of a child's tincan telephone told her what Blanche was thinking.

She smiled and her gold tooth twinkled. Blanche's heart lurched. That tooth had always reminded her of Parnell's with his diamond, but no, no, forget Parnell. He was what had brought her to this pass in the first place. Maybe *that* had been her problem all along, paying attention to men, my God, there had been so many of them, when there were other folks, plenty of other folks, her family, her children, all those women who could have been her sisters, sitting right there in her face big as life—hell, maybe they *were* life—and she had looked right through them like they were water, past them to whatever man was waggling his dick like it was a magic wand that would turn her into a fairy princess with its touch. *Well, you been touched by them wands plenty times, ain't you, woman, and you ain't no princess yet.* But here was Loubella smiling at her. Maybe it wasn't too late.

"You gonna come in the house and sample some of my cake or not?" Loubella was asking.

"Why, I'd be proud to," Blanche answered, rising from her chair and feeling like she was floating. Something had been released in her, and she felt light and wispy as a pink cloud. "And by the way, happy birthday, Miss Loubella."

"Thank you, Miss Blanche." Loubella ducked her head as if she were suddenly shy. Why, yes, Blanche thought. The little girl is still there. We can start over. It's not too late.

Blanche watched Loubella bustling around her neat kitchen, and suddenly the two girls of long ago had swapped places. Now Loubella was the momma, the momma Blanche had never really been to anyone. For the small acts of mothering Blanche had practiced on Loubella had not followed her into adulthood. Now that she thought about it, she couldn't remember ever plaiting her own daughters' hair, though she must have. And she'd certainly never taught Jesse to swim. Who had done all those things—washed their clothes, cooked the countless meals her children must have eaten—because indeed they had grown up. It all seemed like such a blur now, those years of their childhood. She remembered a few snatches, but the pictures in her mind were duplicates of the pictures she'd pasted in a photo album. The kids standing in front of one of her new Cadillacs. All three of them lined up on the porch of River City. Jesse in a new white suit for one of her weddings, she couldn't remember which.

But there were no photographs of the three children sitting with Blanche reading or storytelling or fixing a hem. Did their grandmother Lucretia have pictures like that in her photo album? she wondered. Did people take pictures of a woman serving dinner to her family?

Well, they ought to. Not that she would ever be caught dead in one, but look now, here, at Loubella putting food on the table in front of her. Those sturdy hands carefully placing the little violet-sprigged dessert plate that matched the cup and saucer, they were delivering more than a piece of cake, more like a gift of love.

"Loubella!" Blanche exclaimed suddenly, for her eye had finally caught the diamond sparkler upon Loubella's left hand, and her mind quickly jumped from its maternal meditation back to the more familiar territory of earthy goods. "Good Lord have mercy, where did you get that pretty thing?" And in an instant Blanche, with an eye accustomed to weighing and assessing, had its value appraised as precisely as if she'd examined it with a scale and a jeweler's loupe.

"Isaac." Loubella smiled. "It's Isaac's birthday present to me."

With that, Blanche remembered why she'd come in the first place.

"Where *is* Isaac?" she asked, looking around the room as if he might be hiding behind the sugar canister or underneath the table with its plastic lace tablecloth.

"Oh, he slipped out the back to get some Scotch. Said we ought to have a proper celebration and I'd just run clean out. But I've got some bourbon. Could I sweeten your coffee with a little nip?" And before Blanche could answer, Loubella had poured her a generous dollop, filling her coffee cup to the brim.

"But I thought you said he was here, inside. Didn't you say that a little while ago?"

"He was. He'll be right back. Go ahead, Blanche, drink up."

Blanche took a sip and then another. The dark, sweet coffee and the alcohol warmed her blood even hotter on this July delta night. She could feel it coursing right down to her toes. And the warmth distracted her for a moment from the other questions that had popped into her mind. Like, what did Isaac want? What was the deal he had mentioned? Why had he given her Loubella's address? And what was it between them, anyway, his giving Loubella a diamond as if she were a decent woman?

Loubella answered that last one even before Blanche threw it out.

"That Isaac, he is the sweetest man. We've been keeping company, you know, for quite some time."

"Well, I swear. I never knew that."

"Honey, there's lots of things you don't know about Loubella. It's not exactly as if we been in touch."

Blanche lowered her gaze then. Here it comes. This wasn't going to be as easy as she'd thought.

But in a moment all was calm again. She'd mistaken a passing cloud for a storm gathering. And before she knew it, Loubella was sweetening up her coffee again, and they were leaned back in their chairs, Loubella tucking her feet up, her legs in the circle of her arms, and it was like they were back on the service steps of River City gossiping about folks like Parnell had never come between them, as if his head had never rolled down Front.

"Tell me 'bout your children. What's Jesse up to?"

"Well, I guess he's doing all right. Married. Uh-huh." She paused a moment, thinking about that. And then with pride in her voice said, "He called me today just to say hello."

"He lives in California, doesn't he? They come and visit you?"

"Uh-huh. Once. Stopped by my house." She put her cup down, and this time Loubella didn't even bother with the coffee, just filled it with bourbon, straight up. "Why, I think that day they said they'd been by to see you too."

"That's right."

"Can't say as I thought much of her."

"Why not?"

Blanche just shrugged. You'd have to be mother to a son to understand that.

Loubella rose then, steady as a rock, for no alcohol had passed her lips, just coffee and a few bites of cake. As she skirted the back door, she reached out and tested it, just to make sure. Before Blanche came, she had locked that dead bolt from the inside and dropped the key in her garbage sack. Of course, Blanche didn't know that.

"Way things are these days, you can never be too safe," Loubella said.

Blanche nodded. "Ain't that the truth. Why, just last week, I was reading in the paper about some crazy boys downtown grabbed a woman on her way home, arms full of groceries and . . ."

Loubella wasn't listening, except to a plan she'd run through her mind so many times that it had become a script. She couldn't hear Blanche because she was following that script. Now she read the line that said, "Excuse yourself," and she did.

"Bathroom," she said.

"Sure, honey. Me too, after you."

Loubella closed the kitchen door behind her and headed down a little hall to her bedroom where she picked up the red five-gallon can of gasoline she'd earlier placed inside. She tipped the nozzle, splashed the bed, and began a damp trail that followed her as if to her mamaw's house. In the living room she locked the front door from the inside and hid that key, too, beneath a cushion of her favorite chair. Then she doused the chair, the sofa, the faded Persian rug. After that she did what she'd said, went into the bathroom and relieved herself. For she wanted to be perfectly at ease for this last best part, the cherry on her ice cream sundae.

Then she rejoined Blanche, who had been sitting there drinking another couple of fingers of bourbon that she didn't need. Loubella frowned. She wanted Blanche slowed, but not so drunk that she missed a moment of the impending horror show.

"Honey, I been thinking about what I said about Jesse and that girl, his wife, uh . . ."

"Lily," Loubella said.

"That's right, Lily, and then I was thinking about you and Isaac. You did say—" And then she stopped. "Jesus Christ, Loubella, what *is* that smell?"

Loubella settled herself back at the table and plopped down the can she was still holding, planted it on the floor.

"Gas," she answered.

Blanche jumped up, holding a hand to her breast. "The line's busted!" She reached for Loubella's arm. "Come on, honey, we got to get out of here!"

Loubella smiled at her as serenely as if she'd just gotten up off her knees from prayer and knew beyond a shadow of a doubt that her supplication had been answered.

Blanche saw that and suddenly her blood ran cold.

Well, forget Loubella. She was getting out of here. She pushed past her to the back door and jerked at it. It didn't open. She jerked again. "The door's locked!" she screamed.

Already she was hysterical. This was better than Loubella had even dreamed. She just kept on watching as if Blanche were a picture show, a movie she had waited a long time to see.

"Aren't you going to do something? You just going to sit

there?'' Blanche's voice shrilled with terror and disbelief.

Of course, Blanche had always thought that nothing very bad was going to happen to her, and up until now, she'd been right.

As if in answer, though without saying a word, Loubella stood, picked up the gasoline can, which until now Blanche hadn't spotted, and heaved it toward her, splattering Blanche's baby-blue dress.

Blanche screamed. She stood in one place with her hands in fists atop her head and screamed. You would have thought she could already feel the flames.

''*What* are you doing?''

''What does it look like, Blanche?'' Loubella's words were slow and calm. ''I'm killing you. Actually, I'm killing us both.'' And with that she reached over into a cabinet drawer and pulled out a revolver and placed it before her among the violet-sprigged china and the near-empty bottle of bourbon and the remains of birthday cake. The gun didn't look very much at home.

Blanche was jumping around now as if a fire were licking at her underpants. She whirled and raced out of the room. Loubella could hear her battering at the front door.

''It ain't no use, Blanche,'' she called. ''The doors are locked, and Isaac put bars on the windows last year. You might as well come on back in here.''

Blanche blundered around a while longer before she did as she was told.

She was whimpering. Big tears were rolling down her face. ''No, no, no,'' she whispered over and over.

''You think you can always get your own way, don't you, Miss Blanche? Well, this time you can't.''

''Why?'' Blanche wailed.

''Why what?''

''Why are you doing this to me?''

''Why, Blanche, I can't believe you don't know how *much* I hate your guts.''

Blanche reeled around the room, scrabbling at the things on the kitchen cabinet, grabbed a dish towel, and dabbed at the front of her dress.

"Don't worry about it being stained, honey. Ain't nothing of it going to be left."

Blanche began to scream again. Someone would hear her. Surely someone would.

But it was the night of July Fourth. Hardly anyone was home. And those who were, were mostly drunk. Besides, nobody ever paid much attention to a woman screaming in this neighborhood. They figured whoever she was she was getting what she deserved, and if she didn't, she either ought to get the hell out or pick up a skillet and show the man what for.

"I didn't mean any of it, Loubella, I'm sorry." And she started to cry again, not paying any attention to her dripping nose. "I was gonna tell you tonight, just a while ago, that if I had to do it all over, I'd do it different, I swear."

"That may be true, but those years are already long gone."

"Oh, Loubella." Blanche fell to her knees, scratching on the floor at Loubella's feet. "Please, don't do this."

"Remember when you baptized me in the river?" asked Loubella in a faraway, dreamy voice.

"Yes." Blanche was sobbing, her face buried in Loubella's knees.

"Remember how you prayed that if we drowned, the Baby Jesus would take us straight to heaven with no stops in between?"

"Yes." Blanche's answer was muffled. But in it was just a whisper of hope. Maybe if Loubella could remember those days, when Blanche had been kind, she could find a bit of mercy in her heart.

"Remember how you poured the water over our heads with that old broken cup?"

Blanche nodded. And with that she felt liquid pour all over her hair, dribble down her neck.

But it wasn't river water. It was gasoline—high test.

Blanche jumped up and screamed. And screamed. And screamed. She couldn't stop now. Liquid ran down her legs too. Gasoline and urine mixed together, for Blanche had completely lost control of herself.

"You never should have done what you did, Blanche. Parnell may have loved me, but he married you. He would have given you anything on earth you wanted.''

''I know. I know,'' Blanche moaned.

''He was too good for you, bitch. You know, you're the one who was the whore. I did it 'cause I had to. You did it 'cause you liked it. 'Cause you wanted *everything*. You always was a greedy gut, even as a girl. 'That's *mine*,' you'd say. Licking a biscuit so nobody else would touch it. *'Mine,'* no matter what.''

Blanche kept on moaning. She had stopped twitching around the room and had fallen back in her chair as if she'd returned for another cup of coffee, another drink, except that her head was down on the table buried in her arms, and the liquid running down her face was a mixture of gasoline and tears.

''And Parnell was yours. But those years you took from me—those eleven years, six months, and nine days—that quarter of my life I spent in jail, those wasn't yours to take. *Those* were *mine*.''

''I know. I know.''

''Say you're sorry, Blanche.'' Loubella's voice was very soft and very cold.

Blanche's head snapped up.

''I *am* sorry.''

''But not as sorry as you're gonna be.''

At that, Loubella reached into her wrapper pocket and pulled out a box of wooden kitchen matches. She struck one and dropped it. The floor burst into licking tongues of red and yellow.

In that moment, Blanche saw her chance. Quick as a snake, her hand grabbed the revolver sitting on the table and she fired it without thinking, striking Loubella in the breast.

Loubella reeled backward. Laughter poured from her throat while crimson pumped from a hole in the pale pink wrapper, from right near the spot where her cancer was now cheated from its slower march toward death.

''Thank you, Blanche,'' Loubella whispered, and even as she died, she struck and dropped another match.

It was then that Blanche realized, too late, far too late, that she had shot the wrong person. She should have shot herself.

For a bullet through the brain was much quicker—why, it hardly compared to burning to death.

The gas can exploded then, and flames engulfed her dress, her hair, her face.

She reached one twisting hand toward the revolver, where she'd dropped it on the table. Maybe it still wasn't too late. But it was. For Loubella had loaded only one bullet in the chamber. She'd known that whether she fired it or Blanche did, one was all she'd want or need.

The curtains were on fire now, the rugs, the sofa, the bed, the walls, the floor. And in the midst of it, caroming from one small room to another, from door to window to door, was the fireball that was Blanche. That didn't last very long, though. Soon she dropped and writhed, white teeth showing and glimmers of bone, as beautiful Blanche, blackened like a redfish, fried and crisped and barbecued to a turn, just a little before midnight on this evening of July the Fourth.

a tale of two pretties

by Marilyn Wallace

Part the First: True Confessions

Body Heat

HE ROLLED ONTO HIS BACK AND SHE TRACED THE lines of definition along his triceps. "Only a little while before you check into the drug treatment center. Six o'clock. Three hours. I'm scared, Mickey. What am I gonna do without you?"

"You'll be fine. Vinnie promised me he'd keep an eye on you." He ran a finger along her cheek. "You don't want me wired and wasted, or strung out and wrung out, right? This is a no-fail program, babe. It'll work for me."

Cindy smiled and slid her fingers down the valley of his breastbone. "Twelve weeks apart. At least we'll have plenty of time to think up some proper rewards. For both of us.''

Through the venetian blinds, afternoon sun fell in slats across his chest. How stupid she had been to think that if they moved from Chicago to San Francisco, his problems would disappear. He had found new connections within twelve hours and was back on the same damn roller coaster: cocaine as long as the sun was shining, some kind of downer to get him through the night until it was time to start again. A good residential rehab program was Mickey's last chance to get clean.

Fifty thousand dollars worth of clean.

Picking up and leaving Chicago and coming all the way out here and now living without him for three months would be worth it if it worked. A whole year of him nodding out and falling asleep or being jittery and angry, a whole year of bad sex or no sex . . . Finally, he had agreed; he didn't want to live like that forever.

She jumped off the bed, paced to the window, looked down on a couple dressed all in black as they strolled, arms linked, toward Haight Street. San Francisco was such a dismal city, gray and chilly, not like the sunny California she'd expected. They'd arrived a month ago, at ten minutes to midnight, New Year's Eve, and found a dim and quiet tavern in which to toast new beginnings. The next day the sun had shone for a total of twenty minutes.

She had gotten her bearings quickly—it never took her long to scope out the Right Neighborhood, the Right People—and they started working the insurance scam. Choosing the fanciest homes, telling housekeepers that she was sent to take pictures for insurance purposes. Mickey timed it so that he rang the bell ten minutes after she arrived; when the maid answered the door, Cindy lifted something—a silver this, a gold that—and put it in her camera bag.

It wasn't a bad scam but she hated having to deal with Vinnie. Her contacts in Chicago told her that Vinnie could fence anything, but something about his ferret eyes made her uneasy and contributed to her worries about the immediate future. She'd have to figure a way to work without Mickey. A queasy feeling twisted her stomach at the thought: *without Mickey*. Restless, she reached for the *Chronicle* and scanned the headlines, her gaze lingering on the picture on page three.

Maybe the woman in this picture was the answer. Maybe she could capitalize on the resemblance . . .

"Next time we should get Vinnie involved sooner." Mickey came up from behind her and pulled her against him. "He said he'd help us figure out the best places to hit. What do you think?"

Cindy moaned and slid Mickey's hand down from the waistband of her jeans. "Can't we talk about that some other time, sweetie?" she said as she wriggled closer to him. "There are other things to do now, better things."

Mickey was breathing faster now, pressing up against her. If only she could get him to forget Vinnie—she would handle *him*. He had a soft spot—or was it a hard one? she laughed to herself—for her since that afternoon in the warehouse. She hadn't known *how* making it with Vinnie was going to come in handy; she knew she'd figure it out when the time came. It had been easy enough, afterwards, to convince him to pay her thirty cents on the dollar and to tell Mickey it was only twenty. The extra she put in a separate account; together with the diamond pendant she'd kept back from the last job, they'd have enough when Mickey got out.

"Oh, Mickey, honey, it'll be so nice when you're back." Cindy unbuttoned her blouse and held Mickey's hand up to her breast. "It'll really be like starting fresh."

Breathless

Charlotte Durning stopped at the landing to catch her breath. "But why me, Ed? I don't deserve all this public scrutiny, these stories about my shelties and my claustrophobia. Now my *picture* is showing up in the *Chronicle*. On page three." She pressed a slim, manicured hand to her bosom. "Why am I the scapegoat? It's terribly unfair. All I did was pass on the name of an excellent contractor to a city official who was dissatisfied with the other bids he'd gotten."

His expensively vested chest heaving with exertion, Ed Partridge patted his upper lip and replaced the folded handerkerchief in his pocket. "I wish you would try an elevator again. Maybe you've outgrown your difficulty."

Even the thought of an elevator—doors closing, four walls and floor and ceiling all pressing in on her—brought a sheen of cold sweat to her face. She took another breath, waited for the wave of darkness to pass, whispered a simple, "No, Ed. We'll walk."

He nodded and followed as she started up the stairs again. "Charlotte, my dear, the contractor happens to be an executive of a public corporation in which you are a majority stockholder. The city official has jurisdiction to rule that you can add a penthouse despite the local building height ordinance. Last year, it would have made no splash. This year, San Francisco is on an ethical government campaign and the self-righteous bastards are out to nail you."

Charlotte Durning didn't like the tone of his voice, not one bit. He was her lawyer. She was paying him three hundred dollars an hour, more for court fees and expenses, thousands of dollars in telephone calls. But it would all be worth it if they won.

She *couldn't* go to jail. She'd die.

She'd never last a day. Even in her own home, closed doors and small spaces terrified her. Flying was a trial to which she subjected herself, heavily sedated, twice a year only—for the spring couture showings in Paris and then in December for opening night at La Scala. She never drank anything before or during a flight: those tiny closets they called bathrooms on the planes were the worst. She refused to stay in hotels unless she could have a suite. It wasn't an indulgence so much as a form of self-preservation, she had explained to her accountant.

Jail was unthinkable.

Her throat would swell with fear; she'd choke and die. Charlotte Durning, widow and sole beneficiary of the estate of Preston Durning III (which she surely deserved after putting up with the randy old fart through her best years—all of her twenties, part of her thirties), simply couldn't go to jail. She was counting on Ed Partridge to get her off.

"I used up all my peremptory challenges on single women with children, but I'm still not happy with the jury." An unhealthy red glow mottled his pasty cheeks and a fine line of perspiration sprouted again on his upper lip. "Jury of your peers—hardly any of those around. They're all wintering in Biarritz or Aspen or Cabo.''

Well, she couldn't help it if she was blond, slim, and rich, could she? Surely they'd understand that she had gotten involved in this ugly mess out of pure disinterest. She had seen how two needs complemented each other and she'd brought them together. If that was a crime . . .

How much would it take—a thousand each? Ten thousand? Twelve people on a jury, that would make a hundred and twenty thousand, which would hardly put a dent in her resources. But, really, one juror was all she needed to delay things long enough for the political climate in this fickle city to become more hospitable. Unless she got caught . . .

"I want you to be prepared. A year ago, the same facts and the same defense would have worked. Today—'' When Ed shrugged, his starched collar rose on his wattled neck— "I think we ought to consider the prosecutor's deal. The DA offered to reduce the charge. You'd do three months in a minimum security facility and then it would be over.''

Three months in jail? She'd never survive.

Part the Second: The Birds

Vertigo

Her soup was just the way she liked it. Charlotte Durning dipped her spoon into the steamy saffron-scented liquid and tasted it, then sucked up a long swallow of champagne, blinking away the fizz as she let her gaze wander through the room.

That woman, two tables away—what was it about her? She had an oval face, a not-bad straight brown bob; her green eyes never even looked up from the book she was reading until her salad arrived. When the woman smiled at the waitress, a pang of excitement lapped at Charlotte's tummy, a little flicker she didn't quite understand.

Charlotte brought the spoon to her mouth. Maybe she could cut back to three aerobics classes a week, now that soup was the only thing she could manage to get down. Except for champagne, of course, and coffee. They were getting her through her days and nights. Today was Wednesday, two days after her picture first hit the local papers, and she had reached a desperate conclusion. A straw, maybe, but today she would suggest to Ed that the nice plumber on the jury, the one who—

The woman two tables away pushed her salad plate to the center of the table, reached for her book, leaned back in her chair. She swept her hair behind her left ear. Charlotte stared.

If her hair was blond . . .

If it curled toward her face a bit more . . .

If her foundation makeup was more pink, less peachy . . .

A quick inventory: nondescript black slacks and gray sweater. Turquoise-and-silver ring. Shoes and purse showing signs of wear. Her posture was good; she looked the right shape.

"Charlotte, dear, did you hear me at all?" Ed scooped up a caper and speared a flaky chunk of salmon, stared at his fork, then popped it all in his mouth.

She could hardly catch her breath. A rapture, like the sound of angels singing, filled her heart.

"You must consider your options. The DA is willing to take the reduced charge until court opens day after tomorrow. No later." Ed Partridge's milky white fingers reached for her hand. "I'm your lawyer. I'm the best in the state. But we're losing this one. That's three years instead of three months, and it won't be at the minimum security facility. I strongly advise . . ."

But his words faded. In the past sixty seconds, Charlotte Durning had come to see hope where none existed before.

She stared. The woman was getting up, plucking her scuffed black purse from the chair.

Thank God, she thought as the woman walked toward the rear of the dining room. *She's going to the rest room. Mustn't scare her.* Charlotte measured the woman's height; surely Providence was looking after her once again. "I'm going to the little girls', Ed."

She didn't wait for a nod or a smile from her attorney but scurried out of her seat, following the woman's straight-backed march past the dessert trolley to the rear of the restaurant. The rest room door swung shut; Charlotte sniffed the air before she walked in. *Charlie*. Good, the right sort, the kind who might be open to a proposition.

The toilet flushed; an eddy of fear whirled in the bottom of Charlotte's stomach. She reached into her purse and pulled out a comb and a tube of lipstick. The stall door latch squeaked. Charlotte forced herself to peer into the mirror, forced her hand to bring the comb to the crown of her head.

Footsteps.

Charlotte stepped back to allow the other woman access to the sink. Water splashed; the sweet smell of pink liquid soap wafted through the air.

The other woman, hands still dripping into the rust-stained sink, lifted her head and looked in the mirror.

Charlotte gasped. "My God, it's incredible," she said, her voice a hoarse whisper. She took a step forward.

Staring into the stranger's eyes in the mirror, the heat from their shoulders flicking across the narrow space that separated them, Charlotte felt giddy. The other woman's mouth opened; her lips were moist, her eyes shining with excitement. Charlotte was rocked by a sudden desire to kiss the woman on her identical mouth, to make the difference between self and other disappear. She shuddered, reached over, and brushed the other woman's hair toward her face, noting the tiny lines that netted the outer corners of the woman's eyes. Age was right, too.

"Wow! That's amazing." The other woman leaned closer, then moved out of Charlotte's reach. "Spooky."

There was no wretched regional accent but her voice was thin, a little high. Well, they'd chalk that up to nervousness. Anyone would be nervous going in to plead guilty to bribing a public official. "My name is Charlotte Durning."

"Cindy Carson. Like Kit." Water dripped from her hands into a puddle on the tile floor.

She'd need a good set of acrylic nails—you never knew what those vultures hungry for the beating heart of a public figure would notice.

The woman reached for a paper towel; three fluttered to the floor. As Cindy Carson and Charlotte Durning knelt to retrieve the towels, their heads bumped lightly.

"Sorry," they said at the same time.

Eyes crinkling, Cindy stood slowly; then she laughed, shaking her brown hair. "This is *so* strange. Gotta run or I'll miss my appointment. Bye."

Don't freeze up now, Charlotte thought as she fought a clutch of fear. *She's your only chance and all the signs are right.*

Cindy Carson pulled away from the hold of Charlotte's gaze and reached for the door.

"Wait." Charlotte's eyes teared with relief that she'd finally broken her own silence. "I need to talk to you later. Please. Tell me how I can reach you." She glanced at her watch. She had to be back in court in less than five minutes.

"I, uh . . ." Cindy's quaver trailed off. "Look, you're scaring me." She started for the door again.

"Please. I need your help. And I have a lot of money to pay for it." She reached into her purse and pulled five hundred-dollar bills from her wallet.

Cindy stared at the money but didn't move.

"Meet me at Macy's. Tomorrow at noon. I'm talking about a lot of money. Enough so that, if you were smart, you wouldn't have to worry for the rest of your life."

The faucet dripped noisily. Beyond the rest room walls, the roar of lunchtime conversation rose and fell at the restaurant tables.

"Linens? Sportswear? Electronics?" Cindy frowned and reached for the bills, folded them in half, then jammed them into the pocket of her slacks.

"Beauty salon." She could have spared herself those moments of fright by taking out the cash sooner; Charlotte felt better already. "Fourth floor."

The Lady Vanishes

Charlotte squinted and shook her head. "Look," she said, fluffing the hair toward Cindy's face. "Mine falls forward. Hers keeps curling the wrong way. Can't you do something about it?"

The stylist stepped back. She should have known—anyone who would wear a terrible brown cardigan over that yellow polyester uniform wouldn't have the necessary panache to pull it off. But she couldn't very well have waltzed into her own Union Street salon and directed Bijou to recreate Cindy Carson in her image. Makeup and clothes would have to take care of the rest.

A gnawing fear nibbled at her stomach. How silly to be afraid now, she chided herself. This was going to work to everyone's advantage.

If by some miracle the case went her way or was thrown out of court, then Cindy would keep the $30,000 she'd already been given for her troubles.

But if things went as she expected, Charlotte would deposit $250,000 each month into a Swiss bank account; the bank would print a coded message in the *Chronicle* to let Cindy know that everything was okay. And while Cindy took her place in the facility, Charlotte would live in Cindy's Fillmore Street apartment. When the three months were up, they'd each resume their lives.

"This is better, don't you think?" Cindy flicked a curl down toward her cheek, raised an eyebrow, sat back with her shoulders squared and her neck stretching.

Do I really look like that? Charlotte wondered as she squinted through her dark glasses. *Do I really appear to be so cold and distant? No wonder I have no friends.*

Now the effect was so nearly right she gasped. The sleek blond hair curled into a gentle frame around the Cindy/Charlotte oval face.

Charlotte tried not to watch as Cindy, who had spent ten minutes practicing just before they'd entered the beauty salon, scrawled a signature on the charge slip. The receptionist nodded, tore up the carbons, and went back to her *TV Guide.* Cindy and Charlotte hurried out of the department store onto the crowded street, jostled by the crush of midday shoppers, and started walking.

Three blocks later, they still had said nothing to each other. Cindy stopped in front of Gump's window. "I don't know about this whole trip."

"What do you mean?" Charlotte untied her scarf and let

it fall to her shoulders. She pulled the dark glasses away from her face.

Cindy frowned. "Oh, shit. I don't know."

"Oh, *dear*," Charlotte corrected, her forehead wrinkling in disapproval. "Charlotte Durning would never say 'Oh, shit' in so public a setting. And prison, don't forget, is a public setting. Oh, dear; oh, my; oh, Lord. Any of these. But not 'Oh, shit.' Okay?"

Cindy nodded. "Just a little nervous, I guess. I'm ready for the rest. I'm really hungry, though. You want to pick up some lunch on the way over to my place? Pizza, or maybe some take-out bagels and lox?"

Charlotte's stomach fluttered. "I forgot to tell you. I'm allergic to smoked things. Something in the curing process, I don't know. No bacon. No lox, even though most of it isn't smoked but pickled. No ham. No barbecue."

An annoyed scowl flitted across Cindy's face and Charlotte shivered. Instead of the giggle she expected, Cindy's right eyebrow and the right corner of her mouth rose. She was good, this woman, maybe too good. Charlotte shivered again. She felt inhabited—no, that wasn't quite right. She felt replaced.

Well, that was what she wanted, wasn't it?

Cindy sighed. "That's gonna be a bummer. What *do* you eat for breakfast? I know about the cholesterol rap, but I've been eating bacon and eggs five days a week all my life." She giggled, then frowned. "And the other two days it's bagels and cream cheese and lox."

This whole thing *couldn't* fall apart over the breakfast menu. "Three months of cornflakes and milk—you can put up with that for three quarters of a million dollars. I'll bring some with me tomorrow morning so you can try it." For a minute, she couldn't read the expression on Cindy's face. Then she laughed as she realized that the cant of the head, the pursed mouth, were her own gestures when she was making a difficult decision.

Damn, the woman really had her down cold. Was she so transparent, so easy to mimic?

What did all this identity stuff matter, anyway? She wouldn't be going to jail; that was all that counted.

Rear Window

"Here, I'll take the box of cornflakes. I want you to practice opening the door with this key. It's a little tricky."

Charlotte took the key and looked up as a tan-and-brown pigeon settled on a second-story windowsill. Would there be an elevator? She had forgotten to ask; her throat filled with bile and a cold fist squeezed the air out of her lungs.

"You okay?" Cindy laid a warm hand on Charlotte's bare arm.

"What floor?" Charlotte finally managed to say.

Cindy held up her hand, her fingers spread in the victory sign. "Second. One flight of stairs. You can make it."

Charlotte nodded at Cindy's grin and followed her up the wooden stairs. Cindy's Fillmore Street apartment was in what Ed Partridge would call a marginal neighborhood, with yuppies and upscale restaurants moving the blacks and Hispanics farther into the Mission District or the Western Addition.

Weekends would be noisy. Evenings would be nothing like the cloistered quiet of home, where the back rooms looked out over the lights of the Golden Gate Bridge and the jewellike twinkle of cars crossing the bay.

But it wouldn't be jail, she thought as she wiggled the key in the lock.

"Pull down on the knob and pull the key out just a tiny bit," Cindy directed.

Charlotte jiggled the key but nothing happened. It wouldn't turn. "Oh, shit," she muttered.

"Good." Cindy grinned. "You're getting it now."

The key suddenly felt right; the lock turned, the door opened, and they clattered inside.

Ordinary.

That was the first word that came to Charlotte Durning's mind.

Blessedly ordinary. A Haitian cotton love seat. A pair of rattan chairs with rose-colored cushions. An imitation Oriental on the dull wood floors and lots of green plants in clay pots.

She followed Cindy down the hall. They passed an oval mirror with a carved oak frame. Charlotte pulled Cindy's sleeve.

"What?" She looked annoyed and shrugged out of Charlotte's grasp.

Without saying anything, Charlotte turned Cindy's shoulders so that they both faced into the mirror. It was too unbelievable, not knowing which of the images reflected her own face and which was the other's. Finally, Cindy broke away and hustled to the kitchen.

"The top element of the toaster oven is dead so you have to toast one side first and then turn your bread to toast the other side." She yanked the refrigerator door open, pulled out a package of bacon. "Oh, shi—oh, dear. I think I'll just fry this up and have it all. Before I get in that taxi."

She tossed the package onto the counter and stood a moment too long, hands on hips. Her eyes narrowed. "You never been printed, have you? By the cops. Fingerprints, I mean."

Charlotte raised her eyebrows. "Of course not."

"We'll be okay then. Now sit down and let's turn you into a brunette."

Charlotte watched in fascination as Cindy moved about the tidy kitchen. Maybe she'd learn to cook in these three months. And catch up on her reading and learn to sew or knit. She could do lots of things, without the distraction of board luncheons where the primary objective was to show off how thin you were and how many good deeds you could buy for your good name. No days wasted after late-night parties in which she'd have to fish for questions to ask a fiercely dull diplomat or a boorishly crass manufacturer so that she could be rewarded with the excruciating details of their daily lives.

"What do you do all day? When you aren't looking for work, I mean." Charlotte breathed the ammonia fumes of Miss Clairol Golden Chestnut #390 and squeezed her eyes shut as Cindy dabbed the thick stuff on her head. She could practically hear the other woman shrug and screw up her nose.

"Not much," the voice behind her said. "Whoops. Dripping. Keep your eyes closed."

Charlotte obeyed; the cool touch of the damp cotton swab as it mopped up the hair dye felt . . . what? Sisterly? She didn't have a sister. Her fastidious mother had decided after Charlotte's birth that one such messy event was enough. Charlotte opened her eyes, marveling at the growing embryo of affection she felt for Cindy Carson.

Cindy secured a plastic cap on Charlotte's head with a clip; she set the timer and sat down at the chair across the table.

"I'm a crossword puzzle freak. And I have an herb garden back here. See?" Cindy threw open the window; four wooden boxes filled with lacy greens formed a rectangle on the fire escape outside the kitchen. Sun kissed the soil and sparkled on a white enamel watering can. "Just water them twice a week. Snip the tops of these and use them in omelets. Should be strong and fully grown when I get back."

Charlotte felt a tingle of anticipation.

She would help those brave little seedlings struggle to full fragrant growth. She would do something constructive.

"Mostly," Cindy said as she picked a dried tomato seed from the counter, "I walk. This is a great city for walking. Great bookstores. Places that sell handmade stuff. Cafés. I really like just strolling around and looking in the windows of other people's houses, you know?" She was silent for a moment, her eyes clouded and far away. "You're sure it's going to be three months max? Any more than that—I don't know if it's worth it. Mickey really needs to hear from me— for support, you know. I'm counting on you to mail the letters. To this address." She tapped the yellow note under the plastic sushi magnet on the refrigerator.

"I'm very reliable; of course I'll mail your letters. Look, my attorney says three months. No more, no less."

A siren screamed down Fillmore toward Church Street. She wouldn't back out now, would she? There was no time to do anything else, no chance to make other arrangements. Cindy Carson simply had to honor her commitment.

The timer jangled through Charlotte's thoughts.

"Okay, wrap this towel around your neck and bend over the sink." Cindy tested the water, turned down the hot. "There."

Charlotte closed her eyes. The ammonia smell was awful but the water was soothing. Charlotte gave herself up to the warm water and the light massage of Cindy's fingers on her scalp.

"All done." Cindy wrapped Charlotte's dripping head in a towel. "Here, wash the makeup off your face and we'll go in the bedroom. Light's better in there. You can show me how you do your eyeliner and I'll show you how to use the blusher along your cheekbones."

"*Our* cheekbones." Charlotte beamed. Of course this was going to work. She washed her face, scrunched her drying hair with her fingers, and tiptoed through the living room toward the open bedroom door. Cindy was struggling with the back of the white silk blouse.

My God, she was perfect.

It was like watching a videotape of a former self . . . outside, able to see what other people see, the filters of sensation and internal memory removed.

She was beautiful, with a cool dignity that would keep people at a distance. Charlotte stepped behind her and buttoned the buttons, then stood waiting, silent, solemn.

Again, they both stared at the image in the mirror; for a moment Charlotte felt the dreamy disorientation of a too sudden awakening.

Cindy tittered and they fell into fits of helpless giggles, sliding down to the floor where they swiped at the tears on their own faces and ended by almost drowning in each other's eyes.

Charlotte pulled away first.

Part the Third: The Long Good-bye

The Big Sleep

Two days left—thank God. All the romantic rot she'd told herself about growing herbs and learning to embroider and discovering the quaint niches of the city—how stupid she had been. After a week in Cindy Carson's squalid little apartment, she had missed her sheets being changed twice a week, had longed for just one dinner at Masa's, had cursed as one by one her nails broke. She had forborne the comments of the men as she walked down Church Street. Somehow, between daytime quiz shows and a few Danielle Steel novels, she had managed to pass the time. The best she could say was that it was almost over.

Charlotte put the cornflakes in the cupboard and crushed the empty milk carton before she tossed it in the garbage. As though it had been waiting for her attention, the sun broke through the fog and the street below shimmered in the dappled late morning light. She sprang from the chair and threw the window open.

Must be the dampness that keeps these herbs so green, she thought as she pinched off a leaf. *Certainly nothing I did*. A licorice smell drifted to her—basil? Cindy had planted the seeds and as they grew, she had faded into an insubstantial memory. Charlotte nibbled a corner of the leaf and wondered how accepting someone else's identity would alter her life, beyond this boring familiarity with the ordinary.

Cindy's closet had taught her nothing, had, in fact, been a disappointment. The colors were overdone, ranging from a too-cheery rose blouse to the brightest jewel-green jacket to florals that bloomed with garden hues. And her bookcase: Marques next to Lessing, Tyler beside Hardy, Oliver Sacks and Daphne DuMaurier and Dashiell Hammett. The girl didn't seem to be able to settle down.

Her collection of records was another example of her flightiness. Charlotte had made three purchases and now she ambled to the bedroom, put on her Johnny Mathis album, and settled into the rocking chair to enjoy the classic sounds.

Two more days. If she was careful she'd be able to string the last fifty pages of the book, a story of three orphaned sisters, to the end of her time. She'd resume life as Charlotte Durning—no jail, no cell, no throat filled with fear.

A noise from the front of the apartment startled her. A door squeaked and she heard voices. Heart pounding, she sat still, afraid that any movement might alert the intruder to her presence.

"Cindy?" a voice called out.

A male voice. Someone else had a key to this apartment, someone Cindy never told her about. She would say she was Cindy's sister . . . unless the person who was out there happened to be Cindy's brother or cousin or someone who would know better.

"She's not here. I told you—she usually goes out walking in the afternoon." A different voice, also male.

Johnny Mathis warbled on. Doors slammed, objects clattered to the floor.

"Hey, Vinnie, you don't have to make a mess." The second voice again.

Charlotte finally started breathing again. She hadn't closed the window; the fire escape, while not her favorite means of egress, would do. At least it was open, no small enclosed box. She stood up, held the rocker to keep it from slapping back and forth on the wood floor, and tiptoed to the window.

"No way, Cindy."

She could hardly breathe. A hand grabbed her shoulder, spun her around. She was looking into the narrow face of a small, sharp man with beady eyes.

"I, uh . . ." Maybe she could talk him out of . . . What did he want, anyway? He didn't look like he was related to Cindy; she'd try the sister bit. "Cindy's not here. I mean, I'm her—"

"Look, Cindy," the man growled, "all I want is that diamond pendant that you lifted from the Emerson mansion. The deal was you give me an exclusive on all your stuff and I give you that extra cut. So when I got a hold of that insurance report, you gotta believe I was mad. No broad holds out on Vinnie." He squeezed her arm; she winced in pain.

"Don't hurt her, man. You promised." Wide-shouldered and tall, the second man swayed and leaned against the door frame for support. He seemed to be having trouble keeping his eyes open. "Just find it and let's get out of here, okay? I gotta meet my connection in fifteen minutes."

She wasn't going to stand here and be roughed up by these thugs, whatever they thought Cindy had done. Charlotte screamed; she stomped her feet on the floor and screamed again, trying to break away from the grip of the man with the ferret eyes.

"Shut the bitch up, Mickey. Or I'm gonna have to."

The man called Mickey drew himself upright. 'Don't talk about her like that. I don't like the way you're treating her, Vinnie. You said all you were gonna do was scare—"

Before Mickey could finish his sentence, Vinnie's hand shot out. Something hard cracked against Mickey's temple and for a moment, eyes open wide, he looked like a little boy whose favorite teddy bear had been torn to shreds. Then his eyes rolled back in his head, he clutched his chest, and he crashed to the floor in an unruly heap.

"Fuck piss shit," muttered the other. He looked around, his hand reaching for the leather belt she'd left on the bed when she changed her jeans. When he moved, she bit his hand and screamed again.

"That's it, Cindy. You asked for this."

He grabbed a thick white sock from the pile of laundry on the floor and stuffed it into her mouth, then secured it with the belt.

She was going to gag; she couldn't breathe. She was going to throw up from the fear. Everything went dark for a minute. She started to slump.

"No way. You're not going to pull that shit on me."

He was stronger than she would have guessed. He tied her hands behind her back and pulled her hair when she tried to resist. He dragged her to the far end of the room.

The closet. It was tiny. He was going to put her in the closet. She could choke. She would die. She wouldn't be able to breathe in there. The walls would close in on her. She would be filled by the blackness, crushed by it.

He shoved her inside. She fell onto the shoe rack and tried to right herself; she pounded on the door with her feet. She heard furniture dragging across the floor; he was putting something big and heavy across the door. She pounded again. The air was too thick. She was thirsty and hot and she couldn't swallow.

"Come on, Mickey. Move your ass. I found the pendant."

No, they weren't going to leave her in here.

"Shit, Mickey, if you're not gonna get up, I'm gonna have to leave you here too." She heard steps, then a pause. "Mickey?" the worried voice called, and then silence.

She tried to scream but the sound swelled in her throat until it blocked off her air passage.

Her last thought before her heart stopped was that she would probably be buried in Cindy's embarrassing magenta wool suit. In an open casket.

Farewell, My Lovely

Cindy shoved away the tray of gravy-covered lumps and tuned out the din of the mess hall. One day to go. She could hardly wait to see Mickey again—his bright, clear eyes; his smooth, delicious skin. She deposited her tray on the pile, walked through the metal detector, and followed two blond ponytails out into the yard.

This hadn't been half bad, really, except for being hit on all the time—but that was nothing new. She found a place on the grass and tilted her face to the sun. Mickey couldn't write to her, of course, but the Rich Bitch had passed on all the news from his letters: the shakes and the sweats and the terror of creepy-crawlies on his skin were over. He was learning how to cope with pressure, how to relax, how to think positively. He was training on computers. He was feeling good and missing her.

A tall woman with close-cropped hair meandered toward her.

Cindy closed her eyes to the sight of the woman cruising her on the grass. *Think about Mickey—clean, hard, smelling of Old Spice after his shower, his hair still wet, his terrific smile*, she ordered herself. *Think about our fresh start.*

"Dreaming about your secret lover?"

Cindy opened her eyes and looked down at the brown loafers planted on the grass inches in front of her. "Mmm-hmm," she answered.

"Found out you can live without him, didn't you?"

Cindy scrambled to her feet, shivering at the sight of the grainy skin on the woman's chin and at the idea of living without Mickey. "Shit, no," she muttered as she walked, slowly and deliberately, toward the door.

The months had dragged, but the rest of the day was going to fly by. The separation was almost over. She smiled and hugged herself, a little in triumph and a little in anticipation of seeing Mickey at the apartment.

Sara Paretsky's Chicago provides private investigator V. I.
Warshawski with plenty of tests, but her wit, her agility, and
her toughness prove to be up to the challenges. Named one of
thirteen Women of the Year in 1987 by Ms. *magazine and a*
major force in the establishment of the Sisters in Crime or-
ganization and its first president, Sara also edited two short
story anthologies, A Woman's Eye *and* A Woman on the Case,
and has published a collection of her own short fiction, Windy
City Blues. *Her bestselling novels include* Bitter Medicine,
Blood Shot, *winner of the British Crime Writers Silver Dagger*
award and an Anthony nominee, Tunnel Vision, *and the forth-*
coming Ghost Country,
    In "The Maltese Cat," V. I. develops a pet theory to explain
the disappearance of her client's sister.

the maltese cat

by Sara Paretsky

H

I

ER VOICE ON THE PHONE HAD BEEN SOFT AND
husky, with just a whiff of the South laid across it like a rare
perfume. "I'd rather come to your office; I don't want people
in mine to know I've hired a detective."

I'd offered to see her at her home in the evening—my
Spartan office doesn't invite client confidences. But she
didn't want to wait until tonight, she wanted to come today,
almost at once, and no, she wouldn't meet me in a restaurant.
Far too hard to talk, and this was extremely personal.

"You know my specialty is financial crime, don't you?"
I asked sharply.

"Yes, that's how I got your name. One o'clock, fourth
floor of the Pulteney, right?" And she'd hung up without
telling me who she was.

An errand at the County building took me longer than I'd

expected; it was close to one-thirty by the time I got back to the Pulteney. My caller's problem apparently was urgent: she was waiting outside my office door, tapping one high heel impatiently on the floor as I trudged down the hall in my running shoes.

"Ms. Warshawski! I thought you were standing me up."

"No such luck," I grunted, opening my office door for her.

In the dimly lit hall she'd just been a slender silhouette. Under the office lights the set of the shoulders and signature buttons told me her suit had come from the hands of someone at Chanel. Its blue enhanced the cobalt of her eyes. Soft makeup hid her natural skin tones—I couldn't tell if that dark red hair was natural, or merely expertly painted.

She scanned the spare furnishings and picked the cleaner of my two visitor chairs. "My time is valuable, Ms. Warshawski. If I'd known you were going to keep me waiting without a place to sit I would have finished some phone calls before walking over here."

I'd dressed in jeans and a work shirt for a day at the Recorder of Deeds office. Feeling dirty and outclassed made me grumpy. "You hung up without giving me your name or number, so there wasn't much I could do to let you know you'd have to stand around in your pointy little shoes. My time's valuable, too! Why don't you tell me where the fire is so I can start putting it out."

She flushed. When I turn red I look blotchy, but in her it only enhanced her makeup. "It's my sister." The whiff of Southern increased. "Corinne. She's run off to Ja—my ex-husband, and I need someone to tell her to come back."

I made a disgusted face. "I can't believe I raced back from the County Building to listen to this. It's not 1890, you know. She may be making a mistake but presumably she can sort it out for herself."

Her flush darkened. "I'm not being very clear. I'm sorry. I'm not used to having to ask for things. My sister—Corinne—she's only fourteen. She's my ward. I'm sixteen years older than she is. Our parents died three years ago and she's been living with me since then. It's not easy, not easy for either of us. Moving from Mobile to here was just the beginning. When she got here she wanted to run around, do all the things you can't do in Mobile.''

She waved a hand to indicate what kinds of things those might be. "She thinks I'm a tough bitch and that I was too hard on my ex-husband. She's known him since she was three and he was a big hero. She couldn't see he'd changed. Or not changed, just not had the chance to be heroic anymore in public. So when she took off two days ago I assumed she went there. He's not answering his phone or the doorbell. I don't know if they've left town or he's just playing possum or what. I need someone who knows how to get people to open their doors and knows how to talk to people. At least if I could see Corinne I might—I don't know.''

She broke off with a helpless gesture that didn't match her sophisticated looks. Nothing like responsibility for a minor to deflate even the most urbane.

I grimaced more ferociously. "Why don't we start with your name, and your husband's name and address, and then move on to her friends.''

"Her friends?" The deep blue eyes widened. "I'd just as soon this didn't get around. People talk, and even though it's not 1890, it could be hard on her when she gets back to school.''

I suppressed a howl. "You can't come around demanding my expertise and then tell me what or what not to do. What if she's not with your husband? What if I can't get in touch with you when I've found that out and she's in terrible trouble and her life depends on my turning up some new leads? If you can't bring yourself to divulge a few names—starting with your own—you'd better go find yourself a more pliant detective. I can recommend a couple who have waiting rooms.''

She set her lips tightly: whatever she did she was in command—people didn't talk to her that way and get away with it. For a few seconds it looked as though I might be free to get back to the Recorder of Deeds that afternoon, but then she shook her head and forced a smile to her lips.

"I was told not to mind your abrasiveness because you were the best. I'm Brigitte LeBlanc. My sister's name is Corinne, also LeBlanc. And my ex-husband is Charles Pierce.''

She scooted her chair up to the desk so she could scribble his address on a sheet of paper torn from a memo pad in her bag. She scrawled busily for several minutes, then handed me a list that included Corinne's three closest school friends, along with Pierce's address.

"I'm late for a meeting. I'll call you tonight to see if you've made any progress." She got up.

"Not so fast," I said. "I get a retainer. You have to sign a contract. And I need a number where I can reach you."

"I really am late."

"And I'm really too busy to hunt for your sister. If you have a sister. You can't be that worried if your meeting is more important than she is."

Her scowl would have terrified me if I'd been alone with her in an alley after dark. "I do have a sister. And I spent two days trying to get into my ex-husband's place, and then in tracking down people who could recommend a private detective to me. I can't do anything else to help her except go earn the money to pay your fee."

I pulled a contract from my desk drawer and stuck it in the manual Olivetti that had belonged to my mother—a type-writer so old that I had to order special ribbons for it from Italy. A word processor would be cheaper and more impressive but the wrist action keeps my forearms strong. I got Ms. LeBlanc to give me her address, to sign on the dotted line for $400 a day plus expenses, to write in the name of a guaranteeing financial institution and to hand over a check for two hundred.

When she'd left I wrestled with my office windows, hoping to let some air in to blow her pricey perfume away. Carbon flakes from the el would be better than the lingering scent, but the windows, painted over several hundred times, wouldn't budge. I turned on a desktop fan and frowned sourly at her bold black signature.

What was her ex-husband's real name? She'd bitten off "Ja—" Could be James or Jake, but it sure wasn't Charles. Did she really have a sister? Was this just a ploy to get back at a guy late on his alimony? Although Pierce's address on North Winthrop didn't sound like the place for a man who could afford alimony. Maybe everything went to keep her in Chanel suits while he lived on Skid Row.

She wasn't in the phone book, so I couldn't check her own address on Belden. The operator told me the number was unlisted. I called a friend at the Fort Dearborn Trust, the bank Brigitte had drawn her check on, and was assured that there was plenty more where that came from. My friend told me Brigitte had parlayed the proceeds of a high-priced modeling career into a successful media consulting firm.

"And if you ever read the fashion pages you'd know these things. Get your nose out of the sports section from time to time, Vic—it'll help with your career."

"Thanks, Eva." I hung up with a snap. At least my client wouldn't turn out to be named something else, always a good beginning to a tawdry case.

I looked in the little mirror perched over my filing cabinet. A dust smudge on my right cheek instead of peach blush was the only distinction between me and Ms. LeBlanc. Since I was dressed appropriately for North Winthrop, I shut up my office and went to retrieve my car.

II

Charles Pierce lived in a dismal ten-flat built flush onto the Uptown sidewalk. Ragged sheets made haphazard curtains in those windows that weren't boarded over. Empty bottles lined the entryway, but the smell of stale Ripple couldn't begin to mask the stench of fresh urine. If Corinne LeBlanc had run away to this place, life with Brigitte must be unmitigated hell.

My client's ex-husband lived in 3E. I knew that because she'd told me. Those few mailboxes whose doors still shut wisely didn't trumpet their owners' identities. The filthy brass nameplate next to the doorbells was empty and the doorbells didn't work. Pushing open the rickety door to the hall, I wondered again about my client's truthfulness: she told me Ja— hadn't answered his phone or his bell.

A rheumy-eyed woman was sprawled across the bottom

of the stairs, sucking at a half-pint. She stared at me malevolently when I asked her to move, but she didn't actively try to trip me when I stepped over her. It was only my foot catching in the folds of her overcoat.

The original building probably held two apartments per floor. At least, on the third floor only two doors at either end looked as though they went back to the massive, elegant construction of the building's beginnings. The other seven were flimsy newcomers that had been hastily installed when an apartment was subdivided. Peering in the dark I found one labeled B and counted off three more to the right to get to E. After knocking on the peeling veneer several times I noticed a button imbedded in the grime on the jamb. When I pushed it I heard a buzz resonate inside. No one came to the door. With my ear against the filthy panel I could hear the faint hum of a television.

I held the buzzer down for five minutes. It's hard on the finger but harder on the ear. If someone was really in there he should have come boiling to the door by now.

I could go away and come back, but if Pierce was lying doggo to avoid Brigitte, that wouldn't buy me anything. She said she'd tried off and on for two days. The television might be running as a decoy, or—I pushed more lurid ideas from my mind and took out a collection of skeleton keys. The second worked easily in the insubstantial lock. In two minutes I was inside the apartment, looking at an illustration from *House Beautiful in Hell*.

It was a single room with a countertop kitchen on the left side. A tidy person could pull a corrugated screen to shield the room from signs of cooking, but Pierce wasn't tidy. Ten or fifteen stacked pots, festooned with rotting food and roaches, trembled precariously when I shut the door.

Dominating the place was a Murphy bed with a grotesquely fat man sprawled in at an ominous angle. He'd been watching TV when he died. He was wearing frayed, shiny pants with the fly lying carelessly open and a lumberjack shirt that didn't quite cover his enormous belly.

His monstrous size and the horrible angle at which his bald head was tilted made me gag. I forced it down and walked through a pile of stale clothes to the bed. Lifting an arm the size of a tree trunk, I felt for a pulse. Nothing moved in the heavy arm, but the skin, while clammy, was firm. I couldn't bring myself to touch any more of him but stumbled around the perimeter to peer at him from several angles. I didn't see any obvious wounds. Let the medical examiner hunt out the obscure ones.

By the time I was back in the stairwell I was close to fainting. Only the thought of falling into someone else's urine or vomit kept me on my feet. On the way down I tripped in earnest over the rheumy-eyed woman's coat. Sprawled on the floor at the bottom, I couldn't keep from throwing up myself. It didn't make me feel any better.

I dug a water bottle out of the detritus in my trunk and sponged myself off before calling the police. They asked me to stay near the body. I thought the front seat of my car on Winthrop would be close enough.

While I waited for a meat wagon I wondered about my client. Could Brigitte have come here after leaving me, killed him and taken off while I was phoning around checking up on her? If she had, the rheumy-eyed woman in the stairwell would have seen her. Would the bond forged by my tripping over her and vomiting in the hall be enough to get her to talk to me?

I got out of the car, but before I could get back to the entrance the police arrived. When we pushed open the rickety door my friend had evaporated. I didn't bother mentioning her to the boys—and girl—in blue: her description wouldn't stand out in Uptown, and even if they could find her she wouldn't be likely to say much.

We plodded up the stairs in silence. There were four of them. The woman and the youngest of the three men seemed in good shape. The two older men were running sadly to flab. I didn't think they'd be able to budge my client's ex-husband's right leg, let alone his mammoth redwood torso.

"I got a feeling about this," the oldest officer muttered, more to himself than the rest of us. "I got a feeling."

When we got to 3E and he looked across at the mass on the bed he shook his head a couple of times. "Yup. I kind of knew as soon as I heard the call."

"Knew what, Tom?" the woman demanded sharply.

"Jade Pierce," he said. "Knew he lived around here. Been a lot of complaints about him. Thought it might be him when I heard we was due to visit a real big guy."

The woman stopped her brisk march to the bed. The rest of us looked at the behemoth in shared sorrow. Jade. Not James or Jake but Jade. Once the most famous down lineman the Bears had ever fielded. Now . . . I shuddered.

When he played for Alabama some reporter said his bald head was as smooth and cold as a piece of Jade, and went on to spin some tiresome simile relating it to his play. When he signed with the Bears, I was as happy as any other Chicago fan, even though his reputation for off-field violence was pretty unappetizing. No wonder Brigitte LeBlanc hadn't stayed with him, but why hadn't she wanted to tell me who he really was? I wrestled with that while Tom called for reinforcements over his lapel mike.

"So what were you doing here?" he asked me.

"His ex-wife hired me to check up on him." I don't usually tell the cops my clients' business, but I didn't feel like protecting Brigitte. "She wanted to talk to him and he wasn't answering his phone or his door."

"She wanted to check up on him?" the fit younger officer, a man with high cheekbones and a well-tended mustache, echoed me derisively. "What I hear, that split-up was the biggest fight Jade was ever in. Only big fight he ever lost, too."

I smiled. "She's doing well, he isn't. Wasn't. Maybe her conscience pricked her. Or maybe she wanted to rub his nose in it hard. You'd have to ask her. All I can say is she asked me to try to get in, I did, and I called you guys."

While Tom mulled this over I pulled out a card and handed it to him. "You can find me at this number if you want to talk to me."

He called out after me but I went on down the hall, my footsteps echoing hollowly off the bare walls and ceiling.

III

Brigitte LeBlanc was with a client and couldn't be interrupted. The news that her ex-husband had died couldn't pry her loose. Not even the idea that the cops would be around before long could move her. After a combination of cajoling and heckling, the receptionist leaned across her blond desk and whispered at me confidentially: "The vice president of the United States had come in for some private media coaching." Brigitte had said no interruptions unless it was the president or the pope—two people I wouldn't even leave a dental appointment to see.

When they made me unwelcome on the forty-third floor I rode downstairs and hung around the lobby. At five-thirty a bevy of Secret Service agents swept me out to the street with the other loiterers. Fifteen minutes later the vice president came out, his boyish face set in purposeful lines. Even though this was a private visit the vigilant television crews were waiting for him. He grinned and waved but didn't say anything before climbing into his limo. Brigitte must be really good if she'd persuaded him to shut up.

At seven I went back to the forty-third floor. The double glass doors were locked and the lights turned off. I found a key in my collection that worked the lock, but when I'd prowled through the miles of thick grey plush, explored the secured studios, looked in all the offices, I had to realize my client was smarter than me. She'd left by some back exit.

I gave a high-pitched snarl. I didn't lock the door behind me. Let someone come in and steal all the video equipment. I didn't care.

I swung by Brigitte's three-story brownstone on Belden. She wasn't in. The housekeeper didn't know when to expect her. She was eating out and had said not to wait up for her.

"How about Corinne?" I asked, sure that the woman would say "Corinne who?"

"She's not here, either."

I slipped inside before she could shut the door on me. "I'm V. I. Warshawski. Brigitte hired me to find her sister, said she'd run off to Jade. I went to his apartment. Corinne wasn't there and Jade was dead. I've been trying to talk to Brigitte ever since but she's been avoiding me. I want to know a few things, like if Corinne really exists, and did she really run away, and could either she or Brigitte have killed Jade."

The housekeeper stared at me for a few minutes, then made a sour face. "You got some ID?"

I showed her my PI license and the contract signed by Brigitte. Her sour look deepened but she gave me a few spare details. Corinne was a fat, unhappy teenager who didn't know how good she had it. Brigitte gave her everything, taught her how to dress, sent her to St. Scholastica, even tried to get her to special diet clinics, but she was never satisfied, always whining about her friends back home in Mobile, trashy friends to whom she shouldn't be giving the time of day. And yes, she had run away, three days ago now, and she, the housekeeper, said good riddance, but Brigitte felt responsible. And she was sorry that Jade was dead, but he was a violent man, Corinne had over-idealized him, she didn't realize what a monster he really was.

"They can't turn it off when they come off the field, you know. As for who killed him, he probably killed himself, drinking too much. I always said it would happen that way. Corinne couldn't have done it, she doesn't have enough oomph to her. And Brigitte doesn't have any call to—she already got him beat six ways from Sunday."

"Maybe she thought he'd molested her sister."

"She'd have taken him to court and enjoyed seeing him humiliated all over again."

What a lovely cast of characters; it filled me with satisfaction to think I'd allied myself to their fates. I persuaded the housekeeper to give me a picture of Corinne before going home. She was indeed an overweight, unhappy-looking child. It must be hard having a picture-perfect older sister trying to turn her into a junior deb. I also got the housekeeper to give me Brigitte's unlisted home phone number by telling her if she didn't, I'd be back every hour all night long ringing the bell.

I didn't turn on the radio going home. I didn't want to hear the ghoulish excitement lying behind the unctuousness the reporters would bring to discussing Jade Pierce's catastrophic fall from grace. A rehashing of his nine seasons with the Bears, from the glory years to the last two where nagging knee and back injuries grew too great even for the painkillers. And then to his harsh retirement, putting seventy or eighty pounds of fat over his playing weight of 310, the barroom fights, the guns fired at other drivers from the front seat of his Ferrari Daytona, then the sale of the Ferrari to pay his legal bills, and finally the three-ring circus that was his divorce. Ending on a Murphy bed in a squalid Uptown apartment.

I shut the Trans Am's door with a viciousness it didn't deserve and stomped up the three flights to my apartment. Fatigue mixed with bitterness dulled the sixth sense that usually warns me of danger. The man had me pinned against my front door with a gun at my throat before I knew he was there.

I held my shoulder bag out to him. "Be my guest. Then leave. I've had a long day and I don't want to spend too much of it with you."

He spat. "I don't want your stupid little wallet."

"You're not going to rape me, so you might as well take my stupid little wallet."

"I'm not interested in your body. Open your apartment. I want to search it."

"Go to hell." I kneed him in the stomach and swept my right arm up to knock his gun hand away. He gagged and bent over. I used my handbag as a clumsy bola and whacked him on the back of the head. He slumped to the floor, unconscious.

I grabbed the gun from his flaccid hand. Feeling gingerly inside his coat, I found a wallet. His driver's license identified him as Joel Sirop, living at a pricey address on Dearborn Parkway. He sported a high-end assortment of credit cards—Bonwit, Neiman-Marcus, an American Express plantinum—and a card that said he was a member in good standing of the Feline Breeders Association of North America. I slid the papers back into his billfold and returned it to his breast pocket.

He groaned and opened his eyes. After a few diffuse seconds he focused on me in outrage. "My head. You've broken my head. I'll sue you."

"Go ahead. I'll hang on to your pistol for use in evidence at the trial. I've got your name and address, so if I see you near my place again I'll know where to send the cops. Now leave."

"Not until I've searched your apartment." He was unarmed and sickly but stubborn.

I leaned against my door, out of reach but poised to stomp on him if he got cute. "What are you looking for, Mr. Sirop?"

"It was on the news, how you found Jade. If the cat was there, you must have taken it."

"Rest your soul, there were no cats in that apartment when I got there. Had he stolen yours?"

He shut his eyes, apparently to commune with himself. When he opened them again he said he had no choice but to trust me. I smiled brightly and told him he could always leave so I could have dinner, but he insisted on confiding in me.

"Do you know cats, Ms. Warshawski?"

"Only in a manner of speaking. I have a dog and she knows cats."

He scowled. "This is not a laughing matter. Have you heard of the Maltese?"

"Cat? I guess I've heard of them. They're the ones without tails, right?"

He shuddered. "No. You are thinking of the Manx. The Maltese—they are usually a bluish grey. Very rarely will you see one that is almost blue. Brigitte LeBlanc has—or had— such a cat. Lady Iva of Cairo."

"Great. I presume she got it to match her eyes."

He waved aside my comment as another frivolity. "Her motives do not matter. What matters is that the cat has been very difficult to breed. She has now come into season for only the third time in her four-year life. Brigitte agreed to let me try to mate Lady Iva with my sire, Casper of Valletta. It is imperative that she be sent to stay with him, and soon. But she has disappeared."

It was my turn to look disgusted. "I took a step down from my usual practice to look for a runaway teenager today. I'm damned if I'm going to hunt a missing cat through the streets of Chicago. Your sire will find her faster than I will.

Matter of fact, that's my advice. Drive around listening for the yowling of mighty sires and eventually you'll find your Maltese.''

"This runaway teenager, this Corinne, it is probable that she took Lady Iva with her. The kittens, if they are born, if they are purebred, could fetch a thousand or more each. She is not ignorant of that fact. But if Lady Iva is out on the streets and some other sire finds her first, they would be half-breeds, not worth the price of their veterinary care.''

He spoke with the intense passion I usually reserve for discussing Cubs or Bears trades. Keeping myself turned toward him, I unlocked my front door. He hurled himself at the opening with a ferocity that proved his long years with felines had rubbed off on him. I grabbed his jacket as he hurtled past me but he tore himself free.

"I am not leaving until I have searched your premises,'' he panted.

I rubbed my head tiredly. "Go ahead, then.''

I could have called the cops while he hunted around for Lady Iva. Instead I poured myself a whiskey and watched him crawl on his hands and knees, making little whistling sounds—perhaps the mating call of the Maltese. He went through my cupboards, my stove, the refrigerator, even insisted, his eyes wide with fear, that I open the safe in my bedroom closet. I removed the Smith and Wesson I keep there before letting him look.

When he'd inspected the back landing he had to agree that no cats were on the premises. He tried to argue me into going downtown to check my office. At that point my patience ran out.

"I could have you arrested for attempted assault and criminal trespass. So get out now while the going's good. Take your guy down to my office. If she's in there and in heat, he'll start carrying on and you can call the cops. Just don't bother me.'' I hustled him out the front door, ignoring his protests.

I carefully did up all the locks. I didn't want some other deranged cat breeder sneaking up on me in the middle of the night.

IV

It was after midnight when I finally reached Brigitte. Yes, she'd gotten my message about Jade. She was terribly sorry, but since she couldn't do anything to help him now that he was dead, she hadn't bothered to try to reach me.

"We're about to part company, Brigitte. If you didn't know the guy was dead when you sent me up to Winthrop, you're going to have to prove it. Not at me, but to the cops. I'm talking to Lieutenant Mallory at the Central District in the morning to tell him the rigmarole you spun me. They'll also be able to figure out if you were more interested in finding Corinne or your cat."

There was a long silence at the other end. When she finally spoke, the hint of Southern was pronounced. "Can we talk in the morning before you call the police? Maybe I haven't been as frank as I should have. I'd like you to hear the whole story before you do anything rash."

Just say no, just say no, I chanted to myself. "You be at the Belmont Diner at eight, Brigitte. You can lay it out for me but I'm not making any promises."

I got up at seven, ran the dog over to Belmont Harbor and back and took a long shower. I figured even if I put a half hour into grooming myself I wasn't going to look as good as Brigitte, so I just scrambled into jeans and a cotton sweater.

It was almost ten minutes after eight when I got to the diner, but Brigitte hadn't arrived yet. I picked up a *Herald-Star* from the counter and took it over to a booth to read with a cup of coffee. The headline shook me to the bottom of my stomach.

FOOTBALL HERO SURVIVES FATE
WORSE THAN DEATH

Charles "Jade" Pierce, once the smoothest man on the Bears' fearsome defense, eluded offensive

> blockers once again. This time the
> stakes were higher than a touchdown,
> though: the offensive lineman was
> Death.

I thought Jeremy Logan was overdoing it by a wide margin but I read the story to the end. The standard procedure with a body is to take it to a hospital for a death certificate before it goes to the morgue. The patrol team hauled Jade to Beth Israel for a perfunctory exam. There the intern, noticing a slight sweat on Jade's neck and hands, dug deeper for a pulse than I'd been willing to go. She'd found faint but unmistakable signs of life buried deep in the mountain of flesh and had brought him back to consciousness.

> Jade, who's had substance abuse
> problems since leaving the Bears,
> had mainlined a potent mixture of
> ether and hydrochloric acid before
> drinking a quart of bourbon. When
> he came to his first words were characteristic: "Get the f— out of my
> face."

Logan then concluded with the obligatory run-down on Jade's career and its demise, with a pious sniff about the use and abuse of sports heroes left to die in the gutter when they could no longer please the crowd. I read it through twice, including the fulsome last line, before Brigitte arrived.

"You see, Jade's still alive, so I couldn't have killed him," she announced, sweeping into the booth in a cloud of Chanel.

"Did you know he was in a coma when you came to see me yesterday?"

She raised plucked eyebrows in hauteur. "Are you questioning my word?"

One of the waitresses chugged over to take our order. "You want your fruit and yogurt, right, Vic? And what else?"

"Green pepper and cheese omelet with rye toast. Thanks,

Barbara. What'll yours be, Brigitte?'' Dry toast and black coffee, no doubt.

"Is your fruit *really* fresh?'' she demanded.

Barbara rolled her eyes. "We don't allow no one to be fresh in here, honey, regardless of sex preference. You want some or not?''

Brigitte set her shoulder—covered today in green broadcloth with black piping—and got ready to do battle. I cut her off before the first "How dare you'' rolled to its ugly conclusion.

"This isn't the kind of place where the maitre d' wilts at your frown and races over to make sure madam is happy. They don't care if you come back or not. In fact, about now they'd be happier if you'd leave. You can check out my fruit when it comes and order some if it tastes right to you.''

"I'll just have wheat toast and black coffee,'' she said icily. "And make sure they don't put any butter on it.''

"Right,'' Barbara said. "Wheat toast, margarine instead of butter. Just kidding, hon,'' she added as Brigitte started to tear into her again. "You gotta learn to take it if you want to dish it out.''

"Did you bring me here to be insulted?'' Brigitte demanded when Barbara had left.

"I brought you here to talk. It didn't occur to me that you wouldn't know diner etiquette. We can fight if you want to. Or you can tell me about Jade and Corinne. And your cat. I had a visit from Joel Sirop last night.''

She swallowed some coffee and made a face. "They should rinse the pots with vinegar.''

"Well, keep it to yourself. They won't pay you a consulting fee for telling them about it. Joel tell you he'd come around hunting Lady Iva?''

She frowned at me over the rim of the coffee cup, then nodded fractionally.

"Why didn't you tell me about the damned cat when you were in my office yesterday?''

Her poise deserted her for a moment; she looked briefly ashamed. "I thought you'd look for Corinne. I didn't think I could persuade you to hunt down my cat. Anyway, Corinne must have taken Iva with her, so I thought if you found her you'd find the cat, too.''

"Which one do you really want back?"

She started to bristle again, then suddenly laughed. It took ten years from her face. "You wouldn't ask that if you'd ever lived with a teenager. And Corinne's always been a stranger to me. She was eighteen months old when I left for college and I only saw her a week or two at a time on vacations. She used to worship me. When she moved in with me I thought it would be a piece of cake: I'd get her fixed up with the right crowd and the right school, she'd do her best to be like me, and the system would run itself. Instead, she put on a lot of weight, won't listen to me about her eating, slouches around with the kids in the neighborhood when my back is turned, the whole nine yards. Jade's influence. It creeps through every now and then when I'm not thinking."

She looked at my blueberries. I offered them to her and she helped herself to a generous spoonful.

"And that was the other thing. Jade. We got together when I was an Alabama cheerleader and he was the biggest hero in town. I thought I'd really caught me a prize, my yes, a big prize. But the first, last and only thing in a marriage with a football player is football. And him, of course, how many sacks he made, how many yards he allowed, all that boring crap. And if he has to sit out a game, or he gives up a touchdown, or he doesn't get the glory, watch out. Jade was mean. He was mean on the field, he was mean off it. He broke my arm once."

Her voice was level but her hand shook a little as she lifted the coffee cup to her mouth. "I got me a gun and shot him in the leg the next time he came at me. They put it down as a hunting accident in the papers, but he never tried anything on me after that—not physical, I mean. Until his career ended. Then he got real, real ugly. The papers crucified me for abandoning him when his career was over. They never had to live with him."

She was panting with emotion by the time she finished. "And Corinne shared the papers' views?" I asked gently.

She nodded. "We had a bad fight on Sunday. She wanted

to go to a sleepover at one of the girls' in the neighborhood. I don't like that girl and I said no. We had a gale-force battle after that. When I got home from work on Monday she'd taken off. First I figured she'd gone to this girl's place. They hadn't seen her, though, and she hadn't shown up at school. So I figured she'd run off to Jade. Now . . . I don't know. I would truly appreciate it if you'd keep looking, though.''

Just say no, Vic, I chanted to myself. "I'll need a thousand up front. And more names and addresses of friends, including people in Mobile. I'll check in with Jade at the hospital. She might have gone to him, you know, and he sent her on some-place else.''

"I stopped by there this morning. They said no visitors.''

I grinned. "I've got friends in high places.'' I signaled Barbara for the check. "Speaking of which, how was the vice president?''

She looked as though she were going to give me one of her stiff rebuttals, but then she curled her lip and drawled, "Just like every other good old boy, honey, just like every other good old boy.''

V

Lotty Herschel, an obstetrician associated with Beth Israel, arranged for me to see Jade Pierce. "They tell me he's been difficult. Don't stand next to the bed unless you're wearing a padded jacket.''

"You want him, you can have him,'' the floor head told me. "He's going home tomorrow morning. Frankly, since he won't let anyone near him, they ought to release him right now.''

My palms felt sweaty when I pushed open the door to Jade's room. He didn't throw anything when I came in, didn't even turn his head to stare through the restraining rails surrounding the bed. His mountain of flesh poured through them, ebbing away from a rounded summit in the middle. The back of his head, smooth and shiny as a piece of pol-ished jade, reflected the ceiling light into my eyes.

"I don't need any goddamned ministering angels, so get the fuck out of here," he growled to the window.

"That's a relief. My angel act never really got going."

He turned his head at that. His black eyes were mean, narrow slits. If I were a quarterback I'd hand him the ball and head for the showers.

"What are you, the goddamned social worker?"

"Nope. I'm the goddamned detective who found you yesterday before you slipped off to the great huddle in the sky."

"Come on over then, so I can kiss your ass," he spat venomously.

I leaned against the wall and crossed my arms. "I didn't mean to save your life: I tried getting them to send you to the morgue. The meat wagon crew double-crossed me."

The mountain shook and rumbled. It took me a few seconds to realize he was laughing. "You're right, detective: you ain't no angel. So what do you want? True confessions on why I was such a bad boy? The name of the guy who got me the stuff?"

"As long as you're not hurting anyone but yourself I don't care what you do or where you get your shit. I'm here because Brigitte hired me to find Corinne."

His face set in ugly lines again. "Get out."

I didn't move.

"I said get out!" He raised his voice to a bellow.

"Just because I mentioned Brigitte's name?"

"Just because if you're pally with that broad, you're a snake by definition."

"I'm not pally with her. I met her yesterday. She's paying me to find her sister." It took an effort not to yell back at him.

"Corinne's better off without her," he growled, turning the back of his head to me again.

I didn't say anything, just stood there. Five minutes passed. Finally he jeered, without looking at me. "Did the sweet little martyr tell you I broke her arm?"

"She mentioned it, yes."

"She tell you how that happened?"

"Please don't tell me how badly she misunderstood you. I don't want to throw up my breakfast."

At that he swung his gigantic face around toward me again. "Com'ere."

When I didn't move, he sighed and patted the bedrail. "I'm not going to slug you, honest. If we're going to talk, you gotta get close enough for me to see your face."

I went over to the bed and straddled the chair, resting my arms on its back. Jade studied me in silence, then grunted as if to say I'd passed some minimal test.

"I won't tell you Brigitte didn't understand me. Broad had my number from day one. I didn't break her arm, though: that was B. B. Wilder. Old Gunshot. Thought he was my best friend on the club, but it turned out he was Brigitte's. And then, when I come home early from a hunting trip and found her in bed with him, we all got carried away. She loved the excitement of big men fighting. It's what made her a football groupie to begin with down in Alabama."

I tried to imagine ice-cold Brigitte flushed with excitement while the Bears' right tackle and defensive end fought over her. It didn't seem impossible.

"So B. B. broke her arm but I agreed to take the rap. Her little old modeling career was just getting off the ground and she didn't want her good name sullied. And besides that, she kept hoping for a reconciliation with her folks, at least with their wad, and they'd never fork over if she got herself some ugly publicity committing violent adultery. And me, I was just the baddest boy the Bears ever fielded; one more mark didn't make that much difference to me." The jeering note returned to his voice.

"She told me it was when you retired that things deteriorated between you."

"Things deteriorated—what a way to put it. Look, detective, what did you say your name was? V. I., that's a hell of a name for a girl. What did your mamma call you?"

"Victoria," I said grudgingly. "And no one calls me Vicki, so don't even think about it." I prefer not to be called a girl, either, much less a broad, but Jade didn't seem like the person to discuss that particular issue with.

"Victoria, huh? Things deteriorated, yeah, like they was a picnic starting out. I was born dumb and I didn't get smarter for making five hundred big ones a year. But I wouldn't hit a broad, even one like Brigitte who could get me going just looking at me. I broke a lot of furniture, though, and that got on her nerves.''

I couldn't help laughing. "Yeah, I can see that. It'd bother me, too."

He gave a grudging smile. "See, the trouble is, I grew up poor. I mean, dirt poor. I used to go to the projects here with some of the black guys on the squad, you know, Christmas appearances, shit like that. Those kids live in squalor, but I didn't own a pair of shorts to cover my ass until the county social worker come 'round to see why I wasn't in school.''

"So you broke furniture because you grew up without it and didn't know what else to do with it?"

"Don't be a wiseass, Victoria. I'm sure your mamma wouldn't like it."

I made a face—he was right about that.

"You know the LeBlancs, right? Oh, you're a Yankee, Yankees don't know shit if they haven't stepped in it themselves. LeBlanc Gas, they're one of the biggest names on the Gulf Coast. They're a long, *long* way from the Pierces of Florette.

"I muscled my way into college, played football for Old Bear Bryant, met Brigitte. She liked raw meat, and mine was just about the rawest in the South, so she latched on to me. When she decided to marry me she took me down to Mobile for Christmas. There I was, the Hulk, in Miz Effie's lace and crystal palace. They hated me, knew I was trash, told Brigitte they'd cut her out of everything if she married me. She figured she could sweet-talk her daddy into anything. We got married and it didn't work, not even when I was a national superstar. To them I was still the dirt I used to wipe my ass with.''

"So she divorced you to get back in their will?"

He shrugged, a movement that set a tidal wave going down the mountain. "Oh, that had something to do with it, sure, it had something. But I was a wreck and I was hell to live with. Even if she'd been halfway normal to begin with, it would have gone bust, 'cause I didn't know how to live with losing football. I just didn't care about anyone or anything.''

"Not even the Daytona," I couldn't help saying.

His black eyes disappeared into tiny dots. "Don't you go lecturing me just when we're starting to get on. I'm not asking you to cry over my sad jock story. I'm just trying to give you a little different look at sweet, beautiful Brigitte."

"Sorry. It's just . . . I'll never do anything to be able to afford a Ferrari Daytona. It pisses me to see someone throw one away."

He snorted. "If I'd known you five years ago I'd of given it to you. Too late now. Anyway, Brigitte waited too long to jump ship. She was still in negotiations with old man Le-Blanc when he and Miz Effie dropped into the Gulf of Mexico with the remains of their little Cessna. Everything that wasn't tied down went to Corinne. Brigitte, being her guardian, gets a chunk for looking after her, but you ask me, if Corinne's gone missing it's the best thing she could do. I'll bet you . . . well, I don't have anything left to bet. I'll hack off my big toe and give it to you if Brigitte's after anything but the money."

He thought for a minute. "No. She probably likes Corinne some. Or would like her if she'd lose thirty pounds, dress like a Mobile debutante and hang around with a crowd of snot-noses. I'll hack off my toe if the money ain't number one in her heart, that's all."

I eyed him steadily, wondering how much of his story to believe. It's why I stay away from domestic crime: everyone has a story, and it wears you out trying to match all the different pieces together. I could check the LeBlancs' will to see if they'd left their fortune the way Jade reported it. Or if they had a fortune at all. Maybe he was making it all up.

"Did Corinne talk to you before she took off on Monday?"

His black eyes darted around the room. "I haven't laid eyes on her in months. She used to come around, but Brigitte got a peace bond on me, I get arrested if I'm within thirty feet of Corinne."

"I believe you, Jade," I said steadily. "I believe you haven't seen her. But did she talk to you? Like on the phone, maybe."

The ugly look returned to his face, then the mountain shook again as he laughed. "You don't miss many signals, do you, Victoria? You oughta run a training camp. Yeah, Corinne calls me Monday morning. 'Why don't you have your cute little ass in school?' I says. 'Even with all your family dough that's the only way to get ahead—they'll ream you six ways from Sunday if you don't get your education so you can check out what all your advisers are up to.' ''

He shook his head broodingly. "I know what I'm talking about, believe me. The lawyers and agents and financial advisers, they all made out like hogs at feeding time when I was in the money, but come trouble, it wasn't them, it was me hung out like a slab of pork belly to dry on my own."

"So what did Corinne say to your good advice?'' I prompted, trying not to to sound impatient: I could well be the first sober person to listen to him in a decade.

"Oh, she's crying, she can't stand it, why can't she just run home to Mobile? And I tell her 'cause she's underage and rich, the cops will all be looking for her and just haul her butt back to Chicago. And when she keeps talking wilder and wilder I tell her they'll be bound to blame me if something happens to her and does she really need to run away so bad that I go to jail or something. So I thought that calmed her down. 'Think of it like rookie camp,' I told her. 'They put you through the worst shit but if you survive it you own them.' I thought she figured it out and was staying.''

He shut his eyes. "I'm tired, detective. I can't tell you nothing else. You go away and detect.''

"If she went back to Mobile who would she stay with?''

"Wouldn't nobody down there keep her without calling Brigitte. Too many of them owe their jobs to LeBlanc Gas.'' He didn't open his eyes.

"And up here?''

He shrugged, a movement like an earthquake that rattled the bedrails. "You might try the neighbors. Seems to me Corinne mentioned a Miz Hellman who had a bit of a soft spot for her.'' He opened his eyes. "Maybe Corinne'll talk to you. You got a good ear.''

"Thanks.'' I got up. "What about this famous Maltese cat?''

"What about it?''

"It went missing along with Corinne. Think she'd hurt it to get back at Brigitte?"

"How the hell should I know? Those LeBlancs would do anything to anyone. Even Corinne. Now get the fuck out so I can get my beauty rest." He shut his eyes again.

"Yeah, you're beautiful all right, Jade. Why don't you use some of your old connections and get yourself going at something? It's really pathetic seeing you like this."

"You wanna save me along with the Daytona?" The ugly jeer returned to his voice. "Don't go all do-gooder on me now, Victoria. My daddy died at forty from too much moonshine. They tell me I'm his spitting image. I know where I'm going."

"It's trite, Jade. Lots of people have done it. They'll make a movie about you and little kids will cry over your sad story. But if they make it honest they'll show that you're just plain selfish."

I wanted to slam the door but the hydraulic stop took the impact out of the gesture. "Goddamned motherfucking waste," I snapped as I stomped down the corridor.

The floor head heard me. "Jade Pierce? You're right about that."

VI

The Hellmans lived in an apartment above the TV repair shop they ran on Halsted. Mrs. Hellman greeted me with some relief.

"I promised Corinne I wouldn't tell her sister as long as she stayed here instead of trying to hitchhike back to Mobile. But I've been pretty worried. It's just that . . . to Brigitte LeBlanc I don't exist. My daughter Lily is trash that she doesn't want Corinne associated with, so it never even occurred to her that Corinne might be here."

She took me through the back of the shop and up the stairs to the apartment. "It's only five rooms, but we're glad to have her as long as she wants to stay. I'm more worried about the cat: she doesn't like being cooped up in here. She got out Tuesday night and we had a terrible time hunting her down.''

I grinned to myself: So much for the thoroughbred descendants pined for by Joel Sirop.

Mrs. Hellman took me into the living room where they had a sofabed that Corinne was using. "This here is a detective, Corinne. I think you'd better talk to her."

Corinne was hunched in front of the television, an outsize console model far too large for the tiny room. In her man's white shirt and tattered blue jeans she didn't look at all like her svelte sister. Her complexion was a muddy color that matched her lank, straight hair. She clutched Lady Iva of Cairo close in her arms. Both of them looked at me angrily.

"If you think you can make me go back to that cold-assed bitch, you'd better think again."

Mrs. Hellman tried to protest her language.

"It's okay," I said. "She learned it from Jade. But Jade lost every fight he ever was in with Brigitte, Corinne. Maybe you ought to try a different method."

"Brigitte hated Jade. She hates anyone who doesn't do stuff just the way she wants it. So if you're working for Brigitte you don't know shit about anything."

I responded to the first part of her comments. "Is that why you took the cat? So you could keep her from having purebred kittens like Brigitte wants her to?"

A ghost of a smile twitched around her unhappy mouth. All she said was "They wouldn't let me bring my dogs or my horse up north. Iva's kind of a snoot but she's better than nothing."

"Jade thinks Brigitte's jealous because you got the LeBlanc fortune and she didn't."

She made a disgusted noise. "Jade worries too much about all that shit. Yeah, Daddy left me a big fat wad. But the company went to Daddy's cousin Miles. You can't inherit LeBlanc Gas if you're a girl and Brigitte knew that, same as me. I mean, they told both of us growing up so we wouldn't have our hearts set on it. The money they left me, Brigitte makes that amount every year in her business. She doesn't care about the money."

"And you? Does it bother you that the company went to your cousin?"

She gave a long ugly sniff—no doubt another of Jade's expressions. "Who wants a company that doesn't do anything but pollute the Gulf and ream the people who work for them?"

I considered that. At fourteen it was probably genuine bravado. "So what do you care about?"

She looked at me with sulky dark eyes. For a minute I thought she was going to tell me to mind my own goddamned business and go to hell, but she suddenly blurted, "It's my horse. They left the house to Miles along with my horse. They didn't think about it, just said the house and all the stuff that wasn't left special to someone else went to him and they didn't even think to leave me my own horse."

The last sentence came out as a wail and her angry young face dissolved into sobs. I didn't think she'd welcome a friendly pat on the shoulder. I just let the tears run their course. She finally wiped her nose on a frayed cuff and shot me a fierce look to see if I cared.

"If I could persuade Brigitte to buy your horse from Miles and stable him up here, would you be willing to go back to her until you're of age?"

"You never would. Nobody ever could make that bitch change her mind."

"But if I could?"

Her lower lip was hanging out. "Maybe. If I could have my horse and go to school with Lily instead of fucking St. Scholastica."

"I'll do my best." I got to my feet. "In return maybe you could work on Jade to stop drugging himself to death. It isn't romantic, you know: it's horrible, painful, about the ugliest thing in the world."

She only glowered at me. It's hard work being an angel. No one takes at all kindly to it.

VII

Brigitte was furious. Her cheeks flamed with natural color and her cobalt eyes glittered. I couldn't help wondering if this was how she looked when Jade and B. B. Wilder were fighting over her.

"So he knew all along where she was! I ought to have him sent over for that. Can't I charge him with contributing to her delinquency?"

"Not if you're planning on using me as a witness you can't," I snapped.

She ignored me. "And her, too. Taking Lady Iva off like that. Mating her with some alley cat."

As if on cue, Casper of Valletta squawked loudly and started clawing the deep silver plush covering Brigitte's living room floor. Joel Sirop picked up the tom and spoke soothingly to him.

"It is bad, Brigitte, very bad. Maybe you should let the girl go back to Mobile if she wants to so badly. After three days, you know, it's too late to give Lady Iva a shot. And Corinne is so wild, so uncontrollable—what would stop her the next time Lady Iva comes into season?"

Brigitte's nostrils flared. "I should send her to reform school. Show her what discipline is really like."

"Why in hell do you even want custody over Corinne if all you can think about is revenge?" I interrupted.

She stopped swirling around her living room and turned to frown at me. "Why, I love her, of course. She is my sister, you know."

"Concentrate on that. Keep saying it to yourself. She's not a cat that you can breed and mold to suit your fancy."

"I just want her to be happy when she's older. She won't be if she can't learn to control herself. Look at what happened when she started hanging around trash like that Lily Hellman. She would never have let Lady Iva breed with an alley cat if she hadn't made that kind of friend."

I ground my teeth. "Just because Lily lives in five rooms over a store doesn't make her trash. Look, Brigitte. You wanted to lead your own life. I expect your parents tried keeping you on a short leash. Hell, maybe they even threatened you with reform school. So you started fucking every hulk you could get your hands on. Are you so angry about that that you have to treat Corinne the same way?"

She gaped at me. Her jaw worked but she couldn't find

any words. Finally she went over to a burled oak cabinet that concealed a bar. She pulled out a chilled bottle of Sancerre and poured herself a glass. When she'd gulped it down she sat at her desk.

"Is it that obvious? Why I went after Jade and B. B. and all those boys?"

I hunched a shoulder. "It was just a guess, Brigitte. A guess based on what I've learned about you and your sister and Jade the last two days. He's not such an awful guy, you know, but he clearly was an awful guy for you. And Corinne's lonely and miserable and needs someone to love her. She figures her horse for the job."

"And me?" Her cobalt eyes glittered again. "What do I need? The embraces of my cat?"

"To shed some of those porcupine quills so someone can love you, too. You could've offered me a glass of wine, for example."

She started an ugly retort, then went over to the liquor cabinet and got out a glass for me. "So I bring Flitcraft up to Chicago and stable her. I put Corinne into the filthy public high school. And then we'll all live happily ever after."

"She might graduate." I swallowed some of the wine. It was cold and crisp and eased some of the tension the Le-Blancs and Pierces were putting into my throat. "And in another year she won't run away to Lily's, but she'll go off to Mobile or hit the streets. Now's your chance."

"Oh, all right," she snapped. "You're some kind of saint, I know, who never said a bad word to anyone. You can tell Corinne I'll cut a deal with her. But if it goes wrong you can be the one to stay up at night worrying about her."

I rubbed my head. "Send her back to Mobile, Brigitte. There must be a grandmother or aunt or nanny or someone who really cares about her. With your attitude, life with Corinne is just going to be a bomb waiting for the fuse to blow."

"You can say that again, detective." It was Jade, his bulk filling the double doors to the living room.

Behind him we could hear the housekeeper without being able to see her. "I tried to keep him out, Brigitte, but Corinne let him in. You want me to call the cops, get them to exercise that peace bond?"

"I have a right to ask whoever I want into my own house," came Corinne's muffled shriek.

Squawking and yowling, Casper broke from Joel Sirop's hold. He hurtled himself at the doorway and stuffed his body through the gap between Jade's feet. On the other side of the barricade we could hear Lady Iva's answering yodel and a scream from Corinne—presumably she'd been clawed.

"Why don't you move, Jade, so we can see the action?" I suggested.

He lumbered into the living room and perched his bulk on the edge of a pale grey sofa. Corinne stumbled in behind him and sat next to him. Her muddy skin and lank hair looked worse against the sleek modern lines of Brigitte's furniture than they had in Mrs. Hellman's crowded sitting room.

Brigitte watched the blood drip from Corinne's right hand to the rug and jerked her head at the housekeeper hovering in the doorway. "Can you clean that up for me, Grace?"

When the housekeeper left, she turned to her sister. "Next time you're that angry at me take it out on me, not the cat. Did you really have to let her breed in a back alley?"

"It's all one to Iva," Corinne muttered sulkily. "Just as long as she's getting some she don't care who's giving it to her. Just like you."

Brigitte marched to the couch. Jade caught her hand as she was preparing to smack Corinne.

"Now look here, Brigitte," he said. "You two girls don't belong together. You know that as well as I do. Maybe you think you owe it to your public image to be a mamma to Corinne, but you're not the mamma type. Never have been. Why should you try now?"

Brigitte glared at him. "And you're Mister Wonderful who can sit in judgment on everyone else?"

He shook his massive jade dome. "Nope. I won't claim that. But maybe Corinne here would like to come live with me." He held up a massive palm as Brigitte started to protest. "Not in Uptown. I can get me a place close to here. Corinne can have her horse and see you when you feel calm enough. And when your pure little old cat has her half-breed kittens they can come live with us."

"On Corinne's money," Brigitte spat.

Jade nodded. "She'd have to put up the stake. But I know some guys who'd back me to get started in somethin'. Commodities, somethin' like that."

"You'd be drunk or doped up all the time. And then you'd rape her—" She broke off as he did his ugly-black-slit number with his eyes.

"You'd better not say anything else, Brigitte LeBlanc. Damned well better not say anything. You want me to get up in the congregation and yell that I never touched a piece of ass that shoved itself in my nose, I ain't going to. But you know better'n anyone that I never in my life laid hands on a girl to hurt her. As for the rest . . ." His eyes returned to normal and he put a redwood branch around Corinne's shoulders. "First time I'm drunk or shooting somethin' Corinne comes right back here. We can try it for six months, Brigitte. Just a trial. Rookie camp, you know how it goes."

The football analogy brought her own mean look to Brigitte's face. Before she could say anything Joel bleated in the background, "It sounds like a good idea to me, Brigitte. Really. You ought to give it a try. Lady Iva's nerves will never be stable with the fighting that goes on around her when Corinne is here."

"No one asked you," Brigitte snapped.

"And no one asked me, either," Corinne said. "If you don't agree, I—I'm going to take Lady Iva and run away to New York. And send you pictures of her with litter after litter of alley cats."

The threat, uttered with all the venom she could muster, made me choke with laughter. I swallowed some Sancerre to try to control myself, but I couldn't stop laughing. Jade's mountain rumbled and shook as he joined in. Joel gasped in horror. Only the two LeBlanc women remained unmoved, glaring at each other.

"What I ought to do, I ought to send you to reform school, Corinne Alton LeBlanc."

"What you ought to do is cool out," I advised, putting my glass down on a chrome table. "It's a good offer. Take it. If you don't, she'll only run away."

Brigitte tightened her mouth in a narrow line. "I didn't hire you to have you turn on me, you know."

"Yeah, well, you hired me. You didn't buy me. My job is to help you resolve a difficult problem. And this looks like the best solution you're going to be offered."

"Oh, very well," she snapped pettishly, pouring herself another drink. "For six months. And if her grades start slipping, or I hear she's drinking or doping or anything like that, she comes back here."

I got up to go. Corinne followed me to the door.

"I'm sorry I was rude to you over at Lily's," she muttered shyly. "When the kittens are born you can have the one you like best."

I gulped and tried to smile. "That's very generous of you, Corinne. But I don't think my dog would take too well to a kitten."

"Don't you like cats?" The big brown eyes stared at me poignantly. "Really, cats and dogs get along very well unless their owners expect them not to."

"Like LeBlancs and Pierces, huh?"

She bit her lip and turned her head, then said in a startled voice, "You're teasing me, aren't you?"

"Just teasing you, Corinne. You take it easy. Things are going to work out for you. And if they don't, give me a call before you do anything too rash, okay?"

"And you will take a kitten?"

Just say no, Vic, just say no, I chanted to myself. "Let me think about it. I've got to run now." I fled the house before she could break my resolve any further.

*Wendy Hornsby's has been hailed as writing in the tradition
of Ross MacDonald and Charlotte Armstrong and praised for
her "... skillful sleight-of-hand that borders on witchcraft."
After two books featuring homicide detective Roger Tejeda and
history professor Kate Byrd* (No Harm, Half a Mind), *Wendy
introduced filmmaker sleuth Maggie MacGowen in* Telling
Lies. *Maggie and her supporting cast appear in* Midnight
Baby, Bad Intent, 77ᵗʰ Street Requiem, *and most recently in* A
Hard Light.

*In "Nine Sons," which has been reprinted at least thirty
times in eight languages and received an Edgar Allen Poe
award, a Mystery Scene Magazine Reader award, and Orange
Coast Fiction award, and an Anthony nomination, the Depression and the American Midwest come to life in this star-
tling and moving story.*

nine sons

by Wendy Hornsby

I SAW JANOS BONACHEK'S NAME IN THE PAPER THIS
morning. There was a nice article about his twenty-five years
on the federal bench, his plans for retirement. The Boy Wonder, they called him, but the accompanying photograph
showed him to be nearly bald, a wispy white fringe over his
ears the only remains of his once remarkable head of yellow
hair.

For just a moment, I was tempted to write him, or call
him, to put to rest forever questions I had about the death
that was both a link and a wedge between us. In the end I
didn't. What was the point after all these years? Perhaps
Janos's long and fine career in the law was sufficient atone-
ment, for us all, for events that happened so long ago.

It occurred on an otherwise ordinary day. It was April, but
spring was still only a tease. If anything stood out among
the endless acres of black mud and gray slush, it was two
bright dabs of color: first the blue crocus pushing through a
patch of dirty snow, then the bright yellow head of Janos

Bonachek as he ran along the line of horizon toward his parents' farm after school. Small marvels maybe, the spring crocus and young Janos, but in that frozen place, and during those hard times, surely they were miracles.

The year was 1934, the depths of the Great Depression. Times were bad, but in the small farm town where I had been posted by the school board, hardship was an old acquaintance.

I had arrived the previous September, fresh from teachers' college, with a new red scarf in my bag and the last piece of my birthday cake. At twenty, I wasn't much older than my high-school-age pupils.

Janos was ten when the term began, and exactly the height of ripe wheat. His hair was so nearly the same gold as the bearded grain that he could run through the uncut fields and be no more noticeable than the ripples made by a prairie breeze. The wheat had to be mown before Janos could be seen at all.

On the northern plains, the season for growing is short, a quick breath of summer between the spring thaw and the first frost of fall. Below the surface of the soil, and within the people who forced a living from it, there seemed to be a layer that never had time to warm all the way through. I believe to this day that if the winter hadn't been so long, the chilling of the soul so complete, we would not have been forced to bury Janos Bonachek's baby sister.

Janos came from a large family, nine sons. Only one of them, Janos, was released from chores to attend school. Even then, he brought work with him in the form of his younger brother, Boya. Little Boya was then four or five. He wasn't as brilliant as Janos, but he tried hard. Tutored and cajoled by Janos, Boya managed to skip to the second-grade reader that year.

Around Halloween, that first year, Janos was passed up to me by the elementary teacher. She said she had nothing more to teach him. I don't know that I was any better prepared than she was, except that the high school textbooks were on the shelves in my room. I did my best.

Janos was a challenge. He absorbed everything I had to offer and demanded more, pushing me in his quiet yet insistent way to explain or to find out. He was eager for everything. Except geography. There he was a doubter. Having lived his entire life on a flat expanse of prairie, Janos would not believe the earth was a sphere, or that there were bodies of water vaster than the wheatfields that stretched past his horizon. The existence of mountains, deserts, and oceans, he had to take on faith, like the heavenly world the nuns taught me about in catechism.

Janos was an oddball to his classmates, certainly. I can still see that shiny head bent close to his books, the brow of his pinched little face furrowed as he took in a new set of universal truths from the world beyond the Central Grain Exchange. The other students deferred to him, respected him, though they never played with him. He spent recesses and lunch periods sitting on the school's front stoop, waiting for me to ring the big brass bell and let him back inside. I wonder how that affected him as a judge, this boy who never learned how to play.

Janos shivered when he was cold, but he seemed otherwise oblivious to external discomfort or appearances. Both he and Boya came to school barefoot until there was snow on the ground. Then they showed up in mismatched boots sizes too big, yet no one called attention to them, which I found singular. Janos's coat, even in blizzards, was an old gray blanket that I'm sure he slept under at night. His straight yellow hair stuck out in chunks as if it had been scythed like the wheat. He never acknowledged that he was in any way different from his well-scrubbed classmates.

While this oblivion to discomfort gave Janos an air of stoic dignity, it did impose some hardship on me. When the blizzards came and I knew school should be closed, I went out anyway because I knew Janos would be there, with Boya. If I didn't come to unlock the classroom, I was sure they would freeze waiting.

Getting there was itself a challenge. I boarded in town with the doctor and his wife, my dear friend Martha. When the snow blew in blinding swirls and the road was impassable to any automobile, I would persuade the doctor to harness his team of plow horses to his cutter and drive me out. The doctor made only token protest after the first trip: the boys had been at the school for some time before we arrived, huddled together on the stoop like drifted snow.

Those were the best days, alone, the two boys and I. I would bring books from Martha's shelves, books not always on the school board approved list. We would read together, and talk about the world on the far side of the prairie and how one day we would see it for ourselves. As the snow drifts piled up to the sills outside, we would try to imagine the sultry heat of the tropics, the pitch and roll of the oceans, men in pale suits in electric-lit parlors discussing being and nothingness while they sipped hundred-year-old sherry.

We had many days together. That year the first snow came on All Saints Day and continued regularly until Good Friday. I would have despaired during the ceaseless cold if it weren't for Janos and the lessons I received at home on the evenings of those blizzardy days.

Invariably, on winter nights when the road was impassable and sensible people were at home before the fire, someone would call for the doctor's services. He would harness the cutter, and go. Martha, of course, couldn't sleep until she heard the cutter return. We would keep each other entertained, sometimes until after the sun came up.

Martha had gone to Smith or Vassar. I'm not sure which because Eastern girls' schools were so far from my experience that the names meant nothing to me then. She was my guide to the world I had only seen in magazines and slick-paged catalogues, where people were polished to a smooth and shiny perfection, where long underwear, if indeed any was worn, never showed below their hems. These people were oddly whole, no scars, no body parts lost to farm machinery. In their faces I saw a peace of mind I was sure left them open to the world of ideas. I longed for them, and was sure Martha did as well.

Martha took life in our small community with grace, though I knew she missed the company of other educated women. I had to suffice.

Just as I spent my days preparing Janos, Martha spent her evenings teaching me the social graces I would need if I were ever to make my escape. Perhaps I was not as quick a pupil as Janos, but I was as eager.

Lessons began in the attic where Martha kept her trunks. Packed in white tissue was the elegant trousseau she had brought with her from the East, gowns of wine-colored taffeta moire and green velvet and a pink silk so fine I feared touching it with my callused hands.

I had never actually seen a live woman in an evening gown, though I knew Martha's gowns surpassed the mail-order gowns that a woman might order for an Eastern Star ritual, if she had money for ready-made.

Martha and I would put on the gowns and drink coffee with brandy and read to each other from Proust, or take turns at the piano. I might struggle through a Strauss waltz or the Fat Lady Polka. She played flawless Dvorak and Debussy. This was my finishing school, long nights in Martha's front parlor, waiting for the cutter to bring the doctor home, praying the cutter hadn't overturned, hoping the neighbor he had gone to tend was all right.

When he did return, his hands so cold he needed help out of his layers of clothes, Martha's standard greeting was, "Delivering Mrs. Bonachek?" This was a big joke to us, because, of course, Mrs. Bonachek delivered herself. No one knew how many pregnancies she had had beyond her nine living sons. Poor people, they were rich in sons.

That's what I kept coming back to that early spring afternoon as I walked away from the Bonachek farm. I had seen Janos running across the fields after school. If he hadn't been hurrying home to help his mother, then where had he gone? And where were his brothers?

It lay on my mind.

As I said, the day in question had been perfectly ordinary. I had stayed after my students to sweep the classroom, so it was nearly four before I started for home. As always, I walked the single-lane road toward town, passing the Bonachek farm about halfway. Though underfoot the black earth was frozen hard as tarmac, I was looking for signs of spring, counting the weeks until the end of the school term.

My feet were cold inside my new Sears and Roebuck boots and I was mentally drafting a blistering letter to the company. The catalogue copy had promised me boots that would withstand the coldest weather, so, as an act of faith in Sears, I had invested a good chunk of my slim savings for the luxury of warm feet. Perhaps the copywriter in a Chicago office could not imagine ground as cold as this road.

I watched for Janos's mother as I approached her farm. For three days running, I had seen Mrs. Bonachek working in the fields as I walked to school in the morning, and as I walked back to town in the dusky afternoon. There was no way to avoid her. The distance between the school and the Bonachek farm was uninterrupted by hill or wall or stand of trees.

Mrs. Bonachek would rarely glance up as I passed. Unlike the other parents, she never greeted me, never asked how her boys were doing in school, never suggested I let them out earlier for farm chores. She knew little English, but neither did many of the other parents, or my own.

She was an enigma. Formless, colorless, Mrs. Bonachek seemed no more than a piece of the landscape as she spread seed grain onto the plowed ground from a big pouch in her apron. Wearing felt boots, she walked slowly along the straight furrows, her thin arm moving in a sweep as regular as any motor-powered machine.

Hers was an odd display of initiative, I thought. No one else was out in the fields yet. It seemed to me she risked losing her seed to mildew or to a last spring freeze by planting so early. Something else bothered me more. While I was a dairyman's daughter and knew little about growing wheat, I knew what was expected of farm children. There were six in my family, my five brothers and myself. My mother never went to the barns alone when there was a child at hand: Mrs. Bonachek had nine sons. Why, I wondered, was she working in the fields all alone?

On the afternoon of the fourth day, as had become my habit, I began looking for Mrs. Bonachek as soon as I locked the schoolhouse door. When I couldn't find her, I felt a pang of guilty relief that I wouldn't have to see her that afternoon, call out a greeting that I knew she wouldn't return.

So I walked more boldly, dressing down Sears in language I could never put on paper, enjoying the anarchy of my phrases even as I counted the blue crocus along the road.

Just as I came abreast of the row of stones that served to

define the beginning of the Bonachek driveway, I saw her. She sat on the ground between the road and the small house, head bowed, arms folded across her chest. Her faded calico apron, its big seed pocket looking flat and empty, was spread on the ground beside her. She could have been sleeping, she was so still. I thought she might be sick, and would have gone to her, but she turned her head toward me, saw me, and shifted around until her back was toward me.

I didn't stop. The road curved and after a while I couldn't see her without turning right around. I did look back once and saw Mrs. Bonachek upright again. She had left her apron on the ground, a faded red bundle at the end of a furrow. She gathered up the skirt of her dress, filled it with seed grain, and continued her work. So primitive, I thought. How was it possible she had spawned the bright light that was Janos?

I found Martha in an extravagant mood when I reached home. The weather was frigid, but she, too, had seen the crocus. She announced that we would hold a tea to welcome spring. We would put on the tea frocks from her trunk and invite in some ladies from town. It would be a lark, she said, a coming out. I could invite anyone I wanted.

I still had Mrs. Bonachek on my mind. I couldn't help picturing her rising from her squat in the muddy fields to come sit on Martha's brocade sofa, so I said I would invite her first. The idea made us laugh until I had hiccups. I said the woman had no daughters and probably needed some lively female company.

Martha went to the piano and banged out something suitable for a melodrama. I got a pan of hot water and soaked my cold feet while we talked about spring and the prospect of being warm again, truly warm, in all parts at once. I wondered what magazine ladies did at teas.

We were still planning little sandwiches and petit fours and onions cut into daisies when the doctor came in for supper. There were snowflakes on his beard and I saw snow falling outside, a lacy white curtain over the evening sky. When Martha looked away from the door, I saw tears in her eyes.

"You're late," Martha said to the doctor, managing a smile. "Out delivering Mrs. Bonachek?"

"No such luck." The doctor seemed grim. "I wish that just once the woman would call me in time. She delivered herself again. The baby died, low body temperature I suspect. A little girl. A pretty, perfect little girl."

I was stunned but I managed to blurt, "But she was working in the fields just this afternoon."

Martha and the doctor exchanged a glance that reminded me how much I still had to learn. Then the doctor launched into a speech about some people not having sense enough to take to their beds and what sort of life could a baby born into such circumstances expect, anyway?

"The poor dear," Martha said when he had run down. "She finally has a little girl to keep her company and it dies." She grabbed me by the arm. "We must go offer our consolation."

We put on our boots and coats and waited for the doctor to get his ancient Ford back out of the shed. It made a terrible racket, about which Martha complained gently, but there wasn't enough snow for the cutter. We were both disappointed—the cutter gave an occasion a certain weight.

"Say your piece then leave," the doctor warned as we rattled over the rutted road. "These are private people. They may not understand your intentions."

He didn't understand that Martha and I were suffering a bit of guilt from the fun we had had at poor Mrs. Bonachek's expense. And we were bored. Barn sour, my mother would say. Tired of being cooped up all winter and in desperate need of some diversion.

We stormed the Bonacheks' tiny clapboard house, our offers of consolation translated by a grim-faced Janos. Martha was effusive. A baby girl should have a proper send-off, she said. There needed to be both a coffin and a dress. When was the funeral?

Mrs. Bonachek looked from me to Martha, a glaze over her mud-colored eyes. Janos shrugged his skinny shoulders. There was no money for funerals, he said. When a baby died, you called in the doctor for a death certificate, then the county came for the remains. That was all.

Martha patted Mrs. Bonachek's scaly hands. Not to worry. We would take care of everything. And we did. Put off from our spring tea by the sudden change in the weather, we diverted our considerable social energy to the memorial services.

I found a nice wooden box of adequate size in the doctor's storeroom and painted it white. Martha went up to the attic and brought down her beautiful pink silk gown and an old feather pillow. She didn't even wince as she ran her sewing shears up the delicate hand-turned seams. I wept. She hugged me and talked about God's will being done and Mrs. Bonachek's peasant strength. I was thinking about the spoiled dress.

We worked half the night. We padded the inside of the box with feathers and lined it with pink silk. We made a tiny dress and bonnet to match. The doctor had talked the county into letting us have a plot in the cemetery. It was such a little bit of ground, they couldn't refuse.

We contacted the parish priest, but he didn't want to perform the services. The county cemetery wasn't consecrated and he didn't know the Bonacheks. We only hoped it wasn't a rabbi that was needed because there wasn't one for miles. Martha reasoned that heaven was heaven and the Methodist preacher would have to do, since he was willing.

By the following afternoon everything was ready. The snow had turned to slush but our spirits weren't dampened. We set off, wearing prim navy-blue because Martha said it was more appropriate for a child's funeral than somber black.

When the doctor drove us up to the small house, the entire Bonachek family, scrubbed and brushed, turned out to greet us.

Janos smiled for the first time I could remember. He fingered a frayed necktie that hung below his twine belt. He looked very awkward, but I knew he felt elegant. Everyone, even Boya, wore some sort of shoes. It was a gala, if solemn event.

Mr. Bonachek, a scrawny, pale-faced man, relieved us of the makeshift coffin and led us into the single bedroom. The baby, wrapped in a scrap of calico, lay on the dresser. I unfolded the little silk dress on the bed while Martha shooed Mr. Bonachek out of the room.

"We should wash her," Martha said. A catch in her voice showed that her courage was failing. She began to unwrap the tiny creature. It was then I recognized the calico—Mrs. Bonachek's faded apron.

I thought of the nine sons lined up in the next room and Mrs. Bonachek sitting in the field with her apron spread on the cold ground beside her. Mrs. Bonachek who was rich in sons.

I needed to know how many babies, how many girls, had died before this little one wrapped in the apron. Janos would tell me, Janos who had been so matter-of-fact about the routine business of death. I hadn't the courage at that moment to ask him.

Martha was working hard to maintain her composure. She had the baby dressed and gently laid her in the coffin. The baby was beautiful, her porcelain face framed in soft pink silk. I couldn't bear to see her in the box, like a shop-window doll.

I wanted to talk with Martha about the nagging suspicion that was taking shape in my mind. I hesitated too long.

Janos appeared at the door and I didn't want him to hear what I had to say. Actually, his face was so thin and expectant that it suddenly occurred to me that we hadn't brought any food for a proper wake.

"Janos," Martha whispered. "Tell your mother she may come in now."

Janos led his mother only as far as the threshold when she stopped stubbornly. I went to her, put my arm around her and impelled her to come closer to the coffin. When she resisted, I pushed. I was desperate to see some normal emotion from her. If she had none, what hope was there for Janos?

Finally, she shuddered and reached out a hand to touch the baby's cheek. She said something in her native language. I could understand neither the words nor the tone. It could have been a prayer, it could have been a curse.

When I let her go, she turned and looked at me. For the barest instant there was a flicker in her eyes that showed neither fear nor guilt about what I might have seen the afternoon before. I was disquieted because, for the length of that small glimmer, she was beautiful. I saw who she might have become at another time, in a different place. When the tears at last came to my eyes, they were for her and not for the baby.

Janos and Boya carried the coffin out to the bare front room and set it on the table. The preacher arrived and he gave his best two-dollar service even though there would be no payment. He spoke to the little group, the Bonacheks, Martha, the doctor and I, as if we were a full congregation. I don't remember what he said. I wasn't listening. I traced the pattern of the cheap, worn linoleum floor with my eyes and silently damned the poverty of the place and the cold that seeped in under the door.

We were a small, depressed-looking procession, walking down the muddy road to the county cemetery at the edge of town, singing along to hymns only the preacher seemed to know. At the gravesite, the preacher prayed for the sinless soul and consigned her to the earth. It didn't seem to bother him that his principal mourners didn't understand a word he said.

Somehow, the doctor dissuaded Martha from inviting all of the Bonacheks home for supper—she, too, had belatedly thought about food.

As we walked back from the cemetery, I managed to separate the doctor from the group. I told him what was on my mind, what I had seen in the fields the day before. She had left her bundled apron at the end of a furrow and gone back to her work. I could not keep that guilty knowledge to myself.

The doctor wasn't as shocked as I expected him to be. But he was a man of worldly experience and I was merely a dairyman's daughter—the oldest child, the only girl in a family of five boys.

As the afternoon progressed, the air grew colder, threatening more snow. To this day, whenever I am very cold, I think of that afternoon. Janos, of course, fills that memory.

I think the little ceremony by strangers was a sort of coming out for him. He was suddenly not only a man of the community, but of the world beyond the road that ran between his farm and the schoolhouse, out where mountains and oceans were a possibility. It had been a revelation.

Janos called out to me and I stopped to wait for him, watching him run. He seemed incredibly small, outlined against the flat horizon. He was golden, and oddly ebullient.

Pale sunlight glinted off his bright head as he struggled through the slush on the road. Mud flew off his big boots in thick gobs and I thought his skinny legs would break with the weight of it. He seemed not to notice—mud was simply a part of the season's change, a harbinger of warmer days.

When he caught up, Janos was panting and red in the face. He looked like a wise little old man for whom life held no secrets. As always, he held himself with a stiff dignity that I imagine suited him quite well when he was draped in his judge's robes.

Too breathless to speak, he placed in my hand a fresh blue crocus he had plucked from the slush.

"Very pretty," I said, moved by his gesture. I looked into his smiling face and found courage. "What was the prayer your mother said for the baby?"

He shrugged and struggled for breath. Then he reached out and touched the delicate flower that was already turning brown from the warmth of my hand.

"No prayer," he said. "It's what she says. 'Know peace. Your sisters in heaven wait to embrace you.' "

I put my hand on his shoulder and looked up at the heavy, gathering clouds. "If it's snowing tomorrow," I said, "which books shall I bring?"

Margaret Maron has two major series characters to satisfy
her fans. Sigrid Harald is an unsentimental, compassionate
NYPD detective who appears in eight novels, including Corpus
Christmas, *nominated for an Agatha, an Anthony, and an
American Mystery Award. In 1993,* Bootlegger's Daughter *introduced Judge Deborah Knott, and went on to win an Edgar,
an Agatha, an Anthony, and a Macavity, the first time a single
novel has earned all four awards.* Shooting at Loons *was an
Agatha and Anthony nominee;* Up Jumps the Devil *won an
Agatha. The fifth in the series,* Killer Market, *for which Margaret was given the Key to the City of High Point, N.C.* Shov-
eling Smoke, *a short story collection, will be out soon.*

*In "Lieutenant Harald and the Impossible Gun," a whole
kindergarten class comes under suspicion when Sigrid Harald
focuses on the little details of a case.*

lieutenant harald and the
impossible gun

by Margaret Maron

THE CALENDAR SAID LATE SEPTEMBER, BUT SUMMER
hung on in the city like a visiting uncle who'd overstayed
his welcome and sat out on the front stoop in a smelly sweatshirt, scratching his belly and smoking a cheap cigar all day.
The unseasonable heat had blanketed New York for so long
that the air felt stale and grimy, as if every wino in the city
had breathed it before, replacing oxygen with cheap muscatel
and sewer fumes. Even the trees along the street and scattered through dozens of vest pocket parks drooped beneath
a sun that held in check the cleansing autumn storms that
should strip away wilted, half-turned leaves and leave the
clean grace of bare limbs.

In the air-conditioned coolness of her office, Lieutenant
Sigrid Harald looked up from a report she was typing to see
Detective Tildon standing in the open doorway.

"Could we talk to you a minute, Lieutenant?" His normally cheerful round face wore a look of serious worry. Behind him, equally solemn, stood a younger uniformed

patrolman of similar height and the same sandy-colored hair.

Sigrid pushed the typing stand aside, swung her chair back around to face them and motioned to the chairs in front of her neatly ordered desk. Tildon hesitated a moment before electing to close the door. "Lieutenant, this is my cousin. Officer James Boyle."

As he named his cousin's current Brooklyn posting, the woman acknowledged the introduction with a formal nod.

"Glad to meet you, ma'am," said Boyle, but his heart had sunk at first glance. Tillie had made the lieutenant sound like Wonder Woman and here she was, thin, mid-thirties probably, taller than average, with a long neck and a wide un-smiling mouth. Her thick dark hair was skinned back into a utilitarian knot without even a stray wisp to soften the strong lines of her face.

Boyle was irresistibly reminded of Sister Paula Immaculata, his third grade teacher. Where Sister Paula had worn a long dark habit, Lieutenant Harald wore an equally conceal-ing pantsuit of a shapeless cut which did nothing to flatter. Similar, too, was the way she sat motionless, her slender ringless fingers lightly laced on the desk before her as her wide gray eyes studied him dispassionately. Thus had Sister Paula Immaculata sat and weighed his tales of why he hadn't handed in his arithmetic homework or who had thrown the first punch in that kickball fracas at recess.

"What can I do for you?" asked Lieutenant Harald in her low cool voice; and for the first time since Tillie had pro-posed coming, Boyle felt hopeful. He remembered now that Sister Paula Immaculata had always known when he was telling the truth.

"A man named Ray Macken was shot last night," said Tildon, "and Jimmy—I mean, Officer Boyle thinks he's go-ing to be charged with it."

"Not think, Tillie. *Know*!" said Boyle. "My sergeant gave me the name of a lawyer to get in touch with. A guy who specializes in cases of police shootings."

"And did you shoot this Ray Macken?" she asked mildly.

"Ma'am, I've never fired a gun at all except on the pistol range; but they've got the .38 that killed Ray and it has my fingerprints on it."

"Your own piece?"

"No, ma'am, but it was locked up tight in a property cabinet at the station house and everybody says I had the only key."

Sigrid Harald lifted an eyebrow. "Explain," she said, leaning back in her chair.

The uniformed Boyle looked helplessly at his plainclothes older cousin. His professional training faltered before such intensely personal involvement, as if he simply didn't know where to begin. Sigrid almost smiled as Detective Charles Tildon—Tillie the Toiler to his coworkers—took over with one of his inevitable thick yellow legal pads.

To compensate for his lack of imagination, a lack he was humbly aware of, Tillie followed the book to the letter and was scrupulous about detail. His reports could be a superior's despair, but Sigrid knew that if any vital clues were present at the scene of any crime or had been elicited in a witness's interview, they would appear somewhere in his meticulous notes; and she preferred his thorough plodding to the breezier hotshots in the department who were sloppy about detail and who bordered on insubordination when required to take her orders.

Now she listened quietly as Tillie described Ray Macken, a swaggering native of Boyle's Brooklyn precinct, who'd married the neighborhood beauty and moved to Texas to cash in on the sunbelt boom. His glib and easy manner had started him up half a dozen ladders, but alcohol and an aversion to hard work kept knocking him off.

Three months ago his mother had died and left him the two-family house of his childhood. Since he'd exhausted all the unemployment benefits Texas had to offer, the rental from the top floor and his mother's small insurance benefits were enough to bring him back north to Flatbush with his wife and son.

"He promised her a mansion," growled Boyle, "then he brought her back to an old house that hasn't had a new stick of furniture in thirty years. No air conditioner, no dishwasher in the kitchen, just a beat-up stove and refrigerator from the fifties!"

He lapsed into moody silence.

Sigrid fished four linked silver circles from a small glass bowl on her desk and toyed with them as Tillie resumed his narrative. It was a new Turkish puzzle ring which someone, knowing her fondness for them, had sent to her disassembled. She hadn't quite found the trick of fitting these particular sinuous circlets back into a single band, but it was something to occupy her eyes as she waited for what she suspected was coming.

Emotion always embarrassed her and this was the old familiar tale of high school sweethearts reunited, of a still-beautiful wife who realizes she picked the wrong man, of a young police officer who suddenly falls in love all over again: the secret meetings, the husband's suspicion and jealousy; the bruises where he's hit her in drunken rages.

Then, last night, the tenants upstairs had overheard a loud abusive argument, followed by the banging of the back door as Liz Macken fled to a friend's house. Afterwards, only silence until Ray Macken's body was found early this morning with a .38 bullet lodged just under his heart.

As a woman, Sigrid had remained curiously untouched by love or hate, but as a police officer she knew its motivating force. "Involuntary manslaughter?" she asked.

Tillie shrugged.

"Hey, no way!" cried Boyle. "Liz isn't a killer and anyhow, she couldn't have used that particular gun."

He slumped back down in his chair dispiritedly. "Nobody could have used it except me and I swear I didn't."

"Tell me about that gun," Sigrid said.

"It was four days ago," Boyle began. "Friday, and St. Simon's kindergarten class."

Even though Labor Day had marked the official end of summer vacation, everyone at Boyle's precinct house kept finagling for extra leave time while the heat wave continued and beach weather held. Sergeant Fitzpatrick, the duty officer, had juggled rosters until his temper frayed and he'd made it profanely clear when he tacked up the month's final version that no officer would be excused from duty unless he could produce a death certificate signed by three doctors and an undertaker.

Unfortunately, he'd forgotten about Sister Theresa, which is how Boyle got yanked from patrol duty that hot September morning.

"You'll take over for Sergeant Hanley until further notice," Fitzpatrick had informed him at morning shape-up.

"Hanley?" Boyle was puzzled. Hanley was a real old-timer who was trying to finish out thirty years on the force. He was nearly crippled with arthritis and, as far as Boyle knew, only puttered around the station house and kept the coffee urns full. He'd been on sick leave all week and, except for grousing about coffee, no one seemed to miss him. Boyle was incautious enough to voice that thought to the sergeant.

This earned him a blistering lecture about macho motor jockeys who thought riding around in an air-conditioned patrol car was all there was to being a policeman.

An hour later, a sweaty Jimmy Boyle stood before a blackboard in the briefing room, clutching Hanley's keys, and faced the true reason Fitzpatrick needed a sacrificial goat: Sister Theresa, nineteen wide-eyed five-year-olds, and two of their mothers.

One of those mothers was Liz Macken, cool and lovely in a simple cotton sundress that he'd slipped from her tanned shoulders only a few days earlier in one of their stolen mornings together in his bachelor apartment. As his lover, she made his blood course wildly; today, however, was the first time that he'd seen her in her maternal role and it'd taken him several minutes before he could meet her mischievous smile with a casual smile of his own.

Luckily a fight broke out over a lecture pointer just then and Sister Theresa clucked in dismay as he tried to separate the combatants. Mrs. DiLucca, a six-time grade mother, confiscated the pointer and promised the two kids she'd rap it over their heads if they didn't settle down.

Every September, Sister Theresa taught a unit called "Our Community Helpers" to her kindergarten class at St. Simon's.

Already they had trooped over to the clinic on Arrow Street where a nice nurse had taken their blood pressure and given them tongue depressors, to the local firehouse where they'd slid down the pole and clambered over a pumper truck, and to the branch post office where they'd seen mail sorted and had their hands postmarked with a rubber stamp.

"And today," chirped Sister Theresa, "this nice Officer Boyle is going to show us exactly what policemen do to help our community."

Nineteen pairs of skeptical eyes swung to him and Jimmy Boyle scrapped any thought of giving them a comprehensive view of the department. No way were these kids going to sit still for a lecture on hack licensing, housing violations and the other unexciting details policemen have to keep tabs on. Besides, with Liz sitting there he couldn't concentrate, so he yielded to the kids' appetite for sensationalism and passed out handcuffs for them to examine before herding them upstairs.

The drunk tank was empty for once and a deceptively fragile-looking child got herself wedged between the bars while another shinnied up to the ceiling and swung from the wire-caged light fixture.

He heard Liz say firmly, "Tommy Macken, you get down from there this minute!" and he looked closely at the little acrobat who could have been his son if things had gone differently.

If Liz hadn't thought him dull and square seven years ago.

If Ray hadn't dazzled her with a silky line and visions of the rich life in Texas.

The rest of the hour was just as hectic. In the basement, Boyle showed the children the small outdated lab that no longer got much use since all the complex needs were handled by a central forensic lab elsewhere. They compared hairs under a microscope—Tommy yanked a few from the small blond girl beside him and Liz gave him a quick swat on the bottom. He demonstrated how litmus paper works, then fired several shots from an old .38 into a cotton mattress and retrieved the slugs to show how the markings matched up for positive identification.

"Did that gun ever kill somebody?" they asked eagerly.

Boyle knew they'd be bored with the true story of two derelicts arguing over a bottle of cherry brandy, so he improvised on a television program he'd seen the week before and they ate up the blood and gore. Several grubby little hands had clutched at the pistol, but he put it back in the property cabinet and locked it securely. Of that he was positive.

He had capped the tour by taking every child's fingerprints and warning them mock-ferociously that if any crimes were committed, the department would know whom to pick up. There was a moment of sheepish shuffling and a sudden emptying of pockets.

"Oh dear!" said Sister Theresa as ink pads, handcuffs, a set of picklocks and Sergeant Hanley's keys were returned to him. Liz laughed outright, but Mrs. DiLucca pursed her lips in disapproval.

Upstairs, he had passed out some lollipops from Hanley's desk and managed to wave back as the children filed down the front steps onto a sidewalk shimmering with heat. Sister Theresa had chirped again, "Now aren't policemen *nice*?"

Liz had smiled back at him then, the memory of their last meeting in her eyes, but Boyle didn't think Lieutenant Harald would be interested in that particular detail.

"So you're positive the key to the gun cabinet was still on the ring when the kids gave it back?" asked Tillie.

"It had to be, Tillie, because it was sure there when Sergeant Fitzpatrick asked for the keys this morning. Ballistics got a make on the gun right away and they knew where to go for it. Ever since the kids left, those keys've been locked in my own locker at the station. I stuck them there Friday afternoon and forgot to return them when the sarge said I could go back to my own beat. Nobody needed them. Hanley's still out." Boyle twisted his blue hat in his hands and shook his head. "I just don't see how the gun was taken and then put back."

"No sign of the cabinet's lock or hinges being tampered with?" asked Sigrid.

"No, ma'am," he said unhappily.

"Do you have the M.E.'s report?" she asked Tildon.

Tillie shook his head. "Too soon. But I talked to Dr. Abramson, who did the autopsy. He said the bullet entered about here"—he demonstrated an area just under his left midriff—"and traveled up at an angle to nick the heart and lodge in the pleural cavity. The actual cause of death was internal hemorrhaging. Macken might have lived if he'd been rushed to a hospital in time; instead, he drowned in his own blood, so to speak."

Sigrid looked up from her puzzle ring. "The bullet traveled upward? That means he was standing while the killer sat or—"

"Or the killer stood over him and fired down?" asked Boyle eagerly. "Liz said they had a fight in the kitchen while she was trying to fix herself a glass of iced tea. That old icebox ought to be in a museum the way the frost builds up around the freezer so fast. Ray'd been drinking and he grabbed her. She twisted away and he slipped on a piece of ice and was lying on the floor half-zonked as she ran out the door. What if he never got up? Just lay there till someone who hated him came along and shot him. Liz certainly didn't stop to lock the door. Anybody could've—"

He saw the lieutenant's imperceptible frown. "Yeah," he said, slumping again. "That damn gun."

"Did the tenants or neighbors hear the shot?" asked Sigrid.

Young Boyle shook his head. "No. The neighbors on either side had their windows closed with air conditioners running and the tenants said they slept with a fan that was so noisy it could drown out fire engines."

"Abramson said Macken wasn't shot from close range," said Tillie, reading from his notes. "No powder burns and the fact that the bullet only penetrated four or five inches show that; but there's a bruise around the wound that puzzles him. Maybe he fought with his killer first and got punched there? And all Abramson can give us is an approximation of when the shooting occurred since, like I said, Macken didn't die as soon as he was shot."

Sigrid nodded and resumed her manipulation of the four silver circles. Young Boyle looked at his cousin and started to speak, but Tillie signaled for silence. After a moment, she lifted those penetrating gray eyes and said to Boyle, "What did Tommy Macken give back?"

Boyle looked blank. "Give back?"

Her tone was coldly patient. "In describing the tour you gave those unruly children, you said that several of them had pocketed different items which your remark about fingerprints caused them to give back. What did Tommy Macken take?"

Boyle thought hard, visualizing the scene in his mind. "Nothing," he said finally. "He never touched the keys, if that's what you're thinking. It was the other kids who took things, not Tommy."

"I rather doubt that a child as agile and inquisitive as you've described would have gone home empty-handed," she said dryly.

Three of the silver circles lay perfectly stacked between her slender fingers. Delicately, she inserted a knob of the fourth circlet between the first two and gently rotated it until all four locked into place and formed one ring. She examined it for a moment, then returned it to the glass bowl on her desk with a small sigh of regret at how easy it had been to solve.

Equally regretful was the look she gave Tillie's young cousin. "I'm sorry, Boyle, but my first opinion stands. I really don't see how anyone else could have killed him except Mrs. Macken."

"You're nuts!" cried Boyle. He pushed up from his chair so hard that it scraped loudly against the tiled floor. He glared at Detective Tildon angrily. "You said she could help, Tillie. Is this how? By pinning it on Liz?"

"Sit down, Boyle." There was icy authority in Sigrid Harald's voice. She pushed her telephone toward him. "Someone must still be posted at the Macken house. Call."

Resentfully he dialed and when one of his fellow officers from the precinct answered, he identified first himself and then Lieutenant Harald, who gave crisp suggestions as to where he should search and what he should search for. She held on to the receiver and only a few minutes had elapsed before the unseen officer returned to his end and admiringly reported, "Right where you thought, Lieutenant—stuck down in one of the garbage pails in the alley. It's already on its way to the lab."

•   •   •

"An ice pick?" whispered Jimmy Boyle. "He was *stabbed* first?"

"First and only, I'm afraid," said Sigrid. "It was hot last night. You said she was trying to make iced tea when the fight began. A lot of those old refrigerators only make chunks of ice, not cubes, so it's logical to assume she had an ice pick in her hand. Afterwards, she must have remembered your lecture on rifling marks and pushed that slug into the wound to make it look as if an impossible gun had shot her husband."

"And the blow when she stabbed him with the pick must have made the bruise that bothered Abramson," Tillie mused.

She nodded. "Of course, someone will have to question the boy—make him admit he palmed one of those demonstration slugs and that his mother had confiscated it. He may have bragged about it to some of the other children."

"Sorry, Jimmy," Tildon said, awkwardly patting the stunned young patrolman's shoulder.

Boyle stood up and he still wore a dazed expression. "Not your fault, Tillie." Purpose returned to his face. "I'm still going to call that lawyer the sarge told me about. If Liz did stab Ray, it's got to be self-defense, right?"

"Right," Tillie answered sturdily; but after his cousin had departed, he turned back to Sigrid. "What do you think, Lieutenant?"

She shrugged. "The stabbing might not have been premeditated, but driving the slug into him definitely was. And didn't Abramson say Macken didn't die immediately? The prosecution's bound to bring that up."

Sigrid pulled the typing stand back in place and scanned the half-completed report Tillie had interrupted.

He started to leave, then paused in the doorway. "I didn't think you knew much about kids. What made you guess Tommy took that slug?"

"I have cousins, too," Sigrid said grimly. "They all have children. And all the children have sticky little fingers."

Her own slender fingers attacked the keyboard in slashing precision and Tillie was careful not to grin until he'd pulled the door closed behind him.

a predatory woman

by Sharyn McCrumb

"SHE LOOKS A PROPER MURDERESS, DOESN'T she?" said Ernie Sleaford, tapping the photo of a bleached blonde. His face bore that derisive grin he reserved for the "puir doggies," his term for unattractive women.

With a self-conscious pat at her own more professionally lightened hair, Jackie Duncan nodded. Because she was twenty-seven and petite, she had never been the object of Ernie's derision. When he shouted at her, it was for more professional reasons—a missed photo opportunity or a bit of careless reporting. She picked up the unappealing photograph. "She looks quite tough. One wonders that children would have trusted her in the first place."

"What did they know, poor lambs? We never had a woman like our Erma before, had we?"

Jackie studied the picture, wondering if the face were truly evil, or if their knowledge of its possessor had colored the likeness. Whether or not it was a cruel face, it was certainly a plain one. Erma Bradley had dumpling features with gooseberry eyes, and that look of sullen defensiveness that plain women often have in anticipation of slights to come.

Ernie had marked the photo *Page One*. It was not the sort of female face that usually appeared in the pages of *Stellar*, a tabloid known for its daily photo of Princess Diana, and for its bosomy beauties on page three. A beefy woman with a thatch of badly bleached hair had to earn her way into the tabloids, which Erma Bradley certainly had. Convicted of four child murders in 1966, she was serving a life sentence in Holloway Prison in north London.

Gone, but not forgotten. Because she was Britain's only female serial killer, the tabloids kept her memory green with frequent stories about her, all accompanied by that menacing 1965 photo of the scowling, just-arrested Erma. Most of the recent articles about her didn't even attempt to be plausible: *Erma Bradley: Hitler's Illegitimate Daughter; Children's Ghosts Seen Outside Erma's Cell*; and, the October favorite, *Is Erma Bradley a Vampire?* That last one was perhaps the most apt, because it acknowledged the fact that the public hardly thought of her as a real person anymore; she was just another addition to the pantheon of monsters, taking her place alongside Frankenstein, Dracula, and another overrated criminal, Guy Fawkes. Thinking up new excuses to use the old Erma picture was Ernie Sleaford's specialty. Erma's face was always good for a sales boost.

Jackie Duncan had never done an Erma story. Jackie had been four years old at the time of the infamous trial, and later, with the crimes solved and the killers locked away, the case had never particularly interested her. "I thought it was her boyfriend, Sean Hardie, who actually did the killing," she said, frowning to remember the details of the case.

Stellar's editor sneered at her question. "Hardie? I never thought he had a patch on Erma for toughness. Look at him now. He's completely mental, in a prison hospital, making no more sense than a vegetable marrow. That's how you *ought* to be with the lives of four kids on your conscience. But not our Erma! Got her university degree by telly, didn't she? Learned to talk posh in the cage? And now a bunch of bloody do-gooders have got her out!"

Jackie, who had almost tuned out this tirade as she contemplated her new shade of nail varnish, stared at him with renewed interest. "I hadn't heard that, Sleaford! Are you sure it isn't another of your fairy tales?" She grinned. "*Erma Bradley, Bride of Prince Edward?* That was my favorite."

Ernie had the grace to blush at the reminder of his last Erma headline, but he remained solemn. "S'truth, Jackie. I had it on the quiet from a screw in Holloway. She's getting out next week."

"Go on! It would have been on every news show in Britain by now! Banner headlines in the *Guardian*. Questions asked in the House."

"The prison officials are keeping it dark. They don't want Erma to be pestered by the likes of us upon her release. She wants to be let alone." He smirked. "I had to pay dear for this bit of information, I can tell you."

Jack smiled. "Poor mean Ernie! Where do I come into it, then?"

"Can't you guess?"

"I think so. You want Erma's own story, no matter what."

"Well, we can write that ourselves in any case. I have Paul working on that already. What I really need is a new picture, Jackie. The old cow hasn't let herself be photographed in twenty years. Wants her privacy, does our Erma. I think *Stellar*'s readers would like to take a butcher's at what Erma Bradley looks like today, don't you?"

"So they don't hire her as the nanny." Jackie let him finish laughing before she turned the conversation round to money.

The cell was beginning to look the way it had when she first arrived. Newly swept and curtainless, it was a ten-by-six-foot rectangle containing a bed, a cupboard, a table and a chair, a wooden wash basin, a plastic bowl and jug, and a bucket. Gone were the posters and the photos of home. Her books were stowed away in a Marks & Spencers shopping bag.

Ruthie, whose small, sharp features earned her the nickname Minx, was sitting on the edge of the bed, watching her pack. "Taking the lot, are you?" she asked cheerfully.

The thin dark woman stared at the array of items on the

table. "I suppose not," she said, scowling. She held up a tin of green tooth powder. "Here. D'you want this, then?"

The Minx shrugged and reached for it. "Why not? After all, you're getting out, and I've a few years to go. Will you write to me when you're on the outside?"

"You know that isn't permitted."

The younger woman giggled. "As if that ever stopped you." She reached for another of the items on the bed. "How about your Christmas soap? You can get more on the outside, you know."

She handed it over. "I shan't want freesia soap ever again."

"Taking your posters, love? Anyone would think you'd be sick of them by now."

"I am. I've promised them to Senga." She set the rolled-up posters on the bed beside Ruthie, and picked up a small framed photograph. "Do you want this, then, Minx?"

The little blonde's eyes widened at the sight of the grainy snapshot of a scowling man. "Christ! It's Sean, isn't it? Put it away. I'll be glad when you've taken that out of here."

Erma Bradley smiled and tucked the photograph in among her clothes. "I shall keep this."

Jackie Duncan seldom wore her best silk suit when she conducted interviews, but this time she felt that it would help to look both glamorous and prosperous. Her blond hair, shingled into a stylish bob, revealed shell-shaped earrings of real gold, and her calf leather handbag and shoes were an expensive matched set. It wasn't at all the way a working *Stellar* reporter usually dressed, but it lent Jackie an air of authority and professionalism that she needed in order to profit from this interview.

She looked around the shabby conference room, wondering if Erma Bradley had ever been there, and, if so, where she had sat. In preparation for the new assignment, Jackie had read everything she could find on the Bradley case: the melodramatic book by the BBC journalist; the measured prose of the prosecuting attorney; and a host of articles from more reliable newspapers than *Stellar*. She had begun to be interested in Erma Bradley and her deadly lover, Sean Har-

die: *the couple who slays together stays together?* The anal-
yses of the case had made much of the evidence and horror
at the thought of child murder, but they had been at a loss
to provide motive, and they had been reticent about details
of the killings themselves. There was a book in that, and it
would earn a fortune for whoever could get the material to
write it. Jackie intended to find out more than she had uncovered, but first she had to find Erma Bradley.

Her Sloan Ranger outfit had charmed the old cats in the
prison office into letting her in to pursue the story in the first
place. The story they thought she was after. Jackie glanced
at herself in the mirror. Very useful for impressive old sahibs,
this posh outfit. Besides, she thought, why not give the prison
birds a bit of a fashion show?

The six inmates, dressed in shapeless outfits of polyester,
sprawled in their chairs and stared at her with no apparent
interest. One of them was reading a Barbara Cartland novel.

"Hello, girls!" said Jackie in her best nursing home voice.
She was used to jollying up old ladies for feature stories, and
she decided that this couldn't be much different. "Did they
tell you what I'm here for?"

More blank stares, until a heavyset redhead asked, "You
ever do it with a woman?"

Jackie ignored her. "I'm here to do a story about what it's
like in prison. Here's your chance to complain, if there are
things you want changed."

Grudgingly then, they began to talk about the food, and
the illogical, unbending rules that governed every part of
their lives. The tension eased as they talked, and she could
tell that they were becoming more willing to confide in her.
Jackie scribbled a few cursory notes to keep them talking.
Finally one of them said that she missed her children:
Jackie's cue.

As if on impulse, she put down her notepad. "Children!"
she said breathlessly. "That reminds me! Wasn't Erma Bradley a prisoner here?"

They glanced at each other. "So?" said the dull-eyed
woman with unwashed hair.

A ferrety blonde, who seemed more taken by Jackie's

glamour than the older ones, answered eagerly, "I knew her! We were best friends!"

"To say the least, Minx," said the frowsy embezzler from Croyden.

Jackie didn't have to feign interest anymore. "Really?" she said to the one called Minx. "I'd be terrified! What was she like?"

They all began to talk about Erma now.

"A bit reserved," said one. "She never knew who she could trust, because of her rep, you know. A lot of us here have kids of our own, so there was feeling against her. In the kitchen, they used to spit in her food before they took it to her. And sometimes, new girls would go at her to prove they were tough."

"That must have taken nerve!" cried Jackie. "I've seen her pictures!"

"Oh, she didn't look like that anymore!" said Minx. "She'd let her hair go back to its natural dark color, and she was much smaller. Not bad, really. She must have lost fifty pounds since the trial days!"

"Do you have a snapshot of her?" asked Jackie, still doing her best impression of breathless and impressed.

The redhead laid a meaty hand on Minx's shoulder. "Just a minute. What are you really here for?"

Jackie took a deep breath. "I need to find Erma Bradley. Can you help me? I'll pay you."

A few minutes later, Jackie was saying a simpering goodbye to the warden, telling her that she'd have to come back in a few days for a follow-up. She had until then to come up with a way to smuggle in two bottles of Glenlivet: the price on Erma Bradley's head. Ernie would probably make her pay for the liquor out of her own pocket. It would serve him right if she got a book deal out of it on the side.

The flat could have used a coat of paint, and some better quality furniture, but that could wait. She was used to shabbiness. What she liked best about it was its high ceiling and the big casement window overlooking the moors. From that window you could see nothing but hills and heather and sky; no roads, no houses, no people. After twenty-four years in the beehive of a women's prison, the solitude was blissful. She spent hours each day just staring out that window, knowing that she could walk on the moors whenever she liked, without guards or passes or physical restraints.

Erma Bradley tried to remember if she had ever been alone before. She had lived in a tiny flat with her mother until she finished O levels, and then, when she'd taken the secretarial job at Hadlands, there had been Sean. She had gone into prison at the age of twenty-three, an end to even the right to privacy. She could remember no time when she could have had solitude, to get to know her own likes and dislikes. She had gone from Mum's shadow to Sean's. She kept his picture, and her mother's, not out of love, but as a reminder of the prisons she had endured before Holloway.

Now she was learning that she liked plants, and the music of Sibelius. She liked things to be clean, too. She wondered if she could paint the flat by herself. It would never look clean until she covered those dingy green walls.

She reminded herself that she could have had a house, *if.* If she had given up some of that solitude. Sell your story to a book publisher; sell the film rights to this movie company. Keith, her long-suffering attorney, dutifully passed along all the offers for her consideration. The world seemed willing to throw money at her, but all she wanted was for it to go away. The dowdy but slender Miss Emily Kay, newborn at forty-seven, would manage on her own, with tinned food and second-hand furniture, while the pack of journalists went baying after Erma Bradley, who didn't exist anymore. She wanted solitude. She never thought about those terrible months with Sean, the things they did together. For twenty-four years she had not let herself remember any of it.

Jackie Duncan looked up at the gracefully ornamented stone building, carved into apartments for working-class people. The builders in that gentler age had worked leaf designs into the stonework framing the windows, and they had set gargoyles at a corner of each roof. Jackie made a mental note of this useful detail; yet another monster has been added to the building.

In the worn but genteel hallway, Jackie checked the names

on mailboxes to make sure that her information was correct. There it was: E. Kay. She hurried up the stairs with only a moment's thought to the change in herself these past few weeks. When Ernie first gave her the assignment, she might have been fearful of confronting a murderess, or she might have gone upstairs with the camera poised to take the shot just as Erma Bradley opened her door, and then she would have fled. But now she was as anxious to meet the woman as she would be to interview a famous film star. More so, because this celebrity was hers alone. She had not even told Ernie that she had found Erma. This was her show, not *Stellar*'s. Without another thought about what she would say, Jackie knocked at the lair of the beast.

After a few moments, the door opened partway, and a small dark-haired woman peered nervously out at her. The woman was thin, and dressed in a simple green jumper and skirt. She was no longer the brassy blonde of the sixties. But the eyes were the same. The face was still Erma Bradley's.

Jackie was brisk. "May I come in, Miss *Kay*? You wouldn't want me to pound on your door calling out your real name, would you?"

The woman fell back and let her enter. "I suppose it wouldn't help to tell you that you're mistaken?" No trace remained of her Midlands accent. She spoke in quiet, cultured tones.

"Not a hope. I swotted for weeks to find you, dear."

"Couldn't you just leave me alone?"

Jackie sat down on the threadbare brown sofa and smiled up at her hostess. "I suppose I could arrange it. I could, for instance, *not* tell the BBC, the tabloids, and the rest of the world what you look like, and where you are."

The woman looked down at her ringless hands. "I haven't any money," she said.

"Oh, but you're worth a packet all the same, aren't you? In all the years you've been locked up, you never said anything except, *I didn't do it*, which is rubbish, because the world knows you did. You taped the Doyle boy's killing on a bloody tape recorder!"

The woman hung her head for a moment, turning away.

"What do you want?" she said at last, sitting in the chair by the sofa.

Jackie Duncan touched the other woman's arm. "*I want you to tell me about it.*"

"No. I can't. I've forgotten."

"No, you haven't. Nobody could. And that's the book the world wants to read. Not this mealymouthed rubbish the others have written about you. I want you to tell me every single detail, all the way through. That's the book I want to write." She took a deep breath, and forced a smile. "And in exchange, I'll keep your identity and whereabouts a secret, the way Ursula Bloom did when she interviewed Crippen's mistress in the fifties."

Erma Bradley shrugged. "I don't read crime stories," she said.

The light had faded from the big window facing the moors. On the scarred pine table a tape recorder was running, and in the deepening shadows, Erma Bradley's voice rose and fell with weary resignation, punctuated by Jackie's eager questions.

"I don't know," she said again.

"Come on. Think about it. Have a biscuit while you think. Sean didn't have sex with the Allen girl, but did he make love to *you* afterwards? Do you think he got an erection while he was doing the strangling?"

A pause. "I didn't look."

"But you made love after he killed her?"

"Yes."

"On the same bed?"

"But later. A few hours later. After we had taken away the body. It was Sean's bedroom, you see. It's where we always slept."

"Did you picture the child's ghost watching you do it?"

"I was twenty-two. He said— He used to get me drunk— and I—"

"Oh, come on, Erma. There's no bloody jury here. Just tell me if it turned you on to watch Sean throttling kids. When he did it, were both of you naked, or just him?"

"Please, I— Please!"

"All right, Erma. I can have the BBC here in time for the wake-up news."

"Just him."

An hour later. "Do stop sniveling, Erma. You lived through it once, didn't you? What's the harm in talking about it? They can't try you again. Now come on, dear, answer the question."

"Yes. The little boy—Brian Doyle—he was quite brave, really. Kept saying he had to take care of his mum, because she was divorced now, and asking us to let him go. He was only eight, and quite small. He even offered to fight us if we'd untie him. When Sean was getting the masking tape out of the cupboard, I went up to him, and I whispered to him to let the boy go, but he . . ."

"There you go again, Erma. Now I've got to shut the machine off again while you get hold of yourself."

She was alone now. At least, the reporter woman was gone. Just before eleven, she had scooped up her notes and her tape recorder, and the photos of the dead children she had brought from the photo archives, and she'd gone away, promising to return in a few days to "put the finishing touches on the interview." The dates and places and forensic details she could get from the other sources, she'd said.

The reporter had gone, and the room was empty, but Miss Emily Kay wasn't alone anymore. Now Erma Bradley had got in as well.

She knew, though, that no other journalists would come. This one, Jackie, would keep her secret well enough, but only to ensure the exclusivity of her own book. Other than that, Miss Emily Kay would be allowed to enjoy her freedom in the shabby little room overlooking the moors. But it wasn't a pleasant retreat any longer, now that she wasn't alone. Erma had brought the ghosts back with her.

Somehow the events of twenty-five years ago had become more real when she told them than when she lived them. It had been so confused back then. Sean drank a lot, and he liked her to keep him company in that. And it happened so quickly the first time, and then there was no turning back. But she never let herself think about it. It was Sean's doing, she would tell herself, and then that part of her mind would close right down, and she would turn her attention to something else. At the trial, she had thought about the hatred that she could almost touch, flaring at her from nearly everyone in the courtroom. She couldn't think then, for if she broke down, they would win. They never put her on the stand. She answered no questions, except to say when a microphone was thrust in her face, *I didn't do it.* And then later in prison there were adjustments to make, and bad times with the other inmates to be faced. She didn't need a lot of sentiment dragging her down as well. *I didn't do it* came to have a truth for her: it meant, I am no longer the somebody who did that. I am small, and thin, and well-spoken. The ugly, ungainly monster is gone.

But now she had testified. Her own voice had conjured up the images of Sarah Allen calling out for her mother, and of Brian Doyle, offering to sell his bike to ransom himself, for his mum's sake. The hatchet-faced blonde, who had told them to shut up, who had held them down . . . she was here. And she was going to live here, too, with the sounds of weeping, and the screams. And every tread on the stair would be Sean, bringing home another little lad for a wee visit.

I didn't do it, she whispered. And it had come to have another meaning. *I didn't do it.* Stop Sean Hardie from hurting them. Go to the police. Apologize to the parents during the years in prison. Kill myself from the shame of it. *I didn't do it*, she whispered again. *But I should have.*

Ernie Sleaford was more deferential to her now. When he heard about the new book, and the size of her advance, he realized that she was a player, and he had begun to treat her with a new deference. He had even offered her a raise, in case she was thinking of quitting. But she wasn't going to quit. She quite enjoyed her work. Besides, it was so amusing now to see him stand up for her when she came into his grubby little office.

"We'll need a picture of you for the front page, love," he said in his most civil tones. "Would you mind if Denny took your picture, or is there one you'd rather use?"

Jackie shrugged. "Let him take one. I just had my hair done. So I make the front page as well?"

"Oh yes. We're devoting the whole page to Erma Bradley's suicide, and we want a sidebar of your piece: *I Was the Last to See the Monster Alive*. It will make a nice contrast. Your picture beside pudding-faced Erma."

"I thought she looked all right for forty-seven. Didn't the picture I got turn out all right?"

Ernie looked shocked. "We're not using that one, Jackie. We want to remember her the way she *was*. A vicious ugly beastie in contrast to a pure young thing like yourself. Sort of a moral statement, like."

Carolyn Wheat has been a lawyer for the New York Legal Aid Society, and the New York City Police Department. Currently a full-time writer and teacher of writing, her novels, Dead Man's Thoughts *(nominated for an Edgar),* Where Nobody Dies, Fresh Kills, Mean Streak *(nominated for an Edgar), and the forthcoming* Acid Test, *feature Cass Jameson. Cass is a Brooklyn criminal lawyer who focuses on the plights and pleasures of city dwellers trying to manage life in the Biggest Apple. Carolyn's short stories, which have won an Agatha award and been nominated for Macavity and Anthony awards, are varied and masterful, providing evidence of the range of her vision and voice.*

In "Life for Short," a woman's journey toward her own death takes a decided detour.

life, for short

by Carolyn Wheat

WHEN YOU'RE DYING, YOU DON'T GET TO SLEEP the way you used to. There are tubes. You lie on your back, propped up by pillows, so your overworked lungs grab all the air they can get. At home, you loved curling into a ball, arms wrapped around your body, knees folded up to your chest. Compact, childlike, comfortable. At home, you had a choice.

Nothing here is the way it was at home. Everything's white: sheets, walls, nurses, food. Shrouds.

Excuse that, please. Excursions into morbidity are not appreciated by the living.

I go in and out of consciousness now. It's better that way. Less boring, for one thing. Less pain, for another. Face it, dying wouldn't be so bad if it weren't for the pain. Pain is my pet raven, eating my liver day by day, night by night. (I think often of Prometheus; at least he got fire in return for his pain. What was it I received?)

It grows fatter, sleeker, my black bird, while I waste away

to a weight I haven't known since twelve. If then. I was a tad chubby in my youth.

My youth. It wasn't so long ago, which is the sad part. New nurses sometimes have to leave the room, tears in their eyes, when they see me for the first time. "She's so young," I hear them say in the hall.

It's not true. I'm in early middle age—or what would be early middle age if I were going to have an old age. Since I'm not . . .

Morbidity again. That's what happens when you tumble down the rabbit hole into the world of death. Nothing's the same. The life you once had is stripped away, piece by piece, replaced by a white world with new rules, new importances. Meds are important: how many you take, how often, with what degree of cooperation. Needles are important. Starched white vampires appear at all hours, drawing blood I feel I can scarcely spare at this point. I tell them I gave at the office, but my attempt at humor is not appreciated. The syringe fills with my bright red life as I lie and watch, turning whiter.

It's like a convent, the hospital. You leave the world behind and take vows of poverty, chastity, obedience. Poverty is relative; I probably still have a few bucks on the outside, in the Bank of New York, but what could it buy me? A new liver? A box of Godiva chocolates?

Chastity is pretty much a given. I haven't the strength or the inclination to entertain myself, let alone a man. Once in a while my fingers approach the little mouse between my legs and I pet her. But she doesn't respond; the tiny dancer that used to rouse herself and give me so much pleasure seems to have passed on before the rest of me.

Obedience is the toughie. Never my best thing, and now that too is a given. Nurses must be obeyed. Doctor must be obeyed. My hungry raven must be obeyed. The only thing that breaks the rules is my body, my Judas body. It wets the bed, it throws up the white dinner. It either won't produce the bowel movement Nurse insists on, or it lets go as soon as the sheets have been changed. It embarrassed me terribly at first. How could it not? I was breaking childhood's first taboo, soiling everything, losing control. I cried, blushed, apologized.

Now I take a secret pleasure every time my body makes a mess. It's the only rebellion I've got left.

Except for The Plan.

The Plan keeps me going. The Plan lets my wandering mind focus, gives me a purpose beyond waiting for the next awkward visit from the next old friend who hides her shock at my wasted body and bald head, telling me I look wonderful. The Plan fills the time between crossword puzzles.

I once saw a great crossword puzzle clue: Life, for short. I don't remember how many letters, or if it was across or down. The clue itself entranced me: Life, for short. What could be shorter than life? Who would want an abbreviation for the all-too-little time we spend on Planet Earth?

When I first became a novice in the convent of death, I fought the idea altogether. I wasn't ready. I tried bargaining with the doctors, with my pet raven, with God. Two more years, just two—so I can get the spring list out, make senior editor. Maybe even meet someone. A decent guy, not a New York City bastard. Okay, one year. Forget senior editor, forget the guy. I'll just pick up one-night stands. What the hell, I don't have to worry about AIDS anymore.

When it became very clear I was never going to leave the white convent, I turned my face to the wall and stopped eating. I cried a lot, slow silent tears that slid down my face into my pillow. I cried for everything and everyone I was leaving behind, even people I hadn't thought of for years, like my crazy Aunt Regina and Bobby Slocum, the boy who hit me with a baseball bat in Cherokee Park. Like my fifth-grade teacher, Sister Mary Magdalen, who let me read all my compositions in front of the class. Like Wendy Bentine, who stole my first boyfriend, Harold Kimmerling, in ninth grade. (Terminal illness didn't make me any more charitable; I hoped she'd already died from a brain tumor.)

Then The Plan came to me. I had to die. The script said so. No rewrites. Okay. I can live with that.

Then let *me* write the damn thing, let me direct. Let me choose when and how. Let me kill the horrible black bird before it eats my whole liver.

Tools. I needed tools. Tools of death were all around me, needles, scalpels, poisons. How to get them, that was the rub. Novices in the convent of death aren't allowed near the sacred objects.

I started with pills. Traditional, time-honored method. Slip one under your tongue while you swallow the water, then take it out and hoard it. Pretty soon, I had a nice little stash, ready for use. Pretty soon the hard-faced West Indian night nurse opened my nightstand drawer to hand me a book, found my precious relics, and flushed them down the toilet.

I was too mad to cry. I cursed her out, called her every dirty name I could think of. I went into a tantrum I would have been ashamed to throw at two, kicking and screaming and pounding my chicken-bone arms against the bed. I dislodged all the IVs and ended up spending the night in restraints. Tethered, like the heroine in a silent movie, waiting for the Midnight Special to round the bend, hoping the hero would get there first.

He wouldn't, of course. Not in this movie. In this movie, the villain was going to win. No happy endings here. Very post-modern, this movie.

Part of me hoped the nurse would get fed up and put the pillow over my face as I lay there, helpless to stop her strong black arms.

Not a bad idea. Could I do it myself? Could I, in cold blood, hold a pillow over my face until my lungs stopped gulping air I no longer wanted, no longer had faith in?

Not tonight, not in restraints. Tomorrow night. I'd be good as gold the next day, sweetly apologetic. Dry of bed. A model patient. And the next night, free of restraints, the heroine liberated from the railroad tracks, I'd carefully lift the pillow from under my head and hold it as hard as I could over my face.

"What you standin' there for, like a bump on a log?" Nurse's Jamaican accent cuts through the quiet night. "And poor Mrs. Rosen lyin' in 3B needin' her bedpan emptied? Get a move on, you lazy—" She stands there, hands on her hips, talking in that hard-edged voice they all have, loud enough for the whole floor to hear.

Don't call me lazy, you stupid old bag, is what I want to say but don't. I know Mrs. Rosen needs her bedpan emptied every two hours. Her kidneys are about gone, they say. And so is she.

You can see it in her eyes. Sunken eyes, in a face like a raisin. Like a skinny old hen cooked up for dinner when you killed all the fat ones already.

I walk toward 3B, but I take it slow. Partly to spite that Nurse. Who does she think she is? If she was any good she'd be on days instead of the lobster shift with the losers. By which I don't mean me, because I have ambition, but you should see some of the other orderlies. Real geeks.

But that's not the real reason I don't rush to 3B. Once it was a pleasure to visit Mrs. Rosen, to talk to her, to do for her. Once she was alive.

It's not like I'm afraid of death. Hell, on the C-ward, you better not be afraid of death. It's just that I hate when it takes so long, when a nice lady like Mrs. R starts losing the things that made her special: the way she read the *Times* all the way through every Sunday, then let me have the Arts & Leisure section so I could read about the Broadway plays. The way she laughed when I told her I wanted to be an actor—a nice laugh, like she thought it could really happen and was already excited to think she knew me when I was just an orderly. The way she wrote little cards to her grand-children, block printing for the little one just learning to read. The way she used to knit—or was it crochet?

It's been a long time since Mrs. R's hands moved through the air, her needles clicking, like a spider spinning a colored web.

Nurse is right, of course. Mrs. R's bedpan is full. I lift her real carefully—which isn't hard 'cause she only weighs eighty pounds or so—and slide the pan from under her without spilling on the bed.

Is tonight the night?

I look at her—I take a really good look at Mrs. R, who came in six months ago like a cheerful little sparrow and is now a dead, half-decayed bird you find under fall leaves. I remember her quick fingers, her sharp old-lady eyes, her calling me ''Mr. Barrymore'' after her favorite actor.

I look at the foot of her bed and see the bird. At first, when the patients come in, the birds are like crows, black and kind of scary, but not big. Then they get bigger, fatter, as the patients get skinnier. Finally, when their time is almost up, the bird is a giant, red-eyed vulture waiting to strip the body.

Mrs. R's vulture is bigger than her now. If I don't do something, that bloodred beak will rip the poor lady like a chainsaw.

I've seen it before. I saw it with Mr. Fanelli in 3G, then with Kenny Foster, who was only sixteen when he died. I remember what Kenny's family said the day he finally went: "Thank God, Doctor," his mother said. "Thank God his suffering is over."

They were right to thank God. They were wrong to thank the doctor. It wasn't him saved Kenny from the vulture.

It was me.

And tonight I'll save Mrs. R. It's the least I can do for her.

My best friend Sandy, the one who comes to see me most often, who brings me crossword puzzle books and chocolate milkshakes and news of the publishing world I no longer really care about, is a Zen person.

Sandy told me a story when I first got sick. A Zen story. A man is chased by a tiger. He runs and runs until he finally falls over a cliff, where sharp rocks way below mean certain death. On the way down, he grabs a root and dangles over the rocks, the tiger still snarling at him from the top of the cliff. Death in either direction. He sees two strawberries growing from the side of the cliff. Reaching out his free hand, he plucks them and puts them into his mouth. "How sweet they tasted!"

That was the punchline: how sweet they tasted. I said I wanted my strawberries poisoned, and Sandy laughed un-easily. Clearly I hadn't gotten the point, but I was serious. Poisoned strawberries. How sweet they would taste!

I make it sound as though I was always lucid, always planning. Not true. I went in and out of consciousness with little warning, one minute chatting with an orderly who wants to be an actor. But the next minute, right in the middle of the conversation, there I am going down the rabbit hole into an old memory.

It was like going to the movies, so vivid were the pictures I saw in coma. Sharply real. Yes, I remember, I wore that dress, the not-quite-pink, not-quite-rose that flattered my face as no other shade had ever done. Whatever happened to it?

Sandy was there too, her hair in pigtails, her knee skinned, her tennis shoes coming untied. The exact truth, down to the colors of our bikes, the dank-sweet-rotting smell of the pond behind her house, the way she always said, "Neat-o" when I told her one of my stories.

That night, after the white meal, after the orderly came by to check on me, I was ready. Restraints off, lying calmly waiting for sleep, having kept my vow of obedience and swallowed the red pill.

Suddenly, I was in Marrakesh. The city as real, as vivid as Sandy's blue Schwinn. Narrow, winding streets older than time, dirty children calling in high, shrill voices, mingled smells of spicy lamb and camel dung. The marketplace bustling with veiled women hurrying on scuffed sandals, gleaming brassware glinting at me from under tented bazaars, dust rising into my nose. The wail of the muezzin calls the faithful to prayer from atop a minaret.

Elation fills me. Marrakesh. Here I was happy, here I was alive, fresh, ready for adventure. Here I was fully myself. I enter the dream wholeheartedly, walking the streets, greeting the children, buying a peacock-blue scarf flecked with gold in the marketplace. Drinking hot black coffee out of a tiny cracked cup.

I wake to a poached egg and a bedpan and realize the pillow stayed beneath my head all night.

I realize something else. I have never been to Marrakesh.

I'd planned to go, with Colin, but first the roof on the summerhouse needed fixing and then he met Hilary and we broke up and I didn't want to go alone, so no Marrakesh.

At first my eyes fill with the hot salt tang of regret. No Marrakesh. But was that the truth? Didn't I go there last night, didn't I see all I would have seen, feel all I would have felt? And without jet lag or dysentery.

•   •   •

Mrs. R's family comes to see her and are told the news. It's just like I pictured it: her daughter Rachel says, "Thank God. It was so hard to keep on seeing her like that, day after day." She cries into a Kleenex, and tells her husband to call the rabbi about the service.

The smallest grandchild, the one who reads block printing, the one whose big dark eyes remind me of Mrs. R's, looks up at his mother and says, "Is Nana coming home now?" All Rachel can do is sob harder into her soggy Kleenex and pat her son's head.

I did the right thing. I know I did. It was just like Mrs. R could talk, and said to me, "Please, Mr. Barrymore, please don't let the vulture eat me. Let me go while my children can still remember that once I was alive, that I wasn't always a pile of bones lying on a bedpan."

So I did it. I snuck the extra pillow out of the closet, held it over Mrs. R's face, and let the life ebb out of her. She kicked a little—it's just the body fighting death, like a headless chicken running in the yard—and then she lay peaceful.

I have another friend on the ward. She was an editor at a big publishing house, and knows lots of writers. She used to go to plays all the time, she says. She's not old like Mrs. R, so it's real hard to see her wasting away.

She wants to die. Nurse found pills in her room, pills she was saving. Lots of them do that, while they still have the strength. Why does Nurse have to take them away? Why can't people be put to sleep like old dogs that have chased their last car?

I wish I could tell her not to worry. When her time comes, I'll do the right thing.

In between IV changes and vampire bloodsuckings and watching my raven grow red-eyed with hunger, I glide down the rabbit hole again.

I sit at a table, books piled high around me. Books with *my* picture on the back, *my* name on the front. There are a dozen titles at least, all best-sellers. People stand in line for a few words scrawled on the title page. One after another, they tell me how much my books meant to them, how reading *Ultimate Journey* or *Revenge* changed their lives. The books are my children; I know each one well and remember so vividly how they looked on the screen of my word processor, amber letters flowing after one another in a golden stream of words. Well-crafted words, limned with the care an artist must take, yet reaching so many different people. Characters who lived and grew in my head, the way my stories lived for Sandy as we picnicked beside the pond back home.

It's not the fame I revel in as I sign my name on all those flyleaves. It's not the satisfying ring of the cash register as the buyers shell out top dollar for my words. *My* words.

It's the look in people's eyes when they tell me how real Stella was in *Moonlight Secrets* or how the divorce in *Broken Vows* was just like their experience. It's the hands touching mine, the shy smiles, the enthusiastic replays of my last plot. My hand is cramped, yet I sign on and on, staying after the bookstore closes to autograph stock copies for mailing to special customers.

I wake in a puddle of cold urine.

I can't ring for the nurse. Best-selling novelists do not wet their beds.

There's a world of tears in my chest. My novel attempts lie buried in a cardboard box in my sister's basement in Omaha. Stillborn children. She who can, writes. She who can't—or won't, I never knew which—edits.

The nurse comes and I let her change the sheets and run me a new IV. She gives me a shot and, just as she finishes, there's a Code Blue down the hall. She turns and runs out, leaving me with—a hypodermic. A nice big one, thick and empty. Empty of medicine, full of air, it sits on the edge of my tray, staring at me. Is this a dagger I see before me? Is it really true you can kill yourself by injecting air into your veins?

At least I can find my veins; the vampires have inserted a plastic shunt into my arm to make injections easier. All I have to do is empty that syringe into my vein, let the air bubble float freely through my bloodstream till it hits a vital area—heart, maybe, or fast-fading brain—and I'll have my poisoned strawberries at last.

I slip the needle under the sheets. Not good enough. I reach behind me. This is a slow process, taking much more time to do than describe, but in the end I manage to drag the pillow—extraordinary how heavy pillows are now—to chest level. Using the needle point, I rip threads one by one until I have a hole big enough to slide the hypo through. I bury my newfound weapon in fiberfill, then begin the painful task of putting the pillow back around under my head.

I knock over the IV. It crashes to the ground with a clatter that instantly brings two nurses to my bedside. My heart pounds; one of them is the nurse who left the hypo in the first place. What if she remembers? What if she asks me what happened to it? What if she fluffs the pillow and the needle stabs her hand? My own skinny witch-hand trembles as she comes near me.

The raven sits at the foot of my bed, growing larger and leaner. Not sleek now, not fat, but scrawny, his head bent forward, his beak long. He exudes a rancid-meat smell that makes me want to puke. If I didn't know better, I'd call him a vulture.

I need the needle. I need The Plan. I need a choice.

I smile sheepishly at the nurses and point to the pillow. "Heavy," I say in my tiny "patient" voice. They nod with sympathetic smiles. One lifts my head while the other replaces the pillow behind me. Then they rehook the IV into my blue-veined arms, using the shunt. I wince; the black-and-blue flesh around the shunt hurts every time they touch it, but I don't care now. Nothing matters as long as they don't find the needle.

The careless one looks around the room, her forehead wrinkled. I can see her thoughts as clearly as if a bubble formed above her head: Didn't I leave something here? It's the way I always looked around the apartment before going off on a trip—haven't I left the gas on? Am I sure I packed my hair dryer, and what about the presents for the kids?

I hold my breath. Please, I pray to the gods, or to the vulture on the bed, to whoever will listen, *please* don't let her remember, don't let her search.

At last, shaking her head, she leaves. My breath whooshes out of me, a hot-air balloon coming back to earth a sagging bag of spent magic. Safe. A choice. Free to be or not to be, that truly is the question.

The rest of the afternoon I spend fighting with the raven-vulture. It eats, I cramp with pain. It eats some more, its stink overpowering me as it lunges with blood-soaked jaws at my stomach. I throw up my white lunch into an aluminum pan. The bird's beak is so sharp, its hunger so great that I can't even get to the rabbit hole. There is only reality, which sucks.

Tonight the needle. Into the arm, instead of morphine, 10cc's of air. A nice big bubble to wend its way along the river of my bloodstream, killing me softly.

Two red pills get me safely down the rabbit hole. Dylan sings "Lay lady lay" and I do just that. Lying naked on a big brass bed, my body sleek and ready for love. The night is sultry, a huge moon silvering my milk-white flesh as I lie crosswise on the bed, arms and legs apart to catch every nuance of mimosa-flavored breeze.

He comes into the room. Tall and lean, his face ugly hand-some, his smile twisted, his eyes deep-set and laughing. He puts a cold beer bottle between my breasts. My skin jumps, I shiver with delight as the cold hits my steaming skin. Then I raise the bottle to my lips and take a long draught. He does the same, then lowers his naked body onto the bed next to mine. Our kisses taste of beer.

He runs his callused hand along my body, his touch light as the breeze. I shudder as he strokes my breasts, circling his fingers round and round the tip of my nipple. He licks his finger, lightly rubs the nipple, then blows on it. I curl with pleasure, the tiny dancer between my legs eager to be set in motion by that same finger.

I reach for him, wanting to bury myself forever in the smell of him, wanting to taste his salt sweat, to die in the safe place he makes with his strong arms.

Our lovemaking lasts all night, the heat adding to our pas-sion. He knows just when to touch lightly, when to rub hard. His kisses are long, lingering, deep. We play, like children at the beach. We laugh low dirty laughs, like a whore and her john. We reach sublime heights, sweating human bodies transformed into light-winged, big-souled angels.

As I fall into sleep, my hand softly caresses his cock. No longer erect, yet still a loved instrument of pleasure. His hand cups my breast.

I wake with tears on my face. Never in my life was it like that. Never in my life. Only in my death.

Tonight the needle. I look at the bird perched hungrily on the end of my bed. No trace of raven left, it is all vulture and it waits with terrible patience. When I shoot air into my arm, killing myself, will it die too, or will its horrible body grow fatter, feasting on my remaining flesh?

My new friend is fading fast. In and out of coma. I come in to change the bedpan and see tears on her face. Tears of pain, tears of frustration because Nurse stole her pills. Don't worry, I want to tell her. The vulture won't win. I won't let him.

But I can't say anything. The hospital would fire me. Worse, I'd be arrested, tried for murder. As though you could murder somebody who's already dead, somebody whose body insists on staying alive after the soul is gone. Like the headless chicken. If I "killed" a headless chicken, would anyone call that murder?

All I'm doing is freeing them.

The next day is mostly rabbit hole. I drift from age to age, from what was to what wasn't to what will never be.

I am a grandmother, opening presents on my seventy-fifth birthday, children and grandchildren around me. There's Sally, my youngest. How shy she was, and how self-assured she looks now, sitting next to Derek, her banker husband. My oldest son, Peter, has his father's smile—and now his father's silver-gray hair. How did I ever get this old? And who is the curly-haired child in the red dress? Is it Peter's grandchild Julia or Mandy's midlife baby Andrea? Does it really matter, so long as I have the laughter of children around me, who the children are?

I marvel at all the life I brought forth.

Now I'm a kid, riding a roller coaster, my hands gripping the railing as I plunge into scarifying depths, then rise to heights only to fall again. Every second of the ride I enjoy, from the wind in my hair to the smell of cotton candy to the delicious sense of scared-but-safe I feel knowing Daddy's with me in the front car.

Let's do it again, Daddy, I beg. Sure, Kitten, he says, calling me by the *Father Knows Best* nickname I always wanted. I was never Daddy's Kitten, and he never let me ride the roller coaster twice. Once was good enough for anybody, my real Daddy always said. With my dream-Daddy I ride every ride twice, and I catch the bright brass ring, reaching from the painted zebra on the carousel.

When I next wake up, the doctor stands over me, my frail wrist in his hand, taking my pulse. He shakes his head at the nurse, and I get the picture. Not much more time.

The needle?

The vulture at the foot of my bed is five feet tall now. He gazes at me with hungry red eyes, stinking like a rotted corpse. Should I give myself to him now? Is it time to eat my strawberries?

No. I let myself slip down the rabbit hole. I never could stand not knowing how the story comes out. And there's so much more to do—maybe this time Harold Kimmerling asks *me* to the prom and Wendy Bentine spends the night crying her eyes out. Or maybe Sandy and I will have another giggly picnic by the pond. Or I'll ride up the Zambesi on a barge, my head protected by a pith helmet. And meet a very British wildlife photographer with a crooked smile and long legs, and maybe, just maybe, we'll . . .

Tomorrow I'll put the needle in my arm and give myself to the vulture.

Or maybe the next day. Or the day after that.

I slip into her room around 3:00. Once she said, "In the dark night of the soul, it is always 3:00 in the morning." I knew what she meant. I see a lot more three A.M.'s than most people.

I know she'd want to go at three A.M.

The pillow makes a quiet swishing sound as I edge it from under her head. She doesn't wake, but moans in her sleep. It's the kind of moan that if she was alive you'd think she was having sex, but in the shape she's in it can only mean pain.

The vulture is enormous. It's time.

I'm holding the pillow when I feel something hard inside. I poke around and stab myself on a hypodermic needle. She must have stashed it there, God knows how.

This is one lady who really wants to die. I nod and whisper softly, "I won't let you down. I'll do the right thing." Then I lay the pillow over her skull-face and press ever so gently.

Joyce Carol Oates is one of America's most influential contemporary writers, teachers, and critics. Her novels, essays, poetry, and short stories have earned her a permanent place of honor in American letters. Winner of the National Book Award, the O. Henry prize, the Rea Award, and a member of the American Academy-Institute of Arts and Letters, she has also written several novels of suspense, including Snake Eyes, under the name Rosamond Smith.

In "Extenuating Circumstances," a young woman's monologue reveals the depth of her torment, and her terrible response.

extenuating circumstances

by Joyce Carol Oates

B ECAUSE IT WAS A MERCY. BECAUSE GOD EVEN IN his cruelty will sometimes grant mercy.

Because Venus was in the sign of Sagittarius.

Because you laughed at me, my faith in the stars. My hope.

Because he cried, you do not know how he cried.

Because at such times his little face was so twisted and hot, his nose running with mucus, his eyes so hurt.

Because in such he was his mother, and not you. Because I wanted to spare him such shame.

Because he remembered you, he knew the word *Daddy*.

Because watching TV he would point to a man and say *Daddy*—?

Because this summer has gone on so long, and no rain. The heat lightning flashing at night, without thunder.

Because in the silence, at night, the summer insects scream.

Because by day there are earth-moving machines and

grinders operating hour upon hour razing the woods next to the playground. Because the red dust got into our eyes, our mouths.

Because he would whimper *Mommy?*—in that way that tore my heart.

Because last Monday the washing machine broke down, I heard a loud thumping that scared me, the dirty soapy water would not drain out. Because in the light of the bulb overhead he saw me holding the wet sheets in my hand crying *What can I do? What can I do?*

Because the sleeping pills they give me now are made of flour and chalk, I am certain.

Because I loved you more than you loved me even from the first when your eyes moved on me like candle flame.

Because I did not know this yet, yes I knew it but cast it from my mind.

Because there was shame in it. Loving you knowing you would not love me enough.

Because my job applications are laughed at for misspellings and torn to pieces as soon as I leave.

Because they will not believe me when listing my skills. Because since he was born my body is misshapen, the pain is always there.

Because I see that it was not his fault and even in that I could not spare him.

Because even at the time when he was conceived (in those early days we were so happy! so happy I am certain! lying together on top of the bed the corduroy bedspread in that narrow jiggly bed hearing the rain on the roof that slanted down so you had to stoop being so tall and from outside on the street the roof with its dark shingles looking always wet was like a lowered brow over the windows on the third floor and the windows like squinting eyes and we would come home together from the University meeting at the Hardee's corner you from the geology lab or the library and me from Accounting where my eyes ached because of the lights with their dim flicker no one else could see and I was so happy your arm around my waist and mine around yours like any couple, like any college girl with her boyfriend, and walking *home*, yes it was *home*, I thought always it was *home*, we would look up at the windows of the apartment laughing saying who do you think lives there? what are their names? who are they? that cozy secret-looking room under the eaves where the roof came down, came down dripping black runny water I hear now drumming on this roof but only if I fall asleep during the day with my clothes on so tired so exhausted and when I wake up there is no rain, only the earth-moving machines and grinders in the woods so I must acknowledge *It is another time, it is time*) yes I knew.

Because you did not want him to be born.

Because he cried so I could hear him through the shut door, through all the doors.

Because I did not want him to be *Mommy*, I wanted him to be *Daddy* in his strength.

Because this washcloth in my hand was in my hand when I saw how it must be.

Because the checks come to me from the lawyer's office not from you. Because in tearing open the envelopes my fingers shaking and my eyes showing such hope I revealed myself naked to myself so many times.

Because to this shame he was a witness, he saw.

Because he was too young at two years to know. Because even so he knew.

Because his birthday was a sign, falling in the midst of Pisces.

Because in certain things he *was* his father, that knowledge in eyes that went beyond me in mockery of me.

Because one day he would laugh too as you have done.

Because there is no listing for your telephone and the operators will not tell me. Because in any of the places I know to find you, you cannot be found.

Because your sister has lied to my face, to mislead me. Because she who was once my friend, I believed, was never my friend.

Because I feared loving him too much, and in that weakness failing to protect him from hurt.

Because his crying tore my heart but angered me too so I feared laying hands upon him wild and unplanned.

Because he flinched seeing me. That nerve jumping in his eye.

Because he was always hurting himself, he was so clumsy falling off the swing hitting his head against the metal post so one of the other mothers saw and cried out *Oh! Oh look your son is bleeding!* and that time in the kitchen whining and pulling at me in a bad temper reaching up to grab the pot handle and almost overturning the boiling water in his face so I lost control slapping him shaking him by the arm *Bad! Bad! Bad! Bad!* my voice rising in fury not caring who heard.

Because that day in the courtroom you refused to look at me your face shut like a fist against me and your lawyer too, like I was dirt beneath your shoes. Like maybe he was not even your son but you would sign the papers as if he was, you are so superior.

Because the courtroom was not like any courtroom I had a right to expect, not a big dignified courtroom like on TV just a room with a judge's desk and three rows of six seats each and not a single window and even here that flickering light that yellowish-sickish fluorescent tubing making my eyes ache so I wore my dark glasses giving the judge a false impression of me, and I was sniffing, wiping my nose, every question they asked me I'd hear myself giggle so nervous and ashamed even stammering over my age and my name so you looked with scorn at me, all of you.

Because they were on your side, I could not prevent it.

Because in granting me child support payments, you had a right to move away. Because I could not follow.

Because he wet his pants, where he should not have, for his age.

Because it would be blamed on me. It *was* blamed on me.

Because my own mother screamed at me over the phone. She could not help me with my life she said, no one can help you with your life, we were screaming such things to each other as left us breathless and crying and I slammed down the receiver knowing that I had no mother and after the first grief I knew *It is better, so.*

Because he would learn that someday, and the knowledge of it would hurt him.

Because he had my hair coloring, and my eyes. That left eye, the weakness in it.

Because that time it almost happened, the boiling water overturned onto him, I saw how easy it would be. How, if he could be prevented from screaming, the neighbors would not know.

Because yes they would know, but only when I wanted them to know.

Because you would know then. Only when I wanted you to know.

Because then I could speak to you in this way, maybe in a letter which your lawyer would forward to you, or your sister, maybe over the telephone or even face to face. Because then you could not escape.

Because though you did not love him you could not escape him.

Because I have begun to bleed for six days quite heavily, and will then spot for another three or four. Because soaking the blood in wads of toilet paper sitting on the toilet my hands shaking I think of you who never bleed.

Because I am a proud woman, I scorn your charity.

Because I am not a worthy mother. Because I am so tired.

Because the machines digging in the earth and grinding trees are a torment by day, and the screaming insects by night.

Because there is no sleep.

Because he would only sleep, these past few months, if he could be with me in my bed.

Because he whimpered *Mommy!—Mommy don't!*

Because he flinched from me when there was no cause.

Because the pharmacist took the prescription and was gone such a long time, I knew he was telephoning someone.

Because at the drugstore where I have shopped for a year and a half they pretended not to know my name.

Because in the grocery store the cashiers stared smiling at me and at him pulling at my arm spilling tears down his face.

Because they whispered and laughed behind me, I have too much pride to respond.

Because he was with me at such times, he was a witness to such.

Because he had no one but his Mommy and his Mommy had no one but him. Which is so lonely.

Because I had gained seven pounds from last Sunday to this, the waist of my slacks is so tight. Because I hate the fat of my body.

Because looking at me naked now you would show disgust.

Because I *was* beautiful for you, why wasn't that enough?

Because that day the sky was dense with clouds the color of raw liver but yet there was no rain. Heat lightning flashing with no sound making me so nervous but no rain.

Because his left eye was weak, it would always be so unless he had an operation to strengthen the muscle.

Because I did not want to cause him pain and terror in his sleep.

Because you would pay for it, the check from the lawyer with no note.

Because you hated him, your son.

Because he was *our* son, you hated him.

Because you moved away. To the far side of the country I have reason to believe.

Because in my arms after crying he would lie so still, only one heart beating between us.

Because I knew I could not spare him from hurt.

Because the playground hurt our ears, raised red dust to get into our eyes and mouths.

Because I was so tired of scrubbing him clean, between his toes and beneath his nails, the insides of his ears, his neck, the many secret places of filth.

Because I felt the ache of cramps again in my belly, I was in a panic my period had begun so soon.

Because I could not spare him the older children laughing.

Because after the first terrible pain he would be beyond pain.

Because in this there is mercy.

Because God's mercy is for him, and not for me.

Because there was no one here to stop me.

Because my neighbors' TV was on so loud, I knew they could not hear even if he screamed through the washcloth.

Because you were not here to stop me, were you.

Because finally there is no one to stop us.

Because finally there is no one to save us.

Because my own mother betrayed me.

Because the rent would be due again on Tuesday which is the first of September. And by then I will be gone.

Because his body was not heavy to carry and to wrap in the down comforter, you remember that comforter, I know.

Because the washcloth soaked in his saliva will dry on the line and show no sign.

Because to heal there must be forgetfulness and oblivion.

Because he cried when he should not have cried but did not cry when he should.

Because the water came slowly to boil in the big pan, vibrating and humming on the front burner.

Because the kitchen was damp with steam from the windows shut so tight, the temperature must have been 100°F.

Because he did not struggle. And when he did, it was too late.

Because I wore rubber gloves to spare myself being scalded.

Because I knew I must not panic, and did not.

Because I loved him. Because love hurts so bad.

Because I wanted to tell you these things. Just like this.

In "One Hit Wonder," a has-been recording star tries for a comeback and rebounds into a situation he never bargained for. Gabrielle Kraft, whose Jerry Zalman is featured in several novels, including Edgar nominee Bullshot, Screwdriver, Let's Rob Roy, *and* Bloody Mary, *has been an executive story editor and story analyst at major film studios. From the safety of the northwest, she has written about the wages of pride and the struggle for power in LaLa Land. She describes her short stories as "... the dark side of the Zalman series; if Zalman's is a lollipop view of L.A., the stories are sour pickles."*

one hit wonder

by Gabrielle Kraft

YOU PROBABLY DON'T REMEMBER ME, BUT TEN YEARS ago I was very big. Matter of fact, in the record business I was what we call a one hit wonder. You know, the kind of guy you see on talk shows doing a medley of his hit? That was me, Ricky Curtis.

Remember "Ooo Baby Oooo"? Remember? "Ooo baby oooo, it's you that I do, it's you I truly do?" That was me, Ricky Curtis, crooning the insistent vocal you couldn't get out of your head, me with the moronic whine you loved to hate. Big? Hell, I was huge. "Ooo Baby Oooo" was a monster hit, triple platinum with a million bullets. That was Ricky Curtis, remember me now?

My God, it was great. You can't imagine how it feels, being on top. And it was so easy! I wrote "Ooo Baby Oooo" in minutes, while I was waiting for my teenage bride to put on her makeup, and the next day I played it for my boss at the recording studio where I had a job sweeping up. He loved it. We recorded it with some girl backup singers the next week, and it was alakazam Ricky.

For one long, brilliantly dappled summer, America knew my name and sang the words to my tune. People hummed me and sang me and whistled me, and my voice drifted out of car radios through the airwaves and into the minds of the world. For three sun-drenched months, I was a king and in my twenty-two-year-old wisdom I thought I would live forever.

Then, unaccountably, it was over. Because I didn't have a follow-up record, I was a one hit wonder and my just-add-water career evaporated like steam from a cup of coffee. I was ripped apart by confusion and I didn't know what to do next. Should I try to write more songs like "Ooo Baby Oooo"? I couldn't. Not because I didn't want to, but because I didn't know how. You see, I'd had visions of myself as a troubadour, a road-show Bob Dylan, a man with a message. A guy with heart. I hadn't envisioned myself as a man with a teenage tune wafting out across the shopping malls of the land, and "Ooo Baby Oooo" was merely a fluke, a twisting mirage in the desert. I was battered by doubt, and so, I did nothing. I froze, paralyzed in the klieg lights of L.A. like a drunk in a cop's high beams.

The upshot of my paralysis was that I lost my slot. My ten-second window of opportunity passed, and like a million other one hit wonders, I fell off the edge of the earth. I was yesterday's news. I couldn't get arrested, couldn't get a job. Not even with the golden oldies shows that go out on the tired road every summer, cleaning up the rock-and-roll dregs in the small towns, playing the little county fairs, not the big ones with Willie and Waylon, but the little ones with the racing pigs. I was an instant dinosaur, a joke, a thing of the past.

It hit me hard, being a has-been who never really was, and I couldn't understand what I'd done wrong. I'd signed over my publishing rights to my manager and dribbled away my money. In my confusion I started to drink too much—luckily I was too broke to afford cocaine. I drifted around L.A., hanging out in the clubs nursing a drink, telling my then-agent that I was "getting my head together," telling my then-wife that prosperity would burst over us like fireworks on the glorious Fourth and I'd have another big hit record any day now. Telling myself that I was a deadbeat washout at twenty-two.

Fade out, fade in. Times change and ten years pass, and Ricky Curtis, the one hit wonder, is now a bartender at Eddie Style's Club Dingo above the Sunset Strip, shoving drinks across a huge marble bar stained a dark faux-malachite-green, smiling and giving a *c'est la vie* shrug if a well-heeled customer realizes that he's a guy who had a hit record once upon a sad old time.

But inside, I seethed. I smoldered. I didn't know what to do and so I did nothing. You don't know how it feels, to be so close to winning, to have your hand on the lottery ticket as it dissolves into dust, to feel the wheel of the red Ferrari one second before it slams into the wall. To smell success, taste the elixir of fame on your tongue, and then stand foolishly as your future rushes down the gutter in a swirl of brown, greasy water because of your inability to make a decision.

So I worked for Eddie Style. I had no choice. I groveled for tips and tugged my spiky forelock like the rest of the serfs; I smiled and nodded, but in the abyss I called my heart there was only anger. My rage at the crappy hand I'd been dealt grew like a horrible cancer eating me alive, and at night I dreamed of the Spartan boy and the fox.

I'd wake up every morning and think about money. Who had it, how to get it, why I didn't have it. In this town, the deals, the plans, the schemes to make money mutate with each new dawn. But I said nothing. I had nothing to say. I smiled, slid drinks across the bar and watched the wealthy enjoying themselves, waiting for crumbs to fall off the table. In a joint like the Dingo where the rich kids come out to play at night and the record business execs plant their cloven hooves in the trough at will, a few crumbs always fall your way.

Like when Eddie Style offered me a hundred thou to kill his wife.

Edward Woffard Stanhope III, known as Eddie Style to his friends and foes alike, owned the Club Dingo, and he was also a very rich guy. Not from the Dingo, or movie money, not record business money, not drug money, not at all. Eddie Style had something you rarely see if you float around the tattered edges of L.A. nightlife the way I do. Eddie Style had inherited money.

Edward Stanhope III, aka Eddie Style, came from a long line of thieves, but since they were big thieves, nobody called them thieves; they called them Founding Fathers, or Society, or the Best People. Eddie's granddad, Edward Woffard Stanhope Numero Uno, known as "Steady," was one of the guys who helped loot the Owens Valley of its water, real *Chinatown* stuff. You know Stanhope Boulevard over in West Hollywood? Well, Eddie Style called it Me Street, that's the kind of money we're talking about here.

Trouble was, Eddie Style had bad taste in wives. He was a skinny little guy, and he wasn't very bright in spite of the fact that the accumulated wealth of the Stanhope family weighed heavy on his narrow shoulders. Plus, he liked tall women. They were always blond, willowy, fiscally insatiable and smarter than he was. Chrissie and Lynda, the first two, had siphoned off a hefty chunk of the Stanhope change, and Suzanne, the third blond beauty, had teeth like an alligator. At least, according to Eddie. I didn't know. They'd only been married two years and she didn't come around the Dingo. It was going to take another big slice of the pie to divest himself of Suzanne, and Eddie was getting cagey in his old age. After all, he wouldn't come into any more dough until his mother croaked, and she was only fifty-seven. He had a few siblings and half siblings and such scattered around, so a major outlay of capital on a greedy ex-wife didn't seem prudent.

So, one night after closing, he and I are mopping up the bar—I'm mopping up the bar, he's chasing down mimosas— and he starts complaining about his marital situation, just like he's done a thousand nights before.

"Suzanne's a nice girl," he sighed, "but she's expensive." His voice echoed through the empty room, bouncing off the upended chairs on the café tables, the ghostly stage and the rock-and-roll memorabilia encased in Plexiglas.

"You don't say?" In my present line of work, I've learned

that noncommittal responses are the best choice, and I switch back and forth between "You don't say" and "No kidding" and "Takes all kinds." Oils the waters of drunken conversation.

"I *do* say. Ricky boy, I've been married three times," he said ruefully, "so I ought to know better by now. You see a girl, you think she's..." He narrowed his eyes, looked down the bar to the empty stage at the end of the room and gave an embarrassed shrug. "I dunno... the answer to a question you can't quite form in your mind. A hope you can't name."

"Takes all kinds." I nodded and kept on mopping the bar. Like I said, the Dingo was empty, Eddie Style was in a philosophical mood, and I had a rule about keeping my trap shut.

But he wouldn't quit. "You get married and you realize she's just another broad who cares more about getting her legs waxed than she does about you. I can't afford a divorce," he said, pinging the edge of his glass with his forefinger. It was middle C. "I don't have enough money to pay her off."

I felt my brain start to boil. He didn't have enough money! What a laugh! Isn't that the way the song always goes in this town? I love you baby, but not enough. I have money but not enough. To me, Eddie Style was loaded. He owned the Club Dingo, he drove a classic Mercedes with a license plate that read STYLEY, he lived in a house in the Hills, he wore Armani suits for business and Hawaiian shirts when he was in a casual mood. Oh yeah, Eddie Style had it all and Ricky Curtis had nothing.

"See, Ricky boy," he nattered as he took a slug of his fourth mimosa. "Guy like you, no responsibilities, you think life's a ball. Hey, you come to work, you go home, it's all yours. Me, I got the weight of my damn ancestors pushing on me like a rock. I feel crushed by my own history."

"Sisyphus," I said, wringing out the bar towel. After my divorce I'd gone to a few night classes at UCLA in hopes of meeting a girl with brains. Some fat chance. Even in Myths and Legends: A Perspective for Today, all the girls knew "Ooo Baby Oooo."

"Whatever," Eddie sighed. Ping on his glass again. "I can't take much more of this kinda life." He gestured absently at his darkened domain. "If only she'd die . . ." He looked up at me and shot a loud ping through the empty club. His lids peeled back from his eyes like skin from an onion, and he gave me a wise smile. "If only somebody'd give her a shove . . ."

"Hold on," I told him. "Wait a minute, Eddie. . . ."

He didn't say anything else, but it was too late. I could smell dark blood seeping over the layer of expensive crud that permeated the Dingo. He'd planted the idea in my brain, and it was putting out feelers like a science-fiction monster sprouting a thousand eyes.

For three nights I lay in my bed, drinking vodka, staring out the window of my one-bedroom apartment on Ivar, at the boarded-up crack house across the street, and thinking about money. If I had money, I could take a few months off, vacation in Mexico and jump start my life. I had no future as a bartender at the Club Dingo. If I stayed where I was—as I was—I would never change, and I *had* to revitalize my life or I would shrivel and die. If I could get out of L.A., lie on the beach for a month or two, maybe I could start writing songs again, maybe I could have another hit. Maybe *something* would happen to me. Maybe I'd get lucky. The way I saw things, it was her or me.

Three days later Eddie made me the offer. A hundred thou, cash, no problems. He'd give me the keys to the house; I could pick the time and place and kill her any way I wanted.

"Look, Ricky boy, you've got a gun, right?" he said.

"A thirty-eight." I shrugged. "L.A.'s a crazy town."

"Great. Just shoot her, OK? Whack her over the head, I don't care. Do it fast so she won't feel anything. Make it look like a robbery, steal some jewelry. She's got it lying all over her dressing table; she won't use the damn safe. Christ, I gave her enough stuff the first year we were married to fill a vault; just take some of it, do what you want. Throw it down the drain, it doesn't matter. I just gotta get rid of her, OK?"

"OK, Eddie," I said. By the time he asked me to kill her, it was easy. I'd thought it all out; I knew he was going to ask me, and I knew I was going to do it. Ultimately, it came down to this. If murder was the only way to finance another chance, I would become a killer. I saw it as a career move.

I told him I'd do it. Eddie gave me a set of keys to his house and planned to be at the Dingo all night on Wednesday, my night off. He said it would be a good time to kill Suzanne, anxiously pointing out that he wasn't trying to tell me my job. It was all up to me.

I drove up to his house in the Hills; I'd been there for the Club Dingo Christmas party, so I was vaguely familiar with the layout. It was a Neutra house from the thirties, a huge white block hanging over the edge of the brown canyon like an albino vulture, and as I parked my dirty Toyota next to the red Rolls that Suzanne drove, I felt strong, like I had a rod of iron inside my heart. Suzanne would die, and I would rise like the phoenix from her ashes. I saw it as an even trade—my new life for her old life.

I opened the front door with Eddie's key and went inside, padding silently on my British Knights. My plan was to look around, then go upstairs to the bedroom and shoot her. Eddie said she watched TV most nights, used it to put her to sleep like I used vodka.

The entry was long, and there was a low, flat stairway leading down to the sunken living room. The drapes were pulled back, and I could see all of Los Angeles spread out through the floor-to-ceiling windows that lined the far wall. The shifting shapes of moving blue water in the pool below were reflected on the glass, and in that suspended moment I knew what it meant to live in a world of smoke and mirrors.

"Who the hell are you?" a woman snapped.

It was Suzanne and she had a gun. Dumb little thing, a tiny silver .25 that looked like it came from Le Chic Shooter, but it was a gun all the same. Eddie never mentioned that she had a gun, and I was angry. I hadn't expected it. I hadn't expected her either.

I'd met her at the Christmas party, so I knew she was gorgeous, but I'd been pretty drunk at the time and I wasn't paying attention. Suzanne Stanhope, nobody called her Suzie Style, was a dream in white. She was as tall as I was, and she had legs that would give a lifer fits.

"Eddie sent me," I said brightly. "He forgot his date-book. Didn't he call you? He said he was gonna..." I let my voice trail off and hoped I looked slack-jawed and stupid. I thought it was a damn good improvisation, and my ingratiating grin must have helped, because she lowered the gun.

"You're the bartender, the one who used to be a singer, right?" she asked. "Now I recognize you." She loosened up, but she didn't put down the gun.

This was going to be easy. I'd bust her in the head, steal the jewelry and be a new man by morning. I smiled, amazed that one woman could be so beautiful.

She was wearing a white dress, loose, soft material that clung to her body when she moved, and the worst part was, she wasn't even trying to be beautiful. Here she was, probably lying around in bed watching TV, painting her toenails, and she looked like she was going to the Oscars. Once again I saw the futility of life in L.A. without money.

"Tell Eddie I could have shot you," she said, very mild. "He'll get a kick out of that." She still had the little silver gun in her hand, but she was holding it like a pencil, gesturing with it.

"Sure will, Mrs. Stanhope," I said, grinning like an intelligent ape.

"Oh, cut the crap, will you? Just call me Suzanne." She looked me over, and I got the feeling she'd seen better in the cold case. "You want a drink, bartender? What's your name, anyway?"

"Ricky Curtis."

"Rick, huh?" She frowned and started humming my song. "How does that thing go?" she asked.

I hummed "Ooo Baby Oooo" for her. Her hair was shoulder length, blond, not brassy. Blue eyes with crinkles in the corners like she didn't give a damn what she laughed at. "Ooo baby oooo, it's you that I do...," I hummed.

"So how come you don't sing anymore, Rick?" she asked as she led me down the steps into the sunken living room. I could see the lights of the city twinkling down below and idly wondered if, on a clear day, I'd be able to see my apartment on Ivar or the boarded-up crack house across the street.

"How come nobody asks me?" I said.

She went behind the bar, laughing as she poured herself a drink. Sounded like wind chimes. She put the little gun down on the marble bar, and it made a hollow clink.

"Vodka," I told her.

She poured me a shot in a heavy glass, and I drank it off. I had a strange feeling, and I didn't know why. I knew Eddie Style was rich, but this was unlike anything I'd ever seen before. The sheer weight of the Stanhope money was crushing me into the ground. Heavy gravity. I felt like I was on Mars.

She sipped her drink and looked thoughtfully out the huge windows, past the pale translucent lozenge of the pool toward the city lights below. "It's nice here," she said. "Too bad Eddie doesn't appreciate it. He'd have a better life if he appreciated what he has, instead of running around like a dog. The Dingo is aptly named, don't you think, Rick?"

I wanted another drink. I wanted to be drunk when I killed her, so I wouldn't feel it. I hadn't planned on killing a person, just a . . . a what? Just a blond body? Just a lump in the bed that could be anything? I hadn't counted on looking into her clear blue eyes as the light went out of them. I pushed my glass across the counter, motioning for another drink.

"So why are you here, Rick?" she asked softly. "It was a good story about the datebook but Eddie's too frazzled to keep one. I'm surprised you didn't know that about him. Maybe you two aren't as close as you think."

I didn't know what she meant. Was she kidding me? I couldn't tell. What was going on? I had that old familiar feeling of confusion, and once again, I was in over my head. Did she *know* I was there to kill her? I couldn't let her think that, so I did the next best thing. I confessed to a lesser crime.

"I'm broke," I said shortly, "and Eddie said the house was empty. I was here at the Christmas party and I figured I could bag some silver out of the back of the drawer. Maybe nobody would miss a few forks. It was a dumb idea but it's tap city and Eddie has more than he needs. Of everything," I said, looking directly at her. "You gonna call the cops?"

"Robbery? That's an exciting thought," she said, clinking the ice in her glass as she leaned her head back and popped an ice cube in her mouth. She took it out with her fingers and ran it over her lips. "You value Eddie's things, his life-style. Too bad he doesn't."

"In this town it's hard to appreciate what you have," I said slowly, wondering how her lips would feel, how cold they really were. "Everybody always wants what they can't get."

"Don't they," she said meaningfully as she dropped the ice cube back in her glass. "What do *you* want, Rick? Since you brought it up."

"Me? I want money," I said. As the phrase popped out of my mouth I realized how pathetic it sounded. Like a teen-ager wanting to be a rock star, I wanted money. That's the trouble with L.A. Being a bartender isn't a bad gig, but in L.A., it's just a rest stop on the freeway to fame, a cute career to spice up your résumé.

"That shouldn't be tough for a good-looking guy like you. Not in this town." She refilled our glasses and led me over to a white couch. There were four of them in an intimate square around a free-form marble table. I felt like I was somebody else. I'd only had a couple short ones and I was wondering what she wanted in a man. I wondered if she was lonely.

"Sit down," she said, her white dress splitting open to show me those blond legs. "Let's talk, Rick," she said.

"Sure I married him because he's rich, just like he married me because I'm beautiful," she said, running a finger across my stomach. "But I thought there was more to it than that. He was sweet to me at first. He didn't treat me like some whore who spent her life on her knees. Christ, I'm tired of men who want me because I'm beautiful and then don't want me because I'm smart. Am I smart, Rick?" she asked, pull-ing the sheet around her body as she got out of bed. "Want anything?"

Mars. I was on Mars. You hang around L.A., you think you know the words to the big tune, but you don't. You think you've seen a lot, know it all, but you don't, and as I lay in his bed caressing his wife, I wondered how it would feel to be Eddie Style. Live in his house, sleep with his wife. If I had a room like this, why would I ever leave it? If I had a wife like that, why would I want to kill her? The sheets were smooth, some kind of expensive cotton the rich like; the carpet was soft—was it silk? The glinting perfume bottles on her dressing table were heavy, geometrically cut glass shapes twinkling with a deep interior light far brighter than the city below. If I unstoppered one of those bottles, what would I smell?

She let the sheet drop to the floor as she lowered herself into the bubbling blue marble tub at the far end of the room. I lay in Eddie's bed and watched her as she stretched her head back, and exposed a long white highway of throat pointing to a dark and uncharted continent. I thought about killing her and realized it was too late.

"This is insane," I said.

She laughed. "It's so L.A., isn't it? The bartender and the boss's wife, the gardener and the . . ."

"Yeah, I read *Lady Chatterly*. I'm not a complete illiterate," I told her. "What do you want to do about it?"

"Oh, we could get together afternoons in cheesy motels," she said. "Think you'd like that?"

"Sounds great," I said ironically. "Don't you think you'd find cheesy motels boring after a while? Say, after a week or so?" I got up out of bed, went over to the tub and got in with her. The water warmed me to the bone. "You could come live with me in my one-bedroom. You'd fit in just fine. Course, you'd have to leave this house behind," I said as I slipped my hands underneath her body and lifted her on top of me. "And there wouldn't be much time for shopping since you'd have to get a job slinging fries. Think you'd miss the high life?"

"Probably," she gasped.

"Yeah, I think so too. But we can talk about it later, right?"

"Right," she said, clutching at my back with those beautifully sculpted nails. "Yessss."

Of course, I left without killing Suzanne. Then I went back to the Dingo and yelled at Eddie, which was a laugh since I'd been rolling around with his wife all evening. Funny thing, though. As I stared at Eddie Style, sitting on his usual

stool at the long faux-malachite bar, I felt contempt for him.
He had everything, Eddie did. Money, cars, a beautiful wife.
But he didn't know what he had, and that made him a bigger
zero than I was. Even with all that money.

"Why the hell didn't you tell me she had a gun?" I
snarled over the blast of the head-banging band onstage. I'd
never snarled at him before, and it felt good.

"I forgot," he said, very apologetic as he tugged on his
mimosa. "Really, Ricky boy, I didn't think about it. It's just
a little gun. . . ."

"Easy for you to say," I grumbled. "Don't worry about
it, man. I'll take care of it for you."

But I didn't.

I called Suzanne a few days later, she came over to my
apartment and we spent the afternoon amusing ourselves.

"Why don't you fix this place up?" she said. "It doesn't
have to look like a slum, Rick."

"Sure it does. It is a slum," I told her, stroking the long
white expanse of her back. "You think it's *La Bohème*?
Some sort of arty dungeon? Look out the window, it's a
slum."

"Don't complain, you've got me. And," she said as she
got out of bed and went over to her purse, "now you've got
a nice watch instead of that cheapo."

You think your life changes in grand, sweeping gestures—
the day you have your first hit, the day you get married, the
day you get divorced—but it doesn't. Your life changes
when you stretch out your hand and take a flat velvet-covered
jeweler's box with a gold watch inside that costs two or three
thousand dollars. Your life changes when you don't care how
you got it.

When you're a kid, you never think the situation will arise.
You think you'll be a big star, a hero, a rock legend; you
don't think you'll be lying in bed in a crummy Hollywood
apartment with another guy's wife and she'll be handing you
a little gift. Thanks, honey, you were great.

I took the watch. A week later, I took the five hundred
bucks she gave me "for groceries." You see the situation I
was in? Here I was, supposed to kill Eddie Style's wife for
a hundred thousand dollars, and I was too busy boffing her

to get the job done. Me, the guy who was so hungry for cash that his hands vibrated every time he felt the walnut dash on a Mercedes.

I was swept by the same confusion I'd felt after "Ooo Baby Oooo." Once again I was staring out over a precipice into an endless expanse of possibilities, and I didn't know what to do. I was looking at a row of choices lined up like prizes at a carnival, and the barker was offering me any prize I wanted. But which one should I take? The doll? The stuffed monkey? The little toy truck? Reach out and grab it, Ricky boy. How do you make a decision that will determine the course of your life? A thick, oozing paralysis sucked at me like an oil slick.

All I had to do was kill her and I couldn't do it. When she wasn't around I fantasized about taking her out for a drive and tossing her down a dry well out in Palm Desert or giving her a little shove over the cliff as we stared at the sunset over the Pacific. But when she was around, I knew it was impossible. I couldn't kill Suzanne. Her beauty held me like a vise.

Beautiful women don't understand their power; their hold on men is far greater than they comprehend. Women like Suzanne sneer at their beauty; they think it's a happy accident. Mostly they think it's a commodity, sometimes they think it's a gift, but they don't understand what the momentary possession of that beauty does to a man, how it feels to see perfection lying beside you in bed, to stare at flawless grace as it sleeps and you know you can touch it at will.

The flip side of my problem was that a rich guy like Eddie Style didn't understand that possessing a woman like Suzanne made me his equal. Within the four corners that comprise the enclosed world of a bed, a fool like me is equal to generations of Stanhope money.

"So, Ricky boy, when you gonna do that thing?" Eddie asked me late one night, giving me a soft punch on the arm. He's acting like it's a joke, some kind of a scene. Kill my wife, please.

"Don't pressure me, Eddie; you want it done fast, do it yourself." Now that I was a hired gun, I no longer felt the need to kiss the hem of his garment quite so fervently or quite so often. Weird, what power does to you. You start sleeping with a rich guy's wife, you feel like a superhero, an invincible Saturday morning kiddie cartoon. "If you'd told me about the gun, I would have killed her that first night. Now the timing's screwed up."

This was true, and it creased a further wrinkle into my murderous plans. The vacationing couple was back at work at Eddie's big white house in the daytime, so it was no longer possible to slip in and kill Suzanne even if I'd had the guts to do it. Too many people around.

Besides, I was no longer an anonymous cipher, a faceless killer. I was a piece of Suzanne's life, although Eddie didn't know it. Now that she was coming to my apartment for nooners, I knew we'd been seen together. The elderly lady with ten thousand cats who lived across the courtyard and peeked out between her venetian blinds at people coming in and going out, Suzanne's big red Rolls parked on Ivar—there were too many telltale traces of my secret life, traces that would give me away if I *did* kill her.

So there I was, stuck between skinny Eddie Style and his beautiful wife, and it was at this point that a brilliant idea occurred to me. What if I killed Eddie Style? What if I killed the husband and not the wife? Assuming Suzanne approved of the idea, it would have a double-edged effect; it would cement Suzanne to all that Stanhope money and it would cement me to Suzanne. For I had no intention of allowing her to remain untouched by Eddie's death, if I chose to kill him instead of her.

Turnabout.

But would Suzanne take to the idea of killing her husband? Would she see me as a lout, as a sociopathic lunatic, or merely as the opportunistic infection I truly was? Or would she, too, see murder as a career move?

At night I worked at the Dingo, and though I poured drinks, laughed and chatted with the customers, I was changed inside, tempered by my connection to death. Now that I was concentrating on murder, I was no longer a failure, a one hit wonder. I was invaded by the knowledge that I possessed a secret power setting me apart from the faceless ants who surrounded me in the bar. A few weeks ago, I was a shabby, sad wreck tossed up on the shores of Hollywood with the rest of the refuse, the flotsam and jetsam of the entertainment business. Now that I was dreaming about murder, I was on top again, and I had the potential of ultimate power.

A week later I decided to talk to Suzanne about killing Eddie. I had no intention of bringing up the question directly; I was too clever for that. I planned to approach her crabwise, manipulate our pillow talk in the direction of murder. If she picked up the cue, well and good. If not, I'd have to alter my plans where she was concerned.

It was Wednesday, my night off, and Eddie was at the Dingo. I called Suzanne and said I'd be at her house that night. She wasn't too happy that I was coming over, but I let my voice go all silky and told her I felt like a hot bath.

The white Neutra house was lit up by soft floodlights, and as I knocked on the door, it reminded me of the glistening sails of tall ships flooding into a safe harbor bathed in sunshine.

The door opened. It was Eddie Style. "Do you think you should be here, Ricky boy?" he asked, very mildly.

Not a good sign. I had a moment of fear, but I covered it. I was feeling omnipotent, and besides, I had my .38 in my jacket pocket. "You mean we've got to stop meeting like this?" I mocked. Simultaneously, I knew I was in over my head and apprehension started nibbling at my shoes.

He held open the door for me, and I went inside, automatically stepping down into the sunken living room. Suzanne, wearing a white kimono with deep, square sleeves, was sitting on the couch, a drink in her hand. Her nails shone red as an exploding sun and her face was flat, expressionless. All the beauty had drained out of it, and there was only the molded mask of a mannequin staring back at me from behind a thick sheet of expensive plate glass. Who was she?

Confusion swept me, and I was carried off down the river like a dinghy in a flash flood.

"Here we all are," Eddie said. "Drink?"

I nodded yes. "Vodka."

"Ricky boy," he said as he went behind the bar, "I've had you followed and I know you're sleeping with my wife.

I'm afraid I can't stand still for that," he said slowly. "When the help gets out of line it makes me look foolish and I simply can't allow it to go unpunished." He reached underneath the bar and pulled out the shiny silver .25 Suzanne pointed at me that first night.

Now the dinghy was caught in a whirlpool. "I'm sorry, Eddie," I said. "These things . . . just happen." I indicated Suzanne. "I'm sorry."

"Ricky boy, I know what you think. I've seen you operate." His voice was cold and he was still holding the gun. "You think because I'm rich you can come along, skim a little cream off the top and I'm so stupid I won't notice. You think you're as good as I am, street-smart Ricky boy, the one hit wonder. Wrong, buddy. Dead wrong. You're not as good as I am and you never will be."

The absurd little gun was firmer in his hand, and I had the cold, cold feeling he was going to shoot me. He'd claim I was a robber, that his faithful minion had betrayed his trust. Who'd dare to call Edward Woffard Stanhope III a liar? With his beautiful wife Suzanne by his side to back up his story, why would anybody try?

I looked at Suzanne. Her face was unmoved. I felt empty and desperate in a way I hadn't felt since I'd started sleeping with her. I'd had a taste of invincibility in her bed, but she was giving me up without a backward glance; I could read the news on the shroud that passed as her face. I felt like a fool. What made me think she'd choose me instead of the unlimited pool of Stanhope money? Once Eddie killed me, she'd have him forever. He'd never be able to divorce her; they'd be locked in the harness until the earth quit spinning and died.

"Eddie, that's not it," I said. I heard the helplessness in my own voice. I sounded tinny, like a playback. "OK, man, it was a mistake to get involved with your wife. I know that. I'm sorry." I was trying to sound contrite, once again the serf tugging his forelock. I walked over to him and shifted my right side, the side with the gun in the pocket, up against the bar so neither of them could see what I was doing. Slowly, I dropped my hand and began to inch my fingers toward the gun.

"Yeah?" he laughed, an eerie sound like wind whining down a tunnel. "Tell me how sorry you are."

Confusion butted heads with omnipotence. This was the time, the moment, my last chance for a comeback, and I gave omnipotence free rein as I kept inching my hand toward the gun in my pocket. "Ever try, Eddie? Ever try and fail? You've never had to work, rich boy. You have it all. The house, the wife, the car. You want to own a nightclub? Buy one. You want your wife killed? Hire it done."

Suzanne gasped out loud. "Killed?" she said slowly. "You wanted me *killed*?" she asked Eddie, her voice thick with distaste.

"He promised me a hundred thou to get rid of you, princess. Ain't that a kick in the head?"

"Rick, you were going to kill me?" she asked. "That first night, you were here to kill me. . . ." Now she was thoughtful, pondering her own murder like a stock portfolio.

Eddie Style said nothing.

My fingers closed on the gun and I turned toward him, slowly. "Think about living without that mass of cash behind you, that blanket of money. Ain't easy, Eddie. But you'll never know 'cause whatever happens, you've always got a fallback position. The rich always do."

It wasn't until I said it that I realized how much I hated him, how much I hated his flaccid face, his thin shoulders that had never seen a goddamn day's work, his weak mind that never had to make a tough decision, his patrician arrogance. I pulled the gun out of my pocket, fired and caught him right between the eyes.

I heard Suzanne shriek as blood sprayed out of the back of Eddie's head, splattering the polished sheen of the mirror on the back bar with a fine mist. His body crashed to the floor, taking a row of heavy highball glasses with it, shattering a few bottles. The smell of blood and gin filled the air. I didn't give a damn.

It was all mine. At last I'd turned myself inside out, and the mildewed scent of failure that had clung to me was gone. I was no longer a grinning monkey at the Club Dingo, but Zeus. A king. I was on top, a winner at last.

"Your turn, love," I said softly. "What's it gonna be?

The way I see things," I said, pocketing the gun as I went over and sat down on the couch beside her, "Eddie just struck out and I'm on deck. He's dead, I'm alive and you're rich. Time to choose up sides for the Series."

She shuddered like a stalled Ford. "You killed him. You killed Eddie." Her voice was quiet and she sounded vaguely surprised.

"Yeah. I did. Now, you got two choices. You can do what I tell you to do or you can die."

"I thought you said two choices, Rick. I only heard one," she said carefully. Her voice had changed, and her face was no longer an expressionless mask. "Can I go look?" she asked as she got up and went behind the bar. She stood there for a minute, looking down at her dead husband; then she bent down and touched his cheek. "What do you want me to do?" she asked me as she straightened up.

"First thing I want, I want you to come over here and wrap your prints around my gun," I told her. "That'll keep you in line just in case you get tired of me, some faraway night when we're under the stars on the Mexican Riviera. I'll keep the gun for insurance."

"Don't you trust me?"

"This is L.A. I don't trust anybody who's ever breathed smog. Then I give you a black eye and leave. I won't hurt you, much. You call the cops and say a bad, bad robber broke in and killed hubby. You'll have a rough few months, but I'll take care of the Dingo and we can meet there once in a while. Maybe next year, we'll get married. Think you'd like a June wedding?"

"You're a cold son of a bitch; how come I didn't notice it before?"

"You weren't interested in my mind, Suzanne. Look, baby, now that Eddie's out of the picture we can have it all. Don't you understand, I can't afford to blow this off. I had one hit, I blew it. Usually, one hit is all you get in this town but I got a second chance tonight and I'm taking it. I'm not gonna get another. Ever."

"Why did he want me killed?" she said, looking down at Eddie's bloody body.

"Do you have to know? Money, OK? Isn't it always

money? He said you cost too much and he didn't have enough money to pay you off.''

''Greedy hog,'' she said and made an ugly snorting noise. ''But that's what they all say, right, Ricky boy?''

I walked over to her, very fast, and slapped her in the face, very hard. ''Never call me Ricky boy again, Suzanne,'' I said, a tight hold on her arm. ''Call me honey or sweetie or baby or call me you jerk, but don't ever call me Ricky boy.''

She pulled away from me, rubbing the red spot on her cheek where I'd hit her. ''Why'd you have to hit me? I wish the hell you hadn't hit me. . . .'' Her voice trailed off like a little girl's as she stepped back, leaned against the bar and buried her hands in the deep sleeves of her white kimono. She looked up at me and I saw death in her eyes. My death.

I saw it all and there was nothing I could do. She smiled and seemed to move very, very slowly, though in the back of my mind I knew everything was happening normally, skipping along in real time. The little silver gun slipped into her hand like a fish eager for the baited hook, and I realized she'd picked it up when she'd knelt down next to Eddie's dead body. She aimed it at me and fired. I watched as the gun leapt back in her hand and the bullet jumped straight for my heart.

I felt the slug sink into my body, only a .25, I told myself, a girl's gun, nothing to worry about. But Suzanne's aim was true. I put my hand to my chest and it felt scorched and fiery, like I'd fallen asleep with the hot water bottle on my naked flesh. I took my hand away and looked at it foolishly. Red. I had a red hand. Where the hell did I get a red hand? I was hot and tired and all of a sudden I thought a nap would do me good. Somewhere far away I heard her voice. . . .

''You were right, Rick. In this town, one hit is all you get.''

cold turkey

by Diane Mott Davidson

I DID NOT EXPECT TO FIND EDITH BLANTON'S BODY IN my walk-in refrigerator. The day had been bad enough already. My first thought after the shock was *I'm going to have to throw all this food away.*

My mind reeled. I couldn't get a dial tone to call for help. *Reconstruct,* I ordered myself as I ran to a neighbor's. *The police are going to want to know everything.* My neighbor pressed 9-1-1. I talked. Hung up. I immediately worried about my eleven-year-old son, Arch. Where was he? I looked at my watch: ten past eight. He was spending the night somewhere. Oh yes, Dungeons and Dragons weekend party at a friend's house. I made a discreet phone call to make sure he was okay. I did not mention the body. If I had, he and his friends would have wanted to troop over to see it.

Then I flopped down in a wing-back chair and tried to think.

•　　•　　•

I had talked to Edith Blanton that morning. She had called with a batch of demanding questions. Was I ready to cater the Episcopal Church Women's Luncheon, to be held the next day? Irritation had blossomed like a headache. Butterball Blanton, as she was known everywhere but to her face, was a busybody. I'd given the shortest possible answers. The menu was set, the food prepared. Chicken and artichoke heart pot pie. Molded strawberry salad. Tossed greens with vinaigrette. Parkerhouse rolls. Lemon sponge cake. Not on your diet, I had wanted to add, but did not.

Now Goldy, she'd gone on, *you have that petition we're circulating around the church, don't you?* I checked for raisins for a Waldorf salad and said, Which petition is that? Edith made an impatient noise in her throat. *The one outlawing guitar music.* Sigh. I said I had it around somewhere. . . . Actually, I kind of liked ecclesiastical folk music, as long as I personally did not have to sing it. *And Goldy, you're not serving that Japanese raw fish, are you?* To the churchwomen? Never. *And you didn't use anything from the local farm where they found salmonella, did you?* Oh, enough. Absolutely not, Butt—er . . . Mrs. Blanton, I promised before hanging up.

The phone had rung again immediately: our priest, Father Olson. I said, Surely you're not calling about the luncheon. He said, *Don't call me Shirley.* A comic in a clerical collar. After pleasantries we had gotten around to the real stuff: *How's Marla?* I said that Marla Korman, my best friend, was fine. As far as I knew. Why? *Oh, just checking, hadn't seen her in a while.* Haha, sure. I involuntarily glanced at my appointments calendar. After the churchwomen's luncheon, I was doing a dinner party for Marla. I didn't mention this to the uninvited Father Olson. You see, Episcopal priests can marry. Father Olson was unmarried, which made him interested in Marla. The reverse was not the case, however, which was why he had to call me to find out how she was. But none of this did I mention to Father O., as we called him. Didn't want to hurt his feelings.

My neighbor handed me a cup of tea. I thought again of Edith Blanton's pale calves, of the visible side of her pallid face, of the blood on the refrigerator floor. I pushed the image out of my mind and tried to think again about the day. The police were going to ask a lot of questions. Had I heard from anyone in the church again? Had anyone mentioned a current crisis? What had happened after Father Olson called?

Oh yes. Next had come a frantic knock at the door: something else to do with Marla. This time it was her soon-to-be-ex-boyfriend—lanky, strawberry-blond David McAllister. He had desperation in his voice. *What can I do to show Marla I love her?* Sheesh! Did I look like Ann Landers? I ushered him out to the kitchen, where I started to chop pecans, *also* for the Waldorf salad, *also* for Marla's dinner party, to which the wealthy-but-boring David McAllister *also* had not been invited. Not only that, but he was driving me crazy cracking his knuckles. When he took a breath while talking about how much he adored Marla, I said I was in the middle of a crisis involving petitions, raw eggs and the churchwomen, and ushered him out.

About an hour later I'd left the house. I lifted my head from my neighbor's chair and looked at my watch: quarter after eight. When had I left the house? Around one, only to return seven hours later. The entire afternoon and early evening had been taken up with the second unsuccessful meeting between me, my lawyer, and the people suing me to change the name of my catering business. George Pettigrew and his wife own Three Bears Catering down in Denver. In June it came to their attention that my real, actual name is Goldy (a nickname that has stuck like epoxy glue since childhood) Bear (Germanic in origin, but lamentable nonetheless). What was worse in the Pettigrews' eyes was that my business in the mountain town of Aspen Meadow was called Goldilocks' Catering, Where Everything Is Just Right! We began negotiating three weeks ago, at the beginning of September. The Pettigrews screamed copyright infringement. I tried to convince them that all of us could successfully capitalize on, if not inhabit, the same fairy tale. The meeting this afternoon was another failure, except from the viewpoint of my lawyer, who gets his porridge no matter what.

I nestled my head against one of the wings of my neighbor's chair. Just thinking about the day again was exhausting.

For as if all this had not been enough, when I got home I heard a dog in my outdoor trash barrels. At least I thought it was a dog. When I went around the side of the house to check, a *real* bear, large and black, shuffled away from the back of the house and up toward the woods. This is not an uncommon sight in the Colorado high country when fall weather sets in. But combined with the nagging from Edith and the fight with the Pettigrews, it was enough to send me in search of a parfait left over from an elementary school faculty party.

Not on your diet, I thought with a measure of guilt, the diet you just undertook with all sorts of good intentions. Oh well. Diets aren't good for you. Too much deprivation. But on this plan I didn't have to give up sweets; I could have one dessert a day. Of course the brownie I'd had after the lawyer's office fiasco was only a memory. Besides, I was under so much stress. I could just imagine that tall chilled crystal glass, those thick layers of chocolate and vanilla pudding. I opened the refrigerator door full of anticipation. And there in the dark recesses of the closetlike space was Edith, fully clothed, lying limp, sandwiched between the congealed strawberry salad and marinating T-bones.

I'd screamed. Rushed over to the neighbor's where I now sat, staring into a cup of lukewarm tea. I looked at my watch again. 8:20.

My neighbor was scurrying around looking for a blanket in case I went into shock. I was not going into shock; I just needed to talk to somebody. So I phoned Marla. That's what best friends are for, right? To get you through crises? Besides, Marla and I went way back. We had both made the mistake of marrying the same man, not simultaneously. We had survived the divorces from The Jerk and become best friends. I had even coached her in figuring her monetary settlement, sort of like when an NFL team in the playoffs gets films from another team's archenemy.

When Marla finally picked up the phone, I told her Edith Blanton was dead and in my refrigerator. I must have still been incoherent because I added the bit about the bear.

There was a pause while Marla tried to apply logic. Finally she said, "Goldy. I'm on my way over."

"Okay, okay! I'll meet you at my front door. Just be careful."

"Of what? Is this homicide or is it a frigging John Irving novel?"

Before I could say anything she hung up.

My neighbor and I walked slowly back to my house. The police arrived first: two men in uniforms. They took my name and Edith Blanton's. They asked how and when I'd found the body. When they tried to call for an investigative team, they discovered that the reason I hadn't been able to get a dial tone was that my phone was dead. The wires outside had been cut. This would explain why my brand-new, horrendously expensive security system had not worked when Edith and . . . whoever . . . had broken in. The police used their radio. While I was bemoaning my fate, Marla arrived. She was dressed in a sweatsuit sewn with gold spangles: I think they were supposed to represent aspen leaves.

The team arrived and took pictures. The coroner, gray-haired and grim-faced, signaled the removal company to cart out the body bag holding Edith. Marla murmured, "The Butterball bagged."

I said, "Stop."

Marla closed her eyes and fluttered her plump hands. "I know. I'm sorry. But she *was* a bitch. Everybody in the church disliked her."

I harrumphed. The two uniformed policemen told us to quit talking. They told me to go into the living room so the team leader, a female homicide investigator I did not know, could ask some questions. Marla flounced out. She said she was going home to make up the guest bed for me; no way was she allowing me to stay in that house.

The team leader and I settled ourselves on the two chairs in my living room. Out in the kitchen the lab technicians and other investigators were having a field day spreading black graphite fingerprint powder over the food for the churchwomen's luncheon.

The investigator was a burly woman with curly blond hair held back with black barrettes. Her eyes were light brown and impassive, her voice even. She wanted to know my name, if I knew the victim and for how long, was I having problems with her and where I'd been all day. I told her about my activities, about the following day's luncheon and Edith's questions. At their leader's direction, the team took samples of all the food. They also took what they'd found on the refrigerator floor: an anti–guitar-music petition. Through the blobs of congealed strawberry salad and raw egg yolk, you could see there were no names on it. Edith was still clutching the paper after she'd been hit on the head and dragged into the refrigerator.

I said, "Dragged . . . ?"

The investigator bit the inside of her cheek. Then she said, "Please tell me every single thing about your conversation with Edith Blanton."

So we went through it all again, including the bit about the petition. I added that I had not been due to see Edith, er, the deceased until the next day. Moreover, I was not having more problems with her than anybody else in town, especially Father Olson, who, unlike Edith, thought every liturgy should sound like a hootenanny.

The investigator's next question confused me. Did I have a pet? Yes, I had a cat that I had inherited from former employers. However, I added, strangers spooked him. Poor Scout would be cowering under a bed for at least the next three days.

She said, "And the color of the cat is . . . ?"

"Light brown, dark brown and white," I said. "Sort of a Burmese-Siamese mix. I think."

The investigator held out a few strands of hair.

"Does this look familiar? Look like your cat's hair?" It was dark brown and did not look like anything that grew on Scout. In fact, it looked fake.

" 'Fraid not," I said.

"Synthetic, anyway, we think. You got any of this kind of material around?"

I shook my head no. "Oh gosh," I said, "the bear." I started to tell her about what I'd seen around the back of the house, but she was looking at her clipboard. She shifted in her chair.

She said, "Wait. Is this a *relative* of yours? Er, Ms. Bear?"

"No, no, no. Have you heard of Three Bears Catering?"

The investigator looked more confused. "Is that you, too? I wouldn't know. They did the policemen's banquet down in Denver last year, and they all wore bear . . . suits. . . ."

She eyed me, the corners of her mouth turned down. She said, "Any chance this bear-person might have been waiting to attack you in your refrigerator? Over the name change problem? And attacked Edith instead? Do they know what you look like?"

"I told you. I spent the afternoon with the Pettigrews," I said through clenched teeth. "They're suing me; why would they want to kill me?"

"You tell me."

At that moment, Marla poked her head into the living room. "I'm back. Can we leave? Or do you have to stay until the kitchen demolition team finishes?"

I looked at the investigator, who shook her head. She said, "We have a lot to do. Should be finished by midnight. At the latest. Also, we gotta take the cut wires from out back and, uh, your back door."

I said, "My back door? Great." I gave Marla a pained look. "I have to stay until they go. Just do me a favor and call somebody to come put in a piece of plywood for the door hole. Also, see if you can find my cat cage. I'm bringing Scout to your house."

Marla nodded and disappeared. The investigator then asked me to go through the whole thing *backward*, beginning with my discovery of Edith. This I did meticulously, as I know the backward-story bit is one way investigators check for lies.

Finally she said, "Haven't I seen you around? Aren't you a friend of Tom Schulz's?"

I smiled. "Homicide Investigator Schulz is a good friend of mine. Unfortunately, he's up snagging inland salmon at Green Lake Reservoir. Now, tell me. Am I a suspect in this or not?"

The investigator's flat brown eyes revealed nothing. After a moment she said, "At this time we don't have enough information to tell about any suspects. But this hair we found in the victim's hand isn't yours. You didn't know your phone lines were cut. And you probably didn't break down your own back door.''

Well. I guess that was police talk for *No, you're not a suspect.*

The investigator wrote a few last things on her clipboard, then got up to finish with her cohorts in the kitchen. I didn't see her for the next three hours. Marla appeared with the cat cage, and I found Scout crouched under Arch's bed. I coaxed him out while Marla welcomed the emergency fix-it people at the stroke of midnight. The panel on their truck said: *Felony Fix-up—They Trash It, We Patch It.* How comforting. Especially the twenty-four-hour service part.

An hour after the police and Felony Fix-up had left my kitchen looking like a relic of the scorched-earth policy, I sat in Marla's kitchen staring down one of Marla's favorite treats—imported *baba au rhum.* There's something about being awake at one A.M. that makes you think you need something to eat. Still, guilt reared its hideous head.

''What's the matter?'' Marla asked. ''I thought you loved those. Eat up. It'll help you stop thinking about Edith Blanton.''

''Not likely, but I'll try.'' I inhaled the deep buttered-rum scent. ''I shouldn't. I ate Lindt Lindors all summer and I'm supposed to be on a diet.''

''One dessert won't hurt you.''

''I've already had one dessert.''

''So? *Two* won't hurt you.'' She shook her peaches-and-cream cheeks. ''If I'd had to go through what you just did, I'd have six.'' So saying, she delicately loaded two *babas* onto a Wedgwood dessert plate. ''Tomorrow's going to be even worse,'' she warned. ''You'll have to phone the president of the churchwomen first thing and cancel the luncheon. You'll have to call Father Olson. No, never mind, I'll make both calls.''

''Why?''

''Because, my dear, I am still hopeful that you'll be able to do my dinner party tomorrow night.'' Marla pushed away from the table to sashay over to her refrigerator for an aerosol can of whipped cream. "I know it's crass," she said as she shook the can vigorously, "but I still have three people, one of whom is a male I am very interested in, expecting dinner. Shrimp cocktail, steaks, potato soufflé, green beans, Waldorf salad, and chocolate cake. Remember? Beginning at six o'clock. I can't exactly call them up and say, Well, my caterer found this body in her refrigerator—"

"All right! If I can finish cleaning up the mess tomorrow, we're on." I took a bite of the *baba* and said, "The cops ruined the salad and the cake. You'll have to give me some more of your Jonathan apples. Gee, I don't feel so hot—"

"Don't worry. Sleep in. I have lots of apples. And I'll send a maid over to help you."

"Just not in a bear suit."

"Hey! Speaking of which! Should we give the Pettigrews a call in the morning? Just to hassle them?" She giggled. "Should we give them a call right now?"

"No, no, no," I said loudly over the sound of Marla hosing her *babas* with cream. "The police are bound to talk to them. If they're blameless, I can't afford to have them any angrier at me than they already are. I'm so tired, I don't even want to think about it."

Marla gave me a sympathetic look, got up and made me a cup of espresso laced with rum.

I said, "So who's this guy tomorrow night?"

"Fellow named Tony Kaplan. Just moved here from L.A., where he sold his house for over a million dollars. And it was a small house, too. He's cute. Wants to open a bookstore."

"Not another newcomer who's fantasized about running a bookstore in a mountain town," I said as I took the whipped cream bottle and pressed out a blob on top of my coffee. Immigrants from either coast always felt they had a mission to bring culture to us cowpokes. "Gee," I said. "Almost forgot. Regarding your busy social life, Father Olson called and asked me how you were."

"I hope you told him I was living in sin with a chocolate bar."

"Well, I didn't have time because then David McAllister

showed up at my front door. Wanted to know if there was anything he could do to show you he loved you."

Marla tsked. "He asked me the same thing, and I said, Well, you can start with a nice bushel of apples."

"You are cruel." I sipped the coffee. With the rum and the whipped cream, it was sort of like hot ice cream. "You shouldn't play with his feelings."

"Excuse me, but jealousy is for seventh-graders."

"Too cruel," I said as we got up and placed the dishes in the sink. She escorted me with Scout the cat up to her guest room, then gave me towels; I handed over a key to my front door for her maid. Then I said, "Tell me about Edith Blanton."

Marla plunked down a pair of matching washcloths. She said, "Edith knew everything about everybody. Who in the church had had affairs with whom . . ."

"Oh, that's nice."

Marla pulled up her shoulders in an exaggerated gesture of nonchalance. The sweat-suit spangles shook. "Well, it was," she said. "I mean, everybody was nice to her because they were afraid of what she had on them. They didn't want her to talk. And she got what she wanted, until she took up arms against Father Olson over the guitar music."

"Too bad she couldn't get anything on him."

"Oh, honey," Marla said with an elaborate swirl of her eyes before she turned away and swaggered down the hall to her room. "Don't think she wasn't trying."

The next day Scout and I trekked to the church before going back to my house. Scout meowed morosely the whole way. I told him I had to leave a big sign on the church door, saying that the luncheon had been canceled. He only howled louder when I said it was just in case someone hadn't gotten the word. If I hadn't been concentrating so hard on trying to comfort him, I would have noticed George Pettigrew's truck in the church parking lot. Then I would have been prepared for Pettigrew's smug grin, his hands clutched under his armpits, his foot tapping as I vaulted out of my van. As it was, I nearly had a fit.

"Were you around my house in a bear suit last night?" I

demanded. He opened his eyes wide, as if I were crazy. "And *what* are you doing here? Haven't you got enough catering jobs down in Denver?"

"We don't use the bear suits anymore," he replied in a superior tone. "We had a hygiene problem with the hair getting into the food. And as a matter of fact I am doing lunches for two Skyboxes at Mile High Stadium tomorrow. But I can still offer to help out the churchwomen, since their local caterer canceled." His eyes bugged out as he raised his eyebrows. "Bad news travels fast."

Well, the luncheon was not going to happen. To tell him this, I was tempted to use some very unchurchlike language. But at that moment Father Olson pulled up in his 300E Mercedes 4matic. Father O. had told the vestry that a priest needed a four-wheel-drive vehicle to visit parishioners in the mountains; he'd also petitioned for folk-music tapes to give to shut-ins. The vestry had refused to purchase the tapes, but they'd sprung fifty thou for the car.

Father O. came up and put his hands on my shoulders. He gave me his Serious Pastoral Look. "Goldy," he said, "I've been so concerned for you."

"So have I," I said ruefully, with a sideways glance at George Pettigrew, who shrank back in the presence of clerical authority.

I turned my attention back to Father Olson. Marla might want to reconsider. An ecclesiastical career suited Father O., who had come of age in the sixties. He had sincere brown eyes, dark skin and a beard, a cross between Moses and Ravi Shankar.

"... feel terrible about what's happened to Edith," he was saying, "of course. How can this possibly ... Oh, you probably don't want to talk about it...."

I said, "You're right."

Fancy cars were pulling into the church parking lot. George Pettigrew unobtrusively withdrew just as a group of women disentangled themselves from their Cadillacs and Mercedes.

"Listen," I said, "I have to split. Can you take care of these women who haven't gotten the bad news? I have a dinner party tonight that I simply can't cancel."

I almost didn't make it. Cries of *Oh here she is; I wonder what she's fixed* erupted like birdcalls. Father Olson gave me the Pastoral Nod. I sidled past the women, hopped back in the van, and managed to get out of the church parking lot without getting into a single conversation.

To my surprise, the maid Marla had sent over had done a superb job cleaning my kitchen. It positively sparkled. Unfortunately, right around the corner was the plywood nailed over the back-door opening: a grim reminder of last night's events.

I set about thawing and marinating more steaks, then got out two dozen frozen Scout's Brownies, my patented contribution to the chocoholics of the world. I had first developed the recipe under the watchful eye of the cat, so I'd named them after him. Marla adored them.

Edith Blanton came to mind as I again got out my recipe for Waldorf salad. Someone, dressed presumably as a bear, had taken the time to cut the phone wires and break in. Why? Had that person been following Edith, meaning to kill her at his first opportunity? Or had Edith surprised a robber? Had he killed her intentionally or accidentally?

I knew one thing for sure. Homicide Investigator Tom Schulz was my friend—well, more than a friend—and he often talked to me about cases up in Aspen Meadow. This would not be true with the current investigator working the Edith Blanton case, no question about it. If I was going to find out what happened, I was on my own.

While washing and cutting celery into julienne sticks, I conjured up a picture of Edith Blanton with her immaculately coiffed head of silver hair, dark green skirt, and Loden jacket. Despite being an energetic busybody, Edith had been a lady. She never would have broken into my house.

I held my breath and opened my refrigerator door. All clean. I reached for a bag of nuts. Although classic Waldorfs called for walnuts, I was partial to fresh, sweet pecans that I mail-ordered from Texas. I chopped a cupful and then softened some raisins in hot water. The bear-person had been in my refrigerator. Why? If you're going to steal food, why wear a disguise?

Because if I had caught him, stealing food or attacking Edith Blanton, I would have recognized him.

So it was someone I knew? Probably.

I went back into the refrigerator. Although only a quarter cup of mayonnaise was required for the Waldorf, it was imperative to use *homemade* mayonnaise, which I would make with a nice fresh raw egg. I would mix the mayonnaise with a little lemon juice, sugar, and heavy cream. . . . Wait a minute.

Two days ago my supplier had brought me eggs from a salmonella-free source in eastern Colorado. I was sure they were brown. So why was I staring at a half dozen nice white eggs?

I picked one up and looked at it. It was an egg, all right. I brought it out into the kitchen and called Alicia, my supplier. The answering service said she was out on a delivery.

"Well, do you happen to know what color eggs she delivered on her run two days ago?"

There was a long pause. The operator finally said, "Is this some kind of *yolk*?"

Oh, hilarious. I hung up. So funny I forgot to laugh.

I would have called a neighbor and borrowed an egg, but I didn't have any guarantees about hers, either. Many locals bought their eggs from a farm outside of town where they *had* found salmonella, and hers might be tainted too.

I felt so frustrated I thawed a brownie in the microwave. This would be my one dessert of the day. Oh, and was it wonderful—thick and dark and chewy. Fireworks of good feeling sparked through my veins.

Okay, I said firmly to my inner self, yesterday when you came into this refrigerator you found a body. There is no way you could possibly remember the color of eggs or anything else that Alicia delivered two days ago. So make the mayo and quit bellyaching.

With this happy thought, I started the food processor whirring and filched another brownie. Mm, mm. When the mayonnaise was done, I finished the Waldorf salad, put it in the refrigerator, and then concentrated on shelling and cooking fat prawns for the shrimp cocktail. When I put the shrimp in to chill, I stared at the refrigerator floor. I still had not answered the first question. Why had Edith been at my house in the first place?

She had been carrying a petition. A *blank* petition. So?

My copy had had a few names on it. Edith was carrying a blank petition because I had said I didn't know where my copy was. She came over with a new one.

So? That still didn't explain how she got in.

When she got here, she didn't get any answer at the front door. But she saw the light filtering from the kitchen, and being the busybody she was, she went around back. The door was open, and she surprised the bear in mid-heist. . . .

Well. Go figure. I packed up all the food and hustled off to Marla's.

"Oh darling, *enfin!*" Marla cried when she swung open her heavy front door. She was wearing a multilayered yellow-and-red chiffon dress that looked like sewn-together scarves. Marla always dressed to match the season, and I was pretty sure I was looking at the designer version of Autumn.

"You don't need to be so dramatic," I said as I trudged past her with the first box.

"Oh! I thought you were Tony." She giggled. "Just kidding."

To my relief she had already set her cherry dining room table with her latest haul from Europe: Limoges china and Baccarat crystal. I started boiling potatoes for the soufflé and washed the beans.

"I want to taste!" Marla cried as she got out a spoon to attack the Waldorf.

"Not on your life!" I said as I snatched the covered bowl away from her. "If we get started eating and chatting there'll be nothing left for your guests."

To my relief the front doorbell rang. Disconsolate, Marla slapped the silver spoon down on the counter and left. From the front hall came the cry "Oh darling, *enfin!*" Tony Kaplan, would-be bookstore proprietor.

The evening was warm, which was a good thing, as Marla and I had decided to risk an outdoor fire on her small barbecue. There were six T-bones—one for each guest and two extra for big appetites. I looked at my watch: six o'clock. Marla had said to serve at seven. The coals would take a bit longer after the sun went down, but since we were near the solstice, that wouldn't be until half past six. The things a caterer has to know.

Tony Kaplan meandered out to the kitchen. Marla was welcoming the other couple. He needed ice for his drink, he said with a laugh. He was a tall, sharp-featured man who hunched his shoulders over when he walked, as if his height bothered him. I introduced myself. He laughed. "Is that your real name?" I told him there was a silver ice bucket in the living room. He just might not have recognized it, as it was in the shape of a sundae. You had to lift up the ice cream part to get to the ice. "Oh, I get it!" There was another explosive laugh, his third. He may have been rich, but his personality left a lot to be desired.

When the coals were going and I had put the soufflé in the oven, my mind turned again to Edith. Who could have possibly wanted to break into my refrigerator? Why not steal the computer I had right there on the counter to keep track of menus?

"We're ready for the shrimp cocktail," Marla stage-whispered into the kitchen.

"Already? But I thought you said—"

"Tony's driving me crazy. If I give him some shrimp, maybe he'll stop chuckling at everything I have to say."

While Marla and her guests were bathing their shrimp with cocktail sauce, I hustled out to check on the coals. To my surprise, a nice coat of white ash had developed. Sometimes things do work. The steaks sizzled enticingly when I placed them on the grill. I ran back inside and got out the salad and started the beans. When I came back out to turn the T-bones, the sun had slid behind the mountains and the air had turned cool.

"Come on, let's go," I ordered the steaks. After a long five minutes the first four were done. I slapped them down on the platter, put the last two on the grill, and came in. In a crystal bowl, I made a basket of lettuce and then spooned the Waldorf salad on top. This I put on a tray along with the butter and rolls. The soufflé had puffed and browned; I whisked it out to the dining room. While I was putting the beans in a china casserole dish, I remembered that I had neglected to get the last two steaks off the fire.

Cancel the *things working* idea, I thought. I ferried the rest of the dishes out to Marla's sideboard, invited the guests to serve themselves buffet-style, and made a beeline back to the kitchen.

I looked out the window: around the steaks the charcoal fire was merrily sending up foot-high flames and clouds of smoke. Bad news. At this dry time of year, sparks were anathema. There was no fire extinguisher in Marla's kitchen. Why should there be? She never cooked. I grabbed a crystal pitcher, started water spurting into it, looked back out the window to check the fire again.

Judas priest. A bear was lurching from one bush in Marla's backyard to the next. In the darkening twilight, I could not tell if it was the same one that had been in my backyard. All I could see was him stopping and then holding his hands as if he were cheering.

I sidestepped to get beside one of Marla's cabinets, then peeked outside. I knew bravery was in order; I just didn't know what that was going to look like. Too bad Scout had never made it as an attack-cat.

The bear-person shows up at my house. The bear-person shows up at Marla's. Why?

Oh damn. The eggs.

"Marla!" I shrieked. I ran out to the dining room. "Don't eat the Waldorf salad! There's a bear in your backyard . . . but I just know it's not a real one. . . . Somebody needs to call the cops! Quick! Tony, could you please go grab this person? It's not a real bear, just somebody in a bear suit. I'm sure he killed Edith Blanton."

For once, Tony did not laugh. He said, "You've got a killer dressed as a bear in the backyard. You want me to go grab him with my bare hands?"

"Yes," I said, "of course! Hurry up!"

"This is a weird dinner party," said Tony.

"Oh, I'll do it!" I shrieked.

I sprinted to the kitchen and vaulted full tilt out Marla's back door. Maybe it *was* a real bear. Then I'd be in trouble for sure. I started running down through the tall grass toward the bush where the bear was hidden. The bear stood up. He made his cheering motion again. But . . .

Ordinary black bears have bad eyesight.

Ordinary black bears don't grow over five feet tall.

This guy was six feet if he was an inch, and his eyes told him I was coming after him.

He turned and trundled off in the opposite direction. I sped up, hampered only by tall grass and occasional rocks. Behind me I could hear shouts—Marla, Tony, whoever. I was not going to turn around. I was bent on my prey.

The bear howled: a gargled human howl. Soon he was at the end of Marla's property, where an enormous rock formation was the only thing between us and the road. The bear ran up on the rocks. Then, unsure of what to do, he jumped down the other side. Within a few seconds I had scrambled up to where he had stood. The bear had landed in the center of the road.

I launched myself. When I landed on his right shoulder, he crumpled. Amazing. The last time I'd seen a bear successfully tackled was when Randy Gradishar had thrown Walter Payton for a six-yard loss in the Chicago backfield.

I leapt up. "You son of a bitch!" I screamed. Then I kicked him in the stomach for good measure.

I reached down to pull off his bear mask. Of course, I was fully expecting to see the no-longer-smug face of George Pettigrew.

But it wasn't George.

Looking up at me was the tormented face of David McAllister. I was stunned. But of course. The hand-paw motion. David McAllister had been doing what he always did when he was nervous: cracking his knuckles.

"David? David? What's going on?"

"I'm sorry, I'm sorry," he blubbered, "I didn't mean to hurt that old woman in your house. I just needed Marla. . . . I thought I was going to lose my mind. . . . I wanted to hurt her . . . and whoever she was seeing. . . . I wanted to make them pay. . . . I'm just so sorry. . . ."

Marla and Tony Kaplan appeared at the top of the rocks.

"Goldy!" Marla shrieked. "Are you okay? The police are on their way. What's that, a person?"

Later, much later, Marla and I sat in her kitchen and started in on the untouched platter of brownies. David McAllister had said he figured Marla had asked for the apples for Waldorf salad because she was having somebody else over. (*He knew you better than you thought*, I told her.) He was crazy with jealousy, and I had been no help. Worse, when he was in my kitchen, he had seen "Marla—dinner party" on my appointments calendar. And here I'd thought all he'd been doing was cracking his knuckles. He cut my wires and broke through my back door. He knew I made everything from scratch. (*He knew us all better than we thought*, Marla said.) So he substituted salmonella-tainted eggs for the mayonnaise, to make Marla and her dinner guests sick. When Edith Blanton surprised him, they struggled, and she fell back on the corner of the marble slab I used for kneading. It was an accident. But because David McAllister had broken into my house before his struggle with Edith, the charge was going to be murder in the first degree.

Marla sank her teeth into her first brownie. "Ooo-ooo," she said. "Yum. I feel better already. Have one."

"I shouldn't. I can't." In fact, I couldn't even look at the brownies; my knees were scraped and my chest hurt where I'd fallen on David McAllister.

"Well, you're probably right. If you hadn't gone after that parfait, you never would have found Butterball, I mean Mrs. Blanton. Which just goes to show, if you're going to give up desserts, you have to do it cold—"

"Don't say it. Don't even think it. And no matter how you cajole, I'm not going to join you in this chocolate indulgence."

Her eyes twinkled like the rings on her fingers. "But that's what I wanted all along!" she protested. "Leave more for me that way! Dark, fudgy, soothing . . ."

"Oh all right," I said. "Just one."